Critical Acclaim for
Marcelle Bernstein's

SACRED AND PROFANE

'A psychological thriller and an exploration of prisons both actual and metaphorical . . . Bernstein writes well about people, and she has a good ear for dialogue'
The Times

'Mesmerizing . . . Nuns and prisoners have much in common . . . the close association between the two types of existence form a theme of her brilliant new novel . . . a riveting read'
Manchester Evening News

'Twins are fascinating. They offer a promise of a kind of intimacy only usually experienced by new lovers. But there is also the dread of two people merging so completely that neither knows whose brain had which thought first – or who committed what dreadful act . . . This powerful writer drops the reader into the confusion of blurred identity'
OK Magazine

'Beautifully-crafted . . . delicately written but very powerful. Be prepared to care about these women, to become so involved that you don't want the story to end. And be prepared for heart-stopping moments as some bitter truths are revealed'
Optima

Also by Marcelle Bernstein

NON-FICTION

NUNS

FICTION

SADIE

SALKA

LILI

BODY AND SOUL

Sacred
and Profane

Marcelle Bernstein

BANTAM BOOKS
LONDON · NEW YORK · TORONTO · SYDNEY · AUCKLAND

SACRED AND PROFANE
A BANTAM BOOK : 0 553 40803 8

Originally published in Great Britain by Doubleday
a division of Transworld Publishers Ltd

PRINTING HISTORY
Doubleday edition published 1995
Bantam edition published 1996

Set in Linotype Plantin 10/12pt by
Hewer Text Composition Services, Edinburgh

Bantam Books are published by Transworld Publishers Ltd,
61–63 Uxbridge Road, Ealing, London W5 5SA,
in Australia by Transworld Publishers (Australia) Pty Ltd,
15–25 Helles Avenue, Moorebank, NSW 2170,
and in New Zealand by Transworld Publishers (NZ) Ltd,
3 William Pickering Drive, Albany, Auckland.

Printed and bound in Great Britain by
Cox & Wyman Ltd, Reading, Berkshire

For Felicity and Sister Giles

Acknowledgements

The experts I consulted while writing this book were immensely generous with their time and shared their experience and their insights with me. I am greatly indebted to them all.

Dr Nick Bodkin. Dr Jim Stevenson, Senior Lecturer in Psychology at the Institute of Child Health, University of London, and Nicholas Tucker, lecturer in Psychology at the University of Sussex. Keith Massey. The women of HM Prison Holloway and Zoe Ashmore, Head of Psychology there. Audrey Sandbanks, child guidance counsellor. Marianne Velmans, on twinhood. Manuel Ulacia and Hora'cio Costa. Raymond Kennedy and Joe Mulrooney of the Advent Group of married priests.

My deep thanks go to the Authors Foundation and Hawthornden Castle International Retreat for writers.

To Caradoc King and Jo Goldsworthy.

And – as always – to Eric.

The diary had empty pages thin as tissue and a lock, so no-one else could ever see inside.

She smoothed her hand over blue leather stamped with gold flowers. Gran called them fleurs-de-lys. The gold was real.

But she had to do it. With a kitchen knife, she gouged words deep into the leather. She scorched the letters with the burning tips of matches to make them black and ugly.

It took a long time.

DON'T LOOK

DON'T READ

TURN AWAY

Chapter One

They used to carve it into the door, in the old days, and paint it like a human eye, staring and bright. The eye that never sleeps. The judas hole. The judas, traitorous watcher of the prisoner inside. It was round then. Now it's just a slit with a metal cover.

She was deeply asleep, left hand beneath her cheek, right tucked under her pillow. The sound of the metal sliding back disturbed her and she turned over, pulling the blanket higher.

Thump and sizzle in the black cell. Bonfire smells. She dreamed of fireworks, silver arcs in the night she hadn't experienced for fourteen years. Crackle and fizz of sparklers. Smoke seeped into her dream, wisps of grey round her head. Flickers of light were yellow and white behind her eyelids. The guy's clothes burning now, singeing cloth, acrid fumes catching in her throat so she coughed, coughed again, couldn't breathe . . . Half awake, she struggled to free herself from the covers. She was hot. She was *burning* . . . Oh my *God*!

'Fire! Fire on threes!'

The alarm whooped its warning, the siren sound bouncing back from high walls.

Shouting in the corridor, footsteps running in panic.

'Quick, I think it's Dean . . .'

'Where the hell's the bloody extinguisher . . .'

'Hurry!'

Key in the lock. Light flooding in as the door burst open.

'Christ, where's she gone?'

'Can't see a fuckin' . . . the smoke . . .'

'On the floor – by the window, see?'

'Jesus! Her hair's on fire!'

Hands grasping her shoulders, her legs.

'Wet towels – NOW!'

It sounded as if the whole prison was whooping and yelling. Women were screeching and baying in their cells, banging on their doors, rattling spoons across their barred windows.

'Get the bitch! GET THE BITCH!'

Chanting. Cursing.

'Burn!'

'Burn!'

'BURN!'

They ghosted her out next day. Her cell left empty, blackened and charred. Puddles of dirty water on the cement floor, stink of burned bedding. Her few surviving belongings shoved into brown paper bags. Wait in here. Handcuffs, get in the van. Dingy cramped cell inside it. Sitting on the floor, hour after hour.

Sometimes she stood at the tiny window and stared out. They were on motorway almost the whole journey. She'd forgotten the thrill of travelling at speed, the passing cars, the coaches full of foreign tourists, long distance lorries driven by men with huge elbows sticking out of the windows. When it got dark the lights were so pretty, red and green and white.

She was at the barred window when traffic cones

slowed them almost to a standstill. In a car drawn up alongside the van, two women were staring up at her, talking excitedly. She sat down abruptly, reduced again to an animal in a cage.

The policeman driving the van was nice. He noticed the bandages on her hands, the chopped and scorched ends of hair. He stopped at the Watford Gap service station to use the gents, and came back carrying four hamburgers in red boxes, one each.

'Bet it's bin a bit since you had one a' those.' He handed it through the hatch in the door, watched her face as she opened the polystyrene pack and sniffed the contents. 'Why're we moving you, then?' He winked. 'Fancy a change, did you?'

Kate shrugged and managed a smile through a mouthful of bread and onion. She didn't know the officers travelling with her. One of them, broad in navy jacket and skirt, hair like a brown Brillo pad, said, 'Had to, more like. The girls found out what she done.'

'Oh yeah?' The driver sounded interested. 'What was that, then?' He turned to her again. 'You bin a naughty girl?'

The officer answered for her. But she was used to that, to being treated like a child: it was one of the ways in which they demonstrated their control.

'Don't ask,' the officer said. 'Believe me, you don't want to hear it.'

Chapter Two

The night of Christmas Eve was moist and stifling. It smelled of rotting fruit and the strange heavy flowers that sprang in the convent garden. Through dense shade they thrust, with pouch and sprout of purple and cream. The people here had a name for them, but would not use it in front of the nuns: women giggled behind spread fingers and little boys muttered it to each other just out of hearing.

But in the dark there was only the scent, mysterious and potent as a drug, like nothing Sister Gideon had ever smelled before. Waking to it each morning gave her a headache, took away her appetite. She couldn't even face the flat bread and English honey they hoarded for breakfast. She sat with the sisters in the long conservatory they called the Refectory. She drank herb tea. And beyond the bamboo blinds the garden lay lush and damp, swelling with succulent emerald life.

It made a mockery of the wording of masses in the English missal. That was meant for Europe, for calm and temperate places, not for the drenching sweetness of Guatemala.

'Let the wilderness and the dry-lands exult,' chanted the nuns anyway.

'Let the wasteland rejoice and bloom.

Let it bring forth flowers like the jonquil.
Let it rejoice and sing for joy.'

They'd sung that three weeks ago on the third Sunday of Advent, and she had pictured a jonquil, pale and cold. Nothing so austere here, where butterflies rose like black kites and tiny spinning brilliant birds sucked at flowers with beaks thin as whiskers.

Sister Gideon found her big linen handkerchief and wiped the sweat from her face. The sliver of pain she felt sometimes just below her ribs had been worse lately. Her palms were sticky and the habit prickled uncomfortably under her arms and round her waist beneath her belt. It was the summer habit, but a habit none the less: underskirt and bodice, robe and scapular, head-dress and veil. It was in white, like the mantle she had just put on for the Mass at midnight.

Like the snow which often fell at Christmas, at the Mother House deep in the Welsh hills. She had not seen snow for three years.

Sister Gideon took up her place at the rear of the procession, as the youngest, the most newly professed of them. In her arms she carried the Infant, holding it as carefully as if it were her own. Only it wasn't a baby, but a doll tightly wound in a woolly shawl.

Not so many years ago, the nuns had used an English doll, white and blond and foreign, until they had one sent out from Guatemala City. They'd been so disappointed when it arrived: not the baby doll they had wanted but a haughty señorita with a comb in her long Spanish hair and a yellow dress with black lace flounces. She had been sorry when they cut the hair and rubbed the red from the lips. Under the white shawl, they'd dressed it in a Viyella nightie with a bambi embroidered on the tiny front.

That was when it became dangerous. Now, carrying it,

15

she risked a look. The glistening black eyes were open. In the centre of each glass pupil she could see a tiny point of light, the reflection of Sister Antoine's candle. Her own eyes were brown too, but not this rich dark colour. They were paler, speckled with gold. There were no mirrors in the convent, she only saw her reflection in a window, or in the polished lid of a vaseline tin she used to make sure her veil was straight. Those other eyes she saw when she slept were the same colour as her own. They said, eyes are the mirror of the soul. Sister Gideon stared down into the doll's face, and then with an abrupt movement she tilted the little body back until they blinked shut.

In front of her, the line of candle flames carried by the nuns wavered in the heat.

'The people that walked in darkness have seen a great light; on those who live in a land of deep shadow a light has shone . . .'

Sister Gideon heard those words and thought of someone who lived in deep shadow. Whose days were spent out of the light.

As the nuns paced through the Chapel, there were gasps of excitement: at least a hundred people had crowded into the small building, most of them children, rustling and giggling, wriggling and scuffling.

A hundred years before, nuns of this order had crossed half the world to reach Guatemala. They had come to the green heartland of the Petén, half jungle, half savannah, bringing with them an English god and all their English ways. They tried to teach the Indians to pray in silence, to sing in chorus, to listen and learn. They did as they thought best, they were no more than daughters of their time.

Now the nuns knew better than to attempt to destroy what was old and strong, and they deferred to the people.

16

Who had no use for formality but brought to this service, as they did to all the others, their ceaseless talk, the powerful emotions of their Maya heritage.

Women with smooth coffee skin suckled babies who lay like little gods themselves, swathed in bright cloth against their breasts. Toddlers twisted in the arms of their elder sisters, on the shoulders of taller brothers, on tiptoe. They balanced precariously on the benches, scrabbled for toeholds on the plinth of the statue of St Joseph. One adventurous boy had crawled up the rope they used to open and close the window in the ceiling.

Many wore traditional costumes in piercing colours, but most of the men dressed in cowboy boots and striped knee-length shorts and sunglasses. They smoked prodigiously – though the nuns did not permit them to do so inside the compound – black cigarillos clamped between their teeth, and drank rum whenever they had a quetzal to spend.

The children were whispering among themselves in Quiché, but Sister Gideon caught some phrases in Spanish, which the nuns encouraged. '¡Qué hermoso nene!', '¡ . . . qué precioso! . . .', '¡Mamá, mira, mamá!' were audible above the music.

Sister Oswald, the musician, was playing the piano the order had brought on that first precarious journey. The tone was badly affected by the damp, especially since they were forced to keep its legs standing in buckets of water, or wood-eating insects swarmed up them. She played dexterously, right hand only. With the left she conducted her 'orchestra' of children blowing the painted wooden flutes, giving to this northern music the rare wild sound of their country.

'Alleluia, alleluia, For there is a child born for us, a son given to us.'

Seven-year-old Jorge Amparo stood proudly beside the elderly nun, turning the pages when she nodded. He wore shorts which had once belonged to a very large man, gathered round his hungry body with a piece of cord. His vest was dirty. But he had from somewhere a pair of immaculate white tennis socks and a smile of pride to break your heart. Sister Gideon looked at him and his eyes gleamed bright as the doll's.

Sister Gideon had reached the woven Crib. The nuns and the children they taught had worked on the nativity scene for weeks. Even so, the dark-blue painted sky with the light behind the cut-out Star of Bethlehem inspired all the old thrill and promise of happiness she remembered from her own childhood: *now everything will be lovely*. She knelt to lay the wrapped southern Infant carefully in his winter Crib, between the toy donkey with its laden panniers and the lamb the nuns had knitted for them in Wales, back at the Priory of Our Lady of the Snow.

She had helped the children pull apart rolls of cotton wool to make the snow for the Nativity. Sister Gideon had shown the children how to lay the cotton wool over the straw roof of the manger, beneath the feet of the animals and on the shoulders of the watching Magi as they held their gifts. '¿Qué haces?' the children had asked, gazing at the result. 'What is it? What are you doing?' They loved the idea of snow without comprehending. They said, '¡Muy caliente!' It is warm!

At the other side of the altar was a second, quite different nativity, elaborate and touching and odd. The Indians had made clay figures of the Virgin, St Joseph and the angels. There was an inn, an entire village of minute houses, even the market place. All the figures were brightly painted, and the whole scene was decorated with fairy lights and set against a backcloth of Bacofoil. A

18

visiting priest had brought a tin of chemical snow called *Nieve*, and this had been sprayed over everything. For the week preceding Christmas, there had been a *posadas* each day, with candles and singing and the stable scene carried at the head of a procession.

As the nuns went back to their places, it was the turn of the children. Three-year-old Miguela, holding tightly on to her older sister's hand, had been chosen to add the tiny painted clay baby to the group in the stable. As she bent over the little figures, curling eyelashes swept olive skin. Four weeks ago, her parents had been ordered out of their village house, blindfolded and driven away in a jeep with no numberplates. Everyone except Miguela knew they would never come back.

Sister Gideon looked at the pure white snow. She looked at the sleeping face of the Christ child. She began to clamber to her feet, clumsy for once, she must be tired. As she did so, it was as if something hot and liquid had spilled over inside her, for pain came suddenly, out of nowhere.

She froze, caught in mid-movement, half up, half down. She waited a moment, very still. It must be a stitch, indigestion perhaps. Then she slowly straightened up – and the pain exploded into agony. It clawed deep in her guts, she could feel it twisting and turning.

The sound that forced itself from between her gritted teeth had nothing to do with her will. It came anyhow, without shape or form or any sense but anguish. Among the joyous singing and noise, the out-of-tune piano and bells and the wooden flutes, no-one heard her wordless cry.

She was suffocating in this crowded space, hemmed in by the press of eager bodies, the smell of children's flesh, of the white altar flowers she had helped arrange that morning, and the cheap musky scent called 'Pasión' they all loved, men and women both. She hurried, arms laced across her belly, stumbling away from the altar, back down the chapel, past the happy unnoticing faces. She reached the door, used the weight of her shoulder to push it open.

She must have fresh air. But outside, the damp night was perfumed unbearably by those great flowers. It pressed a black mask against mouth and nose. She tore at the fastening of her white cloak, to be free of its heat. Pain stirred again, a soft slithering at first, that made her catch her breath – and then it leapt. It spiked her from within with such malevolence that this time she could make no noise at all.

She turned her face to the whitewashed wall and vomited.

They put her to bed in her cell. It wasn't much of an effort to get her there, she was so light. The small room was on the second floor, bare white walls and wooden floor.

Sister Gideon could not keep still. She shivered, her body was all little movements and spasms. She said, 'My head hurts,' and her skin was sticky with sweat. The Infirmarian took her temperature. Then she got another thermometer and did it again. She knew these symptoms.

'You didn't forget to use the mosquito net one night, did you, Sister?' Malaria was a real fear here. When the nuns had first opened the mission at the turn of the century, they had believed nets were unnecessary fussiness, and many women had died. Now they had wire mesh on the windows and insecticide sprays and drugs.

'No, no.' Sister Gideon licked dry lips. 'I didn't forget my Paludrine tablets, either.' With a thin hand, she pushed the hair back from her forehead. Like all the nuns, she kept it cut short, trimmed roughly to fit under the head-dress, and it stuck to her head in damp dark tendrils. She had not been eating well for weeks now.

The Infirmarian had seen this, as she saw so much else in her sisters, who were also her charges, noting without comment lassitude, fatigue, heavy eyes. There were illnesses here in the lowlands, catastrophes which could strike at any time. These were so different from anything they knew, so unexpected, that twenty years' experience had still not shown her all of them. Stings and bites from insects they could not even name turned septic with frightening speed. Botflies burrowed beneath the skin to lay their eggs. The hatched larvae, hidden in deep ulcerating holes, gorged on their host. Accidents occurred with the tools the nuns used: machetes and wide-bladed knives took tips off fingers, sliced deep into flesh. And even handling plants in the garden could bring violent allergic reactions: one of the nuns cut down some weeds and the whitish juice blinded her for a week.

The nuns here were enclosed, as they were in the Mother House in Wales. They worked and lived within the large compound. A major part of every day – the early mornings, the best hours, and the evenings – were devoted to prayer. The Infirmarian sighed. Outside, people did not realize that the prayer life was arduous on its own account. Though it gave so much back – beauty, tranquillity, peace of mind – still it cost to stand and kneel for hours at a time when you were exhausted from a day with the children.

No surprise then that Sister Gideon had become ill. In the habit, she had seemed merely over-slim. In her nightdress, she had the knobbly vulnerability of a colt. She muttered, 'Sorry, Sister.'

21

The Infirmarian had never considered the looks of the young woman who had just become not her colleague but her patient. Looks did not matter, it was the inner person who was valuable. But now, in the rough-woven white garment, with her precise profile and the translucent skin you usually saw only in the red-headed, Sister Gideon reminded the older woman of the paintings she had seen on the one foreign holiday of her youth, in small Italian churches.

'You've nothing in the world to be sorry about.' She continued her examination, speaking quietly, not thinking of her own words, using her voice as balm. 'Whatever you've got here, it isn't your fault now. Don't fret, we'll have you up in a couple of days. Just show me where it hurts.' Sister Gideon held her other hand in the air over her midriff, to the left.

'There,' she said. Under the gentle pressure of the Infirmarian's touch, she groaned. Her eyes were closed now, shadowed beneath from lack of sleep.

'No swelling.' The nun was speaking to herself now. Her delicate fingertips told her there was nothing abnormal here: no heat, no distension, no hint of inner disorder or disease. She finished and helped Sister Gideon rebutton the long cotton nightdress. The younger woman said faintly, 'I'm so cold. Why is it so cold?'

'I'll get you another blanket.' She tucked the mosquito net in more firmly round the narrow bed. 'I'll be back in a moment.'

Twenty-four hours later. Sister Gideon was no better. The Infirmarian discussed the problem with her Superior.

'How is she?'

'It's hard to say, Mother. What happened in Chapel – and she's clearly in pain but . . .' Sister Paul hesitated. 'It doesn't hang together. She has no temperature, it's absolutely normal, I couldn't believe it, I took it with two thermometers, to be sure. Yet she's shivering with cold as if she had a fever. I can't find a thing wrong with her.'

The two women looked at each other. The corridor where they stood took the full midday sun and was almost unbearably hot.

'But the pain?'

'That seems to have abated. Nothing for seven hours now. If she had the right symptoms, I'd say appendicitis perhaps. But not without a temperature, some swelling. Even the whites of her eyes are clear.'

'Does any other ailment look like this?'

'Maybe something viral,' the Infirmarian sounded doubtful. 'In this climate you never know. I'll keep an eye on her for a couple of days. Dr Gomez will be here on Friday for the clinic anyway. If she's not better by then.'

The Infirmarian slept in the cell adjoining the Infirmary with both doors open. Tired as she was, she was woken just after three by Sister Gideon's restless muttering. She sat up almost before she was awake.

'Yes, what is it?'

She could just make out words now. They made so little sense, she thought at first she was still asleep. And then the fear she heard in the voice from the next room prickled the skin on her arms. 'Whatever . . . ?'

'Screel din!' Sister Gideon called. Her voice was strange, shrill and childish. Stricken with panic. When the Infirmarian reached her, and spoke her name, it was obvious the younger woman was asleep. She lay absolutely still, but in the bedside light her cheeks were smeared with tears. 'Screel *din!*'

Chapter Three

'Screel din!'

Half a world and fourteen hours away, in North London, Prisoner Number T307805 lay curled on her narrow metal bed in Holloway Prison.

'Screel *din!*'

She woke on a bitter surge: *Oh, God! What now?*

Someone had just shouted to her, cried out in panic the awful childhood warning, used the words she had not heard for so many years.

A wave of old anger and resentment choked her like black mud, anger she couldn't contain or control, trailing despair in its wake. She sat up abruptly and her sudden movement woke Blue. She had drawn the curtains and his hoarse voice came out of the dimness.

'You're gorgeous you're sexy I love you. You're gorgeous you're sexy . . .'

'Shhhhh,' she hissed. Offended, he fluffed his wings and knocked his bell against the cage bars.

Blue and the others were the best thing that had happened to her in prison. Something to look after. At first, she had assumed him dead in the fire at New Hall. It was only thanks to the prison psychologist here in Holloway that after two weeks he had been allowed to follow her. And those weeks without him had shown her how much she had needed someone to love.

She reached out for the mug she'd put beside the bed. She'd got some orange juice left. The mug was decorated like a cross-stitch sampler. It said, HOME SWEET HOME.

Going for reports happened every four months: it was tender, and it hurt, to talk about what had happened. They wanted to discuss personal, private things: they were looking for repentance. She had to say the same things over and over again as different people considered her case.

In the brief time she had been here, the psychologist had unexpectedly given her several sessions. Laura Pegram had explained better than anyone before about the nightmares. The ones where she was desperate to go home, the ones where she was back there, in the house, in the garden, but no-one recognized her. She had sobbed with the effort of describing the feelings they brought with them.

Laura Pegram listened while Kate struggled to explain the blinding anger she felt. And then she'd said, 'We can do something about this, you know.'

Now Kate was dutifully attending the Management of Emotions course, working through long hours of Creative Thinking and Values Enhancement and Critical Reasoning. She was learning not to stifle her feelings, as she had struggled to do for so long, but to let them out, release the poison. She was already proud of herself because it seemed to be working. She'd believed that after all she could move on from what had happened. From what had been done.

But those hardly heard words ('Screel din! Screel din!') had woken all the old fury again. She knew they were intended to alert her to something, they were a communication, a reaching out: the mental energy that had sent them sparked like electricity in her brain.

She'd had enough, she refused to accept any more. If there was a threat, it was not to her. What could they do to her that they had not done already? The fire, the attack on her two months before, had not been her fault. Even so, she was certain it had already set back her chances of parole. She faced the prospect of another year, or two, or more, before it was even raised again.

But she *had* heard the words, and that meant she'd changed nothing. Nothing, in all this long endless time. She thought of what she hadn't been able to tell Laura Pegram. Or any of the parade of psychologists before her. She thought of the thing that must never be said. And she thought, I'll go out of my mind.

She breathed lightly, the way she'd been learning to do in Meditation, let her limbs go soft. Breathe. Breathe. Relax.

When she felt calmer, she opened her eyes. Yesterday she had tucked a printed card under the edge of her mirror: *What's a nice girl like me doing in a place like this?*

The place she was in now was the only place she had. A prisoner's cell in Holloway was her only private space among more than five hundred inmates. And even there she could be observed, at will, from outside through the glass observation panel. Still, it was her home, all ten by twelve feet of it.

Ten by twelve feet in which she was locked from eight o'clock at night for twelve hours. Ten by twelve in which she worked, listened to the radio, slept, cried, drank coffee, ate bowls of muesli, despaired. Ten by twelve in which she could retreat into fantasy, masturbate, plan, read. Or give up.

Plenty did. She could tell: those who didn't take baths when they were allowed to, or use the washing machines to keep their clothes clean. They never exercised unless they were forced to, they viewed everyone with sullen resentment.

Kate understood their behaviour was one of the few forms of protest open to them. They were treated like children, often by guards younger than themselves. They had no control, no voice. Dignity was denied them: everyone called them 'girls', even guards young enough to be their daughters. They were excluded from any decision about their fate, they were excluded from reality.

But none of them was further from reality than Kate. At twenty-six she had been inside for fourteen years. For almost half her life, ever since that March afternoon when the judge had pronounced sentence in the stuffy St Albans courtroom and added, 'Take her down.'

That was exactly what they had done. She had been taken down. She had been depersonalized, degraded, denied. They had taken so much away from her besides freedom: innocence, laughter, love. Prison had got into every part of her life. She would never be free of what had happened. It had destroyed her teenage years. She did not know how to talk to a man who was not a gaoler. Her family links, always few, were now virtually non-existent. Only her grandmother had visited regularly, and for the months before her death last year she'd been too frail to travel.

Before – and for a long time after – the trial, Kate had gone over it and over it: how it had happened, how she could perhaps have stopped it. She was obsessed by it. She saw it like a film for which she invented different beginnings, different middles, different dialogue. But she could never change the ending.

And then gradually, the days and months and years moved on, taking her with them. She was a long way now from that frightened child travelling speechless in the police van away from the court, while the crowds outside howled hate and ran alongside it and thumped the metal sides.

Prison had given her some things, after all. All those endless discussions – with psychologists, psychiatrists, senior prison staff – about why she was there, and the kind of person they hoped she would become. The kind of person she wanted *herself* to become. She had really looked at herself, in a way few people ever do. And the experience had given her a maturity beyond her years.

It had taught her, too, that she could survive living among people who'd terrify anyone outside. Here, in Holloway, she was meeting yet another collection of them. There were seventeen lifers. Like Jan, who had strangled the man she lived with while he slept. She had used her bare hands. Inside, she'd tattooed a writhing flower pattern all over the backs of them, down every finger, round each nail, as if this would transform them from dangerous to decorative. She had wound cotton thread round a needle point, dipped it in blue ink, then pushed it through her skin. She had done this again and again and again, over months, a million tiny stabs, until there was no more skin left to embroider.

Nita was another lifer, doing ten for aggravated assault. The day after Kate reached Holloway, she'd nearly taken the head off a prison officer with a brick stuffed into a sock.

Prison had educated Kate in other ways. She was halfway through her Open University psychology course, although she was finding it harder since the move to Holloway. Most of her essays had gone in the fire, all her books were new, without her notes and markings. But she persevered, not least because it gave her a role other than that of prisoner: she was a student.

She struggled to feel like one. At Cookham Wood she'd started wearing a lot of black: high necked black sweaters over black leggings, little black boots. She still did. It was only the staff, in prison, who had to wear uniform.

And over the years she had tried to make each one of her cells feel the way she supposed a student's room would be. All round her now were heaps of books from her course piled on table and floor. The burn-out at New Hall had cost her all the personal possessions she had painstakingly collected for so long – the two soft pink pigs, the mouse in check trousers, her soapstone Buddha, the lamp from Granny, her Led Zeppelin and Doors tapes, her posters. Holloway's emergency funds had bought her a new Walkman, and a member of the gym staff had given her a flask for hot water, so she could make tea or coffee in her cell. It had stickers on it, Ron Jon Surf Shop Cocoa Beach Florida. Some people had postcards all over their walls, from friends. But Kate had been a prisoner too long. She had no friends outside.

Kate lay down again and buried her face in her arms. The cell was if anything overheated – it had a large radiator – but maybe she was getting a cold, there was always something going round the closed and stressed environment. So she'd put on her furry robe, searching for comfort in the warm material.

The robe had been found for her by the two upright elderly ladies who ran the WRVS shop upstairs. All the clothes were clean and pressed, and all showed very faintly the outlines of other bodies. But her own dressing-gown had been so badly scorched in the burn-out they'd chucked it.

Hard to believe that had all been only seven weeks ago. She had arrived at Holloway late on November 6, the day after the burn-out. She'd been exhausted and in some pain – her hands were burned as she grabbed her smouldering hair – but they were only minor injuries. The true hurt was emotional: the shock of finding how much they hated her. She wondered who had told them the real reason she was inside. The secret.

When the police van delivered her to the bright green door of Holloway Receptions it was half past seven at night. The Receptions Officer, a plump Manchester woman with a bad cold and blue eyeliner, directed them to a neonlit room to the right of the entrance, with a high counter. Officer Ellis took her details – name and age, crime and sentence, where previously held – from the escorting officer, as though Kate were not to be trusted on these things.

Then she said, 'Right, Dean. You're Number T307805. Don't forget it.' She read out the list of jewellery she could keep – a plain ring, a pair of earrings, a necklace with a pendant, three bracelets, a watch. Kate, who possessed only the last of these, said 'Thank you' anyway. She had learned a long time ago that to be polite was easy for her and made things more pleasant.

Officer Ellis looked at her bandages.

'What happened to your hands?'

The escort officer explained about the burn-out. Officer Ellis said, 'We'll get the doctor to have a look at them for you.'

Before that, though, they did other things. A second officer gave her a scratchy brown towelling dressing-gown and pointed to a curtained cubicle. On the wall a huge cartoon girl lifted her skirts and showed her suspenders and grinned. Kate stood facing this stupid image while the officer said to her back, 'Everything off, please. Shoes too.'

Kate waited and the officer whisked the curtain closed. The room wasn't really cold but there were goosebumps all over her skin. When she took off her shoes and socks the floor gritted under her toes. They hadn't given her any slippers.

She unzipped her track suit very slowly, it was hard to get the bottoms off with bandaged hands. T-shirt next. Bra. She sniffed the dressing-gown before she put it on: someone else had worn it.

Tiredness and hunger – the hamburger was all she'd had for hours – heightened her sense of smell, and this place smelled bad. Cigarette smoke and vomit and women's bodies too long unwashed, all overlaid by disinfectant. She came out of the cubicle and sat on a bench against the wall. The stained wood was pockmarked with drawings and words. She wondered what they'd used to scratch so deeply.

A black woman sat on the next bench, also in a dressing-gown. Her shoulders were rounded and she was rocking and talking quietly to herself. Kate could hear the three officers outside discussing the hours they'd been working.

'I started at six-thirty yesterday morning, didn't get off till ten at night,' one of them said, and yawned.

'Today's bin a bugger an' all,' said the second woman. 'What about that pair did the shop in Camden, the state of them? Some people.'

'Didn't mind the smell. It was the yellin'.'

'Can't wait for Thursday,' another voice said, 'I'm gonna get pissed out of me mind an' sleep for a week . . .'

Officer Ellis called her out into the main room. 'You're

lucky tonight. When we're busy in here, we have maybe eighty women coming in, and sixty going out, more sometimes.' She was suddenly brisk. 'Robe off, please.' She added, trying to lighten things a bit, 'You can do a tap dance if you like, give us a twirl.'

Kate turned round stiffly. She understood this had to be done. She'd been in enough prisons by now to know that everyone was searched every time they entered or left – even if they were going to court. Some places even searched you after a solicitor's visit. Although, brought under escort from New Hall, she'd hardly be carrying a weapon. Drugs were a possibility, everyone knew Holloway had a problem with the number of users they had. This search, though, wasn't really designed to find drugs. It was significant and disturbing, it provided a ritualized humiliation, yet another way of demonstrating to her where she stood, how she was regarded.

'Come on,' the officer said, 'do it properly. Stick your arms out.'

Kate complied. She was used to these procedures, but not reconciled to them. She did it, because all these people were around her in uniform. They said, take off your clothes. But really, they were stripping you of everything: you couldn't keep your dignity with your knickers off.

Naked before the uniformed officers with their keys, the symbolic token of their control, she had nothing to protect her. In this secret world of prison, she was laid bare.

'Right,' said the Receptions Officer. 'Put on the dressing-gown and wait over there. The nurse'll want to weigh you.'

Weighed and measured, she went back into the cubicle. As she passed, the third officer, who hadn't spoken to her before, said, 'You'll be OK. It's not bad here.'

32

The unexpected kindness in her voice was almost worse than the orders. Kate knew what was going on. She was the lowest level in the hierarchy, subject to the authority of everyone, from the Chief Governor to the newest officer. She had no control over her existence. And this place was so big: New Hall had maybe a hundred and fifty prisoners against Holloway's five hundred and more.

She had no idea what faced her here. In all the places she'd been – Bullwood Hall, Cookham Wood – the girls had plenty of stories about Holloway. She remembered what they'd said about the women staff, and her hands shook so badly she couldn't fit together the ends of the zip in her track suit.

Officer Ellis was sorting through her belongings in their big paper bags, mopping at her nose with a large tissue. 'You're allowed three sets of clothing with you officially. But you can have five if you want. You can change them over once a month, you get permission to come down to Sanctuary.'

Sanctuary was like a giant lost property office near the entrance at Receptions. *Parcels and Property* said the notice on the door. *9.15–11.30 a.m. 1–2 p.m.* Big clear plastic bags on rows of open shelves held clothes, bedspreads, bright African cottons. Kate saw a rolled red umbrella and wondered how long it would be before its owner needed it again.

They took her photo in an empty room. Front face. Profile. She'd read that Muslim women believed the photographer would then possess their soul. Kate looked into the lens with her mind as blank as her eyes. When later she saw the photograph they'd taken that evening, she scarcely recognized the closed face that gave nothing away.

She was given a pack of wash things – a comb and

toothbrush, a face cloth, SR toothpaste, two plastic sachets of shampoo and a bar of soap without a wrapper, in the sort of brown paper bag used for sanitary towels. The short winceyette flowered nightie they lent her had been washed many times, and the towel was worn. On the wall a sign read: *Wigs are not allowed in possession. Weave-ons and Extensions only. Governor's instructions.*

They still weren't finished with her.

'In here.' She was put in the large holding room, with glass observation panels and tables. She sat on another bench and they gave her tea in a plastic cup. There was another form, more questions. Then the doctor, middle-aged and tired, who unwrapped the bandages on her hands to give them a cursory glance.

'These must be dressed again. You'll need help to have a bath, you mustn't get them wet. We don't want any more problems. You've enough on your plate, young lady.' He looked down at her notes, pushing horn-rimmed glasses back on his nose. 'D'you want something to help you sleep? You must have been very upset by what happened.'

He wore a white coat over his clothes, she could see the silky gleam of his tie. He was quiet and civilized.

She said, dully, 'Not really.'

He looked at her as if she were a moron, and she was too tired to care. How could she explain to this man? The fire had only been a bit of it. She hadn't told anyone about the other things. She wasn't about to start now.

Sometimes she lost track of the secure units and prisons in which she'd been held. It didn't much matter where she was, though. One thing was always the same. It was all right until they discovered what she had done. And then it began. There was no way to explain what it was like. Sometimes they faced you. Sometimes they came from behind.

Once, her arms were wrenched back by people she couldn't see. She was pushed on to her knees, head forced down a stinking lavatory pan: at least two of them must have used it deliberately first. Head pushed even further by a hand on the back of her head. The brown-stained pottery bowl hard and cold and painful on forehead and nose, eyes squeezed shut. The obscene horrible greasy feel, the reek, the *taste* of excrement in her hair, on her skin, her lips, up her nose . . . The endless pause, impossible to breathe, no air, no *air*.

'We *know*, you stinking shit cunt.' And the plug pulled and the water gushing, pumping stuff up into mouth and throat, eyes and hair streaming, gasps choked off . . .

Kate looked at the doctor and her eyes filled as all the strain and hurt of the week hit home. He nodded and wrote on his pad.

'Valium, then.'

She said softly, 'I hate taking pills.'

'We give it in liquid form.' He looked at her from under his glasses. 'Otherwise you might store up your pills and take them all at once, if you were a very silly girl, hmmm?' He doodled on a pad, talking more to himself than to her. 'Wonder if we should keep you apart from the others for a bit . . .'

'I don't want to go on Rule 43. Please.' Experience had taught her what would follow. In the pecking order of prison, Rule 43s were right at the bottom. Prison staff always told her, never tell what you did. Say you're in for burglary. So when other inmates learned she'd been kept separated for her own safety, there was always someone who would make it their business to leak her story. She'd had boiling water chucked over her at Bullwood Hall. In Styal one night, they'd given her four freezing baths. At Cookham Wood they'd shoved her down the stairs, and when they'd seen she was only bruised, had carried her back to the top and thrown her down again. A broken collar bone that time. Still, as she'd been told, could have been worse.

The doctor nodded. 'No, don't worry, not Rule 43. Just the medical wing for twenty-four hours. Till your hands are healed and you're a bit stronger, OK?'

As Kate was finally led away, clutching her belongings in brown paper bags, she'd heard Officer Ellis say reflectively, 'Ordinary looking little thing.'

'Expect her to have horns, did you?' another voice asked.

'Wouldn't have surprised me.'

Prison penetrated every fibre of her body.

At first, she used to think everyone coming towards her wanted to kill her. Because she was under constant surveillance, she imagined they were all talking about her.

And the noise. Cries and echoes, shrill whistles and bells. Radios blasting raucous music. Women's raised voices in the corridor outside, penetrating and intrusive. '*Don' come near me, ya fuckin' yella bitch* . . .' Cell doors opening and crashing closed on metal. The rows that broke out over drugs or stealing, and raged until the screaming combatants were dragged apart and rushed back to their cells.

In Holloway, some of the racket came over the walls: workmen digging beyond the gates in Parkhurst Road, drilling hour after hour. An engine endlessly running on one note. The dangerous drone of the police helicopter hovering above, causing the inmates to glance sideways at each other: some bloke broken out of Pentonville down the Caledonian Road.

Prison was metal and concrete and stone. Holloway was grey and institution blue, and red brick perimeter walls banded with white. These buildings were high and bleak, despite all their efforts to humanize them. Despite the thin grass in the central yard they called 'the village green'. Despite the murals of Portmeirion and tropical islands painted on the walls in the Visitors' Room, the mugs of instant coffee in the psychologist's office, the Arts and Crafts shop full of jewellery and pottery made by the prisoners.

Kate Dean turned her head. The last occupant had hung flowered curtains over the cell window, over the thick unbreakable plastic they used instead of glass, coated with a white glaze like thick fog. The light was odd, paler than usual. She clambered off the bed and opened one of the vertical slits, so narrow she could just about see the block opposite. Then she had to pull it almost closed, because Blue flew out of his open cage and clung to the front of her robe.

It was snowing. Nothing spectacular, just wispy flakes that turned immediately to dirty water on the glistening roofs. She wished it would fall thick and perfect as a Christmas card. She tucked her hands into her sleeves and tried to imagine what it must be like outside.

Chapter Four

Father Michael Falcone drove his body the length of the empty pool, his shoulders a muscled wedge cutting through chlorinated water with a sure grace he lacked on land.

Seven . . . Eight . . . No thoughts here. Nothing but exhilaration at the massive pressure of water against chest and thighs, the sound in his ears of his regular gasps for air.

Twelve . . . Fourteen . . . Streams of water filleted back from his upraised arms. The steady pattern of his movements – right arm left leg, left arm right leg – were a reassurance. The leg was almost healed now. In water at any rate it was as good as ever.

Eighteen . . . Twenty . . . It was a dull April morning outside, but in here lights were set into portholes in the pool sides below the water, their beams emphasizing every wave and ripple. It was humid and steamy as a tropical aquarium, totally insulated from Central London.

Twenty-five . . . Twenty-eight . . . Father Michael began to slow down: he wasn't as fit as he had been. Or as young.

Thirty-two . . . Thirty-four . . . He would be thirty-four on his next birthday. Holy shit! Where did the time go?

Thirty-six . . . Time had intruded now. He had a lot to do today.

He increased his pace. Forty-one . . . Forty-two . . . He turned on his back and floated, waiting to catch his breath. He could hear voices in the changing rooms, the sound of a shower, but he still had the water to himself and no-one else was in sight. A very small boy in bright shorts galloped out and tore at top speed towards the deep end of the pool. He carried a yellow plastic board and a pair of blown up fluorescent red armbands.

The priest wiped his face clear of water, pressed his hands through unruly black hair now sleeked to his head. He moved to the end lane and started his next lap, anxious to finish before the pool filled up. He swam every morning when he didn't have early mass.

Forty-five . . . Forty-six . . . His right hand reached for the curve of tile at the pool's end, push and turn and off again.

He heard the splash as the child bellyflopped into the water, and the waves slapped against his own face. He was irritated by this: he finished before nine to avoid the young families, and he still had seven minutes to go.

Forty-seven . . .

'MARK!'

The woman's scream was loud enough to reach him over the sound of his splashing. He paused in mid-stroke, shook his head to clear his eyes and looked behind him.

'Oh God! MARK!'

She was at the edge of the pool with a baby girl in her arms, staring down. A young mother, mid-twenties, in a black swimsuit. Clutching her daughter tightly, she was starting down the steps. Alerted by her screams, an attendant was already running towards her.

Father Michael was faster. A dozen strokes took him

to where the little boy was flailing wildly out of his depth, sinking below the surface, his mouth open to scream but taking in water.

Michael grabbed the boy's arm above the elbow, but the child was too panic-stricken to hold on to him. Slippery as a fish, he struggled to avoid the man's grasp, churning up the water around him like a frenzied puppy. The big overhead lights burst on and the priest saw his blue eyes were staring and sightless from shock. With astonishing strength he wrenched his bony little arm away, sank back again under the water. The priest sank down too, eyes open, reaching out for the twisting, writhing boy. The child's frantically kicking foot caught him hard in the groin and he expelled air in an involuntary wordless shout: the sharp pain made him want to retch.

In the moments it took him to recover, the boy had dropped further away from him beneath the water. Michael forced himself down, eyes open. Somewhere above them on the poolside there was activity and movement, but beneath the illuminated water Michael could hear nothing.

There was an ache like an iron bar in his chest but no time to surface for air. Then the boy was rising and when the priest lunged out again, he got the child firmly round the waist, held him close enough to avoid the kicking legs and kicked out himself, propelling them both upwards. It took twenty years before they broke the surface in an explosion of water. There was a roaring in his ears and he couldn't see.

He floundered wildly for a moment, guided by shouts from somewhere above his head. Then, thank God, his foot made contact with the side of the pool.

Waiting hands grasped the child, who let out a wordless howl of protest. In his fear, he didn't know what was happening, only that he was being torn from his rescuer. He clung frenziedly, arms and legs twined round the man with amazing strength. Unable to speak, holding on to the edge of the pool with one hand, Michael tightened the arm that held the boy, to reassure him.

Voices at the poolside shouted, urgently:

'Come on now, let's get this towel round you.'

'Up you come, son, give us your hand.'

The voices fell on deaf ears. Michael hung in the water, the boy's wet head still buried against his chest. His heart was bursting: from the effort, from relief, from the tenderness he felt for this child. Not until his mother reached down for him ('Marky, come to Mummy, come on!') did the boy loose his grip on Michael, let himself be lifted from the water.

The priest held on to the curved tiles. He was shivering violently despite the clammy heat. Above his head someone was giving orders.

'. . . get his head down, well down, he's swallowed a lot of . . .'

Something touched his back and he looked round. The yellow plastic swimboard was bumping against him, bobbing on the disturbed surface of the pool. Still carefully balanced on it, incredibly after all that activity, were two fluorescent red armbands.

When he came out of the water one of the attendants, a smoothly tanned Australian, put a towel round his shoulders.

'You did great. Good on yer. You go and warm up under a shower now, we'll look after the kid.'

The woman was sitting on the ground, the boy leaning back weakly against her, his face white and his hair plastered flat against his skull. He looked even smaller than before, not more than four years old. The little girl was crouched by her brother's feet, holding on to them with both hands. The woman looked up at him and she had the same blue eyes as her son, red now from crying. Even distraught, she was pretty, light brown curls shining with youth.

'I'm sorry.' She shook her head. 'I'm so sorry.'

'No,' he said, sombrely. 'I'm the one who's sorry. I saw he was by himself, I should have kept an eye on him. I'm not . . .' he paused. 'I'm afraid I'm not used to children.'

She didn't seem to hear him. 'I don't know how it happened. I just never let him near the water on his own, I've told him and told him. But he's so *quick* . . .' Her voice trailed off into little gasping sobs of relief.

Father Michael squatted beside her.

'Don't worry now. He's safe, he'll not do it again. You can't have eyes in the back of your head.'

Impulsively, she reached up and put her free arm round his neck and kissed his cheek. She seemed not to notice the instinctive reaction he couldn't help, the way his jaw set and his shoulders tensed: it was a long time since any woman had been so openly demonstrative towards him.

'Thank you. *Thank* you. I'll never forget what you did for us.' She drew back a little. 'You look as if you've had a shock as well. Will you be all right?'

He spent a long time under a hot shower. The boy's frantic grasp had scratched the skin of his chest and shoulders, the weals stinging as he washed off the chlorine. When he got home, he'd put on witch-hazel cream. He rubbed his hair dry, dressed in trousers and shirt, then the black scholar's robe with its long shoulder wings. His hands quivered as he did up his white neckband.

He was in the foyer ready to leave when the three of

them came out of the First Aid room. The woman, still in her black swimsuit with a towel round her shoulders, glanced towards him without recognition or interest, her gaze passing over the priest's clothes, the Roman collar. She never even looked at his face.

Father Michael sat at the big desk and stared out of the window. It was a typical Central London view of tiles, slender spires, distant office blocks, and after years in Africa it delighted him. He was here by chance. He had been staying at Jesuit House, the order's London headquarters in Mount Street, where he bumped into an old friend, one of half a dozen men he knew who had left the priesthood. He was off to Kuwait for six months, and suggested Michael might like to use his flat while he was away. The two attic rooms overlooking a roof terrace were simply furnished – but luxurious to Michael.

He tried to drag his mind back to the page he was working on but the words never lifted off the paper into his mind. All he could see was the little blond boy running towards the pool, all he could hear was the smack of his body hitting the water. The whole incident had left him unaccountably shaken.

That poor woman had kissed him for saving her son. She should have slapped his face.

He had seen a small boy playing alone. He had known himself to be the only adult present. Why hadn't he realized the little boy was far too young to jump into eight feet of water? Any other man would have had the commonsense to see what might happen. But not him. He had felt no concern, nothing but annoyance at the child's presence.

Father Michael shoved his papers away with a violent gesture. What kind of selfish monster had he become?

43

He had cut himself off from the swirl and movement of life. Swimming in that pool this morning had been like swimming in a tropical aquarium. He saw himself circling round and round it for ever, imprisoned behind a bubble of glass. Feeling nothing, touching no-one.

It wasn't meant to be like this. It had not been isolation he sought, but integration. He had tried to love more, not less. Something had gone terribly wrong.

He had wanted to be part of each individual – but he was part of no-one. He had thought he would be able to change lives – and through his own lack of concern, he had nearly watched one lost.

He had made his vows at the seminary with only the normal degree of fear: God did not expect the impossible. The vows were practical, they would free him for his work. They were the keys to open up his life. Through them, he would immerse himself in the love of God.

Poverty was easy. Possessions had never interested him much, they held you back and he wanted to go forward. He had been living in one room in a rented house with a group of friends before he entered the seminary: he'd made a small ceremony out of giving away odd pieces of furniture, a couple of prints, clothes. In many ways, he had fewer problems than most people struggling to bring up children, pay for housing and heating, buy essentials, afford a holiday. He had everything he needed.

He was far more conscious of his vow of obedience, living under regulations like a soldier in barracks. Maybe he could decide where to have his evening meal or what he wore: dress rules had been so relaxed that now novices even wore blue jeans for mass in the Church of the Gesu, the ancient baroque church of the Jesuits in Rome. But the big decisions in his life were taken for him and without him: the work he would do, the country in which he did it.

Perfect Jesuit obedience was the glue bonding that clever and scattered group, the 'Pope's Men'. It held them together for more than a thousand years of worldwide power and influence. At twenty, Michael Falcone had tried ardently to follow the demands of Inigo de Loyola, to let himself be kneaded like a lump of wax, to be part of that mystical union of hearts and wills.

But the Society of Jesus, like every other religious group, had begun to change before he ever joined them. It was no longer the disciplined and intellectual force it once had been. In the eighties, change accelerated and Michael Falcone changed with the others. Thirteen years on, he found his vow of obedience chafed each day like a badly fitting shoe.

Father Michael shivered again. He had walked back from the pool as usual and eaten the same simple breakfast he always made of cereal and fruit, wholemeal toast and tea. That had been two hours ago. He went across to the long sideboard where a tray had been left ready, and switched on the kettle. He put two spoonfuls of ground coffee into the filter and leaned against a cupboard, arms folded, waiting for the water to boil.

The day was still dark, he ought to turn on the light, but the grey suited his gloomy mood. He might have saved the child, but he could only see that he had failed. The incident at the pool could serve as a metaphor for his life: he was no longer capable of seeing what was before his eyes. He was going under.

For all these years he had put a high value on thoughts and theories, pursued abstract ideas, gone to bed exhausted by argument, discussions. His mind had been satisfied. His heart was another matter. He had become cold and isolated, incapable of involvement, of real caring. Years of spiritual training had cut him off from his own feelings. He had tried to live the life of angels – and forgotten that he was only a man.

But his body had not forgotten. It was thirty-four years old and strong, and yet for all this time its needs had been ignored and suppressed. He had not come to terms with still being sexual despite being 'Father'. He hadn't faced the needs and desires of his body, only denied them. As he had denied the symptoms of despair he would have detected in another man a long time ago.

Celibacy had been the most exciting of the three vows. It was the most spectacular promise, the greatest renunciation. He had seen it as part of a miraculous process, the search for perfection.

It was a challenge: *Come, follow Me.* By accepting, he knew he would never be alone. He would come as close as a man could to living in Christ if he became celibate.

In retrospect, he had spoken the words without any understanding of what it would mean for him as the years went by. Full of faith and enthusiasm, he believed what he was told: his calling singled him out and set him apart. He was better than the angels.

That was how it had felt, at first. He had chosen to remain free of all human ties so he could devote himself to others. He was to be a sign of God in the world, for he had made a passionate commitment to Christ.

He was younger then and more idealistic, totally committed and excited by the future waiting for him. His one brief love affair had ended with enough bitterness to convince him he would never find happiness with a woman. He told himself – he really believed – that satisfactions of the flesh weren't important to him: ideas

were. A man could be spiritual or he could be sexual –
but not both.

So he had ignored any problems which were merely
physical. He had dismissed the headaches, promising
himself to go for an eye test soon. He decided the
depression that came down whenever he had a moment's
leisure was due to tiredness. And that in turn was caused
by sleepless nights, which he was sure were brought
about by overwork. He never allowed himself to admit
to unhappiness, because then he would have had to deal
with the consequences.

What happened this morning had jolted him out of
lethargy. If that child had died, it would have been due
to his negligence. Maybe no-one else would have blamed
him but he would always have known. He could not risk
another failure. He saw again the child's mother at the
poolside cradling the boy in her arms. She had been beside
herself with worry and still she had found the time and the
emotional energy to be concerned with his well-being, to
ask how he felt. She had, in a way, taken his role, spoken
his words.

Four months ago, when he crashed the motorbike and
broke his leg and the order had sent him home, his life
had changed. In the long hours at his disposal, he realized
his former frantic busyness had enabled him not to think.
In all honesty, he had deliberately taken on work for just
that reason. Now, compelled to reluctant inactivity, he
was forced at last to face up to all his doubts and questions,
the emotions and desires he had struggled to suppress.

Her skin had been very soft and warm beneath his hand.
Her thighs were rounded and white, and her breasts had
pressed against the black stuff of her swimsuit. His body
ached, just at the memory.

He saw her face, in the foyer, when he stood before

her dressed as a priest and she didn't recognize the man. It was as if he had become invisible, without value.

But a priest was not a man. He was always a priest. The bishop had put his hands on Michael's dark head during the ceremony of ordination.

'*Tu es sacerdos in aeternum.*'

Thou art a priest for ever. After the order of Melchisedech.

During his time as a Jesuit, he'd seen a lot of his friends walk away from the order. In the past twenty years the number of men and women leaving religious life had been first a trickle, then a flood. Now it had steadied, but the departures continued, as people found they could no longer bear to have their personal lives ordered by Rome.

For many, it was the vow of celibacy and chastity which finally tipped the scales. Like him, they understood it was only one of the threads of their commitment. It was not the end, only the means, a necessary sacrifice. But it had come to seem outmoded and out of touch with normal life. They could not handle it any longer.

Father Michael thought of the child in the pool this morning, the small wet body in his arms. If he were to marry, it would be a mortal sin: his union would never be recognized by the Church. Any child of his would be considered illegitimate.

The kettle boiled and switched itself off. He didn't move.

Tu es sacerdos in aeternum.

It is always going to be like this. I will be alone always, every day and every night, until I die.

Chapter Five

She could smell them even before they crowded into the compound. She could detect their scent long after they had gone.

The garden was loud with the scraping of cicadas as Sister Gideon locked the door of the low building they used as a schoolroom. Even now, hours later, she smelt the scented oil, rich as fruit, the young Indian women used on hair and skin. Under it, the hint of urine from the babies slung so casually on their hips. The brown burnt odour they brought with them came from the leaves of the sapodilla trees they chewed to a soft paste. The nuns said, that was what made them so happy.

While she taught the children to add and subtract and write their names, their mothers sat outside on the open verandah breastfeeding their babies and chattering. They were sturdy and vivid in their home-woven clothes and she couldn't look at them enough. Their hair was long and straight, blue-black as Parker's ink in her pen at school. They prized their strong noses, and thought beauty lay in crossed eyes. When she'd first seen how they tied a bead on a thread into the hair of the babies, so it dangled between their eyes, she'd been horrified. The Infirmarian had warned, leave them be, you'll not change the beliefs of a thousand years overnight.

Sister Gideon had started brushing the verandah. Almost immediately, she had to pause to get her breath. She tried not to think of the physical distress she was enduring. There was nothing wrong with her, nothing. Maybe it was just overwork: they'd been busier than ever, these last months. And the work was vital.

Still, they could spare her for ten minutes. She perched on the top step. She sat neatly, knees together, arms linked round them. As always, she sat in one corner. As always, unconsciously, it was the left side she chose. She gripped her left wrist tightly with her right hand, thumb uppermost.

They all did far too much. Because the need was here, but not enough nuns and not enough time to do it all. Their school was the only one within reach of three hundred families. It was important both to them and to the people it served. With an education, these peasant children might perhaps be able to hope for more than a life of grinding poverty and toil.

Sister Gideon knew they were not educating savages. Two hundred and fifty years after Christ, the Mayan civilization had been at its peak. They were sculptors and astronomers even then, mathematicians and potters and weavers of textiles. Their architects had built wonderful cities of stone. There, they held their ceremonies and buried their kings.

A century ago, when their order arrived among these people, the nuns believed they could bring salvation to the Maya Indians through Christ. Now they knew better. The Christianity here was coloured and shaped by the many Mayan deities the people would not relinquish. They even gave Christian figures the names of their own gods. The same gods they had once placated in chilling rituals, hurling living human sacrifices into deep wells, slaughtering them upon carved altars.

Yesterday, the child Gloria had seized Sister Gideon's hand and pointed to the convent's old wooden St Joseph.

'Iapec,' the child had whispered, awed.

'No,' Sister Gideon had protested. 'Poor St Joseph, you don't want to change his name.'

Later that afternoon, when she was in the kitchen, she asked Ester. A tough, leathery little woman of no age anyone knew, her plait still fiercely black, she never seemed to stop working.

'What did Gloria mean, calling St Joseph that name?'

Ester didn't pause in her scrubbing but she lifted her head for a moment and her eyes were quick and black.

'Is not San Joseph. Is Itzamna.'

'Who is Itzamna?'

'Lizard House.' She spoke the name almost with reluctance and scrubbed faster, the skin of her hand red from hot water.

Sister Gideon opened her mouth to explain once more to Ester about the Holy Family. And closed it again.

The Indians prayed with the nuns for their crops. Then they would go to their own altars, hidden on the edges of the land they cultivated. They beseeched Chuc to send the rain they needed. For an abundant harvest of maize, they danced before Ah Mun. In order that that sun god would look on them, they offered Kinich Ahau their own blood, secretly, spattered on pieces of bark.

When the rains came, and the maize ripened, the nuns held their Thanksgiving service in the whitewashed chapel. The Indians sang and prayed with them. But it was Chuc and Ah Mun who once more had ensured their

51

survival. It was Kinich Ahau's warmth that had lifted the crops from the earth.

Sister Gideon understood why they sweetened the ground for him with their blood. It was all that remained of the old ways, the bitter sacrifices. These people had all but forgotten the origins of their rituals, yet repeated them generation after generation. The Indians worshipped a hundred and fifty gods. Before she left for Central America, when the nuns on furlough back at the Welsh convent spoke of the mission and told how there was a different god for every act, Sister Gideon used to wonder, why ever would they want ours?

When she made the long journey to the Petén, they had stopped one night in a town she couldn't pronounce, with a fine old colonial mission church dominating the dusty pink main square. Early next morning they had gone there for mass.

Inside, she had her first glimpse of the intensity and strangeness of the faith in this distant place. Among clouds of incense, the figures of saints stood in their niches, as they always did, only they were no saints she recognized.

All of them were dark-skinned and swathed in women's clothes, though one wore a stove-pipe hat. They were short and stocky as the Indians themselves, they had the same big bare brown feet. Many of these, she saw, were stained like the palms of their outheld hands with painted stigmata. The sight of the dark wounds was painful to her.

These people had been conquered centuries before the nuns arrived. But their 'pagan' cults had never been eradicated as the Spanish Inquisitors intended. They were thousands of years old, and they would not be extinguished. They had simply been absorbed into the voluminous folds of the new faith.

Old gods do not vanish. Old bloodstains only fade.

Chapter Six

'Outta my way, ya stuck up lil' slag.'

Kate moved aside and Carla slammed down two more huge tins of baked beans on the worktop. There was plenty of room, but you didn't argue with Carla, and certainly not at six in the morning. She bristled with aggression, and though not a big woman she demanded a great deal of space. Under her white kitchen overall she wore powder-blue track suit bottoms with a pale-pink stripe, bare feet in grubby light-green trainers. Kate thought it curious, that a woman capable of extreme physical violence should choose to dress herself in baby colours. The other girls treated Carla as they would a bear, giving her a wide berth, taking pains not to annoy her.

'Thanks,' Kate said. 'I was just coming to get those.' Carla's words had been unpleasant but not the tone: Carla was in a good mood. And she liked Kate. If she hadn't, she would have jostled her out of the way.

Kate tipped the contents of the vast saucepan she was stirring into a long metal dish. Her hands were healed now. Using oven gloves, she slid this into its compartment in one of the heated metal trolleys. According to the blackboard on the wall with its chalked menus and special orders (22 vegans, 5 low fat, 70 no pork), breakfast today was sausage and beans for 466 people. Each unit made its own toast upstairs and tea was brewed up there as well: the wing cleaners made it with water from the boilers, in big metal teapots.

At £7 a week, the kitchens paid inmates the highest wages in the prison, but they earned it: the night patrol woke them to start breakfast at five. Apart from the permanent kitchen staff, there were twenty-four inmates on kitchen duty each day. Kate wasn't normally one of them, but the prison was in the middle of a flu epidemic. She had been doing it for just five days, and she couldn't get the cabbagy smell of the washing up gloves out of her skin.

Kate was filling the saucepan with more tinned beans when Bob came over. He was one of the kitchen officers, a sallow, worried-looking man who could have been any age between twenty-four and forty. He'd been nearby when Carla swore at her. Now he said, the firm order hidden in the question, 'Carla, take over here, will you?' He turned to Kate. 'Miss Shaw says, if you've had breakfast, you can start chopping onions with Iyabo.'

Kate stood back without protest. Carla grimaced. 'Bloody beans,' she said, 'I hate soddin' bloody beans.' But she picked up the wooden spoon. Kate went to the glass fronted office at the back of the enormous kitchens, behind the banks of ovens. She opened the door and smiled at Miss Shaw, the officer in charge. They had already exchanged their 'Good mornings': Miss Shaw, who had been running the kitchens for seven years now, was always down here by six a.m., and remained on duty till five o'clock and probably much later. She spent a lot of her time making up menus, ordering in food, doing the books. She was emotionally – though not physically – a Jewish mother figure who had somehow managed to end up single and in the prison service. She was an unlikely

54

cook anyway, being very tall and impossibly skinny. Olive Oyl, Kate thought, even to the enormous feet.

Miss Shaw believed in the importance of food for people whose lives were so drab. 'You handle food,' she said, 'like love and hamsters – very carefully.' The trouble was – as Kate knew, but suspected Miss Shaw did not – most of the girls would have preferred hamburgers and chips every day, strong curries, fry-ups: the sort of food they were used to.

Prison meals went round the building on the trolley route, pushed along the concrete corridors linking the prison blocks. The girls either ate in small communal dining rooms or – in the case of trusted inmates with more freedom of movement – in the TV rooms, even their cells. Food might be eaten two hours or more after it was sent out on the trolley, after sitting in the hot plates kept in heated metal cupboards on each unit. By then, what had been tempting in the kitchens was reduced to half empty tins crusted with gravy.

Kate had never complained about the meals, though, even at prisons where it was far worse than here. She listened to the others grumbling and quietly got on with liver and onion casserole, or vegetable pie and chips, or roast chicken and chips. She loved rock-cakes and the farmhouse sponge the kitchens turned out in ranks of huge metal dishes. Holloway used to bake its own bread, but now the kitchens only made rolls themselves, using 96 kilos of flour at a time.

It never occurred to her that she liked prison food because it was all she could ever remember eating: alone among the inmates of this vast place, she had no basis for comparison.

Now she went to get a knife from the narrow cupboard which was locked by a prison officer every night after checking each item, unlocked again first thing in the morning. Each knife – long, curved and all catering quality – had its own slot. In order to take one, you replaced it with your brass tally so an officer could see at a glance who was using which knife.

She selected a kitchen devil for the onions. This, of course, was why Bob had asked Carla to switch jobs with her. If Carla was in a bad temper, he didn't want her with a possible weapon in her hands. Anyone applying for kitchen work had to be approved first, and Carla had been behaving well for a long time. Her violence took the form of verbal abuse these days, Kate had heard she'd calmed down a lot. But you couldn't blame Bob for being cautious.

Kate rinsed her hands in cold water and salt, which Miss Shaw reckoned reduced the onion smell, and went to the chopping table where Iyabo Odeh was working with an open sack of onions beside her.

''Morning,' she said, and got a slow, shy smile in return. When she smiled, Iyabo's lips turned outwards like a fleshy flower. A lot of Nigerians did kitchen work and kept very much to themselves. Iyabo was younger than the others, she looked about twenty. She didn't speak much and Kate felt sorry for her. She started peeling and slicing, forced herself to keep her hands away from her watering eyes.

'Heard anything yet?' she asked.

'No letter. No nuthin'.' Iyabo's voice was small and despairing. 'Nuthin',' she repeated.

'Maybe tomorrow,' Kate said, but both of them knew there would be nothing tomorrow, either.

Iyabo had been in Holloway about a month longer than Kate, just one of many women induced to fly to England with drugs smuggled from Nigeria. She had been told to take her baby with her as cover, but at the last moment had left the child with her mother: now she was desperate to get back to them. She would be deported at the end of her sentence, but that was a long way off.

Kate said, 'Perhaps your mother will write soon.'

'She don' know to write.'

'You said your sister could.'

The Nigerian woman shook her head. 'No. No use. My sister gone wid her man now.'

Iyabo never referred to her child's father. Kate felt an odd affinity for this silent young woman, whose few visitors were not anyone she loved, but from the befriending organizations for African women: Kate had shown her how to fill in visiting orders.

Kate sliced onions mechanically, lost in her thoughts. She filled in very few for herself, these days. Gran had always been her chief visitor, and Kate missed her terribly, more than she could have believed. There was no-one else.

Long ago, when she was in the Young Offenders Unit, Dad used to come regularly to see her. These days a new young family took all his time and energy: Kate had two half-brothers she didn't know. Long before he had stopped visiting, they had run out of things to say. She wasn't part of his life anymore. She wasn't part of anyone's life.

Kate tried to shut her mind to the cries of warning (*Screel din!*) that came to her more and more frequently – three or four times, some days. She didn't want to hear them, to acknowledge what was going on. Not anyone's life, she told herself.

They'd been peeling and slicing for twenty minutes. Kate never noticed Carla coming towards them, carrying the heavy saucepans to the sink. She didn't see Iyabo, unaware, step back into her path.

All she heard was Carla's roar of anger as she dropped

a saucepan, and Iyabo's shriek, and the sudden horrified silence in the huge kitchen.

Like a punch-drunk boxer, Carla rolled back on her heels and the beefy arms came up in front of her chest. Before the Nigerian girl could move, one vast hand was at her throat and the girl's head was slammed against the wall.

Officer Nelson was a senior officer, a middle-aged black man with an athlete's supple walk. He seemed never to hurry but he was there almost instantly, at Carla's shoulder. Another, less experienced man might have put a hand on Carla, and Kate knew what could have happened then.

But Officer Nelson spoke very quietly, so quietly no-one else heard what he said. Nothing happened for a long, long moment, while Iyabo's eyes rolled back in her head from fear.

Then Carla's body gradually relaxed, the tension went out of her, and the black girl, unexpectedly released, slid down the wall to the floor.

'AAAaagh!' A second later, there was another bellow from Carla as Bob and Miss Shaw grabbed her from behind, wrenching her arms behind her back. She was wild and screaming, it took both of them to wrestle her to the floor. Bob sat on her chest while Miss Shaw and Officer Nelson snapped her into handcuffs.

Kate had gone over to Iyabo, who was too stunned to speak. The whole episode had taken less than two minutes.

'Let's have a look.' Miss Shaw was there, feeling the back of Iyabo's head, looking at her throat, inspecting her hand. She'd held on to her kitchen knife through the attack and the blade must have slipped between thumb and first finger: blood was bright on the pink skin.

Kate said, 'Hold it up. Up!' She grabbed a piece of paper kitchen towel and tried to staunch the flow. Iyabo was moaning softly.

Miss Shaw held a clean J-cloth under the tap at a nearby sink. Iyabo's eyes were huge, there was a rim of white round the velvety dark iris, like a frightened pony. Miss Shaw said briskly, 'She can walk all right . . . Kate, you know where the clinic is? You're both due a break anyway.' Miss Shaw turned to the Nigerian girl. 'If nurse says it's all right, go back to your cell for the rest of the day. I'll telephone your unit now and tell them you're to rest.'

The nurse was efficient but unfriendly. Silently she washed, disinfected, bandaged. 'Tetanus up to date?' When Iyabo looked blank, the nurse dabbed her arm and injected her swiftly.

On Iyabo's unit, Kate made them coffee in the empty kitchenette and they drank it in silence. They were both still wearing the white kitchen uniform and the white peaked caps that were made upstairs in the sewing room, and sent out as orders to other prisons. Iyabo was holding her hand cradled close to her body, and Kate saw there was blood smeared on Iyabo's lapel. The Nigerian girl followed her glance.

'I wash it.'

She led the way along the corridor. Iyabo's cell was a bleaker replica of Kate's. The posters had belonged to someone else, the only books were a couple of black women's magazines. Beside them, the Foreign Prisoners' Resource Pack telling Iyabo her rights and giving basic information about the courts, immigration and deportation. Kate wondered if she had read it. On a chest of drawers a handbag mirror with chipped edges was propped beside a tube of skin cleanser, a deodorant and a bottle of shampoo.

Iyabo went to the basin and started scrubbing the bloodstain with a nailbrush. Kate sat on the bed and drank her coffee. A photograph of a small smiling naked boy was stuck to the wall. Iyabo had shown this to her before, her son Akande. Just below, on a cupboard top was the only other personal item in the room: a strange wooden statue about nine inches high.

'Did you bring this with you?' Kate was about to touch it, then drew back her hand. The little man – the genitals were most specific – had markings on his cheeks, just as Iyabo did. Eyes, mouth and nose, even the ears, were well defined, and the legs were planted wide apart on a wooden base. The carved detail was intricate and somehow eerie. Perhaps because the room was so empty of possessions, it was a powerful little presence.

'He is ibeji.' Iyabo said it so softly Kate could hardly hear.

'Ibeji? What's that?'

Kate noticed the painted box placed in front of the little man. It had once contained Simple soap, she could make out the wording through the yellow watercolour. Two artificial flowers, painstakingly cut and sewn of blue satin, lay on the box like an offering on an altar.

'Is ibeji a god?' she asked.

Iyabo turned round, very serious. 'Not a god, but very strong.' She touched the photograph of the smiling baby with a tender forefinger, and Kate saw the surface of the photograph was smeared where she must kiss it goodnight. The Nigerian woman touched the cheek of the statue with the same caress.

'This is Obawa,' she said. 'My son.'

Kate was lost. 'But your son is called Akande.'

Iyabo sat down on the bed. 'Ibeji means two. This is my son Obawa.'

'I didn't realize you had two boys.'

'Two just the same. Same face, same eyes, same hands.' She leaned forward and patted the little carved hand. 'This is my son who has gone away.'

There was a long pause. Kate said quietly, 'He died.'

'Oh no.' Iyabo was emphatic. 'Oh no. He din' die. He jus' gone away.' She put her coffee mug on the floor, and cradled the injured hand. 'He gone away three years now,' she said. 'He came to me after Akande, a long time after, a day maybe. An' then he got very tired an' he gone away.'

Kate said, 'You mean – you had two babies. Twins? Is that what you mean?'

Iyabo nodded firmly. 'It's good. He near to spirits now. So my mother show me, an' I keep Obawa close, so he don' get angry. I carry everywhere. I wash him. I dress him. He like pretty things, see?' She showed Kate the tiny bright beads threaded round the wooden neck. 'I sing to him, in the night. An' I dance wid him.' She got up, and held the little figure carefully in front of her at waist level, facing Kate. She started to dance, swaying her hips, her shoulders, humming softly. It was a lullaby. Kate watched her move. Iyabo was unaware of her cramped surroundings, lost in her small ritual of devotion.

'An' then one day,' she went on, 'he will come back to me an' Akande. He needs his brother or he never be happy. Obawa will be borned again, no problem.' Her eyes were shining. 'It's good to have an ibeji. He take care of us.'

'Yes,' said Kate, 'of course he will.'

And she thought, Gone away.

Just like her.

Chapter Seven

St Agnes, pray for us.

She followed Sister James in procession across the compound. A flock of tiny parrots the colour of limes rose squawking into the evening sky, and the cooling air released damp scents from the earth.

St Michael, pray for us.

It had been a hot, harried day. That was always a worry: it was hard not to fall asleep when you were tired.

St Peter, pray for us.

On the edge of the compound, where the trees were very dense, they formed a dark green tunnel which flowered only at the high tips, young fronds of silky green and silver. Beneath, the foliage was brown and there was a rich, cloying smell of wet vegetation. It was dark in there now, and fireflies – *luciernagas* – glimmered in the shadows. She caught small, fierce night sounds.

St Benedict, pray for us.

The nuns carried lit candles, but they did not need them. Ix Chel was the moon goddess. Huge and low she hung above the convent, her glowing golden face at every window as they passed.

St Jerome, pray for us. St Catherine, pray for us.

They reached the Refectory, where the evening meal was laid out ready for them. Before each place a pottery bowl, with its hardboiled egg and piece of flat bread covered with a plate. A handleless cup, a godet, stood beside it. Long platters held sweet peppers and beans.

St Ambrose, pray for us. St Clare, pray for us.

The nuns placed their candles on the long tables. They had their own electricity generator in the compound but used it as little as possible. It was ancient and unreliable and expensive. They had long ago decided its use was a luxury. The nuns must not be seen to set themselves above the people they served, who survived on so little.

The candle flames were invisible in the moonlight pouring through the glass roof of the conservatory where they ate. It cast sharp shadows behind the benches and beneath the table. It caught at the silver of crucifix and profession ring. It gleamed on the white habits. It shadowed their eyes, hollowed their cheeks. It turned their skin to chalk.

St Jude, pray for us.

So no-one noticed how pale Sister Gideon had gone, quite suddenly, as grace finished and the nuns seated themselves to eat and listen to the reading from the Book of Job. No-one saw how she crumbled her bread into the bowl, and chopped her egg into little pieces without eating any.

When they reached puddings – dried pineapple and apricots, a bowl of oranges and bananas – she muttered her apology, scrambled over the bench and hurried from the room, the back of her hand pressed against her mouth.

A little later, Sister Paul came to her cell. Sister Gideon had not lit her paraffin lamp and the only light was the one bulb hanging in the corridor.

'Has it started again, Sister? The same pain?'

'I don't know. I can't tell.' Sister Gideon's hands were

shaking. The Infirmarian slipped a thermometer into her mouth and held the thin wrist to take her pulse.

'Everything seems normal. It's been two weeks since you were last ill . . . Try taking a couple of aspirin and we'll see how you are in the morning.'

Only when she was alone did Sister Gideon let herself rock backwards and forwards in pain, wrapped in her own arms. No-one heard the small, childish words she whispered to herself, sitting on her bed, watched only by Ix Chel. Even if they had, they wouldn't have understood them. Just one other person spoke that language.

The moon floated higher above the steep thatched convent roofs. Now its green white glare leached all colour from the land. Sister Gideon got very cautiously to her feet and moved to the window so she could see it, flat and round, a circle cut out of indigo cloth. She could never imagine becoming accustomed to the nights of Guatemala, pure and deep and stretching to infinity, crusted with stars burning cold.

Something bumped and whirred softly against her head. Startled, she jumped back. A huge moth buffeted itself against the blind, a panicked prisoner. It finally settled high in one corner, draping wings of gold-dusted gauze across its furred body.

After a while the pain lessened, as she had learned it did. She unpinned the back of her head-dress and released the white headband. With a sigh of relief she ran her hand through short strands of sweat-damp hair. She undressed, putting her habit on its hanger, smoothing the folds, meticulous and quiet. She moved as carefully as a woman balancing a bowl of boiling liquid, so as not to set off the inner turmoil again.

Normally she washed before going to bed, because of the heat, standing in the large empty bathroom using the primitive shower with its head like a watering can and its long metal chain. But tonight it was as much as she could do to lower herself gingerly onto the bed.

She had a whole series of tricks to stop herself from falling asleep. She would dig her nails into her palms, or the soft flesh of her upper arms or thighs. She chanted all the many psalms she knew. Anything, to ward off the moment of unconsciousness.

She had always had nightmares, as long as she could remember, red and black terror. They got worse just before her twelfth birthday. She was able, now, to see they were part of the hurt, of all she'd lost.

The child Sarah had never understood what happened to her when she was asleep. She would wake in a screaming panic, not knowing where, or who, she was. It was as if she had gone outside her own body and been disturbed before she could get back. Sometimes, she would be very cold as she crouched shuddering on her bed.

Because her cries frightened the other girls, they had put her in a room on her own. Sarah never asked herself how Mother Joseph knew. But the old lady would come from her cell on the next floor, behind the door lined with green felt. She would be there within minutes in her long thick convent nightclothes, her bunchy night-bonnet, to murmur reassurance. Sometimes – when it was very bad, when she couldn't stop trembling – Mother Joseph would pull her close and hold her safe, although the nuns weren't supposed to do that. The child would be tense and taut – and then she would nuzzle into the consoling arms, seeking the human warmth she so desperately needed.

Mother Joseph would rock silently until Sarah's breathing had slowed and her heart beat quietly. Sister Gideon could still remember her childish surprise that the elderly nun who always looked so stiff should be so soft to lean against, could still smell the antiseptic soap the nuns used.

The dreams that came now were not like those. They were slow and still and heavy, they made her feel she was being buried alive. There were doors she could not open, high walls that moved close together to shut her in. And huge painted open eyes, watching her secret self.

She knew, even in her sleep, these were not her dreams. She understood she was looking out of someone else's eyes. But that didn't lessen their horror or her fear.

In the corridor outside, Sister Gideon heard the rustle of the white habits. One belonged to the Infirmarian, she recognized the click of the drugs cabinet keys she wore on her belt. The whispers were almost too low to catch.

'. . . not good, Mother, I don't like . . .'

'. . . have to send her back home . . .'

'. . . no choice, really . . .'

'. . . going on for nearly three months . . .'

'. . . such a dreadful journey but . . .'

Sister Gideon lay on the very edge of her bed, eyes wide and fixed on the window, hearing different whispers beyond another door:

'. . . *far too late to try that, poor woman* . . .'

'. . . *lost a lot of blood* . . .'

'. . . *know what she used?*'

'. . . *found its body on the floor under a towel, my God, those kids must've seen* . . .'

'. . . *sssshh, they'll hear* . . .'

She watched the blind where the great dark moth clung unmoving. The people here said if you saw one in a room, death would follow. But surely that had all been a long time ago.

The moth stirred and opened wings the colour of memory.

In the end, Sister Gideon couldn't hold out against the exhaustion of the day. She slept with her right hand beneath her cheek, the left tucked under her pillow.

St Bridget, pray for us. St Cuthbert, pray for us.

Chapter Eight

'Mother Emmanuel, good morning – how nice to hear you.'

Father Michael Falcone hastily took his feet off the desk as he identified the voice on the telephone. Mother Emmanuel had that effect on people. She might be sitting two hundred and fifty miles away in her Welsh convent, but he could feel her gaze resting on the run-down state of his shoes. He'd take them in for resoling tomorrow.

In the meantime, he removed the unlit panatella from between his lips and tossed it onto one of the piles of manuscript pages littering his desk. It wasn't that Mother Emmanuel would object to him smoking. But there was a rigour about her, she knew what had to be done, and more often than not, she managed to do it despite being almost seventy.

'This is an unexpected pleasure,' he added. It was no less than the truth. Despite her retiring lifestyle, Mother Emmanuel was a considerable figure, and he had known her by repute, though he owed their friendship to his broken leg. Four months ago he had been thrown from his motorbike in Zaire, while travelling to the school where he taught, and the Provincial proposed he take long leave and go home to England.

He'd welcomed the opportunity to work on his book.

This cherished project – he was interested in the phenomenon of modern pilgrimages, and their rise in popularity since the fifties – had been started several times and put aside because of his commitments. This would be his chance to do some real research, and begin writing.

He had only been in London a short time when his superior had asked if he could be persuaded to do a favour for another diocese. Would he consider taking over as parish priest at a small town on the Welsh–Shropshire border, just for a month? He would live in the priest's house, have the use of his car. Not a lot to do, so his leg would continue to heal nicely. Oh, and he would also be priest to the Priory of Our Lady of the Snow.

He had not relished the prospect as the local taxi drove up the wet road into the hills beyond Welshpool. He reached the winding, overgrown drive where a one-room lodge spouted smoke at the gate. Heavy trees met overhead to form a dark green tunnel – and then, at the end, the solid ugly house standing foursquare in a ramble of rhododendrons. Beyond it, the ground fell away so he could see three rivers winding flat and silver in the valley far below.

The Priory of Our Lady of the Snow was for contemplative nuns and the life of prayer. It was the only European house of the order, which also did missionary work in Central America, in Guatemala; there, too, the nuns were enclosed. From within their compound in remote and inaccessible country, they ran a school for Mayan children. These women would live for years at a time in Guatemala, then return to the Welsh house to renew their physical and spiritual strength. He smiled to himself as he recalled the quaint expression they used – going home on furlough. At a time when religious orders were turning themselves upside down in their efforts to meet the modern world on its own terms, Our Lady of the Snow decided to make no concessions. They kept the strict rules of perpetual enclosure, of silence. They retained their medieval clothes and pattern of day.

The nuns of Our Lady of the Snow gave up everything to God, trusting that even in these troubled times, they would survive. Their faith was justified. In common with other contemplatives – the Carmelites, Benedictines, Poor Clares – they lost a handful of nuns, while women left active orders in increasing numbers. The majority stayed, though they were of course the older women.

Perhaps because the life they led was so austere, so timeless, these enclosed nuns kept their hold on the public imagination. There was about their lives, and the way they looked, a quality of drama and beauty which more modernized orders, with their uninspired adapted habits, their jobs as social workers, entirely lacked.

Our Lady of the Snow had just one novice until the day they agreed to let a television company in to make an hour-long documentary. Afterwards, four new entrants arrived within a few months. Five young women more than balanced the ageing community. Suddenly the old house felt alive again.

The nuns thanked God joyfully for their new young novices. Father Michael privately considered His instrument was undoubtedly Mother Emmanuel. In common with many priests, even of his generation, he retained a measure of scepticism about the intellectual capacities of nuns: many of the older men still regarded them as priests' housekeepers. But Mother Emmanuel showed him otherwise. At first, she had been strictly formal and it was always 'Father Michael'. But their friendship had deepened rapidly. He had never come across a woman of such powerful understanding. When she told him one day that in her twenties she had corresponded with Jung about her dreams, he decided she was truly remarkable.

Now she gave that quick laugh of hers, that belied her age.

'You may not be so pleased to hear me when we've talked.' Her voice changed and softened and he thought, she's the most godly woman I know, and one of the oldest, and yet she turns on her charm like a seventeen-year-old girl. And it always works. 'Is this a good time?'

'I'm only too delighted to have an excuse to stop work. I've a lecture to give next month and I'm out of practice.'

'You're giving it in Rome?'

'No, London. I'd be halfway up the curtains otherwise, it'd have to be in Latin.'

'And the leg's healed properly? We didn't like seeing you hopping around on crutches.'

'I've graduated to a rather elegant walking stick. I don't really need it, but it looks good.'

'Well, I hate to bother you, only I've something particular worrying me.'

'You're well?'

'Good Lord, Michael, it's not for myself.' She made it sound as though illness in her was unthinkable. As indeed it was. 'I wouldn't be troubling you with our little problems, but I've a nasty feeling this isn't so little. One of our order has recently been sent home to me from Guatemala and I'm very concerned about her . . .'

Using one hand, he re-ordered his piles of manuscript pages and found a blank pad. He kept his steel Parker behind his ear. It was a habit he'd picked up in childhood, when as a schoolboy he would help in his grandfather's shop. The priest jotted down odd words, phrases, as he listened. Occasionally he asked a question.

71

'Well,' asked the prioress at the end. 'How does it sound to you?'

'Strange. It sounds strange.' He rubbed the side of his nose with an impatient finger and caught himself up – now why was he doing that? It was a gesture which in someone else he'd interpret as doubting what he was hearing. Not for a moment did he doubt Mother Emmanuel. Only there was something not quite right here.

He picked up the chewed panatella and stuck it back in his mouth.

'You say she's had X-rays, all the routine tests, and nothing shows. So the next time she has one of these attacks, what happens?'

'Dr Bevan says, maybe exploratory surgery. We're all getting very worried, it's been going on four months now, since Christmas. She was sent home in March – just after you went back to London, in fact.'

As he listened, he flipped the calendar.

'I could get to you on Thursday, around two o'clock. Is that all right?'

'You know there's a guest room always ready for you, Father. We'd welcome a visit from you and that's the truth. I'll have Sister Gregory keep your lunch on the Aga, in case you haven't eaten.'

He grimaced. Convent food was a source of considerable amusement to masculine communities. All religious were supposed to treat it with monastic disdain, but that didn't prevent the serving and consumption of some splendid meals in monasteries and seminaries. Women religious, however, took the injunction to quite painful extremes: in many a convent he'd been offered fish fingers and pre-sliced white bread with a cup of tea.

'Don't you trouble Sister Gregory,' he said. 'I'll grab something on the train.'

When he arrived at the Priory of Our Lady of the Snow, the nuns were reading in their cells before the afternoon's work. But Sister Rosalie had been waiting for him. He was slightly surprised when she did not show him as usual to the Visitors' Parlour. Instead, she silently led the way through a small door and up a flight of back stairs to what had once been servants' rooms above the kitchens, and were now used as an infirmary. Cut off by a long corridor from the main convent, the separate entrance allowed the local doctor – not of course permitted to enter the enclosure proper – to visit nuns in his care.

Looking for the Infirmarian, Sister Rosalie knocked on a couple of doors without success. She opened the third, and peeped in. Father Michael happened to be just behind her. The moment before he drew back, as Sister Rosalie whispered 'Sorry, Sister,' and closed the door, was long enough for him to see the woman in the narrow convent bed.

Pale curtains had been pulled against the daylight and the room was quiet. Sister Gideon lay on her side, turned away from him, curled under the sheet, knees drawn up the way a child sleeps. He couldn't see her face, only the averted head muffled in the odd old-fashioned bonnet the nuns wore at night to hide their hair.

It was quite obvious that, even if they could not explain it, her illness was real. Her body seemed scarcely to lift the cover, her breathing was quick and shallow. The white sleeves of her nightdress exposed frail wrists. Her hands, folded against her cheek, were thin and pale, as though she had done nothing for many weeks.

He was to wonder later, when he knew her much better,

73

how he could possibly have known then how lovely she was? Her luminous eyes, her strong cheekbones, the curve of her jaw.

In the dim room she was like a woman sketched in faint pencil. The long slender lines of her limbs, her fragility, disturbed something he thought he'd buried safe and deep.

Father Michael had joined the Jesuits straight from school, knowing almost nothing of women. Without sisters or brothers, the only young person in an ageing family, he was shy and inarticulate in the presence of girls. He was useless at parties, and lack of money kept him out of pubs. When his friends boasted of what they'd done and who to, he just kept quiet.

His father had left them long before, and his mother's efforts to talk to him about sexual matters embarrassed them both. So he relied for information on novels and films. Soft-porn magazines and photographs illicitly circulated at school had both thrilled and repelled him. He'd kept some hidden under his mattress and would go through them when no-one else was home. He had a ritual to heighten his anticipation, drawing the curtains and putting on a bedside light before opening *Penthouse* or *Mayfair*.

Pouting girls wore black leather, satin, chains. They cupped their heavy breasts and gave rounded bottoms to his stare. They parted their thighs for him, exposing secret hair, touching the mysterious folds of their sex. His own would throb with an awful excitement.

Real girls were a different matter. He had far less self-confidence than they did. At sixteen, during a firework party, he tentatively kissed Penny Hanham: her mouth tasted of toffee but his attempts to touch her breast were defeated by the toggles on her duffle coat. They'd kissed again, a bit later, and held hands in the cold garden. Her father had given him a lift home.

Next day she'd turned her head away when he smiled at her in Maths, and gone off giggling with her friends after the lesson. He was certain they were laughing at him. He longed for a Mrs Robinson, for a sexually voracious older woman looking like Anne Bancroft, but there were no candidates for the role in Wells that he could see.

He was still a virgin when he was sent to Rome to study Theology at the Gregorian University. He was by now indoctrinated enough to consider his chastity a positive virtue. It would allow him the freedom to love many people. He was a torchbearer for the eternal life, and he felt free and brave as Don Quixote.

The first years of study at the Greg had been a revelation. He'd taken himself too seriously, of course, observing every rule with all the fidelity he could muster. Which in those days, he reflected, was a lot. Keep the Rule and the Rule will keep you. He read Dom Marmion and Dom Lahoda, he desired only to be clay in the hands of the Potter.

He lived at the International Scholasticate, a magnificent private house at Porto Mercale. There were forty-five of them, young men from all over the world – America, France, Tanzania.

All lectures were to be in Latin. He had to learn Italian. As well as the language, Jesuits adopt the garb of the priests of the country. It was almost like wearing a disguise. In what time he had from his studies, he walked the city confident in his dark soutane, brown eyes shadowed by the wide black Borsalino hat.

But then something unforeseeable happened. He found that the more he saw of the hierarchy in action – be-ringed

75

bishops, cardinals clothed in crimson complacency – the more he realized the Catholic Church was the most exclusive male club in the world. And celibacy was part of the lip service paid to that club. The line of command was totally male: from the Pope to cardinals, bishops and then priests. He knew this must be wrong. Women were half the human race but they were not considered here. It did not reflect society as he knew it to be, but its effect upon that society was immense.

Where once he had accepted easily, now he began to question everything.

As he matured, he had to struggle not to think of the ravishing young women he passed in the streets of Rome as sexual beings. An elderly spiritual director at the seminary explained that there were decent parts of the body, less decent parts – and indecent. It was a mortal sin to touch the indecent parts of a woman's body. Michael thought of the forbidden flesh exposed to his gaze in his darkened bedroom when he was fifteen.

He had always known it was never going to be easy to respond to that stupendous invitation: 'Come, follow me'.

But there were times when he thought, no, it's impossible. Times when he found himself conjuring up those taut, unlined, unreal bodies to lie against his own. Lust would surge up in him with the imagined pressure of ripe breasts, flat bellies. Sometimes desire grew and peaked and took him down. He set himself limits: if these imaginings made him ejaculate, he went next day to the confessional.

The director advised that, when Michael found himself thinking about women, he visualize them as a mass of blood and bone and muscle, so he wouldn't be 'led on'. Michael, then twenty-two, decided he preferred poor old St Benedict's method of chucking himself in the nettlebed.

When he found himself actually breaking his vows and making love to Francesca Gardelli – something he still could not quite believe had happened, though he had confessed it often enough – nettles would not have been of the slightest use.

Michael had grown up experiencing very little physical closeness from his family. Like his mother, he gave it scant thought. So he could not have said why his life felt so incomplete. It was only much later he understood perhaps this need came from the father he had scarcely known.

Francesca was alluring, twelve years older than he, married but separated. She made all the running. It was the first time he had been fully intimate with a woman. The relationship had lasted only briefly before she ended it. But it was as if he could suddenly speak a language he'd heard people whispering before but never understood.

This same sexual drive was a sin in the eyes of the Church, something a priest must crush and overcome. There were techniques for emotional and intellectual control. There were techniques for physical control. And by now, he knew them all.

More than ten years had passed since then. He felt his character, his personality, hardening. He recognized that many of the traits he saw in himself were repressive. Always neat, he had become obsessively so. Each morning he made a detailed list of what he had to do, each evening ticked off completed tasks. He clung to his regular routine, it was the spine holding him upright.

Since the accident, he had found himself increasingly at a loss without his protective framework. Where the core of his life should have been, something felt hollow and sad. He was lonely as an atom in space.

Standing in the doorway of the darkened room where Sister Gideon lay, his emotions bore no relation to anything he'd known before.

It struck him – and not for the first time – how ridiculous it was that a man should be cut off from the society of women. He saw the line of hip and thigh under the covers and thought, that a curve of flesh could affect him like this. He wanted to comfort her. He wanted to protect her.

He stepped back into the corridor.

His mind's eye saw the exposed and vulnerable nape of her neck below that absurd bonnet.

God help him. He wanted to touch her.

The Infirmarian bustled down the corridor, a clipboard of notes in her hand, her smile of welcome as firmly in place as the veil held on with black kirby grips.

'It's very good of you to come and see us, Father. But I think Sister Gideon's asleep just now. We're worried about her, I know Mother's told you.' The welcoming smile faded. 'To be quite honest, I'm at my wit's end. She had a particularly bad day yesterday – kept saying she couldn't see, everything was "fuzzy", she said, like webs over her eyes. We got Dr Bevan in, of course, but he couldn't explain it.' She made a small, anxious sound. 'What a worry it all is.' She paused, then offered, 'I could wake her for you. Only she didn't get much rest last night.'

He seized the excuse with relief. 'No, don't do that. I'll speak to Mother Emmanuel first.'

Sister Rosalie led him silently through the convent to

the prioress's empty room. 'Reverend Mother says please to excuse her, Father, she won't be long.'

The priest waited at the long, uncurtained window. Even now, in spring, it was chilly in here, and he recalled with a shiver that in winter it had been cold as charity. Perhaps, recently returned from Africa, he'd felt it more than most. Though they had only the most primitive central heating in the house, even that was rarely, if ever, switched on: oil was expensive. He turned the handle and finding the glass door open, walked down wrought iron steps into the walled garden.

It was still too early for the old-fashioned cottage flowers the nuns loved, the lupins and marigolds. He walked to the sunken rose-garden where in summer the now stark bushes would be surrounded by catmint, so the blooms blazed in a blue mist. Standing among them, he thought about Rome.

The city hit him like a gloved fist: it took him weeks to collect his wits. After that, for the four years he spent there, Rome was his.

He followed the immense flight of stone steps that billowed from their narrow beginning in the Trinita di Monte to the Piazzi di Spagna, and the Egyptian obelisks in dusty-rose granite. He found magnificent muscled Roman statues in neglected courtyards, while outside cars and scooters raced and hooted: two worlds never touching. He watched live chickens squawking on market stalls, and flower and vegetable sellers sprinkling the pavements with cooling water. There was water everywhere in Rome. Creamy squares shimmered with its reflected light, ripple and bubble of countless fountains.

It seemed sometimes that everything in Rome came to him through his nose. He could smell babies in the narrow back streets where lines of washing crisscrossed overhead and women called their children with harsh musical cries. In the Via Veneto in the evenings, as the fashionable parade of Romans took their *passegiata* past the glittering windows of elegant barbers and expensive dressmakers, he could smell money. And in dark candled churches, imbued with centuries of incense, he could smell God.

It had been the scent of roses that drew him that day after the philosophy lecture – given like all the others in Latin – had finished early. He'd gone for a walk and wandered by chance into the hard narrow streets of Trastavere, where bent women filled carafes of water at street pumps and little boys ran barefoot.

It was hot, the long Roman afternoon recess, and his wide black Borsalino hat was tight. The shadowed rose garden offered a respite, led him on into the Church of St Cecilia. It was early ninth century and built over often since then. Bits of antiquity could be glimpsed in chancel-screen and spandrel. It hung overhead, in the airy spaces of transept and triforium. It lay buried underfoot in crypt and vault. He could smell it in the naves and in the ambulatory: old leather and faded tapestries and melting wax.

Evening had drifted down while he was in the church. Through stained glass the sky had deepened to the colour of the lapis lazuli necklace in the window of his grandfather's jewellery shop all those years ago. The alcoves and arches of the ancient place faded into sepia as the lights in chapel and chancel glowed.

He'd rested on a gilt chair while a discreet loudspeaker conveyed the end of a service from the convent next door. And then someone began to play an organ with a tone so thin it might almost have been a spinet. The music was like the sorbet he'd bought earlier from a street vendor, the lemon wincingly sharp and sweet. Bach, *Jesu joy of man's desiring* . . .

He stood in front of the altar. Below it lay the body in pure marble of the saint, Cecilia. Beside it was the sculptor's statement, carved in the sixteenth century: Stefano Maderno's description of how he had copied the incredibly preserved woman's body, martyred and embalmed in AD 230.

She lay there still. On her side, knees drawn up, the lines of her limbs fine and slight beneath ivory marble draperies. He stayed a long time, gazing at the body that had once been flesh. He made out the curve of her hip, the long sweep of her thigh. She could have been sleeping. But then he saw the narrow clasped hands were tied.

Normally, he hated such things, hated the sentimentality, the blank staring eyes. But there were no eyes here. The slim head was turned away from him, and muffled. It was a beautiful piece of work, full of emotion and delicate tact and pain.

For Cecilia, with musical skills so great they said an angel had fallen in love with her, had been blind.

Chapter Nine

There were days when Kate was furious because the sun came out. Tuesday was one of them. It was not yet seven a.m., and the narrow strip of sky through the plastic window was clear and pale and fresh. She did not see how she could endure any longer the excruciating pain of being buried alive.

It was a kind of mourning. Unlike many other convicted women, she had no children to cry for, no lover. In the first years, she had to deal with the loss of her mother. Now, she grieved for the life she had not had: she mourned time.

Prison was a stopping of time. Day or night, whenever they wished, she was subject to the gaze of her guards. And with such scrutiny came control. All around her there was violence as women fought against it, struggled to keep a sense of themselves. But Kate never became violent. Instead she sought permission to swim.

Wearing a track suit over the regulation swimsuit, with her towel round her neck, she went down to the blue-tiled swimming pool. She hurled herself into the water, making the great griffin symbol of Holloway embossed on the bottom shudder.

She would churn up and down until she was blinded and breathless. Then she pushed herself further and faster.

Finally, spent and emptied, she reached a place of calm deep inside.

There were days when whatever she did, depression would bring exhaustion. It was no less real for being illusory. All she wanted to do was stay isolated in her cell, in her bed, to escape briefly in sleep.

Authority interpreted this as non-compliance. When she missed a dental appointment she had specially requested, because she had slept through it, she was given a misconduct ticket. They said she had no valid reason for staying in her cell. No-one ever told her that an increased need for sleep is a recognized symptom of depression, or suggested that depression itself was a valid response to being locked away for all those years.

There was a knock on her door. Val stood there, in gym kit. 'Ready?'

Val had asked her to partner her yesterday, and Kate had forgotten. She started to make an excuse. 'Look, I don't . . .'

'OK,' Val broke in, almost as if she had expected rejection. The minute she'd gone, Kate felt guilty. She changed into the grey-blue vest and shorts. She liked Val. The older woman had the cell next door. On Kate's second evening, she'd knocked before the doors were locked at eight.

'It's hard to sleep here,' she said, and gave Kate a small sachet. She'd laughed at her expression. 'It's a camomile tea bag, twit. Got a kettle?' Kate shook her head. 'I'll get you some hot water.'

Over the next couple of weeks, Kate learned that Val was doing three for fraud, using stolen cheque cards to buy clothes and toys for her children. She lived for their weekly visits from the children's home, accompanied by a care worker. Although when they'd gone, she would fall into bleak despair.

'I never got nothing for myself,' she said once. 'You'd think they'd take that into account, when they're sentencing. But they don't.'

Downstairs, in the Olympic-sized gymnasium, Kate joined her. Side by side, not speaking, the two women stepped on and off the box, on and off, in mute companionship. Not until they'd jogged the circuit twenty-five times, showered and changed, did they speak.

'What's wrong?' Val asked, towelling her straight dark hair.

'Nothing being out wouldn't cure.' Kate pulled on a black plimsoll.

'You will be. It wasn't your fault, back at New Hall. They can't blame you for the burn-out.'

'It was trouble, though. Maybe they thought I'd got mad, said something . . . God knows how they work.'

'No. You'll be out long before me.'

Kate stared at her. 'But you've only got another few months.'

Val shrugged. After the effort of the gym, she seemed listless. She finished tying the laces in her trainers. 'Yeah. Well. Right now that feels like forever.' She got up. 'I'll see you.'

'Val.' Kate reached out a hand towards the other woman, stopped short of touching her. 'You all right?'

Val shook her head. 'Got a message the lawyer wants to see me this afternoon. I didn't request it so . . .' There was no need for her to say any more. Both of them knew it meant only trouble.

'Kate, Miss Dempster says she needs another body to staff the Visitors' Room canteen at three. Got that?'

Kate had had no visitors since arriving in Holloway. She didn't want to sit in the tiny canteen in the Visitors'

Room, pouring coffee at 25p a time for other women's husbands and lovers and mothers, selling KitKats to other people's children.

The corridor which inmates used to get to the Visitors' Room had half a dozen glass panelled doors leading to small interview rooms. These contained a desk and a couple of chairs and were used for private meetings with police or legal advisers.

As she passed, Kate saw Room C was occupied. On the other side of the reinforced glass a large and beautiful black woman was seated, shapely legs crossed high. She wore a black wool suit with gold buttons. Perfectly groomed, her glossy hair was coiled in a bun and she held a sheaf of papers. She was shaking her head with a resigned expression. As Kate watched, she opened a black leather briefcase. The woman to whom she was speaking – clearly her client – seemed small in comparison, round-shouldered and dejected. Her head was bent, Kate couldn't see her face. She recognized Val by her purple cardigan.

'They've given him the kids. They don't hardly know him and they've handed them over like they didn't have any feelings. He comes back from bloody nowhere, not so much as a birthday card for them for two years, not a penny to help feed them . . .' Val's harsh whisper went on and on.

Kate didn't speak, there wasn't anything she could say. Val's common-law husband had applied for custody, as was his right. He was taking them back to Newcastle to live with him and his mother, and there was nothing Val or her solicitor could do to prevent him.

'Because I'm in Holloway,' Val said bitterly. 'But I'm

in Holloway because he didn't give us any money. I didn't know where he *was*, I couldn't even of asked him . . . Oh God, it's not *fair!*'

She pulled herself together with a visible effort. 'I'm going to lie down,' she said. 'You're all right, aren't you, Kate?'

'Don't bother about me. Of course I am. It's you I'm worried about. Why don't you ask to speak to the Governor? Maybe he could do something.'

Val's voice was flat. 'No use. Pete's offering a home and family, any court would say that's better than being in care. What hurts is that even when I'm out, I'll never get my kids back.'

'Of course you will,' said Kate, with a certainty she didn't feel.

The two women looked at each other. Val got up. 'So long as you're all right,' she said again.

At eight-twenty p.m., when the unit officer checked her cell as usual, Val was lying on her bed with her eyes closed.

Unobserved, she took the long laces from her trainers and tied them together to make a strong double cord. She knotted this round her neck. She wound the other end of the loop around the washbasin taps. She turned the taps as tightly closed as she could, hurting her hands, so there would be no mistake. Then she simply sat down.

By eight-forty p.m. she was dead.

If they had found Val sooner, Kate knew what would have happened, and the knowledge made her almost thankful her friend had succeeded. They'd have put her in the strips, that was how they dealt with all attempted suicides. In doing so, they denied the pain and punished the sufferer yet again.

But Val had made her last decision, and carried it through: an act of the self turned against the self.

Kate had been in the strips once, in Cookham Wood, and she had a puckered scar on her lower lip as a reminder. It was after a fight with Glasgow Rita, who'd been caught bringing drugs in on a ferry from Holland. Rita talked about nothing but jellies and eggs and tems and smack, but she decided Kate's crime was beyond the pale. She attacked her with a piece of broken glass from a smashed marmalade jar during Association. Kate fought back and both of them were wrestled down by the staff and hauled away.

She would not forget that grubby room with a dim fluorescent light above the door, fixed in an iron cage and never turned off. They took all her clothes – everything – and in return gave her a shift dress of tough nylon and a stained blanket. The bed was made of plastic foam, and even the radiator was padded. There was a metal lavatory and washbasin, both streaked with dark blood. Someone with a sense of irony had written the whole of Psalm 136 on one wall.

> *For it was there that they asked us,*
> *Our captors, for songs,*
> *Our oppressors, for joy.*
> *'Sing to us,' they said,*
> *'One of Zion's songs.'*

On the second day, she got her clothes back and they moved her to an ordinary seg cell, with a metal bed bolted to the floor. A round table and two chairs were made out of card. Former occupants had passed the time scrawling on the furniture, covering the yellow surface with the silent insults of graffiti. *Fuck them   One on them*

They took her to the Adjudications Room. The Governor asked her questions, listened to her answers, read her behaviour report and finally said, no charge. But I think we have to move you on. For your own safety.

In the corridor, waiting for an escorting officer, there was more card furniture stacked, all scrawled on. She read it for something to do, until she saw her own name and the continuing threat.

> *Rita H woz ere*
> *27 days remission + 3 days*
> *for punching her in*
> *the face – 2 stitches*
> *rotten cunt*
> *Kate Dean you're a dead girl*

The card with Val's details was removed from her cell door hours after her death. Her name wasn't mentioned when the head check was done, when the whole establishment was frozen at midday. They disappeared her, as if she had never existed.

A bouquet of flowers was sent in from outside, with Val's name on. The unit officer divided up the bunch and put them in different rooms. Stunned, Kate asked the officer why she did it, why she hadn't left the bouquet as it was: a remembrance of a life. The woman walked away as though she hadn't heard. Then she came back. 'We don't want the girls worrying about a death,' she said. 'It'll only upset them.'

The officer didn't use Val's name. She did not say, she's

not worth mourning over. Her attitude made it plain. Her death was Val's final act, but she was not allowed to own even that.

Officer Jansen was pleasant enough, not an uncaring person. Kate realized then, this is how they see us: this is how they cope. And it could have been her. *Kate Dean you're a dead girl.*

Then and there Kate decided: nothing mattered but getting through to the end of her sentence, getting out. She didn't know how long that would be. But if it was a year – or two, or three – she would do it. She had survived this long.

On Tuesday evening, Kate lay and thought about Val, and camomile tea. Wordless shrieks echoed from the Muppet House over the way, on and on, painful as a wet finger drawn down glass.

She must have drifted off at some point, because she was wrenched awake to a sensation of frantic misery. Strands of a dream that was no dream floated on the surface of her mind. Cruel images. Bitter actions. They were almost more than she could bear.

She was very cold, though she knew the cell was uncomfortably warm. She had felt it before, this sensation of losing touch with her body. When she got out of bed and looked in her little mirror, her face was white, her eyes huge.

She turned away. And in that second, in the poor light, it was as if she glimpsed someone else in the glass: she almost spoke a name aloud.

Oh, God, not again. Not again.

This had been going on for weeks now. At first, she had refused to acknowledge what was happening. What was being done to her. She cursed it, fought it, she willed it gone. But somewhere deep inside her a warning struggled up to the level of consciousness: Take *care*! Something terrible is coming!

It came harsh as the cry of a watchman in the night. Screel *din*!

Chapter Ten

'Penny for them!'

The low voice at his side made Father Michael jump. Mother Emmanuel smiled and said, 'I didn't disturb you? You seemed very far away.'

'Mother! It's good to see you.' He greeted with real pleasure the upright figure, almost regal in her dark robes. 'I was thinking about . . .' What? About a third-century saint, whose tenderly carved body had sprung back to mind when he saw Sister Gideon?

'Did the Infirmarian tell you Sister is very low today?' She began to move towards the beehives and the lines of small wooden stakes holding twine and neat labels to mark the new planting. Falling easily in step with her long stride, he slid a look at the still-handsome profile. She could never have been merely pretty, he thought, with those commanding eyes set in deep sockets: it was a face expressive of power. He wondered, fleetingly, how it would be for her when she no longer held office. But of course, the title Mother would always be hers.

'I'm not at all sure she'll be able to talk with you,' the abbess went on. 'When had you planned to go back to London?'

'Thought I'd catch an early train tomorrow. But as long as I'm there by the end of the day, that's fine.'

'If we give her till the morning, I'm sure a short chat wouldn't be too much for her.'

'I've a lot of questions. But you must have many of the answers yourself. That'd save time.'

'She was mainly under the care of our novice mistress when she entered. All I really know of her myself is what I've seen these last two months.' She stopped by a long garden bench of weathered wood. Taking a voluminous white linen handkerchief from somewhere within her habit, she dusted the seat for them both with a couple of quick flicks. The housewifely gesture made him smile, but he kept his amusement to himself.

She opened the slim blue file she carried. 'This tells us nothing out of the ordinary and certainly doesn't help. She was a pupil at our boarding school from the age of, let's see, thirteen. Sarah Grayling, she was then. Quiet girl, too quiet according to one of her reports.' She turned over a couple of pages, scanning them quickly, then paused. 'An odd thing. Her birth certificate is missing. It should certainly be in here – the order could not have accepted her as a novice without it. We've searched everywhere, we've been through dozens of papers. I've never known one lost before and it's most irregular.'

'Maybe it's at the Guatemalan house?'

She shook her head. 'They take only their passports with them. Given the political situation out there, they might be thrown out of the country at any time. Or worse.' She shrugged. 'Oh, well, it'll probably turn up.'

'What else does the file tell us?'

Mother Emmanuel turned over a couple of pages, scanning them quickly. The heavy amethyst ring of office gleamed on her left hand, and he noticed the edges of her nails were dark, probably from the garden. His first sight of her six months ago had been driving their antiquated tractor in the field.

'Very sad family background – her mother was a suicide, that's the main reason she came to us. She had a bad time adjusting to life at boarding school, which was to be expected. But apparently the emotional problems went on far longer than anticipated.'

She placed the papers on top of the file and straightened them carefully. As though, the priest thought, by doing so she could tidy up the problems they recorded. 'It's a difficult enough age anyway,' she continued, 'particularly for a girl. Thank God *I'll* never be pubescent again.'

'You and me both, Mother. How old was she when she decided to enter?'

'Young. One of the keen ones.' She smiled at him. 'The sort that give me the heebie-jeebies in the night.'

He couldn't help the quick explosion of laughter. '*What?*'

'Come on, Father Michael. I've known many a nun entered at fourteen, and none the worse for it. But I've seen plenty of others, started off in religious life full of high ideals, and a few years later they were banging their heads against the walls. I was eighteen myself, and looking back, it was ridiculous they ever took me so young. Now they feel as I do: best sow your wild oats first and come in with no regrets.'

'D'you have regrets?' The idea that this elderly religious might not be perfectly content had never crossed his mind.

She gave him the quick, candid look that was so surprising in a woman of her age. 'I do,' she said firmly, 'and so does everyone who's honest with themselves. I know I was meant for this life and no other, and that makes it easier. I do thank God for my early vocation: I

93

pretty much live with Him now. But yes, there have been times when it hurt, to realize I would never have what other people take for granted: the love of a man, my own child in my arms.' She paused, her finger still keeping her place in the file, her face alight with a mischievous smile. 'Don't worry, I'm not hazarding any guesses about *your* wild oats, Father.'

He remembered something Father Bernard had told him about the Mother Prioress: she was said to have an infallible eye for vocations. 'She only has to look at a new arrival,' the old man had claimed, 'to know if the girl will persevere. She gazes at her intently and sometimes she'll say, "No need to unpack that child's bag." They say she's rarely wrong.'

He thought, she could ask me anything she wanted, I'd answer it.

'I was too young.' It felt like the confession it was. 'I should have waited. I've come to see that in the old days adolescence was over at seventeen, so early vocations might have worked. But now we have an extended student life – I've friends in their thirties still taking university degrees. So these days there's no clear self-image, no cut and dried idea of your own personality until you reach your mid-twenties.'

'Until Vatican II,' she observed, 'sixteen was considered a perfectly acceptable age to enter. And the orders took them in without blinking, so long as there was no mental illness, and they had a current medical certificate. The only bar used to be illegitimacy.' She caught his expression. 'Oh, we didn't say, no bastards.' He blinked at the word, but she sailed on oblivious. 'Only it was felt they'd have an unstable family background. And another thing, you had to have middling good looks.'

'You're not serious?'

'Indeed I am. If you wanted to join a teaching order, or any that went out into the community, they could refuse you if you had, say, a birthmark across your face. They said, you'd be representing the community.'

'At least we can now test entrants properly before we accept them.'

Mother Emmanuel nodded. 'It's made a big difference to us: what a lot of heartbreak could have been saved if we'd been able to send people to take their psychologicals in the past. You see them for what – two sessions, sometimes three – and you often spot problems that might not have shown up until well into the novitiate. And if we have to turn them away then, it's a failure in their lives. That's bad for all of us.'

He said, a trifle sadly, 'Psychologists can only do so much. They can tell you an entrant is normally sound, reassure you that she's not seeking a refuge or running from something. They can tell you how she relates to others. But they can't see everything, unfortunately. Who interviewed Sister Gideon?'

Mother Emmanuel went back to the file. 'No-one who saw her at that time is available. Some have left the order, a couple are on the missions. Two more have died. As I said, I knew nothing of her personally until these last months. Coming into the order from the school, of course, when she'd declared her interest, she'd have lived half in, half out of the convent. She'd have observed some of the rules, like silence at certain times. She would have changed into the black dress and white veil of a postulant when school finished at four.'

'But even with all that, she should still have seen a psychologist.'

'Yes.' Mother Emmanuel frowned down at the file. 'Mother Joseph would have been headmistress then. She shouldn't have held the post by rights, she was past retirement age. But she was incredibly active and we were short of people with her teaching qualifications.' She glanced up at the priest and shrugged. 'As an older woman, of course, she was perhaps less concerned than she should have been with the new methods of recognizing vocations.'

'Where is she now?'

'In a Sussex retirement home. Run by nuns, of course. Normally we keep our people with us, but she needs a lot of care. I tried to ask her on the phone about Sister Gideon, but no use, I'm afraid. She remembers what happened fifty years ago, but not fourteen . . . that's how it gets when you're pushing eighty.'

'Why don't I go and see her?'

She looked at him thoughtfully. 'You've read my mind. Would it be too much to ask you to help us with this? The more we look at it, the more difficult it all seems.' She clasped her hands and he knew by the formality of her words how hard she found it to ask him. 'We really do need someone who's able to move around freely. I could perhaps have asked old Father Martin.' She gave him a quick, mischievous look and added, 'Though perhaps not. But there is really no-one else I'd trust.'

'You didn't have to ask,' he said, 'I'd already offered.'

'It'd take time, though. And you've already come all this way for us.'

He said easily, 'No problem. My time is pretty much my own while I'm working on this book. No-one will mind if I take a day or two.' He grinned. 'I think even I get to have a bit of a holiday.'

'It won't be much of one,' Mother Emmanuel said regretfully. 'And we're more grateful than I can say. But there's one problem . . . I hardly know how to raise this with you . . . Sussex is a long way away and we really haven't the funds for travelling and so on.'

'I'll pay,' he offered.

She was simultaneously relieved and taken aback. 'Father Michael, I couldn't let you do that.'

'Yes, you could. What are we talking about – train fares, maybe a couple of nights away. Years ago when my mother died, all the money from the house and so on went to the order. If I ask the bursar now for expenses to help you and Sister Gideon, I don't think there'll be any difficulties.' He gave his slow smile. 'It seems a worthwhile reason to me.'

'I believe it is.' Mother Emmanuel leaned back in her chair. 'You know, Father Michael, I never cease to be amazed and gratified by the way the good Lord works. This morning, I had no idea how we'd sort this problem out. And here you are, offering time and money.'

He looked at her with real affection: she did not see her own hand in this at all. He would never be capable of such humility.

'I'll go tomorrow,' he said. 'And what about the school? Would any of the teaching sisters remember Sarah?'

'If they're alive, they're in Guatemala – we closed the school years ago. Falling vocations meant we were spread too thin, and we decided to concentrate on the mission. The school building fetched a great deal of money.' She clicked her tongue. 'Leaving it was a wrench, though. And we're required to keep pupils' work for a certain number of years – the tea-chests we filled with exercise books, you wouldn't believe. They're all stored away in the cellars here.' She opened the file again. 'The novice mistress at the time Sarah Grayling entered, died last year, God rest her soul. But I did find this.' She handed him a document, thin yellow pages stapled together. 'It's a report on Sarah when she first applied to enter. It would normally be presented to a council of eight of our sisters, under the guidance of the provincial superior. And the novice mistress who prepared the report would not have had a vote.'

It was an exhaustive document, the subject identified only as 'S.G.'. He read it, skipping parts, reading others carefully. 'S.G.', it said, 'is a pleasant though noticeably reticent girl of eighteen. She has been a pupil at our Chelmsford school since she was thirteen years old. It took her a long time to settle at the school. She was sent to board with us following the unexpected death of her mother and her father has since remarried. There is little contact with him, and what there is does not seem to make her happy.

'During her first two years at the school, she needed a considerable amount of special care and attention from the staff. Understandably, since her mother died very suddenly, she experienced great grief and loneliness. She was going through a most difficult period of her life, even without this additional trauma. At that time she rejected all the overtures of her fellow pupils and kept very much to herself. There were long periods when she could not sleep and anti-depressants were finally prescribed. After this she improved. She still does not have any close friends in the school. During the holidays she has occasionally stayed on in school: her father has a new young family and there is not always room in their house for her.

'S.G. is academically capable – "A" level subjects are Maths, Science, French and R.E. She is unwilling to continue on to university, though she may change her mind when her results are known.

'Personality test – tentative emotional balance, low self-confidence. Low self-esteem. Some inability to relate

98

to others. Tends to be very austere in interpersonal relationships, has some leadership qualities but lacks self-discipline. During the interviews she was at times reticent. She clearly carries a good deal of self-doubt and has still to make more use of her talents. In my view, it is doubtful that she would make a good religious.'

Father Michael read the last sentence twice. Mother Emmanuel was watching him carefully.

He said, in total disbelief, 'You're telling me that after a report like this, the order still accepted her as a novice?'

The prioress folded her hands slowly in her lap. 'I am very well aware that Sister Gideon would have flunked any stringent tests. I'm aware she entered in despair. But, Father, you and I both know it is possible that even negative reasons may none the less lead to a genuine vocation.' She reached into the file again for a large piece of white card, handwritten. 'A couple of years ago, the BBC made a programme about nuns, and they came to us for part of it. Sister Gideon volunteered – no question of pressure – to say why she entered. She had to write it out before the programme so she could read it for them. A voice-over, I think they called it.' She adjusted her glasses. 'Listen to this. "*I was eighteen and still bitterly upset about Mum dying. It was years ago, but I couldn't seem to get over it. I thought perhaps if I went into the convent properly, I might find a bit of happiness. At least I'd be safe. And once the doors had closed behind me, I felt at peace. I knew I was in the right place. I was where I deserved to be.*" '

She looked up at the priest. 'That sounds sincere enough.'

'I still don't understand,' he said carefully, 'just why the council of sisters under the provincial superior let her in despite such a report.'

'They have informal discussions, question and answer sessions. They had time to get to know her. She must have shown some quality that convinced them.'

Father Michael looked doubtful. 'I suppose so. Can I take the file, Mother? Just in case something suddenly jumps out at me.'

She handed him the blue file. 'Oh, one more thing – will you celebrate mass for us, in the morning?'

Enclosed nuns do not eat in the presence of outsiders, men or women. Mother Emmanuel had told him how, when in the old days ('long before even my time, Father') their missionary nuns returned to England for a few months' rest after perhaps five years in Guatemala, they were not permitted to take their meals with the rest of the order. They were treated as visitors. 'Honoured visitors,' remarked Mother Emmanuel, 'but visitors.'

He ate alone in the guest room, the file open on the table beside him. The extern sister served him silently, ladling out the thick soup that was made every day, from the perpetual stockpot. Then it was baked convent eggs and mashed potato with parsnips, a huge mound because he was a man, and must therefore be hungry. After the prunes and custard they brought milky Coffee Hag in a handthrown pottery mug. He was a coffee addict, drinking it hot and black and Colombian, and to him this was tasteless as tea. But he knew it was a luxury the nuns would deny themselves.

It was still light after compline and evening prayers. At nine-thirty p.m., the old house was wrapped in Great Silence. He walked the convent drive, up and down, up and down, smoking one of his short black cigars. In the squat little house beside the closed gate, he could see old

Mr Dunbabbin, the handyman, as he sat brooding beside his coal fire.

It was late when he returned to the guest room. It had once been an outbuilding, a dairy, opening on what was now the inner courtyard of the convent. The nuns had bricked up the old door and windows and opened new ones on the far wall to make an entrance on to the driveway. The single room was austere, but he was prepared to bet it was a palace compared to the nuns' cells. A narrow bed was covered with a flowered cotton quilt. Handmade curtains matched it, and the stone floor was covered with thin jute. On one whitewashed wall there was a painting of St Winifred, on another a palm cross.

One of the original shallow stone sinks had been left in place and covered with a piece of wood to turn it into a table. It held an electric kettle and a small handmade bowl filled with old-fashioned pot-pourri. He unpacked his small case and put his hip flask on the table. When he'd showered in the tiny bathroom, he poured a minute amount of Jack Daniels.

But as he tried to get comfortable in the bed that was too short for him, his mind still fiddled and fumbled with the words on the white card, the odd little phrase Sister Gideon had used when she described her vocation.

He decided it was arrogant. Strange, that, coming from a young woman with low self-esteem.

'I was where I deserved to be.'

His last thought before sleeping was that in an hour or two, the nuns would be rising for Adoration of the Night.

Chapter Eleven

'Why am I so angry?'

Robina Knight slouched on her chair, massive thighs in tight jeans splayed wide. There were words written all the way up the skin of her arms, disappearing under the sleeves of her striped jumper: swear words and curses and pleas. *Hands off this woman* and *bastard* and *life sucks* and *torch me*.

Kate had never seen anyone demonstrate such visible hurt.

'I can't control it, know whatta mean?' Robina talked as she looked, her sentences shapeless and haphazard. 'An' if somethin' happens, somethin' I'm not expectin', like, I can't get my head aroun' it, know whatta mean? An' then I get afraid I'll do it again, like, an' they'll throw away the key, next time.' Robina rubbed her hands over her cheeks so hard she pushed up the skin and her eyes vanished into folds of orangey flesh. 'I'm so *angry*.' She dropped her hands and asked the psychologist, almost piteously, 'If I talk about it, will that stop the anger?'

Laura Pegram was the focus for the group in the Psychologist's Room. On the white easel behind her the word TARGET was written in big red letters. Underneath was a list: Management of Emotions. Values Enhancement (Dilemma Game). Critical Reasoning. Cognitive Skills.

Kate liked her, liked the mass of frizzy blond hair which gleamed under the fluorescent light, the vivid short-skirted suit. She wore tiny gold earrings and a pendant necklace. She had calm eyes and a confident smile.

All the other psychologists and psychiatrists Kate had met over the last fourteen years had seemed to her far more disturbed than she was. Like the man at New Hall who always interviewed wearing a track suit, belly bulging through the red vest, with a lit pipe clenched between his teeth. Or before him, at Bullwood Hall, the tiny middle-aged woman with bad teeth who constantly interrupted her, trying to get her to admit things her parents had done to her, things which Kate knew had never happened. It was as if she had already come to a decision about Kate, and merely wanted confirmation.

Mrs Pegram was different. She asked sensible questions and listened very carefully. She never ordered anyone about, but instead made firm requests. You found yourself doing exactly as she wished, but without any resentment. Now she said, 'Well, do you think talking helps the anger? What about you, Rose?'

No-one deserved the name less. Rose was fat, too, but flabby where Robina was solid. Her clothes all seemed too small, a lot of heavy white flesh showed between her jeans and her short T-shirt. The narrow red weals of slash marks scarred both her inner wrists and her watch had to be held on with grubby white bandages.

She shook her head dully. Kate had only once heard her talk with animation, and that was when she'd described how it felt to set light to a building: rejected at home, her response had screamed '*Look* at me!' Rose had described the act of arson lovingly, dwelling on the details, building up to the final, climactic moments when the flames took hold, lingering on the sense of freedom and release afterwards. But now she had no words, no interest in what was going on.

'Dilly?'

Dilly was a teacher from New Zealand doing six years for importing drugs and bitterly resentful.

'The only thing that'd help me is being left alone.' She crossed her arms defiantly over her chest, crossed her legs, turned her head away.

The psychologist responded with professional smoothness. 'Think about it, we'll talk again next session.' She twisted in her chair. 'How about you, Kate?'

Kate surprised herself. 'I do want to talk about it.' She hesitated. 'Only . . .' Her eyes flickered towards Robina and Rose sitting opposite.

Laura Pegram looked at her thoughtfully, glanced at the clock on the wall, between windows set too high to see out. At the end of the session she asked Kate to wash up the coffee cups.

'I've got some time free now,' she said, when Robina and the others had gone. 'Can you stay? I'll phone and tell your unit.'

The psychologist spooned coffee granules into two mugs. 'Robina's doing really well. She couldn't have recognized her anger a few months ago, let alone acknowledge it.' She kept her eyes on the electric kettle. 'She's taken two years to get this far. But she's been putting it into words all this time, only she couldn't say them.'

'She wrote it on her skin.'

'Yes. You realized?'

'Lots of people do stuff like that. There was a girl in New Hall with only one eye. She pulled it out herself.' Kate shuddered at the recollection of the woman's sunken lid.

104

'Self-mutilation is an inverted form of control, can you see? The woman wants to hurt herself worse than the prison possibly can. That way, *she*'s got the power, not us.' The psychologist picked up the kettle. She didn't look at Kate. 'It's good you've stopped scratching your arms. That was anger, wasn't it?'

Kate spoke to her back. 'That wasn't a prison thing. I always did it. Even when I was little.'

'Why?'

'It was always when I was frightened, so I suppose it must have been a reaction to stress. It was kind of a vicious circle, because then Mum used to smack us for it.' She didn't seem to notice the plural. 'So we did it in the cupboard.'

Laura waited, then she said, 'The cupboard?'

'Where we hid. When they were fighting.'

'Your parents? But they were fighting each other. They didn't hit you.'

'No,' said Kate, loyally. Laura turned from the kettle, her eyes were blue and searching. Kate met them and her own dropped. 'Yes.' She had never been able to admit it before. Her voice quivered as it must have done all those years ago.

'Both of them?'

Kate was immediately defensive. 'Dad would *never* hit *us*.' She seemed unaware how much her inflections revealed.

Laura Pegram sat down on the far side of the table, sipped her coffee. The silence went on and on. At last Kate said, 'The question under all this is why did it happen? That's what you want to hear. You all do.'

The psychologist just nodded. The hand Kate couldn't see crossed two fingers as she willed the girl to go on.

'I don't know, not any more.'

'Did you know then?'

Kate said slowly, 'I remember things, I dream all the time. Only I can't tell. Are they my own dreams?' There was desperation in her voice. 'How can I be sure?'

Laura Pegram recognized the effort she was making. It was what the psychologist had been working for since Christmas, but they'd never got this far before. Why today? she wondered.

She said, 'Remember I told you, there are always little ripples, before it happens? People don't just do things out of the blue. It builds up over a period of time.'

Kate nodded. 'I've been trying to go back. You were right, there were lots of things. Lots. Dad had left us, he said he was never coming back. And Mum wouldn't talk at all, she wouldn't go out, she just lay in bed with the curtains drawn. The only thing, she kept saying, *It's your fault he's gone.*' Kate swallowed painfully. 'And it was. I was such a little devil, I used to drive them both mad. Mum didn't love me, I always knew that.' Her voice tailed away. 'She never wanted me, even. She told me and told me.'

Finally Laura Pegram said, 'Maybe you were naughty *because* she didn't love you.'

'But to hurt someone else just because . . .' Kate's voice was breathless, her eyes wide. 'I'm so sorry, so sorry. So sorry for the poor . . . For Aaron.'

Laura had never heard her speak the name before.

'When they said all those things in the court, all those things that'd been done, I couldn't bear it,' Kate went on. 'I couldn't bear to hear them.' Suddenly it was coming out, the hidden past. She put the mug of coffee on the floor beside her and brushed her face hard with her forearm, the gesture of a small child. 'I'd give anything for it not to have happened.' She was crying herself. 'It was such an awful

106

thing to do. So *cruel*!' The word burst out of her. 'How could anyone . . . how could *anyone* . . . Oh God, if only that part of my life had never happened!' She wrapped herself in the circle of her own arms and bent her head.

There was no mistaking Kate's remorse. Sorrow and regret showed in every line of her body.

The psychologist watched her with compassion and relief and only a touch of triumph. Now they could move on.

Chapter Twelve

Morning prayer is a paean of praise to the new day. At six o'clock, the nuns were already in chapel. The office would be followed by the Mass. Father Michael prepared himself for the sacrifice of praise and thanksgiving in the small sacristy, taking what he needed from wooden cupboards and shelves.

He touched the long piece of cloth, the amice, to his head for the ceremonial moment, dropped it over his shoulders and tied it around his waist: *Place, O Lord, on my head the helmet of salvation*. Then the alb of pure white linen, to cover him head to foot in white: *Make me white, O Lord, and cleanse me*. The white cincture then around his waist to hold the end of the narrow stole, *Give me back, O Lord, the stole of immortality*, which he placed round his neck and across his chest, symbolizing the suffering of Christ and His obedience. He regretted they no longer pinned the maniple from the left arm, as Christ was bound in the Garden of Gethsemane. *Be it mine, O Lord, to bear the maniple of weeping and sorrow that I may receive with joy the reward of toil*.

He paused, listening to the sound of the nuns in their choir.

'It is good to give thanks to the Lord,
To make music to your name O Most High . . .'

The timeless plainchant of early morning, the pure voices of the hidden women, were like a benediction.

He turned to the chasuble, the principal vestment for celebrating mass. Sister David had placed ready for him the great mantle which would cover him back and front. She had been embroidering it for two years, working in joyful shades of yellow and blue. It hung from a brass hook on an old-fashioned wooden hanger stamped with the unexpected legend: Redwood & Feller Limited London Tailors By Appointment to Her Majesty The Queen.

He tested the weight of it on his hand. It was heavy with gold thread and equally heavy with meaning. This garment, more than any other, symbolized his calling, the justice and humility, the charity and peace that must mark his life.

Father Michael took the chasuble from its hanger, folded back the thick silk and gold encrusted fabric and pulled it over his head. For a moment he was lost in its bulk, in the smell of rich new material. Ten years ago, he had done this for the first time, dizzy from his twenty-four-hour fast.

You have not chosen me, but I have chosen you and ordained you.

The mantle fell of its own weight smoothly to his knees. He stood with bowed head, marked out for ever as a man who had accepted the yoke of Christ.

The nuns in the choir had fallen silent. In a moment, he would enter into the mystery of the Eucharist. He would remove the Sacred Host from the Tabernacle. He would hold the chalice of precious blood and take into his hands the bread of angels.

In the sanctuary Father Michael picked the smoking brass censer from its stand. Holy communion was his armour of faith, his shield of good purpose. He opened the door of the sacristy and moved into the formal and sacred choreography of the Mass.

There was a note from Mother Emmanuel on his breakfast tray, propped against the pewter vase holding a spray of young leaves: Sister Gideon will be happy to see you ten a.m. in the Visitors' Parlour.

He crossed the gravel drive to the main house and entered the front door, which always stood open. Inside, he faced the locked enclosure door, set with the heavy wooden 'turn', the revolving cupboard which brought in letters and small parcels without the 'duty' nun ever having to show herself. On its right, the parlour door stood open in readiness.

The convent had retained its formidable double grille which divided the square room completely in two, separating the nuns from their worldly visitors. The outer grille was made of broad dark painted wooden slats, horizontal and vertical, forming squares about six inches across. The inner grille was of finer slats, the openings smaller. Not so long ago, an opaque black curtain had hung between the two, almost totally obscuring any sight of the nun within – or indeed, of the visitor without. Mother Emmanuel had told him months ago that when first she entered, even for the twice yearly visits of their own families, the nuns had also worn a heavy black veil over their faces.

'It was a nightmare!' she had said, laughing. 'We must have frightened the living daylights out of them. It made black witches out of us!'

He had replied, 'It was cruelty.'

At first, she had protested. 'It is not for lack of affection we have left them, but because God called.'

'But for your parents . . . terrible, never to see your faces again.'

110

'It was a sacrifice we made for *their* happiness. To increase them in the love of God.' Then she softened. 'You're right, of course. It was absurd, ridiculous. Too extreme for modern women. We have kept many things, but the black veils have gone.'

Now he could see through clearly. Through a tall window he could even glimpse shrubs in the nuns' garden. Beside it, three hard upright chairs were placed in a meticulously measured row facing him. On his side, there were three chairs upholstered in brown leatherette. The room smelled faintly of beeswax and baking.

Two women entered, one slightly behind the other. Slowly, watched anxiously by the Infirmarian, Sister Gideon sat down. Then she got up again and moved her chair, quietly but deliberately, several inches to close up the space between it and the next chair. He thought perhaps the floor was uneven, though it looked smooth enough. Seated, she looked at him. She wore glasses, little round gold frames that would have fitted a child. The light from the window fell across her face and the lenses gleamed, so he couldn't see her eyes or their expression. He said, 'Sister Gideon. Good morning.'

There was the slightest hesitation before she answered. 'Good morning, Father. I apologize for keeping you waiting.'

He gestured with an open palm. 'Not at all. I'm just pleased to see you on your feet.'

She smiled at that, and her eyebrows went up. 'Well, more or less on them.'

The Infirmarian said, in the brisk tones of someone accustomed to cheering people up, 'I'll leave you two to your chat.' She turned to Father Michael. 'Father, you'll press the bell if you need anything?'

When she had gone, he pulled his own chair forward,

to get a better view through the impeding slats of the heavy grille.

She was, he knew, twenty-six. All he could see of her face framed in the white linen triangle of the wimple looked both younger and older than that. She was too pale, and the skin under her eyes was dark from lack of sleep. She was too thin, even under the bulk of scapular and robe. But the skin was unlined, almost translucent.

The shape of her head was outlined by the close-fitting head-dress. Without the distraction of hair, the bone structure was emphasized – cheekbones, jawline. She turned her head and he noticed the striking nose, narrow and slightly bumpy.

When she removed her glasses and slipped them into the capacious pocket beneath her scapular he could see that her eyes, set very wide apart above fine cheekbones, were light-brown with curious flecks of golden light, making them very alive despite her obvious tiredness. She had, he thought, a guarded expression. But perhaps that was just the effort of focusing on him. Her mouth was a complete contradiction: full and young and oddly sweet, an honest mouth. Dry lips, slightly puckered.

He was staring at her very hard, he realized. For a moment he remembered that particularly irritating precept of St Ignatius: *Do not look into the eyes of a woman in the habit.* He could never decide whether, in the twentieth century, it was more of an insult to the nun or the priest. And where else, faced with a habited nun, was the person? Only the face and hands revealed anything.

'How are you today?' he asked.

Again, that slight hesitation. 'Much better, thank you. Just a headache.'

'That's a big improvement, isn't it?'

She said nothing.

Everyone had been treating her with great care. He had decided before she came in that there was another approach.

'Have you any idea,' he asked, deliberately harsh, 'just what this illness is all about?'

She closed her eyes for a second as if in protest at the attack. Her voice was low. 'I do not.'

He persisted. 'Did you want to come home, maybe, from the mission?'

Her eyes opened, and there was hurt in them. This time, he could see the effort she had to make to speak. 'I know what you're implying, and you're quite wrong. I love it there.' She added with dignity, 'But if I had wished to leave, I was perfectly capable of making the request. There was no need to make myself ill.'

'I'm sorry. But this whole business has a lot of people very worried.'

Something he couldn't read flickered in her face, was gone. 'I honestly don't intend it.' She looked at him properly, as if she was seeing him for the first time. 'Can you help me, Father?'

He said slowly, 'I can try.'

'How? How can anyone help me? I can't even help myself.'

'Mother Emmanuel and I have talked about everything we could think of, starting from your schooling. There's nothing in your reports to cause concern. When you first came to the school, of course you were upset about your mother. That's normal. But maybe there's something else, something the nuns don't know about.' He got up, and went close to the grille, holding the bars. 'Something that happened a long time ago to upset you? It's possible, you know, to have an emotional reaction many years after an

113

event. If we could find what it was, we could maybe clear all this up.'

He could actually see her eyes darken with fear. He added, carefully, 'But to do that, you'd have to be prepared to talk to me. I don't need to tell you whatever we discussed would be absolutely between us. Will you do it?'

She said, finally, 'I'd rather not. It was all such a long time ago.'

'What was?' he asked quickly.

That pause again. '*You* said, something a long time ago.'

He shook his head. 'Dr Bevan can't find any physical cause for all you're going through. And it can't go on, can it? The next stage – if you don't get better – seems to be elaborate medical tests. He's very opposed to going that route. He says – I'm sure he's told you this already – he believes maybe the answer is in your own mind.'

Sister Gideon nodded.

'So – do you think he might be right?'

The shrug was so slight he scarcely caught it. He watched her carefully. This woman, who had lain on her bed in the exact pose of a medieval saint, now sat as if carved in stone.

Emotions can be expressed in all the ways a body moves. Even in stillness itself. He knew – from her posture, the curve of her shoulder as if shielding herself from him – he *knew* Sister Gideon was withholding something.

He said, very quietly, 'Try to think, please. It might have seemed a small thing, but maybe it worried you more than you thought at the time. Were you ever bullied, and didn't want to tell the nuns? Did you see something on the mission, perhaps? Guatemala can be a terrifying place. I once saw soldiers . . .'

She interrupted him. 'Stop, please, Father. Don't go on. It's nothing like that.' Her hands were out of her sleeves now. She put her left hand palm upwards on the seat of the chair beside her. Very slowly, the way she might have stroked a much loved cat, she rubbed the back of her hand against the upholstery.

'All right then,' he said, 'what about your family? Tell me about them.'

She asked miserably, 'What d'you want to know?'

'Well, what was your father's job? Were you all happy together? Where did you go for holidays?'

Sister Gideon fumbled in her pocket for a moment and brought out her glasses. She rubbed them against her habit and then put them on again, as if retreating behind their slight protection.

She said finally, 'We were just ordinary. An ordinary family.'

'Come on,' he said, impatiently. 'You can do better than that.'

'No. I don't remember.' She looked up at him with the frowning, contorted face of a desperate little girl. 'I don't *remember*.'

He was a compassionate man. What had she been, twelve, thirteen, when her mother died and her world fell apart.

He said quietly, 'Sister Gideon, I'm sorry.'

She drew a deep breath. He saw she'd gripped her left wrist tightly with her right hand. It was an odd pose, thumb uppermost.

'I can't,' she said. She rose to her feet. 'I *can't*. Please excuse me, Father. I don't mean to be rude.'

She turned and walked slowly from the room.

Damn it. It hadn't gone at all the way he intended. He knew less about her, not more. Father Michael sighed and stuck his hands in his pockets, tipping his chair back onto two legs, staring at the ceiling and frowning.

As he got up he glanced again, incuriously, through the grille at the two chairs Sister Gideon had placed side by side so they were touching. Odd, the way she had rubbed her hand against the seat.

He was almost at the door of Mother Emmanuel's office when it occurred to him that it had been the only unnecessary movement she'd made.

He saw her again with his mind's eye. Only this time, he remembered it differently. On the underside of her wrists, there was something he had seen but not registered. Something cruel, something savage. What? What was it?

His hand was lifted to knock on the prioress's door when he let it drop to his side. With a pang of dismay, he registered short white scars on her pale skin, and drew in his breath. He saw them crisscrossing her wrists and up her inner arms, revealed as the wide sleeve of the habit dropped away.

Father Michael knew what they meant: he had scars of his own. His shoulders, the backs of his legs, still bore traces of old pain. But he couldn't see them, and seldom thought of them.

In his first years as a Jesuit, he had used the discipline as a penance for his faults. He had pushed onto his index finger the metal ring with five chains suspended from it, each chain ending in a hook. He thrashed himself for the period of time laid down in the Rule, though it was never permitted to draw blood. In those early days his spiritual director was an elderly man who stood firmly by the old ways. Any feelings that were even remotely sexual must be excised. Only the discipline, regularly used, could subdue imagination and memory.

116

It did not subdue imagination. Pain and sexual pleasure, he discovered, are too closely intermingled. Nor memory. He would never forget Francesca Gardelli, and he didn't want to.

He had met her ten years ago when, in an elegant shop on the Via Condotti, he had bought a wallet of burgundy leather for his mother's birthday. The young woman who sold it had smiled and answered the young seminarian's halting Italian in her charming English.

Somehow, he found he had agreed to meet her for a coffee. In the street, she scarcely reached his shoulder. She did almost all the talking: about the city, her job, her flat. And, briefly, about her husband Renato. He had chosen to work in Milan despite her dislike of the north. That was why they had decided to separate. Now – she shrugged delicately – she did not know . . .

He thought the risks were all his. The fear certainly was. He couldn't bring himself to accept what she was so clearly offering, afraid he would find he wasn't a man any longer, that all those years of denial had killed something in him.

He had almost ceased to see himself as masculine. Perhaps it was the result of the atmosphere of suppressed sexuality in the seminary. It seemed to him that after years of separation and segregation from them, he could no longer respond to any woman in the way a normal man would.

Then one afternoon, preparing an essay, he read Bernard of Clairvaux on women: 'Their face is as a burning wind, their voice the hissing of serpents.' That ancient nonsense decided him. He slammed the book shut, and went out to find a public telephone.

Francesca's experience made up for his ignorance: with her, at least, he could do anything. The fact that

117

he was committing a mortal sin never ceased to hurt him. But there is nothing, he discovered, like the thrill of the illicit.

He made his confession – the first of so many – admitted his repentance, repeated an Act of Contrition. 'Oh my God, I am truly sorry for having offended Thee . . .' He received his penance and was told to go in peace.

His state of grace would last a week, ten days. At the first opportunity he could contrive – and they were rare – he went back to Francesca's bed. It didn't matter that out of it, they had nothing in common. Francesca demonstrated that all the stuff he'd been inculcated with in the seminary and before, about decent and indecent parts of the body, was more absurd even than he'd imagined.

He had somehow supposed that a woman's body would be shiny and hard as the forbidden photographs of his darkened bedroom when he was fifteen. Even in his desperate excitement, he was astonished to find how warm she was, how soft.

He didn't think he was in love with Francesca. What he felt was more lustful, more carnal than that: he was in thrall to her. She made him ecstatically happy for four months and deeply depressed for almost two years after she said, 'Michael, I'm sorry, it's over.'

She went to Milan, to Renato. It wasn't, she explained, that she loved Renato more than him. But – she gave that delicate shrug of hers – she was thirty-one years old and 'I must have a baby,' she said.

She had waited, but he had said nothing. And then it was too late. He was jealous of Renato, even jealous of the baby she had maybe borne by now. He lived with his heart strung tight in his chest, an ache that pervaded every day, every thought. He couldn't imagine being without the raw hurt of it.

For a long time, bitterness had been his strongest emotion. It took him more than two years to work through it, to regain his self-control. And he gained, too, in unexpected ways. He found he was left with a sure belief that there was no substitute for full sexual love – and the knowledge that it was not meant for him.

Despite everything, he still felt he was meant to be a priest. His lapse might even make him a better one. Now he was no longer on the outside, looking in.

So Father Michael knew how he had earned his scars. What had Sister Gideon done, to deserve hers?

Mortifying the flesh, like so many relics of the past in religious life, had been largely abandoned now. The more extreme penances – metal chains with tiny spikes worn around the hips beneath the clothes, the wooden crosses studded with blunt nails worn against the skin on shoulder or back, where the habit would press them into the flesh – were viewed with positive disfavour. But there were many who still kept their disciplines in their cells, packed away in black cloth purses they sewed themselves.

Anticipation had been almost the worst part for him. And the confusion, for the very act of penance – the hurt, the violation of your own body – could stimulate and act as substitute for the sexual feelings it was intended to suppress.

He wondered whether Sister Gideon had used the discipline on herself in the name of spiritual growth. Or whether it was to expiate breaches of the Rule, real or imagined, in the belief that sorrow for sin is the next best thing to innocence.

Just as the body of Christ was crushed, let us learn how to subdue our bodies.

*   *   *

119

Mother Emmanuel said, a little stiffly, in answer to his unwelcome question, 'If anyone here wishes to use the discipline, she may do so. We don't encourage it, not these days.' She gave a wry smile. 'We've heard of Freud even in here, you know. But if a professed nun should choose to discipline herself, then of course that is her decision.'

'Does Sister Gideon use it?'

'Most unlikely, I think. My young black veils very rarely try it, these days. Why ever do you ask?'

He told her of the marks he had seen. 'These were old scars, Mother. Not recent. Done years ago, I'd say.'

The prioress sighed. She sounded tired suddenly, and the lines round her mouth had sharpened. She looked down at her hands, at her ring of office set with the huge amethyst, incongruous against the surprisingly weathered, work-worn skin of her hands. Of course, he thought, she was a stone-carver.

'No, those marks are not from the discipline. We should have told you. But we didn't want to drag all that up again. She was just a schoolgirl when it happened.'

'When *what* happened?'

The prioress's fingers went instinctively to the cross at her waist. 'She tried to kill herself. Slit her wrists. We found her in time, thank God.'

'Why did she do it?'

'Her mother had just died by her own hand, God rest her soul. It wasn't such a surprise that she should want to do the same. I believe they were close.'

'The marks I saw,' he said slowly, 'went right up her arms on the inside. You don't slit your wrists like that, Mother.'

'The school doctor spent a lot of time with her. It was simply an expression of her grief, he said. And she's never

120

so much as referred to it since.' She smiled at him. 'She was scarcely thirteen. Remember what we were saying about girls of that age? It's an emotional time.'

'I'll take your word for it,' he said.

Chapter Thirteen

It was a vast building in two acres of West Sussex. The taxi took four minutes to travel along the unweeded drive beneath a double row of elms and gave Father Michael plenty of time to take in the architectural absurdity looming at the end of it. The Holy Family Nursing Home was a Victorian folly, but it looked like a Bavarian Schloss escaped from its native mountains. Round turrets decorated the green-tiled roof, shutters guarded the many-paned windows.

A slip of a girl in the modern habit of her order – navy skirt and blouse, triangular black head-veil – led him through wide corridors which smelled of old age and hot closed rooms.

Mother Joseph sat erect in her high-backed chair. One leg rested stiffly on a footstool, several cushions supported her back. A gnarled hand grasped a walking stick. Her eyes were heavy-lidded and sombre in a face as lined and creased and brown as a leather glove. She was one of the old school of nun, he recalled, the indomitable women who had spent their lives on the missions. Mother Emmanuel had told him the story, famous in the order, about the worst storm in Guatemala anyone could remember. Mother Joseph had prayed diligently for survival, put the metal feet of her bed into two pairs of rubber wellingtons for protection from lightning and gone to sleep.

He sat down in a small armchair and began to explain his visit, but she interrupted. 'Yes, yes, they told me. Sister Gideon, poor girl.'

There was more than impatience in her voice; there was, he sensed with surprise, direct antagonism. He decided to disregard it.

'There seems to be nothing wrong with her physically, so we have to assume the problem is in her mind. But she hardly says anything – certainly nothing to enlighten either Mother Emmanuel or me.' He took the slim blue file from his briefcase. 'So then we went through this.'

Mother Joseph held out an imperious hand and he gave her the file. She riffled through it, but he sensed she was only going through the motions.

'Can you tell me any more about her?'

She didn't answer and he asked again, shouting louder.

'I heard you the first time,' she said sharply. 'I'm not deaf. The answer's no. I'm very sorry, but there it is.'

He leaned forward, dropped his voice, let his help-lessness show. 'We really need your help,' he said. 'This young woman is in a terrible state. If I can't do something for her, and soon, there's no knowing what might happen.'

This time he connected, but only just. She shook her head. 'Forgive me, but I have the very strongest reasons for not wishing to discuss Sister Gideon. Maybe someone else could help you.'

He caught the softening in her stance and pressed on: 'We've traced the eight sisters who considered her original application to the order. Three have died, two have left religious life and we can't reach them. The other three are on the missions. We've written to them, but it could be weeks before we hear. And we're running out of time. Sister Gideon is going rapidly downhill. She's in constant pain, she scarcely eats, she's a sick woman.'

'You're not telling me she's going to die of this imaginary illness?'

'That's exactly what I am telling you. I don't believe it is imaginary, for one thing. The pain she endures is real, there's no doubt of that.'

He caught the cynicism in her eyes behind the thick lenses. He thought, does she believe me? At that moment the pink hearing aid he'd noticed behind her ear suddenly emitted a high-pitched buzz. He waited while she fiddled with it, suddenly reminded of her age.

When she seemed satisfied, he asked, 'Mother, you are familiar with psychosomatic illnesses?'

'Father Michael, I may be old but I'm not stupid. Please don't patronize me.'

'Now it's my turn to say, forgive me. I only meant . . .'

'I see exactly what you meant. I imagine there have been developments since my day. Is that what you're going to tell me?'

He said, with relief, 'It's now accepted that psychological problems and mechanisms underlie all illnesses – and despite all the impressive technical advances, what causes them in the first place is still a mystery. Some have very clear beginnings in the mind. Many skin conditions, for instance, reveal stress. Let's consider Sister Gideon's illness in this light. She can't – or won't – understand it herself. I need to find if there's anything in her background which might explain what's happening to her. She could be reliving some bad experience. If we could get at this, then we could give her appropriate treatment, psychiatric treatment.'

He touched the blue file. 'The report on her original application to the order shows quite clearly that she was a troubled child when she arrived at your school. I know the mother died, and that might be the cause, but she is able to speak of her quite calmly now. I'm convinced there's something else. And if there is, you would know it.' He looked hard at the lifted chin, the obstinate, determined jaw, and suddenly he knew how to play it. 'Unless,' he added carefully, 'you've forgotten.'

The long silence was broken by a young nun bringing a tray, which she set between them. Fresh coffee in a small percolator, a plate of chocolate and ginger biscuits. In a sudden change of mood, the old lady gave him an enchanting smile.

When Mother Joseph resumed talking, it was as though she had never said 'no' to him. She began abruptly, almost in the middle of events.

'It was a terrible business. We didn't really know it all, you understand. The child came to us under some sort of cloud, we knew that much. The Bishop dealt with it all, and there was a lot he kept to himself. He was a good man.' She crossed herself, and sighed. 'I remember thinking at the time, how all the trouble aged him. He took it into himself, you see.'

'What trouble?'

'All this to-do with the girl's family. I don't know why it became so personal with him, but it did. Anyway, it seemed the father was a bit of a bad lot, if you follow me. Involved with other women. That was why that poor woman did away with herself, God rest her soul. The girl was in such a way when she first came to us, I thought she'd go out of her mind. She couldn't sleep, we could never leave her in the dark, even in a dormitory with five other girls. She would waken from nightmares and all she did was just shiver like a little animal, crouched on her bed. It was dreadful to see her.'

Mother Joseph turned her head. Very quietly she said, 'I was close to her, then. I was the only one she wanted. In the daytime, in school, it didn't seem too bad. She didn't make friends, exactly, but the other children tolerated her all right. But those dreams . . .' She locked her trembling hands together on her lap to keep them steady. 'They weren't a child's dreams, you understand. They were terrible beyond the telling.'

He saw that her skin had paled, and red blotches of emotion stood livid on her cheeks.

'She never spoke of them in the night.' She kept her voice level. 'It was as if they were too dangerous to be let out. Anyway, when she woke she didn't speak. She never even cried. She'd just hold my hand against her forehead as if . . .', the half-laugh held despair and amazement, '. . . as if I was a lucky charm. We weren't supposed to have emotional involvements with the children, you know how convent schools were run even a few years ago. But that child was stretched to breaking point. She touched my heart.'

She fell silent. He looked at those tired eyes and thought, what this woman has seen.

'What happened?'

'We got her through it. By the grace of God. Time went by, she moved further from . . .', he caught a fractional hesitation, '. . . from her mother's death. The nightmares became less frequent, though I don't think they ever stopped altogether. But as she grew older – fourteen, fifteen – she was able to cope with them. She was allowed to get up and go to the kitchen to make herself a cup of tea and talk to the cats. Poor little soul.' She wiped below her right eye with the back of her hand and a tear glistened on freckled skin. 'Poor lost little girl.'

He had a brief mental picture of a younger Sister Gideon, barefoot in a cold kitchen, clutching a cat for comfort against her hideous dreams.

He asked, 'What were her dreams, d'you remember?'

He knew, before she answered, that she did. She had loved that desolate child, had comforted her night after dreadful night. Even the ancient woman she now was could tell this story lucidly. Those dreams, which made her tremble even to speak of, she would not have forgotten them.

'I don't remember, I'm afraid.' She said it without apology and he knew she lied.

'That's a pity.' He had to force himself to keep calm, to keep his voice even, not to show his frustration. 'They might be relevant.'

She frowned. 'I really don't think I should be talking about this. The Bishop said, we were never to discuss it. He said, she was going to be punished enough, it was not for us to judge her. We were to pray for her, but we weren't to speak of her.'

He was completely lost. 'Her? You mean you were to pray for Sarah? And why was she to be punished?'

She focused on him and shifted in exasperation. 'Of course, not Sarah.' Irritated, she used the name for the first time. 'Not Sarah. The sister.'

'The *sister*?' He held the file in his hand, he knew it backwards. The old girl's mind was wandering, he shouldn't have bothered her. 'There are two little half-brothers, from the father's common law marriage. No mention of a sister. That kind of detail is always known, it's important. But it's not in the file.'

'The Bishop would have had it removed.'

'*What?* Why?'

She looked at him as if he were mad. 'He was the Bishop. He did what he thought best. We would not have questioned him.'

'This sister. What was her name?'

She shook her head.

'Was she older than Sarah, than Sister Gideon? Or younger?'

Behind the thick lenses, an odd expression he could not decipher flickered for a moment. 'I don't remember,' she said again.

'You said, you were to pray for her but not speak of her. You said she would be punished. Why, for God's sake? She can only have been a child herself.'

'I cannot answer that. I promised the Bishop and I will not break my word.'

'Even to save Sister Gideon's *life*?'

She sat silent, coffee and biscuits forgotten. She rocked herself gently forward and back. She had gone very pale, and the lines from nose to mouth had deepened into tracks of sorrow. He waited, his mind racing. What was this all about?

When she finally spoke her voice had changed. She sounded frail and querulous, an old lady who needed to be left alone.

'You don't understand, Father Michael. I made the promise in the first place in order to save that same life.'

For a long time neither of them spoke. Father Michael put his head in his hands and rubbed his fingers through his hair.

'Mother Joseph,' he said finally to the floor, 'I'm sorry to have bothered you. I appreciate your position. You want to continue to protect Sister Gideon and you think silence is the way to do it. You're wrong, but there's nothing else I can say.' He took the blue file from the table, still without looking at her, started to get to his feet. 'I just hope you can live with the consequences, that's all.'

Her walking stick was suddenly thrust in his way. 'So you don't know about the trial?'

'My God! What trial?'

She said heavily, 'You're right, Father Michael. I'm a stubborn old fool. I don't want this on my conscience as well, not at my age. I haven't time any more for emotional baggage where I'm going.'

He demanded urgently, 'Whose trial? What's all this about?'

'I told the truth, you see. I can't give you any details. If ever I was aware of them, I've blotted them out of my mind. All I can tell you is that it was dreadful.'

'*What happened?*'

'It was her sister, not our little Sarah. The sister was the one. Even though she was a child, what she did was so appalling they gave her a public trial. That doesn't usually happen, does it? But that's the way it was. She was sent away to one of those secure units for years and years.'

He crossed the room to the fireplace. In the huge grate, logs were piled. He very much wanted to smoke but the place was full of smoke alarms.

'You *must* remember what she did! Mother, I need to know. There could be something here that is affecting Sister Gideon now, years later. Think, please. Try to remember. It must have been in the papers. Or on television . . .'

Mother Joseph said reprovingly, 'You're forgetting, Father. We're a religious order. The Bishop warned me it was the headlines in all the newspapers. But we didn't see them. He decided that in order to protect Sarah, we were not to take even *The Times*. It was a boarding school, so it was quite easy to control what the girls read. We'd only one television set, of course, the girls were allowed to watch the occasional programme under supervision.' Her face softened. 'Though I seem to remember good behaviour was rewarded by watching *Ready, Steady, Go* on Saturday afternoons. But nothing else. And we simply took the radios away until the Bishop said it was all over.'

If it hadn't been so serious, he could have laughed. 'This is unbelievable. It's nonsense. What about the parents?'

She said, 'You must remember, Father, things were different in those days, not so free and easy. We're talking about fourteen years ago. And it was a convent school, very disciplined. We protected our children from anything we considered sordid or unsuitable. That's what the parents wanted too.'

'Someone would have known.'

'Why so? I remember when I was younger, we never took newspapers in the convent at all. Just the Vatican newspaper, *l'Osservatore Romano*, and the *Catholic Herald*. Even during the war, we hardly heard what was going on. Do you know, it wasn't till oh, years later I found out about our young king giving up his throne for an American woman, a divorcee . . .'

Father Michael put up a hand to stop her flow of reminiscence. 'Hold on a minute. Are you really telling me the Bishop never discussed something so serious with you? And anyway, people would have recognized her name and realized who she was.'

'The Bishop knew what he was about. He did everything in his power to make sure the innocent child didn't suffer because of her guilty sister. And no-one ever connected the two girls.' She helped herself to a ginger biscuit. She dipped it in her coffee first to soften it, and it seemed to take her a long time to swallow.

He planned his next move as he waited. Mother Joseph had said the crime was so terrible Sarah Grayling's sister was tried although she was a child. In that case, there would be newspaper reports. Grayling was a fairly unusual name, he knew it was about fourteen years ago. He'd go to the Press Association in Fleet Street on Monday and look up reports of the trial.

Mother Joseph broke into his thoughts. '. . . and of course,' she said, 'it was to protect her that he changed her name to Grayling.'

'He *what*? You're telling me she's not Sarah Grayling, after all!' He thought for a moment. 'Who is she, then? What *is* her name, for God's sake?'

Mother Joseph drew herself even more upright in her chair, annoyance stiffening every line of her thin body.

'There's no call for blasphemy, Father. And I have no knowledge of her former name. If he did not see fit to give me details, I would not have dreamt of questioning him. Why should I?'

Father Michael ran an impatient hand through his hair. The more he found out, the more complicated it all became. He was a man who required order, method, rational thinking in order to function. And he was being led by the nose through a farrago of nonsense.

'This is absurd. Look, Mother Joseph, even a Bishop can't rename someone on a whim.'

She looked at him and the moist eyes sparkled. 'You think not? Then let me tell you, young man, I don't have to read your tea leaves to know you'll never become one. And if you're not aware of the extent of a Bishop's power, I'd have thought at least you would have known something of English law.' Her smile held

131

malice. 'And I always understood you Jesuits to be such great intellectuals.'

He made a positive effort to keep calm. He came back and sat down again opposite her. 'Just what are you saying, Mother?'

'Anyone can choose what surname they use, so long as it isn't changed for fraudulent reasons. You can just decide to call yourself Loyola and it will be perfectly valid. From the law's point of view you just have to always use Loyola in everyday life.'

'I can't believe that would work for legal documents? Officials always need bits of paper.'

'She was a child. There were no legal documents.'

He thought, the old girl is an opponent, after all. I was right first time. He said, musing, 'But the order sent Sister Gideon to Guatemala. She'd have had to produce a birth certificate for the passport office.'

He remembered a problem brought to him once by a woman with an illegitimate child who'd wanted to change the baby's surname when she finally married. 'And,' he added triumphantly, 'there's no way you can alter the name on a birth certificate more than twelve months after registration. The Bishop would have had to prove Sarah was known as Grayling during those twelve months, produced a GP's registration card or a post office book in that name. Which,' he concluded, 'would have been quite out of the question.'

Mother Joseph appeared unimpressed. 'But you see, in the unusual circumstances, the passport office were quite happy to accept a note confirming that Grayling was the name by which she was commonly known. That is the law. It merely had to be signed by a respected member of the community such as a solicitor, or a doctor. Or a clergyman.' She tapped his knee with the end of her walking stick. 'I think we can therefore take it that the Bishop's name was perfectly acceptable, don't you?'

He thought for a minute. 'What about Sarah's father? What did he have to say about all this?'

She sighed. 'As I said, there'd been trouble between the parents. He wasn't close to Sarah, either. He very rarely visited, and we were almost glad, she'd get herself so excited.' Her voice dropped. 'And then afterwards, she'd be so quiet, all the happiness drained away. Sometimes she'd even ask him to go before she was due back in school. Then she'd have nightmares again. I don't recall that she ever went to him for holidays. He was always travelling on business. He *said*. Anyway, we had plenty of room for her. And plenty of love.' She pinched her lips. 'So I'm sure he couldn't have cared less, when the Bishop asked for his consent to a name change.' A thought struck her. 'Of course, now I think of it, he must have agreed — he called himself Mr Grayling.'

The priest sat in silence.

'Shocked, are you, Father?' She shrugged. 'We all used to be given different names when we entered religious life. It was a form of de-personalization, of course, loss of self. Some orders still do it, though it's losing favour. I was Enid Gower once.' Her voice quavered, high and childish. 'Enid Gower, 53 Leverton Road, Liverpool. Please could you help me find my way home? I don't like it here.' She added, in her normal voice, 'She's Sister Gideon now, anyway.'

He was disconcerted but not surprised. He got to his feet. 'Mother Joseph, I think maybe I should be going now. You've been very . . .'

There was a knock on the door and the nun who'd brought coffee put her head round it.

'Father Michael, it's been a long time, I'm afraid

133

Mother Joseph must be getting tired. She's not used to talking a lot these days.'

The old prioress waved her away. 'Just a minute, child. We're nearly done. I've something more to tell the father here. In *secret*!' She winked theatrically. When the door closed again she gave him a sly sideways look.

'I just wanted to tell you the important thing. The only thing about Sarah and her sister that really matters.' She leaned forward, conspiratorial and – he saw with despair – hopelessly crazy.

   'O'er the rugged mountain's brow,' she recited,
    'Clara threw the twins she nursed,
And remarked, "I wonder now
    Which will reach the bottom first?"'

Chapter Fourteen

'Jaffa! Jaffa! Whur are ya?'

The voice bawled again from one of the cells up on Fours, magnified by the canyon-like buildings. It was almost five in the afternoon. Kate was sitting on a bench as the last of the sun disappeared from the village green, her regulation swimsuit spread beside her to dry.

Jaffa answered the shout in a hoarse voice, not like a woman's at all. 'Wha'ya say? Wha'? Ah carn 'ear ya!'

'But everyone else can,' a man's voice said with irritated humour.

Kate looked up to see Mr Jarrow standing there, holding a large cage containing a young parrot, its plumage brilliant red and blue. He smiled down at her.

'Kate Dean, isn't it? Busy?'

'Been swimming,' she said reluctantly, with a movement of her head towards her wet suit – it didn't do you any good if the girls saw you chatting up a governor.

He seemed all right, though. Better than most of them: he was one of the few governors who actually moved around the building. The rest kept to the offices and their computers. Their physical presence was not required to control the inmates. There were around two hundred and twenty-six officers, maybe a dozen of them men. Then thirty-six senior officers, and twelve principal officers. Of these, five of each were men. But the ten governors were all male, and probably the only time you ever saw them was if you were in trouble, up before them on Adjudications.

'Ah yes, so I see.'

Kate wore a baggy sweater which accentuated the long neck, and sleek wet hair defined the shape of her head, curling tendrils clung to her cheeks and forehead. Something in his voice made her blush. She never wore any makeup, though cosmetics were allowed in Holloway now, and the stain of colour lit her face.

'I'll escort you back to your unit,' he said. 'I want to talk to you.'

Her heart sank. Mr Jarrow had never spoken to her before, so why now? She tried to think what she could have done in the last few days to merit a governor's intervention. Nothing she knew of. And she didn't need escorting. Because of her previous record, they'd made her a redband almost immediately. She wore the piece of bright material on her wrist, with that awful photo they'd taken when she entered set into it as identification. Within limits, she could move around as she wished, and unlock certain doors closed to others.

'But first,' Mr Jarrow went on, 'I want this gent boarded out for the weekend. Can you deal with him?'

She got up obediently.

'Bought him from here for my daughter,' he went on, looking at the bird, not at her. All the other officers kept their eyes on you, all the time. '. . . decided she wanted a mountain bike instead,' he was saying. 'I've got fond of him now though.' He stuck a finger through the bars. 'He gets very excited about my sandwiches at lunch time.' The bird watched his finger with a sardonic eye. It sidestepped, gave a sudden shriek and pounced. David Jarrow yelped and pulled his hand back sharply. Despite herself, Kate giggled.

'I'm still not parrot-trained,' he said ruefully, as she took the cage from him. The wooden aviary behind them on the village green housed dozens of birds, mostly grey and black cockatiels. They were well-kept in two vast cages. Several of the inmates looked after them, as Kate did for six hours a week. She knocked for Rowena to let her in.

Kate hung up the parrot's cage, checked its water and added a few sunflower seeds. She lingered at the nesting boxes where a budgie had just hatched two tiny pale babies, smaller than toy Easter chicks on chocolate eggs. She loved it in here, the flutterings and whirrings and sudden soft calls.

Mr Jarrow got up when she went outside and the courtesy made her blush again. She thought he was old, mid-forties maybe. But she liked his quiet voice, his stillness.

Apart from her father, and one of her solicitors, the only men Kate knew were her gaolers. Mr Jarrow was one of them but he didn't behave like one. Walking back to A4 he said, 'You swim with the autistic kids? You like doing that, don't you?'

'I've just started.' The children were brought in once a week from a nearby special school to use the pool. 'I'm teaching Liam. He's not very responsive yet, but he'll get there. It just takes patience.'

She watched him from the corner of her eye as he nodded. With his beard, he reminded her of pudding bowls they'd had when they were little. Eat every scrap, Mum said, and then you can see him. And sure enough, right in the centre of the bowl every time, under yogurt or banana or custard, was the bearded figure in blue with a stick over his shoulder and his belongings tied in a bundle on the end. There was a winding road behind him, between two green hills. Home is the sailor, went the poem beneath it, home from the sea, hoping he'll be in time for his tea. Out of that thought she asked him, 'Aren't you here late? Won't your tea be ready at home?'

Mr Jarrow grinned at her serious expression. 'D'you know, Kate, I've been in the prison service twenty-five years and I don't think anyone has ever worried about my tea-time before!'

Embarrassed, she felt herself flush again. She was angry at her inability to cope with his teasing: men frightened her.

'Sorry,' he said, 'I'm not laughing at you. It was a nice thought, I appreciate it. But I'm not in a rush. And you've got time to talk for five minutes, haven't you?'

Kate said nothing. He knew very well she had. He planned the timetable, didn't he?

'Tomorrow morning I'm due to take a group of visiting magistrates around. They've already told me they want to see the cell of a "lifer". I'd like to show them yours.' He paused. 'Would you mind?'

She didn't know which surprised her more – the request, or the polite way he made it.

'Was that what you wanted to talk to me about?' He nodded. She couldn't understand him. 'Why did you ask?' she said. 'Why didn't you just *tell* me you were going to do it?'

'That's not the way I do things.' He sounded almost cross. 'You're studying psychology. You know about gender roles and patterns of authority. Well, I don't want to intrude my presence on you in your own cell just because I can. I think you should control at least this

138

small area of your life. Unless . . .', he gave her a quizzical look, '. . . you give us reason to think otherwise.'

He stood back while she used her own key to unlock the corridor door on her floor. She waited for him to go through first but he gestured with his head: after you.

'Another thing,' he went on, as they walked round the concrete hallway along which they made the regular trolley runs with heated food for each unit. 'Mrs Pegram initiated a more thorough enquiry. Did she tell you?' Kate shook her head. 'Well, we've discussed your case with the people back at New Hall. Mrs Pegram made recommendations to the governors here. The Parole Board have been told all about the burn-out, that you were asleep at the time. Now this is all strictly unofficial, but I wanted you to know . . .' He paused while they passed a cleaner, slopping water on the concrete with a surly expression. Kate daren't let herself think. *What?* '. . . provided there are no setbacks of any sort, you will be released in two months' time.' He looked down at her and added, 'Congratulations.'

She heard what he said, but could make no answer. She wouldn't let herself believe this time. Not until it happened.

There was a knock on her cell door at ten a.m. next morning. Unusual: the kangas just peered through the hatch. All the cells on A4 were unlocked, and she waited for someone to come in. When no-one did, she opened it. David Jarrow was outside, standing on the far side of the corridor, arms folded. Not crowding in like the officers did but respecting her privacy. Kate smiled at him, appreciating the small courtesy.

She felt oddly proprietorial: she had tidied up, Blue was in his cage. The well-dressed, middle-class men and women – she wondered what the collective noun would be for magistrates, a bench perhaps – had to enter her cell in two groups, there were so many of them. They didn't say much to her but even so managed to be both patronizing and nervous, as if she might fly at their throats.

They stared curiously at her Open University books and notes, at her basket of Body Shop bath gels and shampoos, and she had to explain the inmates were permitted to spend up to £10 a month on personal items. A woman wearing tweeds and pearls asked about Kate's course and was visibly shaken by her answer. ('Psychology?' she repeated, her voice rising. 'Really?') One elderly man, red-faced and waistcoated like Farmer Giles in a children's book, peered at her intently, then went back outside the door and read her information card. Then he stared at her again, up and down, clearly trying to fit the information it contained with her appearance.

'Why do you have no photographs of your family, I wonder?'

Kate swung round. The woman who had spoken was brown-haired, slight, with a gentle smile. She even looked kind. But a kind person would never have asked such a question, never have opened up that particular wound. She opened her mouth and started to say, trying to overcome her shaky voice, 'I . . . never had . . .' and suddenly David Jarrow was at her side, his own voice curt, as if reprimanding the woman for overstepping the limits he had set.

'There was a fire, unfortunately. Kate lost almost everything. I expect her photographs were destroyed too. Now, ladies and gentlemen . . .'

'Good Lord,' a man's voice broke in, 'whatever have you got here?'

By Kate's window there was a faint scratchy sound from

the sick bird crouched like a ball of dingy cottonwool in a nest of old sweater.

'I brought him in from the aviary,' she explained. 'He needs feeding every couple of hours, I couldn't get out at night so . . .'

She went over and picked him up. As she did so, one of the women gave a little shudder of distaste. 'It looks so dirty,' she said, when Kate looked at her.

'He's ill. That's all. He'll be fine in a day or two.' She felt fiercely defensive, though whether of herself or the quail, she honestly couldn't tell. Two years ago, she had never so much as touched a live bird. It had been Sarah who loved birds, at home. When she was in that first secure unit, a twelve-year-old girl taken from her home and family and set down among terrifying strangers, she'd begged repeatedly to be allowed a hamster. She imagined herself holding the little creature between her palms, feeding it, feeling its warm fur. She longed for it with a desperation so great she thought she'd die if she didn't get it. She even had a name ready for it: Flower.

But the regulations forbade it. You could have a bird, she was told, caged birds are permitted. So she'd saved up her birthday money for a budgerigar, and she'd had one ever since, always called Blue. Wherever she'd been, they'd teased her: Birdgirl of Alcatraz.

'I suppose it's good for you to have a bird to look after.' The woman who said this invested it so heavily with meaning, the unspoken hung in the air: *considering why you're in here.* She was dressed in pale clothes, clearly expensive. As she spoke, she brushed imaginary flecks from her skirt. As though, Kate thought furiously, the place was dusty. But she kept her thoughts to herself, and it was Mr Jarrow who answered for her.

'Certainly it is,' he said quietly. 'Everyone needs something to love.'

Kate had promised herself a long time ago that she would never love anyone again. It was too risky, love. It made you do things you regretted for ever. So when she was twelve years old, she set her face against it.

It was an easy enough decision, where she was. You had to be hard in a Young Offenders Unit, or God help you. Hard and tough. Let them see you cry and you were done for. Let them think you were weak, and you'd be everyone's victim. She learned that for sure: there were victims and there were aggressors. And she didn't want to be either.

She lay in the special darkness of Holloway, the sky a dull glowing orange from millions of reflected city lights. It was not a night for sleep. Her pillow was so hard her ear hurt. The mattress felt thin and lumpy. She thought of someone else who lay on a hard bed, in a small room.

The child who was her mirror image. Whose eyes were her eyes, brown flecked with gold. Who wore one green glove and one blue mitten, while she wore one blue mitten and one green glove.

Such total submersion in the other's being, they divided the two sides of a complete personality between them, and never even knew they were doing it. Each of them a half person. A split egg.

Two imaginative little girls left alone together for long hours.

Go and play with your sister. I'm too busy . . . Inventing their private world where grownups and commonsense and don't do that and be careful didn't exist.

Nightmare nights and dragoned days. Feeding on each other's fantasies, frightened by each other's fears.

Smothered screams in empty rooms and faces leering from the pattern on the wallpaper.

Screel din. Screel *din*. Words only two people understood: *Something bad is coming!* Childhood terrors now buried deep. But not deep enough.

Kate stared at the wall. Against the scratched cream emulsion she conjured up the face she had recognized in the mirror before she learned to recognize her own reflection.

The perfect one, the centre of her universe. The only person in all her world who never rejected her, never disapproved.

There was a loud crash in the corridor outside, a smothered exclamation. 'Fuckin' 'ell.' She recognized Edie, one of the night patrol. The budgerigar woke and stirred and muttered.

'. . . gorgeous you're sexy I love . . .'

Chapter Fifteen

'. . . *won't you stay awhile and save my life . . .*'

The soft, insistent voice was mesmerizing, very seventies, perfect music to shave by. Father Michael Falcone considered his lathered-up reflection in the bathroom mirror. The white foam made his skin very dark, his eyes almost black: he looked foreign even to himself. He picked up his razor and started beside his right ear.

'. . . that Dory Previn knows what it's all about . . .' Wogan's voice interrupted his reverie and he hastily turned the radio knob with his left hand, spinning through the channels, catching an assortment of voices.

'. . . as the cloud continues to break . . .'

More music, flamenco rendered by session musicians closer to Acton than Andalusia.

'. . . five ounces of broccoli provides as much Vitamin C as two pounds of oranges . . .'

'. . . Danish prime minister is today hosting an international . . .'

Rising as always at six, he'd already heard the news twice, the first time before going for his swim. He twisted further. A repetitive beat hit the same note over and over and he tried again. A lot of laughter and a woman's voice saying, 'Sex in the head is always better, orgasm every time. Why d'you think people read my books?'

Finally he found some real music, speaking of ice and empty places.

He wiped the mirror free of steam with the towel on his shoulder. Electric razors were fine when he travelled, but there was nothing to beat a badger-hair brush and Floris shaving-cream. It was a luxury he permitted himself only rarely, and a block would last more than a year.

Father Michael's desire had always been to live a simple life of prayer and work, and one of his few vanities was the belief that he was a simple man. Only there were too many contradictions in his personality for that.

He liked to eat, but forced himself to be abstemious. He drank very occasionally, but chose the most expensive whiskies. He loved to smoke dark Dutch panatellas, so he rarely allowed himself to light one.

The black Jesuit gown suited his olive skin, gave him height. It conferred authority, status, and in it he moved with assurance. His nose was strongly curved, his lips well-sculpted and slightly down-turned. His hands – the only other part of him visible in the gown – were square, with blunt fingers, his father's hands.

When he went home to the small English town of Wells where all his family lived, he appeared – and felt – utterly different to everyone else there. The Pelhams were conventional, conservative, chilly. His mother rarely spoke of Rainaldo Falcone, the prisoner of war she had met when she was seventeen. Michael had been an adult before he pieced the story together: how his father had urged her to accompany him back to Italy, but she always refused. The cool English prettiness that had charmed Rainaldo later drove him away: when Michael was seven he had gone, alone.

Michael was left with a couple of photographs and the memory of his father's hugs, his big white teeth when he laughed. It stunned the whole family when Michael adopted his father's Catholic faith. He could hardly explain it to himself, it was just something he had to try.

Only when he was sent to Rome was he able to comprehend his father's restless unhappiness in England. Even the smallest things had flavour there: groups of middle-aged men congregating volubly in cafés, eating olives and hard country bread dipped in their oil. He would have given a great deal to talk to his father then, but it was too late for that by ten years.

Rome changed him. Not only emotionally, but physically. He looked increasingly Italian, so that people meeting him for the first time there were puzzled to find he spoke the language with hesitancy. It was only when he went home to Wells that he was made aware of how fast he talked, how much he used his hands and body for emphasis.

Father Michael held the skin of his jaw taut, enjoying the coarse glide of the blade, the clean morning feel. The day was already neatly laid out in his mind. He ticked items off to himself while the Sibelius climbed, climaxed, fell away. Lecture notes to finish, Farm Street for mass at eleven. But first, phone Mother Emmanuel to tell her about that bizarre interview with the old lady in Sussex. Demented she may be, but she had told him a surprising amount. He thought with pity of the unhappy child she had described, bewildered by dreadful dreams.

Was Sarah Grayling going through her own torment – or someone else's? Was old Mother Joseph really telling him something with that twin rhyme?

'. . . see that twins are nature's genetic experiments. Identical twins are the same person, separated into two in

146

the womb. This splitting takes place *after* the single ovum has been fertilized by one sperm . . . Scientists don't know what causes this, but it's not a genetic message, it isn't in the genes . . .'

For a moment he gaped at his reflection, so pat was the timing. 'Fraternal twins, on the other hand,' the pleasant Canadian voice continued, 'occur when two eggs are released into the Fallopian tubes at the same moment, and fertilized by two different spermatozoa. They share the womb, the birth date. But they look and behave more or less as normal siblings.'

'In your programme, Professor,' the interviewer said briskly, 'you say twins are nature's genetic experiments. What exactly do you mean by that?'

'Every baby has a genetic programme laid down in the forty-six chromosomes. Half from the father through the sperm, half from the mother through the ovum. This programme interacts with the environment to control the child's future development: as an embryo, a foetus, an infant, a child and an adolescent – and through to old age.'

'And this control extends throughout life, Professor?'

'That is so. Where the genes are identical – in monozygotic twins – it's so profoundly powerful that even if they're separated at birth and raised apart, they resemble each other in everything. In fact they actually resemble each other *more closely* if that happens.'

The interviewer laughed. 'Really?'

'When twins're together, they themselves accentuate differences – they react off each other. There was a French researcher in the sixties, a Professor Zazzo . . .'

Father Michael splashed his face with cold water.

'. . . phenomenon he named the "Couple effect" . . . choose roles . . . competent one, clumsy one . . . one twin

147

artistic, the other good at sports . . . people encourage this as a way of telling them apart.'

He groped for his towel.

'It's when they're brought up separately that they become really interesting, though.' The Professor's voice was really enthusiastic now, he was into his stride. 'They're material for all the nature versus nurture arguments. Separately, you see, identical twins behave instinctively. And as they're identical, they have the same instincts.'

Father Michael wrapped a towel round his waist. Carrying the radio, he went into the kitchen behind the silver Venetian blinds. He switched on the kettle.

'. . . both will choose to paint, or play football, or whatever. There are literally hundreds of documented cases, and these are examined in the first of our television series tonight.'

'I understand one of the most remarkable stories is of two male twins. Tell us about them,' suggested the interviewer.

'Each was reared by one of the parents and were ignorant of the other's existence. Jack was brought up a Jew on an Israeli kibbutz, Oskar as a Catholic in Nazi Germany, so perhaps we can see why.'

The interviewer gave an audible gasp.

'When they were finally reunited at the age of forty-seven,' the Professor went on, 'they wore identical blue shirts with epaulettes, and square wire-rimmed glasses. Both had the same moustaches . . .'

Father Michael pressed the button on his coffee grinder. Over the noise he just caught,

'. . . style of walking . . . sitting . . . rate of speech . . . spicy foods. Both dunked bread in their coffee.'

The interviewer said, 'I'm gobsmacked, Professor.'

'Both,' went on the Professor, 'stored rubber bands on their wrists. And both,' he finished, 'flushed the lavatory before *and* after they used it.'

'I wonder,' said the interviewer, 'what gene that was? Thank you, Professor Schon, for being with us this morning. And Professor Schon's series will be starting on BBC-1 at nine thirty-five tonight.'

Chapter Sixteen

Kate heard something one night which frightened her more than anything before or since.

She was not even sure where it had been. Perhaps because she'd hated being there so much, she thought it was Styal. The girls were divided into small houses, four to a bedroom, with no officer there at night. So it was then the aggression surfaced.

Some time in the early hours Kate had been woken by scuffling outside in the corridor. She hauled herself onto one elbow: the other three beds still held their sleepers.

Was it burglars? Styal was a closed prison, it'd be harder to get in than out. And there was nothing here anyone would want.

But she already knew it wasn't an outsider. There was no crack of light beneath the door. Whoever was out there could find their way easily in the darkness.

It was impossible to tell how many people. Three at least, from the muffled noises. She could even make out someone breathing heavily, it made her think of Jude, with her snuffles. Then she heard the whimper, a pathetic little yelp like a whipped puppy. But no animals were ever allowed in the houses.

Kate lay down again, too wise by now to interfere. Something – or someone – thudded repeatedly against a wall. There was the creaking sound a bed makes under too great a weight.

Kate held her breath. After a long time, there came a single frantic cry, swiftly stifled. The silence which followed was more awful to her than the sound.

She stayed absolutely still. Only she couldn't stop the images that filled her mind. Horrible, tormenting thoughts she couldn't hold at bay.

Frightened and unhappy, she dug her nails deep into her arms without noticing. After a long time, she heard the weeping begin. She finally drifted into a restless doze from which she woke frequently. Every time, the sobbing was still going on.

In the morning, the occupants of the next room had seemed normal enough. No incident was reported. Kate never knew for sure what had happened. What had been done, or to whom.

She understood and accepted lesbians in prison, they all did. But it provided a warning she never forgot.

There was an unwritten rule at Styal, a lesbian activity rule. When they wished to enforce it, L.A. could mean anything the officers chose. Playing cards with someone. Sitting on a bed. Giving a friend a casual hug. They'd split houses and move women on suspicion if they found what they called 'unspecified marks on the body'.

The authorities created a taboo which forbade the physical manifestation of love between women. It was banned not just as sexual activity but as a demonstration of solidarity among the inmates. Prison rules, as Kate had long ago learned, were there to destroy the people they had formerly been. *Take her down*.

The prison service, run by men mainly for men, decreed that the only acceptable feminine sexuality was traditional and subservient. A lot of the girls here fitted that pattern:

working-class, underskilled, poor. They were mostly in for shoplifting, breaking into cars with their boyfriends, stealing credit cards.

Holloway was once staffed solely by women within the building. Now there were a number of men, though still very much a minority – if you didn't count all ten governors. Kate heard girls teasing the uniformed staff, inviting them into their cells: 'Come on then, darlin', I won't eat yer, unless yer very lucky . . .'

The men had no problem dealing with this. The women were behaving in a stereotyped and expected way. Sometimes they were disciplined, often they were simply ignored.

'They can't help it, poor sows,' said Noonie. 'They miss it, see? Sex.' Noonie was only her nickname, she was really Officer Nairn, a big cheerful woman from a Scottish mining village with eyes like bits of sky. She'd even asked the authorities – unsuccessfully – if she could have 'Noonie' on her official badge. She said to Kate, 'The only ones in here who never even think about it are the brass.'

There were always prostitutes in Holloway from nearby King's Cross. It was said they arranged with the police when they would be picked up, when it suited them to lose a week's earnings.

They came in wearing leather shorts and black fishnets and high patent boots narrowing to wicked points. On platform soles so steep they could scarcely balance, and hair down their backs or frizzed a mile high. No coats even in the coldest weather. They looked twenty from behind: when they turned, all but the very youngest of them had forty-year-old faces and eyes as stony as the streets they worked.

Once processed, they more or less merged with the other

inmates. Some of them were foul-mouthed and many weren't very bright. Others had a feisty toughness they could have turned to advantage in another line of work. Fate had tricked them, though, put them in inadequate homes and lousy schools, given them teenage pregnancies and men who lied. But they knew how to take care of themselves. Only the ones with small kids at home paid up. The rest preferred seven days in Holloway to forking out seventy quid: it was a bit of a rest for them in here. A chance to stand up, the kangas said.

When Kate was eighteen and they told her she had to leave Bullwood Hall she'd cried. She hadn't liked it there: it was run very strictly on almost Victorian lines. Though she had no visitors other than Dad and Gran, it was awful being stuck out in the sticks. But it was at least familiar. She had noted the dangers, she knew the score.

At twenty-one, she entered the adult prison system. Her solicitor then had been nice. John Eldridge had said to her, 'Watch out for the women officers, OK?' He thought because she hadn't answered, she hadn't understood.

'*You* know,' he said, clearly embarrassed. 'Lesbe friends.'

She'd looked at his smooth grey suit and close-shaved pink cheeks with an odd expression. She'd been inside since before she was thirteen. The talk that went on among the kids, the information and gossip that was passed around, would have made his hair stand on end.

A lot of the women officers in Holloway had female partners in the prison service. At Christmas, it was all change and plenty of tears. Sometimes there was a bit of a scandal about a kanga carrying on with an inmate. There were a lot of these relationships, Kate knew. Everyone did. It was probably the possibility of just such a liaison that brought a number of the officers to Holloway in the first place. The view among the inmates was, if it made the people involved happier, what was wrong with that? You had to get by somehow.

It was only a problem if a couple behaved stupidly. Just after Kate arrived here, an officer tried to get her lover out. The plan was for the girl to go missing, they'd search for her outside. When they'd moved out beyond the walls, she would smash a glass door, get into the corridor and from there through a window with bars not properly fixed. A grappling iron made out of toilet roll holders removed from the walls was to get her down from the flat roof to the road outside.

In the event they caught her right at the beginning, after the headcheck had shown someone missing. She was hidden in a kitchen cupboard in the tea-making room in Education. It had been a joke for weeks: *So that's what they teach them in Education.*

The high-ups didn't like to sack an officer for conducting a lesbian relationship with an inmate. The publicity would do no-one any good. So if it had just been a lover's tiff, then there'd be a bit of a talking to in a governor's office. The officer would decide she'd rather try another line of work. Sometimes the inmate would be moved quietly on.

That was how it worked, and you lived with it. A lot of the time, the relationships were caring and very important. And like the girls said, at least you don't get pregnant.

But there was another side to this world of confined women in which she lived, a brutality she tried not to think about. It didn't often intrude on her, but whenever it did, Kate was conscious that she had to grow another layer of indifference, of hardness, to cope with it.

When Kate first got to Holloway, they fixed the typed information sheet on her door.

Convicted Prisoner Number/T307805
Age/26
Location/A4
Name/Kate Dean
Date of conviction/
Details of sentence/
Work for which fit/kitchen, gym
Special notes/

Several of the spaces were left blank. She had assumed it was as a kindness, a protection for her. Then she saw they often didn't bother to fill them in.

She had thought, this is all they need to know of me. I won't give them any more. But when Blue and the others followed her from New Hall she had added her own neatly printed sign: Please don't leave my door open, my birds are out.

She was astonished to find she had written in the possessive: *My door. My birds.*

If she had learned one thing in prison, it was that she had to keep part of herself private. If she had no secrets from them – the officers, the governors, the system – she would become their creature. It didn't matter how small the secrets were.

One of hers was an object she wasn't supposed to have, a tiny ornamental pearl-handled penknife. It had once been on a keyring and her father had brought it with him on a visit years ago: he'd found it in one of her desk drawers when he was emptying it to sell. She kept it in a packet of tissues which looked unopened.

Kate weighed the knife. The pearly handle glinted

different colours, and felt cool and smooth in her palm. It was little more than a toy, it scarcely cut paper. But the fact of its possession gave her a little dignity because they *didn't know*.

There was one other secret: one that had at all costs to be kept from the other inmates – just what she was serving life for. Of course, it always got out in the end. That's why they had moved her so many times. She wasn't a Cat – a prisoner, that meant, that was a danger to public and state. But she was closed category, and could only be sent to certain prisons. So she'd gone from the Closed Young Offender Institution for Females at Bullwood Hall in Essex to Styal, from Cookham Wood in Kent to New Hall near Huddersfield. And finally here.

Kate tucked her penknife into the tissue packet, stuck down the Cellophane and slipped it into the drawer beside her bed. She yawned and stretched and picked up her towel and toilet bag.

In the corridor she passed Officer Cavell. She was pleasant enough to them, but intimidating: she rarely smiled and looked as if she'd never made a wrong move in her life. Immaculate and elegant even in the navy skirt, white shirt and epaulettes, the long chain attached to her belt and holding her passkeys looped round her slim hip. Her discreet gold jewellery included a wide wedding band. Blonde hair was cut sharply just below a strong jaw, her grey eyes were beautifully made up.

'Off for a bath?' she said.

You were supposed to clean the bath after you used it: Kate cleaned it before as well. The rooms were spartan – lino floor, a single wooden chair to put your stuff on, a couple of tiled showers that ran dangerously hot – but at least they were rooms.

156

'Hiya,' Ruth said, going into the next-door bathroom. 'Give mine a go, will you?'

'Sez who?' She swilled the bath round for the last time, put the plug in and started running the water. Ruth, cleaning her bath, said through the open door, 'In Risley, we had communal bathrooms, did I tell you? And the taps were on the outside, so the officers had to run them for you. It didn't really matter though, because they didn't have plugs.'

'What did you use?'

'You wadded up loo paper. But after about two minutes it started disintegrating. The water ran out and you were left covered in bits. And in Pucklechurch it was slop out, potties, washing in cold water. Ugh.' She shuddered. She pulled her door shut and then opened it again and stuck out an arm.

'Can I have a lend of that strawberry stuff?'

Kate handed the Body Shop bottle through the door. 'How could I refuse anyone who's suffered such privation?'

Ruth giggled. Kate thought again, how ridiculous that studious, anxious Ruth, in her long ethnic cotton skirts and horn-rimmed glasses, should be here doing six years. With a group of friends, she'd broken into an animal testing centre and smashed a door down. No-one hurt even, but property was more important than people.

Kate was wrapping a towel round her wet hair when she heard the first deep bark. Quickly she finished dressing and hurried back to her cell. Bloody rottweilers. They'd brought them in from Pentonville again for a spin.

Holloway was full of drugs: the problem was keeping away from them, not getting them. Mostly small time, though there were a couple of big dealers. One had been pointed out to Kate: a quiet-looking dark woman in her thirties who dressed like a secretary. Drugs were brought in on children, or inside babies' nappies. Visitors, knowing they couldn't be searched, would crotch them.

Everyone knew a crackdown like this was more for form's sake than what they'd find. The minute the first dog barked, the stuff was down the lavatory or scattered from the windows. There was no way the staff could hope to eradicate drugs from prison life. And they helped anyway to keep the lid on things. But the intention of the spin was complex. As much as anything, it was done to remind prisoners they had no place of concealment.

She'd fed the birds, shut them into their cages and was working on her James-Lange essay by the time they knocked on her door. By now, they would have gone through the cells of any real suspects, the rest was a matter of form. The handler, a slight man with a pale face and leather gloves, stared round without moving from the doorway. The dog padded in, enormous in the cramped space, and lifted his head. She said quietly, watching him, 'He can smell the birds.'

'Yop. Let me see what you feed them on.'

He looked into the cages while she took the plastic bag of seed from her cupboard. He held it out to the dog, who sniffed and turned away, bored.

'That it?'

'Yes.'

'Take that towel off your head.'

She handed it to him.

'Shake your head. Hard.'

She did that, too.

"Kay.'

She worked at her essay uninterrupted until eight o'clock when the unit officer called, 'Rooms, ladies, please.'

The doors on this floor were locked only from now until the early morning. When they gave orders here, it was usually polite. A4 was a unique unit: all thirty-two women had signed a contract to be of good behaviour and abide by all the rules. With this went the privileged redbands worn on the wrist allowing the wearer to move around the prison, while every other inmate had to wait for doors to be unlocked. But with even relative freedom came responsibility, and if a redband got thrown off the wing for any reason, she would never get back here.

All down the hall, doors were clanging closed, keys turning. Officer Cavell passed her door without locking it. A couple of minutes later, she returned and opened the hatch.

'A word, please.' She let herself in. 'Aren't you the lucky one?' she said.

Biro in hand, not understanding, Kate looked up at her. Officer Cavell pushed the door shut behind her and stood with her back to it.

'I meant, they didn't find it.'

'Didn't find what?'

The officer lifted perfect arched eyebrows. 'Your little penknife. The one you keep in the pack of tissues.'

Officer Cavell leaned against the door, her arms behind her back. 'A kid's knife really, isn't it? You must have had it a long time.' She lifted a hand and examined her nails. 'It must mean a lot to you.'

Kate drew a face under the sentence she was writing . . . *theories of emotion* . . .

She asked very carefully, 'How did you know I had it?'

Officer Cavell's expression was impossible to read. Her voice sounded as though she thought it funny, but Kate didn't think she was joking.

'That's for me to know and you to find out.'

Kate thought about this. 'When did you find it?'

'Oh. Weeks ago.'

Kate gave the face eyes and a mouth.

'I've told no-one,' Officer Cavell went on, 'in all that time.' Kate had never heard her voice so soft. 'They wouldn't like it,' she went on. 'They might take you off the unit. We wouldn't want that. Not now. Not at this point.'

Kate drew a tear under one eye and filled it in with blue biro.

'It's such a tiny knife,' the officer went on. 'But think of the harm owning it could do you.' She moved and glanced at her watch. 'I'd better get back to the office. You have a think.'

'A think? About what?'

Officer Cavell smiled faintly. 'Don't be dense. About me. About why I didn't shop you over the knife.' Her perfume was rich in the small room, too expensive for Kate to recognize.

'See you later,' said Officer Cavell.

Kate didn't move from her desk for a long time after she'd gone. She did think about Officer Cavell: the wide wedding ring she wore, the lace bra you could see through her uniform shirt, the feminine scent. The firm, trained body and those grey eyes, considering and cool.

Screel din! Danger coming! Was this what it had all been about? A useless warning, then.

She supposed she could go to one of the governors – Mr Jarrow, maybe – and tell him everything. But she discounted it. If she was believed, she might escape the threat of Officer Cavell, but would expose her possession of a knife.

Kate treasured the illegal little knife. Partly because it was forbidden, partly because nothing else had accompanied her every move. Possessions had been broken, or stolen, or lost, but not the knife. And it had allowed her some peace of mind. It was a weapon, however inadequate. Just knowing it was there gave her confidence, though she had never used it and never would.

The peace of mind had been wiped out by Officer Cavell's words. Kate filled in another tear: she knew what she had to do. There was no way she was going to start a relationship with that woman.

Kate was a product of the prison system, shaped and conditioned by confinement. Her sexual needs had never been allowed, her choices had never existed. For her, this was not a question of right or wrong, of loving or not. Officer Cavell was attractive and assured. If Kate became her woman, she would gain a measure of protection.

And there would be risks. Of blackmail, of exposure and – even more frightening – of involvement. Kate was no fool. Like everyone else, she'd heard of girls who, released, had immediately offended again to get back to their lovers.

She'd been right to set herself against love, when she was twelve. Love was the most dangerous thing of all, and she wanted no part of it. For the first time in fourteen years, an end was in sight. Mr Jarrow's words to her last week had re-awakened an instinct she had lost a long time ago – the desire for freedom. She was not going to do anything to jeopardize that.

But Officer Cavell didn't know of this new determination. She only knew Kate treasured the little penknife, and she thought she could use that to her own advantage.

Kate reached over to the drawer beside her bed and took out the tissue packet. She removed the knife and held it smooth and cold in her hand one last time. Kate valued it so highly not because it brought her happy memories – it didn't – but because it was the only thing she had left of the time before prison, her sole remaining link with childhood.

She had held it tight in her hand when the rows had raged downstairs. She always believed the things they screamed at each other, she always thought the house would be empty in the morning. It comforted her, to know she could protect them both.

Nights full of noises, lights, things smashing. Mum screaming and going, oh, no! *No!* Heavy lumps of words to hurl at each other.

Her fault, all her fault. Making him so angry, making her so sad. She should have been better, should have had neat hair, clean books like hers, ruled lines, red ticks. Well done! Good work!

The front door banged. The bed shook, the window rattled. She woke up, whispering, what is it, why are you crying? Crying herself, half asleep. What's the matter now, I'm frightened.

Come into my bed, baby, warm and close and safe. My sister, my love.

There was a copy of *Bella* on Kate's bed, tattered after going the rounds on A4. She spread it open and sellotaped the knife securely against the centrefold staples, next to a picture of Rod Stewart's first wife complaining about her breast implants.

Quickly, so she wouldn't have time to regret it, she opened the opaque vertical slat of her window. Rolling the magazine up, she hurled it out as far as she could. It was raining heavily, which was all to the good. The magazine would lie unremarked in the gap between the

162

blocks, where everyone chucked their rubbish – half-eaten food, used tampons, tea bags – and eventually, next time there was a clean-up, it would be stuffed in a plastic sack and binned.

She closed the window and sat down again at her desk. She had nothing but her wits, now. And just one secret left.

Kate put the packet of tissues open on her table where Officer Cavell would see them when she returned. With a sigh she sat down again and tried to concentrate on work. But she found herself doodling those weeping faces again.

Noonie had told her of the inscription on the original foundation stone of the first Holloway: *May God preserve the City of London and make this place a terror to evil-doers*.

If she was an evil-doer, then this place was supposed to be a terror to her. But it was almost over, now. Not long to go. Not long.

Perhaps she would believe that in the morning. Tonight, still on the dark side of fourteen long years, it was beyond her.

Kate filled in another tear.

Chapter Seventeen

The old rectory at Somerford was a handsome Edwardian house no vicar could ever have afforded to heat against Suffolk winters, when the wind sliced in straight from the Stour. Even now, in April, it was chilly waiting in the porch.

Father Michael conjured up from the name, qualifications and the voice he had heard on the radio two days ago, what Professor Victor Schon would be like: in his sixties, tall and white-haired, with the ascetic bony features of his Viennese parentage.

The man who opened the door was in his early forties, short and broad in baggy green corduroys, worn moccasins. He had unruly red-brown hair and the knowing, fleshy face of a stand-up comedian.

'Father Michael? Did you have a pleasant journey? Sorry to drag you all the way down here . . .' The cordial warmth turned platitudes into genuine welcome. 'I was just about to make some tea – I'll only be a second.' He waved a hand towards a worn leather Chesterfield. 'Make yourself comfortable.'

Father Michael looked round the elegantly proportioned room with velvet curtains at long windows, dark painted walls almost hidden by pictures. Every surface – tables, bookshelves, the large director's desk in the window – was awash with newspapers and open books. Medical journals, old copies of *The Spectator* and an untidy manuscript lay on chairs.

Professor Schon came back, carrying two mugs of tea and a packet of Co-op bourbon biscuits on a tin tray decorated with an owl. He kicked some plastic building bricks aside and sat down.

'Now then,' he said eagerly, without further preamble, 'tell me about your strange young woman.'

'We're at our wits' end,' Father Michael finished. 'And I'm an incompetent detective – but how can anyone's past be wiped so clean? There doesn't seem to be any way in. Mother Joseph may be senile, but she more or less told me the girl is a twin. Then I heard you talking about these strange links between separated pairs.' He paused. 'Thinking about it, I did notice one or two odd things about her, that didn't make any sense at the time. But if she had a twin, they became understandable.'

'What sort of things?'

'When I talked to her, she always made a great business of pushing two chairs together. Then she sat very primly right at one end. The Infirmarian mentioned she sleeps the same way, always on the edge of the bed, on the same side. It really is as if she was leaving room for another person. If you ask her a question she waits just a minute too long before she answers. She's heard, all right, it's not that. It's as if she was waiting for someone else to speak for her.'

'How old are the women now?'

'Twenty-six.'

'And when they were parted?'

'When they were thirteen, I think. At least, that's the age Sister Gideon was when she went to the order's boarding school.'

'You say no-one remembers anything about a twin sister?'

Father Michael grimaced. 'It's been very effectively hidden, either deliberately or by accident. God knows I've tried. The Bishop's dead, the Diocesan Office have no record of any siblings.'

'The present head of the school must have access to information about former pupils.'

'The order closed the school a few years ago. The local council rents the building now as offices. Apparently a lot of old school stuff is still stored in the basement – pupils' work, their exercise books, paintings that won prizes. They kept registers – in which Sarah Grayling's name appears, incidentally – and certificates, and those long group school photographs.'

'You've obviously tried to get Sister Gideon to tell you who she is?'

'Sarah Grayling, she says. Of course I looked in her file first, and the gaps are very noticeable. Stuff that should have been there is missing. I couldn't believe there was no birth certificate. She could never have been admitted to the order without producing that. So where is it?'

Victor Schon asked, 'The family?'

'The mother was a suicide, a surviving grandmother died a couple of years ago, there's only the father left. For a few years he wrote to her, and visited. From what the nuns know, he seems to have started another family and just lost interest in her. We've no idea where he is, or even the real family name: he used Grayling when he visited. Apparently the Bishop himself forwarded the girl's letters to him.'

'And I guess you didn't find anything about any trial?'

'If there was one. Mother Joseph couldn't give me

any details at all about it. Just the rigmarole about how information was suppressed in the convent. There's no doubt that sort of thing happened, particularly in the women's orders. But maybe it's all in her mind, who knows? We rang the Home Office, but they could find no record of any offence at all committed by a child named Grayling. They even tried their probation files.'

Father Michael rubbed his face with his palms in exasperation. 'I've nothing to go on, nothing. Just a woman looking as if she's at death's door. I heard you on the radio, but I thought of talking to you when I read your article in the *Guardian*. You spoke of the two-year-old twin who was in hospital for eye surgery. The child at home screamed out in pain at the moment of the surgeon's incision.'

'Sympathetic pain's a really mysterious phenomenon.'

'Surely there's got to be a link between the fact that Sister Gideon is a twin and this illness. But what is it?'

'I wonder,' said the professor slowly, 'if you realize what you've got into here. Have you any idea how close twins can be? I tell you, they can be real eerie, they're often close in ways we don't even know about.' He tipped his chair back onto two legs and rocked reflectively. 'There've been some interesting results from the work University College recently did with twins. They found all sorts of things are more likely with members of identical pairs – coronary heart disease, diabetes.' He paused, and added quietly, 'The incidence of schizophrenia is greater, too.'

'I don't know what she's suffering from, but not that. And of course we don't know what sort of twins these two are.' He put his mug down on the table. 'We don't even know if this mysterious sister is *alive*.'

Professor Schon said, 'If your Sister Gideon isn't physically ill, and if she's suffering as you describe, then

I'd lay odds the sister is still around. Though God knows what sort of state she's in. The last we heard, she was a thirteen-year-old kid who did something dreadful enough so her sister's identity had to be changed, presumably to prevent repercussions.'

He reached behind him and pulled out a crumpled rag doll. It had a beaming face under tousled yellow wool curls. He turned it upside down and its long skirt fell back. In place of legs, there was another head, sad-mouthed, with straight black hair and tear drops painted on white cheeks.

'Mother committed suicide,' he said, 'Father's disappeared. Daughter has been completely cut off from everyone she knew or loved.' He leant back, stretched. 'Not exactly the best start in life.'

A yellow Renault with a large cartoon duck on the bonnet came down the drive and stopped in a spray of gravel. A minute later the door burst open and several small children converged shrieking and giggling on Professor Schon, climbing onto his knee, sitting on his feet. A woman's voice shouted, 'Hi, darling, be there in a sec.'

'Now,' said Professor Schon, calmly, 'where was I?'

Father Michael coughed. 'Professor, I don't honestly think . . .'

'Oh, ignore this bunch of hoodlums. They're just troublemakers, the lot of 'em.' He wrestled a small blond boy off his shoulder. 'Right, Hugh, any more of this and it's bread and water for tea.'

'You always say that,' observed his sister, looking up from tying knots in the professor's shoelaces, 'but he never gets it. Mum says—'

An older boy burst out, 'Daddy, you promised to take us fishing this afternoon, can we still go?'

'I said I will and that's what I'll do. But I'm talking to Father Michael right now. Go and play for a bit and when I'm ready we'll get the bait.'

There was a chorus of 'Pooey bait!' 'Disgusting!' 'Slimy *worms*!' as the professor almost disappeared under a heap of little bodies. He was rescued by his wife, who merely spoke the word 'Children!' in an awe-inspiring voice.

The professor slid his arm around her waist. She was small, with glossy swinging hair, wearing a maternity smock.

'Zoe's the boss here, as you can see,' Schon said. 'The only trouble is, she will keep having these babies.'

'Right, darling.' She grinned at him. 'You don't have anything to do with it, of course.' He caught hold of her hand and kissed it. Father Michael suddenly felt like an intruder. He looked down into his cup. For a moment he couldn't identify the emotion which engulfed him. Then he recognized it, the old familiar enemy. It had been a long time since he'd felt such loneliness.

'Move it, people,' Zoe said briskly, 'that's enough, Daddy's busy.'

The professor rubbed his cheek where someone had planted a wet kiss.

'Look, Adrian's right, I did promise them fishing. Why don't you stay overnight, then we'll have all the time we need.'

He sat at the long table, watching Zoe slice raw beef on an old butcher's block, fair hair swinging across her face as she worked. The shelves of a Welsh dresser held jars of homemade jam, tattered cookery books, a collection of pestles and mortars. In front of him was a lump of blue pastry on a child-sized board and a red school exercise book. The printed space on the front had been filled in with laborious capitals, LOUISE SCHON CLASS 7a HISTORY. He opened it. Louise had eight out of ten for half a page about castles and a drawing complete with moat and drawbridge. That was on the last page. Opposite, on the inside cover, the child had written her name over and over, the letters ornamented with squiggles and dots and lightning flashes in bright pentel colours. LOUISE SCHON LOUISE LOUISE LOUISE LOUISE SCHON SCHON SCHON. The biggest name of all was surrounded with smiling daisy faces.

Zoe looked up from her slicing.

'I don't remember doing this,' he said, showing her the book.

'Boys don't, I've noticed. Just the girls. Here.' She handed him a vast maroon and white striped apron. 'Want a go?'

When she saw the speed with which he cut and trimmed mushrooms and peppers she said, 'You'll have to excuse me, I don't know anything about priests. Except that they have housekeepers.'

'Not any more. I decided a long time ago that if I wanted to eat well I'd have to feed myself. Anyone can cook a chop and peel potatoes.'

'Victor can't. Correction, Victor could, but doesn't.' Her smile held both love and irritation. 'He claims to be a new man but that's self-delusion.'

'There are a lot of you to look after,' he observed.

She gave him a wicked smile. 'More than you think. This is Victor's second family. This one . . .' she put her hand on her rounded stomach '. . . will make seven. They're his life, his work, his hobby,' Zoe spoke with protective intensity and he found himself envying Victor Schon.

It had never occurred to him that a man would relish the

company of children as the professor so clearly did. His own father existed for him only in a couple of photographs, foreign and smiling beside his prim English wife, holding the hand of the three-year-old Michael.

'Oh I won't be a nun, no I won't be a nun . . .'

The professor broke off his tuneless humming when he heard the other man's footsteps.

'Sorry about that. God knows where I heard it. But it's a perennially interesting question, isn't it? Why does a young girl go into a convent?'

'Some do go in from convent school. Fewer and fewer, these days. All religious orders, men and women, are in the same boat. Just not enough vocations to support the work they want to do.'

'Hard to imagine a modern woman wanting to live locked away.'

'Convent walls,' observed the priest, 'have always been intended to keep the world out, rather than the nuns in. Though I believe in the Middle Ages people were quite keen on snatching them away.' He smiled, conscious of pedantry.

The professor grinned back at him. 'I stand corrected.'

'It's certainly the general impression that the Church keeps them under lock and key. I think it's more a legacy of the Victorian suspicion of Catholics than anything else. At any rate, the enclosed orders are a tiny fraction of the women in convents. Most of them don't live in marble mother houses any more, either. You're far more likely to find them living with five other sisters in a semi in Camden and working with the social services.'

'Hold on – you said Sister Gideon taught Mayan children in Guatemala. An enclosed missionary is surely a contradiction in terms.'

171

'Oddly enough, the nuns there *are* enclosed. Once they reach the mission, everything is provided within the compound, and they don't move beyond it. In the old days they travelled out draped in heavy veils and invariably died there. They were heroic women.'

The professor said, 'Audrey Hepburn and Peter Finch, who could forget? OK, so given all this, how much contact would your Sister Gideon have had with her twin – always supposing there is one?'

'Very little. An occasional visit years ago, perhaps letters now.'

Absent-mindedly, Victor Schon picked bits off a French loaf. 'You do realise,' he said, 'that I specialize in developmental, psychological, abnormal behaviour in children. I really *want* twins to be like other kids, so I can use them as controls to demonstrate other facts. But when all's said and done, they're different.'

He took a couple of olives from a dish. 'Even if they're not identical, twins come to resemble one another the older they get. In looks, intelligence, height. And the reason is pre-birth environment, in the womb.' He forgot to eat the olives and instead waved them for emphasis as he spoke. 'You can get twins who look incredibly alike, yet they're not identical, not monozygotic. It's something you don't even know without running skin-graft tests. Though some guy at Tulane University has developed a way of analysing hand and footprints that determine twin type. Newborn twins may be quite different in all sorts of ways: different weight, length, physical characteristics. Now, if the birthweight difference in the two is between, say, three pounds and six pounds – more than two kilos – that means there's been a shared placenta.'

While he was speaking Zoe came back into the kitchen.

She picked up her glass of wine from the dresser and leant against the pine cupboards to listen.

'*Think* about it,' her husband said. 'Even the blood supply has been through one twin before it reaches the other. They've shared even that: two babies where there should have been only one. How close can you be to another human being?'

Zoe took a box of matches and lit a parchment-coloured candle in an ornate, tarnished silver stick, used the same match for the second candle. Her husband moved the candlesticks so that the two little flames glowed steadily, one at either end of the long table.

Father Michael asked, 'Your stories of matching behaviour in separated pairs – could these be hoaxes twins set up between them?'

'It's hard to argue with such a mass of available evidence. There really is too much to put it down to any kind of manoeuvring. Twins who may have only recently discovered each other's existence turn up for their meeting in identical clothes, do their hair the same way. They find they both fell downstairs at fifteen and broke an ankle. They do the same jobs, marry at the same age, give their children identical names. They'll both have cats called Tiger, wear seven rings on one hand . . .'

'Hold it,' said Father Michael, 'that's impossible.'

'Far from it.' Schon rapped four fingers on the table. 'These are all bits of different documented cases. It's been recorded that both will hate water, or suffer from claustrophobia, chainsmoke the same brand cigarettes. They even marry people with the same names.'

'I suppose,' Zoe started to laugh, 'I suppose you could say, similar tastes would account for much of that.'

'Not for having a similar accident at the same age. Not for giving birth at the same time – which is a particularly well-documented phenomenon. What about separated sisters who met their husbands in the same place, or took jobs working for the same company? There's a pair of twins, mixed-sex, who didn't even know they were twins till they were in their mid-thirties. They had married on the same day within an hour of each other. No scientist could accept such coincidences time after time.'

'Maybe these things come in the same category as people dreaming events before they occur,' Zoe said. 'I do that.'

Father Michael said, 'But that's pre-destination: God determines every event beforehand.'

The professor shrugged. 'Even without believing in God, one can feel there must be some sort of pattern.' He swallowed his olives and sent them down with half a glass of wine. 'The explanation may be that there are laws and patterns operating which we haven't even begun to suspect.'

'Or perhaps,' said the priest, 'these twins have an extraordinary degree of telepathic communication, of empathy with each other. Natural powers that in the rest of us have been suppressed, so we don't know what they are or how to use them. And maybe these strange people, developing differently, have access to them.'

'Supernatural powers?' Zoe asked.

'Yes. I don't mean ghosts and demons, but supernatural in the *real* sense of the word – not explicable by the known laws of nature. How else can you explain pain transference?'

Victor Schon got up and scrabbled around among the papers at the end of the table until he found a folder containing photostatted sheets. He sat down and flipped through them.

'With some things, like health problems – migraine

headaches starting at the same age, or heart murmurs, or wearing the same prescription glasses, having trouble with the same knee – well, you'd expect that. They're essentially one and the same person.'

He tapped the photostatted pages. 'These are the pain transference stories that'll be in next week's programme. Australian twin sisters: one dies in a road crash in the middle of the night, the steering wheel through her chest. Apparently at the same time the second twin wakes in her bed screaming with terrible pains in her chest. She dies in the ambulance taking her to hospital.' He paused. 'But *she* wasn't injured. And this one: twenty years ago in a Finnish village, twin sisters died within minutes of each other, for no apparent cause.'

Zoe said, 'They could've been very old.'

'They were twenty-three,' her husband said. 'And there are other cases where one twin has died a violent death, and the other has died at almost the same moment, when they could not possibly have known what had happened to the twin.' He pulled one of the candlesticks towards him so the flame flickered. Licking thumb and forefinger, he pinched it out.

'Let's take it a step further,' he went on. 'They're engineered the same, like two watches. When one breaks down, the other is probably going to as well, for the same reason. And at the same time.' He leaned across and extinguished the second flame.

The room was still. Upstairs, a child called. Zoe put down her glass.

The professor said quietly, 'It looks as though Sister Gideon is suffering her sister's pains, and we know she's in a serious condition. The sister might die directly from her illness. Sister Gideon is also at risk, either from the

175

cause itself, whatever it turns out to be. Or from some sort of psychic or emotional shock.'

Father Michael blew out his breath. 'You're saying these two could live or die as one person? Heaven help us!'

'It's a definite possibility. Your Sister Gideon and her twin, whoever and wherever she is, are a biological time-bomb.'

Next morning, Father Michael woke earlier than usual. Birdsong started with a few solitary calls, and then the room was awash with sound and growing light. Dark shadows paled until he could make out flowered wallpaper and the few pieces of furniture the room possessed: a carved wardrobe, a dressing table with an oval mirror, a long blanket chest at the foot of the bed.

He must have fallen asleep again, because the next time he looked, Victor Schon was sitting on the blanket chest. He wore a faded red brocade dressing-gown. His feet were bare and his hair was rumpled and he was already talking.

'. . . realized something in the night that I'd like to share with you.'

Father Michael hauled himself to a sitting position. 'Wha'?'

'Oh, sorry . . .' Schon sounded genuinely surprised. 'Thought you were awake. I brought your coffee.' He pointed to the tray placed on the floor. 'Well, as I was saying, that stuff you told me about Sister Gideon and the convent. The way she lives. The enclosure, the strict timetables, the rules . . . it's all quite obvious, it's as clear as daylight. She's as good as said it.'

Father Michael passed a hand over his hair and yawned.

'I must be very stupid. She's said nothing about all that . . .'

'She doesn't need to. The woman's a twin, isn't shè? A mirror image. So she's put herself, as near as she can, in the same situation as her sister. Dammit, man,' his voice rose with excitement and as he gestured, the coffee slopped unheeded from his cup. 'Don't you see, she's been telling us all the time where her sister is!'

Chapter Eighteen

'Exercise books?' asked Mother Emmanuel in bewilderment. 'You want her old school exercise books?'

All the packing cases were numbered, their contents neatly listed on the foolscap pages Mother Emmanuel had taken from the files. Sarah Grayling's final year books were in the middle of number 211, maybe fourteen of them parcelled in brown paper and string. He went through them fast, knowing what he wanted now.

Nothing in Maths or Science. She must have found those the hardest subjects, where she needed to concentrate. French was the same, the pages all neat and clean.

But her English and History, and particularly the Religious Education books, had elaborate drawings inside their covers. He could just see the child listening to lengthy Scriptural explanations and doodling the flower faces, the shells, the stars. SARAH SARAH SARAH. No surname anywhere. Until he opened the narrow spelling book and saw it beneath a list that finished with '. . . guilefulness, guiltlessness'.

There were no bright rainbows here. Just rows of jagged lines zigzagging round the name, drawn heavily in black and red.

SARAH DOWNEY.

*　　*　　*

He reached Fleet Street just after eleven. He remembered narrow side streets where great bales of off-white paper were winched up for the presses, and the smell of printers' ink was the prelude of tomorrow's excitement. It had a different feel to it these days. Now it was all Japanese banks and boutiques, girl clerks buying tights in their lunch hour, sandwich bars. He went into Boots for some paracetamol: he thought he was probably going to have a headache.

He got as far as Barclays Bank before he realized he'd passed the entrance and went back to No. 85, the Press Association/Reuters building. He identified himself to the doorman and was signed in for the cuttings library. He stared at an old photograph of Sophia Loren inside the lift until they reached the sixth floor. He followed the signs down a stifling corridor to a big room full of desks, telephones, people and newspapers. The clerk he'd telephoned yesterday handed over a couple of tattered brown files bulging with clippings. 'Nasty story,' he said conversationally, his soft Irish voice taking the sting from the words.

Father Michael blinked. 'I don't know. Was it?'

'Yeah. I remember thinking at the time, such a nice kid she looked. Real little girl next door.' He gave Father Michael a glance of curiosity and speculation that made the priest explain quickly,

'I've come across someone who was involved. Someone who needs help.'

'Ah.' Satisfied, the man pointed towards a desk and showed him the Xerox machine. Father Michael settled himself at the wooden desk. Notes were pinned to the rough wall above it, boxes of cuttings were piled high on top of filing cabinets. Even the floor was littered with bits of newspaper.

He sat for a couple of minutes, willing himself to begin, held by a mixture of dread and a horrible fascination. It was going to be bad, worse even than he'd feared.

The latest cuttings were on top. So the first file began with the front page of the *Sun* on the morning after the trial ended. Most of the page was taken up with what was obviously a family photo of a little laughing boy, his arm round the neck of a pet dog. In big black letters beneath it the words: TERRIBLE TWIN SLAYS TODDLER.

His blood ran cold. He understood the meaning of the commonplace phrase for the first time: the physical sensation of pain and despair, the chill tingling in arms and legs.

Dear God. Of course! The story had led on every front page, popular daily and broadsheet alike. He'd been in Rome then, and even the Italians were talking about it, speculating, condemning. That a child – a girl – could be capable of such an act of evil, of original sin. Much of the sensationalism had centred on her having committed the murder just after her twelfth birthday.

He made an effort and went on reading. The *Daily Mail* ran an out-of-focus photograph of a very young girl in a dark school regulation swimsuit, sitting on a wooden breakwater on an English beach. He stared for a long time at the face he knew so well and not at all, the face of Sister Gideon's twin.

She held a self-conscious pose, one thin leg drawn up and embraced by narrow arms, caught in that brief and pretty pause between childhood and becoming a woman. Clear eyes were half hidden by a fringe of hair and a strand blew across the smiling, secretive mouth. The first time he'd seen the likeness, as he passed a newspaper stand in the Piazza del Pantheon all those years ago, he'd assumed she was the victim. She had smiled out at him then in the glittering Roman morning, and he had looked back at her with compassion.

Such a picture on the front pages could mean only one thing and he knew the promise of that smile would never be fulfilled. It was a victim's face, without aggression or guile, without defence or defiance. The sort of photo they printed all too often, accompanying stories of girls who had been found buried in woods, or raped and dumped on a motorway, stabbed in parks in broad daylight. He read the story much later in the day as he drank bitter black coffee after a moral philosophy lecture. If he had not read it for himself, he would never have believed that was the face of the murderer. He made an unconscious sound, a grunt of denial.

The story must have been a sub-editor's dream: they'd had a great time with the headlines. TERROR TWIN GETS LIFE. The *Sun* story was brief. MONSTER WITH THE PRETTY FACE. They had concentrated on photographs of the victim's mother, a thin woman with carelessly bundled hair, supported by an older man, probably her father. 'Twelve-year-old killer twin Katharine Downey today received a life sentence for the manslaughter of the little boy she was looking after. "It's not enough," said the victim's distraught mother, Pat Keller, outside the court. "She killed a defenceless baby. She doesn't deserve to live. She'll go home one day. My Aaron's gone for ever. And her mother's got another daughter, another child to love in the meantime. I've lost my only baby." '

The *Daily Telegraph* headline was no less hysterical. BABYSITTER TWIN KILLS CHARGE. The article underneath was more detailed, though.

181

'Six months ago, on a dark October evening, twelve-year-old Kate Downey went to a neighbour's house to babysit while Tom and Pat Keller went to the cinema. Both twins knew two-year-old Aaron well, and had looked after him many times during the previous year. But this was to be the first time Kate had been entrusted with him in the evening. The night was exceptionally cold, so her mother drove her the short distance to the Kellers' house at seven o'clock.

'She was never to go home again.

'The events of that dreadful night have unfolded in court over the last seven days. They have made harrowing listening. The description of the pretty twin girl who saved up her babysitting money to buy presents for her family has had all the elements of a horror story as normal everyday events spiralled inexorably into tragedy.'

There was a long article on the feature pages of *The Times*, written by a well-known male novelist the day after the verdict was announced. The headline read 'BROKEN HEARTS'.

'On a rain-laden grey afternoon in March, Mr Justice Harlow enters the panelled-hush of St Albans Crown Court at two p.m. precisely. He wears a red robe trimmed with ermine, with frilled white sleeves, and an elaborate white wig. He takes his place on the raised dais. To his left in a lower seat the Clerk of the Court wears black morning dress.

'Already standing in the dock directly facing him is the Accused. Her tawny hair is pulled neatly back into a pony-tail, and shines under the lights. She is dressed in a fresh white blouse with a soft grey cardigan over it. Beside her stands a social worker. When the judge is seated and they follow suit, you can tell the bottom of the dock has been raised so the defendant can see over the brass rails: Katharine Downey is only twelve years old.

'She has been here for the last seven days for five hours a day. Because of her age, Judge Harlow decided the court would sit from ten a.m. until three-thirty p.m., to coincide with school hours. During that time, she has heard the case against her spelled out in dreadful detail. Evidence has been given by pathologists and forensic scientists.

'It must be a terrible ordeal for any child to hear such material. But the Accused must hear everything that is said for and against her. That is the law.

'Throughout all this, every eye has been on Katharine Downey. She is a pretty girl, her fine-boned face dominated by winged eyebrows over long and unusually beautiful brown eyes. She fidgets, clearly an energetic girl unused to sitting still for long periods. She looks with interest at the people who enter the witness box, at the barristers seated in front of the judge's dais. They are usually solemn but just occasionally, during intervals, they joke among themselves. One who never does this is the young Queen's Counsel who is defending her, David Maddox.

'Kate Downey glances briefly towards the men and women who crowd the public gallery, the area fenced off at the back of the court. If she knows that relatives of the murdered baby boy sit there, she gives no sign. Sometimes, too, she looks towards the Press benches. Her gaze is thoughtful and intelligent: it is clear she is well aware what is going on.

'People react to appearances, no matter how much they believe otherwise, no matter how professional, how well trained they may be. Kate Downey looks like everyone's ideal daughter, the perfect pupil. It is hard to see this young girl as the personification of evil.

'Witnesses have testified to her outgoing personality. Bright, talkative, so unlike her reticent twin. In court, when she speaks, there is something more. It is as if the characteristics they have described are exaggerated, dramatized. She was almost eager at first, almost too willing to answer the questions, to explain.

'Roy and April Downey sit behind their daughter, ordinary people in extraordinary circumstances. He wears a grey suit, white shirt, blue tie. His hair is bushy, somewhat unkempt. Although he is a well-built man, he looks shrunken and desperately tired. Despite that, it is clear his daughter's good looks come from him. And perhaps something else: even at tense moments, he sits without moving or reacting. He is a jobbing builder. Outside the courtroom he smokes incessantly, cigarette held cupped inside his palm.

'Mrs April Downey has more grey in her hair than he does. She must have been pretty, now she is pinched with worry and so white the blusher stands in hectic patches on her cheekbones. Her clothes are unremarkable – a blouse with a ruffled neck beneath a brown jacket – but she looks rumpled. She is never still. An embroidered handkerchief is crumpled in her right hand and she uses it to dab her eyes. Sometimes the tears become loud sobs and then she has to leave the court, halting the proceedings. Quite often, she gives gasps which might be horror at what she hears. In the quiet courtroom, they are surprisingly loud.

'They seem isolated, not really a couple. They do not speak and rarely even glance at each other during the long hours in court. On the rare occasions when Kate turns to look at them, her father smiles back. Her mother wipes away a tear and nods, trying to be encouraging. Neither of them reaches out to touch Kate, although she is only a few feet away. Perhaps she is not the ideal daughter they wanted, after all.

'Kate has cried, but only once or twice. The first time, and most noticeably, was when Prosecuting Counsel described the death of Aaron Keller, and the child's tiny bloodstained pyjamas, patterned with little grey elephants, were held up in the well of the court. Then Kate Downey's head sank down towards her lap as she wept silent tears.

'Sometimes, towards the end of the long afternoons, when the central heating makes the building airless and stuffy, her shoulders have drooped in fatigue. She is only a child, after all, and this is no place for a child.

'To the judge's left sit the eight men and four women of the jury, all treating this case with the utmost seriousness, visibly concentrating on every word. They say when a jury has found against the defendant, the men and women of the jury do not look at him or her as they file back into court from the jury room.

'Today we wait for the jury to deliver their verdict, and watch them come into court behind the foreman. Not one person looks towards the dock. Among the family of the murdered child, Pat and Tom Keller hold hands tightly, their heads close together.

'Kate Downey watches her barrister's face. Her own is alert, calm. Almost as if she were a spectator, not the focus, of this awesome occasion. David Maddox QC is considering the point of a pencil he holds between his fingers. Briefly, he glances at her with a small smile.

'The room is utterly silent as the Clerk of the Court, seated just below the judge, gets to his feet.

' "Members of the jury. Are you all agreed upon your verdict?"

'The foreman is in his forties, a countryman from his

sensible tweed jacket with leather elbow patches. He looks straight across the courtroom at Mr Justice Harlow. He does not glance at the Accused as he answers.

' "We are."

' "Do you find Katharine Downey guilty or not guilty of the murder of Aaron Keller?"

' "Guilty of manslaughter," the foreman says. And then, speaking louder over the rustles and whispers, "Because of diminished responsibility."

'There is a wail of anguish from April Downey and the sound of a body falling as she slides to the floor in a faint. The low murmur in the courtroom becomes a babble. Roy Downey is on his feet, trying to lift his wife. A policewoman is already moving towards them. Judge Harlow turns his head, the light catching his horn-rimmed glasses so his expression is hidden.

'And Kate Downey turns too, looking behind her at her mother's collapsed body.

'This is the most harrowing and important moment of her young life. In a few minutes, Mr Justice Harlow will pronounce sentence and she will know her fate.

'This girl is a twin, sharing everything with her sister, having nothing that is unique to her. Her birthday, her face, the colour of her hair are all shared with someone else. Defence Counsel has suggested that perhaps one of the reasons for this crime was a desperate attempt to prove she was a separate person, that she could indeed do something big by herself.

'But if that was her intention, then even at this last moment Kate Downey is forestalled. Because, at the instant when she could have expected to be the sole centre of attention, the spotlight is once again seized by someone else.'

★   ★   ★

Father Michael sat for a long time, his hand over his eyes, grateful for the old-fashioned fan whirring on the table not far away. He found himself looking at a section of the coroner's report from the post mortem. '. . . throat was cut to the bone by a sharp instrument, from right to left; all the membranes, blood-vessels, nerves and air tubes were completely divided. There is no doubt that the cut was made by a single sharp, clean incision . . . stabs on the body . . .'

Sickened, Father Michael turned the page, but he saw the words anyway. 'Penetrated the pyjamas . . . wounded outer wall of the stomach . . . wound four inches deep . . .'

Dear God. The everyday language made it worse. He got up. In the green-tiled gents, the mirror over the basin gave him back his shock as he splashed his face with cold water.

And this was the woman he was going to try to track down, to save? For a moment, he wondered, should he leave her be? If it was God's will that she died, who was he to interfere?

Then he remembered Professor Schon telling him about twins dying within minutes or days of each other. No. It was Sister Gideon he had to save.

He took a paper cup of water back to the desk and drank it slowly, staring at an assortment of straggling plants. Then he went back to his cuttings. After several more newspaper reports of the trial, he came to a more recent piece in the *Guardian*. It was written in 1989 by one of those bleeding heart liberal writers on the women's pages, headed 'Tragedy of Terrible Twin'. He read intently, hoping it would shed some light for him. Much of it was an interview with a woman who specialized in treating pre-menstrual stress.

Father Michael had only the vaguest idea what this was – something to do with the monthly cycle. When he'd finished, he was better informed. They had analysed Kate's blood at the same time in her monthly cycle as the murder had been committed. It had apparently revealed an extremely low level of progesterone.

The figures seemed meaningless but the expert claimed this strongly suggested that Kate, young as she was, suffered pre-menstrual syndrome of sufficient severity to lead to temporary loss of control. 'Such an abnormality could substantially impair her mental responsibility. It's quite clear that the judge didn't think pre-menstrual tension was a significant factor in this case. The evidence of her state was simply discarded.'

The article went on to discuss the exact nature of pre-menstrual tension in its most severe forms, quoting cases where women had, in this state, murdered their own children. The evidence was that Kate Downey had killed while under the malevolent influence of her body rhythms.

Father Michael flipped the cuttings now, catching odd phrases. 'Twelve-year-old twin Kate Downey displayed no emotion at the Crown Court today', 'happy, smiling little boy who lived his short life to the full', 'accused to be assessed by prison medical staff . . .', 'Police scuffle with enraged protesters as Katharine Downey leaves the court . . .'

Father Michael paid £45 at the desk for his use of the library, picked up the sheets he'd photocopied and left the building. He stopped at the first pub he reached – The Cheshire Cheese – and went inside. He took his Jack Daniels to a dark booth and lingered over it, trying to come to terms with what he had learned in the last two hours.

He must find Katharine Downey in order to save her sister. And if, in the course of doing so, he saved a murderer as well, so be it. He was not the power. He was merely the instrument.

Chapter Nineteen

Gate fever, they call it.

She fell asleep one night and then woke suddenly, with no idea of the time. The silence was dense and deep. But prison nights were never silent.

For one wrenching moment, she believed she had died. She didn't know where she was, she couldn't see or hear anything. She had no sense of her body at all, none of the little odd sensations – a stiff shoulder, a cramped foot – that normally come with waking.

The old panic grabbed her by the throat. It tightened the muscles of her chest and constricted her lungs. Her narrowed air tubes whistled as she gulped, desperate for oxygen.

But she heard the whoop in her own throat, and knew at least she was alive. She made a huge effort. Keep calm, let go, relax.

She could smell the stuffy feathery heat of her birds in the airless room. Air. God, she must have air.

She struggled to sit up, clambered clumsily out of bed. The rough carpet grated against the soles of her feet, she stubbed her toe on the chest of drawers in her haste. Disturbed, Blue spoke huskily out of the darkness, 'Hallo darling,' and fell silent.

She reached the window, pushed the thin curtains aside.

The narrow frosted panels were already opened as wide as they would go.

Kate pressed her face against the vertical pane. She caught the rumble of night traffic on the Holloway Road, the sing-song siren of a distant ambulance. She could just make out the dim lights of D1 block opposite. Prison nights were never dark.

She stared up at the sky. The misty fluorescent orange glow of millions of lights reflecting against low clouds was the nearest London got to darkness. No stars.

She took several deep breaths. She could smell petrol fumes and cigarette smoke – and something else, something clear and clean. She stuck one arm out of the narrow window, palm up. Drops of rain burst cool on her skin. She rubbed her hand over her face and the rain and her tears were the same.

She didn't know where the howl came from. It started somewhere deep down in the roots of her. It climbed and clutched and tore its way out of her choked throat.

'OUT!' She heard it with a shock. As if it was not her voice, as if she had not willed it. Behind her in the dark cell the terrified birds whirred wildly in their cages at the sound. 'LET . . . ME . . . OUT . . . OF . . . HERE!'

Gate fever had started for her a few weeks ago, soon after Mr Jarrow told her about her parole. The moment she was given her release date, she was terrified. She was walking on fragile ground: if she made a mistake, got into any trouble . . . she couldn't bear to think what might happen. She worried about things that had never crossed her mind before: would someone outside object to her release? She'd heard of that happening. Suppose they changed the law, or found some forgotten offence which would cancel her parole? Suppose another inmate decided to get back at her for some imagined slight?

191

Like Dot. Whose inmate lover, already sensing rejection in favour of Dot's friends waiting on the outside, had concocted an elaborate fantasy of thieving and drugs to extend her sentence. It hadn't worked, but it could have done. Kate didn't think anyone inside would care that she was going, but you never knew. She worried anyway. Suddenly, she had something to lose.

She would lurch between ecstatic expectancy at the thought of the bedsitter which would soon be hers, the job she would soon be doing, the friends she would make – and utter despair, deeper than any she had previously felt in prison, because she did not know what might be lying in wait for her out there.

The last fourteen years would never be expunged. Her offence would always be held on the police national computer. Any other crime would be deleted if the person did not come to the attention of the police after twenty years. But her record would never be deleted. It would always be there, like a deadly mould, with the power to spread itself over all her days.

She had realized early on in her prison existence that she must accept her life sentence. There was no question of her case being reopened, of any appeal. They might as well have put a neon sign over her door saying NO EXIT. The killing had happened. And she had faced reality, accepted what had been done to her, and why. She had set about making a life for herself inside, doing the best she could.

And as she matured, she discovered that acceptance co-exists with hope. She had hope, and so she could survive. Val hadn't survived, because hope had died before she did.

Kate didn't think she believed any more in the God she had imagined, somewhere, when she was a child.

But she learned hope was also a spiritual power, a belief. She hoped for a real life again. She told herself, soon she would be free. Soon she would walk away from here, and it would all be behind her.

Often, during the long years Kate had passed in confinement, she'd heard some woman or other, desperate for her lover or for drugs or her children, shouting from her window.

For Kate, it was none of those things. She was screaming out the wild anger she couldn't control, the fury at everything that had been taken away from her and would never be given back.

Freedom was a word she'd never said. Not even to herself. She had coped with its loss by forgetting she had ever possessed it. But it was coming closer now, she could almost reach out and touch it. A few more weeks of good behaviour and she could leave this cell behind her. And as it slowly became a possibility, its absence became unbearable.

She hadn't anticipated that she would suffer from gate fever. Though they'd warned her often enough. Years ago, when she'd first heard inmates talking, she had assumed it was an illness. Then she had learned it wasn't physical, but a state of mind. Now she had it. And she'd been right the first time.

Gate fever took many forms. An odd thing happened to time. It had been scarcely noticeable. Nothing to worry about. Cleaning the showers in the gym took hours – until she checked and found it was still only ten o'clock. She waited all evening for Ruth to come in so they could go over their OU essays together. Then Ruth protested, I wasn't late, what're you going on about? Eight, we said. Bloody hell, it's only ten past now.

Even in the aviary – where she always forgot the outside

world and more than once had to race back to A4, and occasionally lost pay or privileges as a result of lateness – even there, something odd happened. It took far longer than usual to check the nesting boxes, clean out the two big cages, sprinkle fresh shavings from the Pentonville carpentry shop and change the water. She'd hurry out, cross the village green at a trot, certain she was late, only to find she was on time.

Joannie – in and out of prison all her life – told her, 'Don't fret, girl. It takes people different ways. Me, I always get dead happy. Gate happy.'

Someone, Kate couldn't remember who, had years ago sent her a tiny packet, with Japanese writing on. The contents resembled pencil sharpenings. Drugs? But it had passed the censors. She'd smelled the stuff, tasted it – nothing. Only then did she see instructions in English on the other side. Sprinkled in a glass of water, the sharpenings soaked up the liquid and expanded into stylized bright flowers.

So the prospect of freedom, denied for so long, flowered in her mind. The nearness of it taunted her, bringing intense frustration with the changeless routine that was her life. Minutes dragged into hours, mornings yawned into afternoons. Nights gaped endless because she woke every hour, and it was never dawn.

The huge cry came again: 'OUT . . . I MUST . . . OUT!'

It took all her strength, left her trembling and sick. She let herself slide to the floor to huddle awkwardly under the window.

'Let me go,' she whispered to the wall. 'Please, please. Let me go.'

As if it was the start of a conversation, a brisk voice replied, 'You should be in bed, Kate. What're you doing down there then?' Edie had opened the spy hole and was peering in. 'All right, are you?'

Kate opened her eyes. It was an effort to speak. 'Yes, I'm fine, Edie. I must've fallen asleep down here.'

'Hear that yelling a minute ago? Some poor cow gone and done 'er 'ead in. Enough to scare the knickers off you.'

Edie was a tiny woman with blue eyes in a shrivelled face and improbable yellow hair. She was one of the Night Patrol, the dozens of civilian women in the area who came in to guard the prisoners as they slept. They wore uniform and regarded themselves as part of the prison service, and the jobs got passed around among families, going to aunts, sisters, daughters.

Edie had always worked nights at Holloway, the prison was a major part of her life. The job had lasted longer than her marriage and her children's childhoods. She relished the strangely intimate relationship between gaoler and gaoled, the sense of power it gave her to sit at the officer's desk, wear the passkeys on her belt.

Edie sympathized with Kate because she was a bit of a night-bird too. She didn't know that Kate had slept with the total unconsciousness of childhood until the trial. That was when the nightmare had started. It was always the same – the bereaved parents chasing them through the garden, pursuing them. She began sleeping light as a rabbit, a hunted thing, waking often. So she and Edie would chat when the others were asleep. Edie felt protective because Kate was young and seemed impressionable, and she kept herself nice, not like some of the others. Suddenly suspicious of Kate's silence, she flashed her torch onto her face.

'Hey,' she said, 'it was you. It was *you* screamin' just now.'

Kate turned her face to the wall. Edie waited a minute and then Kate heard the key in the lock. 'Come on then, upsadaisy!'

The surprisingly strong arm round her back brooked no argument. Kate found herself sitting on her bed with Edie beside her. The woman's arm was still around her. Kate sat stiff and quiet. Edie whispered, 'Carryin' on like that.' Her hoarse Rothman's whisper smelled of peppermint. 'Whatever was you thinkin' of? What a state you're in, you poor little scrap.' Kate started to laugh – she was at least a foot taller than Edie. But it came out as a sob and then she was, she was crying, her head on the little woman's shoulder, her body shaking. Edie made sympathetic noises, as if she were her own child.

Kate couldn't remember the last time anyone except Gran had held her. They were not a family who touched. Her parents had never demonstrated affection towards each other and though her father occasionally patted her shoulder or kissed her cheek, even this dwindled away as she reached eleven, twelve. Her mother drew back from even the slightest physical contact.

But somewhere buried in memory where she dare not look, she'd been enclosed by arms that might have been her own, had turned her face into a shoulder that could have been hers. But that was in forgotten time.

At thirteen, fourteen, fifteen, there had been no casual hugs, no touches, no goodnight kisses. No-one smoothed her hair or wiped a smudge off her cheek. All through those years when a child needs to be held, to be stroked and babied, reassured by more than words that she is lovable and loved, Kate had been isolated in small rooms.

So even now, as Edie tried to comfort her, Kate was stiff and unyielding, buttoned into herself. Gradually, though, the tears stopped. She sniffed and Edie

196

said, 'They're sayin' in the office you'll be on the out soon.'

Kate nodded. 'I've got my Discharge Board tomorrow.'

'That's what this is all about, right?'

'I'm scared. I want it and I'm frightened of it, both together.'

''Course you are.' Untrained, almost unschooled, Edie none the less knew instinctively what she was dealing with here. 'You've done all right inside, made a life for yourself. Teachin' kids to swim, the governors love all that stuff.' She rubbed a hand over Kate's ruffled hair, smoothing, soothing. 'That's your trouble, see? If you fit into prison life, if you can cope with all the shit they dish out, then it's goin' to be harder outside, know what I mean?'

'Edie, don't.' Kate laid her head on the woman's shoulder.

'Don't fret, girl, you'll be all right. You'll have to find a new way of doin' things, that's all. Learn to work stuff out for yourself. All this time you've been doin' what you're told and yessir nosir. Now it'll be different. But you want different, don't you?'

Kate sniffed. 'Yes.'

'Right then. Just remember, you don't get anythin' for nothin'. Everythin' costs. Everythin'.' Edie patted Kate's arm with brisk affection and stood up. 'I'm makin' a cuppa. Want one? I got those chocolate whatsits from Sainsbury's.'

'Please.'

'Into bed then, there's a good girl.' Edie paused, one hand on the door, and added warningly, 'And quiet about this, mind. I'll be out of a job if they knew I was playin' Florence bloomin' Nightlight.'

Her brusque kindness was more welcome even than

the tea would be. Kate climbed clumsily back into bed. Edie's key turned in the lock.

Ten minutes before lock-up the following evening, David Jarrow knocked on the door of her cell. Scrupulous as always, he waited on the far side of the corridor.

When she opened the door he didn't enter, but moved forward and leaned his shoulder against the door frame. 'I'm off on holiday tomorrow. Thought I'd say goodbye now.'

For a minute she couldn't think what he meant. He grinned at her puzzled expression. 'I won't get back till after you've gone. You're to be congratulated, you know. Your tariff is for 1997. Early release is recognition of how well you've done.'

'Thanks. I still don't really believe it, though.'

'You'll be signing your release papers in the governor's office soon. You'll believe it then.' He was watching her face. 'I'm told you're going to spend the first month with your Dad and the family. That's good to hear – they'll be pleased to see you.'

The way his voice rose made it almost a question, and it was one Kate found she couldn't answer. David Jarrow read her expression and added, 'You haven't taken up your home visits for a long time, have you? That's maybe a pity: it's all part of the leaving process, d'you see?'

'It was difficult . . . the children . . .'

'All sorted now?'

'The probation officer in Bristol went and talked to him and arranged everything. And she's found me a bedsitter for when I move on.'

David Jarrow took out his pipe from an inside pocket. She could see there was no tobacco in it, but he put it between his lips anyway. *Home is the sailor.*

'Maybe that's not such a good idea,' he said slowly. 'If I were you, I think I'd find somewhere to live with a friend, soon as you can manage it.'

'Who?' she asked simply.

He rubbed the bowl of the pipe between his fingers. 'You're right,' he said finally. 'You've had enough time to think, you don't want a bloke like me telling you what to do.'

'I'll phone and tell you how it works out, shall I?'

There was a pause. 'No, Kate, I wouldn't do that if I were you.' At the hurt look in her eyes he added, making a joke of it, 'The prison governor's book of unbreakable rules says, don't encourage dependency.' He dropped the jovial tone and said seriously, 'Don't look to come back here, Kate. I mean that. Try to forget about us.'

Kate folded the one sweater she was taking as small as she could. The day of her Discharge Board had been the real beginning of her release, but she had been unable to shake off the depression that had gradually developed.

'I won't forget,' she said, not looking behind her at the man who was still her gaoler. 'It'll always be with me. As long as I live.'

'Yes,' said David Jarrow. 'I know.'

Chapter Twenty

'Out of the depths I have cried to you O Lord,
Lord hear my voice.
Let your ears be attentive to the voice of my
     pleading . . .'

Upstairs in the Infirmary, Sister Gideon, who was
supposed to be in bed, supported herself against the
wooden shutter. As she watched, the entire community,
two and two, passed beneath her window as they walked
round the inner courtyard. It was eleven-thirty a.m. and
time for lunch.

'My soul is longing for the Lord more than the
watchman for daybreak.'

Beside Mother Emmanuel was Sister Aelred with her
sticks. Her tiny body was riddled with arthritis, but her
great spirit almost managed to ignore it. Sister Antonia,
whose singing transformed their choir into something
sublime, and who never even thought of herself as
possessing a real gift. She was followed by Sister Louis and
Sister Josse, the two French members of the order, and
behind them came Sister Vincent with that odd jerky gait,
seeming as always to be tightly controlling her temper.

'Let the watchman count on daybreak and Israel on
the Lord . . .'

The voices faded as they reached the Refectory. The last nun to enter would pull the door carefully behind her, lifting and releasing the metal catch without a sound: even something so simple as closing a door is an act of the love of God. That would be Sister Davina. She was not the youngest woman in the house, but the last to join them. Your life only began when you entered the enclosure: therefore, the most recent arrival was the youngest, whatever her age in the world.

Sister Davina would be sitting at the foot of the last of the three long pine tables, facing inward towards each other. Before each woman would be a pottery bowl and a boxwood spoon, the handleless godet and a tiny brush for crumbs.

Upstairs, Sarah stood before the small table bearing her lunch tray, head bowed in prayer.

'Bless us and these your gifts, which of your bounty we are about to receive, O Lord, Amen.'

She pinned the large white linen napkin around her neck, as they all did, to protect their immaculate starched white wimples, entirely forgetting she was wearing the soft night bonnet. She lifted her soup spoon to her lips. Even this was more than she wanted, but convent soup was their staple diet, absolutely delicious and made from anything that came to hand, stirred into a rich and perpetual hotpot on the Aga. Downstairs, her sisters were eating fish. They had it once a week, if they could afford it. Cheese and eggs the rest of the time.

Her spoon clattered in the bowl, loud in the silence. It would be silent in the Refectory downstairs, too, except for the steady voice of the nun who was the day's Reader. The women signed their needs, laying an index finger on the table to request that a bowl be passed to them, raising one hand, finger and thumb held together in a circle, for the water jug or the teapot. Since medieval times, silent religious had communicated during meals like this.

It was one thread of the steady, continuous rope which had pulled her since she first went to the order's boarding school, long before she was at ease with the language and customs of convent life. The nuns performed exactly the same tasks, at the same time of day, wearing precisely the same clothes, as their predecessors hundreds of years ago.

Theirs was an old-fashioned order, scarcely changed by the recommendations of the Second Vatican Council. The nuns still had almost no contact with the world. They received the Eucharist through the grille in their private chapel, and letters and goods from outside were placed in the turn, the revolving wooden cupboard at the priory door. Occasional visits from family and friends were conducted through the grille in the convent parlour.

Sarah shied away from that thought. It had been years – *years* – since Dad had come to see her. She swallowed her soup with an effort. Nothing had any taste these days. And they tried so hard to tempt her appetite with wafer-thin slices of homemade cake, bowls of creamy custard. She shifted uncomfortably: she'd lost so much weight now, it hurt to sit in a chair. Without a mirror, of course, she didn't know how she looked, but she could tell from everyone's faces how worried they were about her, though they did their best to hide it.

She was still sipping her soup when the door downstairs opened and she heard the first words of the de Profundis.

Mother Emmanuel would by now have finished the last of her dates and nuts, and risen to her feet. She did not glance at her community: if she had finished, then so had they. It was the imperiousness which went with her office. Reverend Mother represented God in the priory, and obedience to Him begins with obedience to her.

It was the most difficult of the three vows, Sarah thought, struggling to finish her wholemeal bread, as Sister Mark had asked. As a small act of mortification, she had spoiled the taste by sprinkling it with too much salt. The other vows, of poverty and chastity, had been taken care of when she entered: there was no possibility within the enclosure of breaking them. But obedience was different. Every day, in a thousand ways, you were called on to fulfil that vow. The will must be subjugated totally to the will of God. Love of self is the greatest unhappiness.

That at least had been easy for her. She had always loved someone else better than herself.

'Requiem aeternam dona eis, Domine,' recited Mother Emmanuel.

'Et lux perpetua luceat eis,' answered her nuns.

Their voices grew louder as they left the Refectory, still chanting. She could see them in her mind's eye as they processed back round the courtyard, where in the middle the linden tree flowered. Sister Matthew, with the great dark eyes of her Spanish mother. The ample figure of Sister Julian, bearing witness to her love of cooking. Bulky Sister Peter, whose fingers, shapeless as sausages, produced the most exquisite handiwork. And Sister Thomas à Kempis, the professional musician who had brought her skill and her magnificent harp here, to the service of God alone.

'Requiescat in pace.' May they rest in peace. The benediction floated up to Sarah's window, so she was soothed and reassured. The formal, beautiful pattern of life imposed by the Rule answered a deep need.

There was form and order here, so essential to the enclosed life, and to her. It was like a continuous, endless design. So long as she was part of that design, she would be safe.

Chapter Twenty-one

It had taken ten days and a letter from the diocesan office to convince the Home Office that Father Michael was genuine.

'We have to be very careful.' Corinna, the pleasant girl in the Press Office of the Prison Department, had telephoned him finally to say his request had been granted. 'With crimes in this category, there's always the chance of someone trying to get to the inmates for rather dubious reasons . . . I'm sure you understand.'

'Not a pretty thought.'

'But the way things are. Anyway, Holloway has ten governors, and Governor Five is the man you want to see. He's at a conference this week in Denmark, but I've arranged a meeting for you next Monday at eleven. His name's David Jarrow.'

It was only when he reached Parkhurst Road that he remembered the place had been rebuilt twenty years ago. He'd been expecting the forbidding entrance gates he'd seen in photographs, the griffons with their gyves and keys, the battlements and turrets and castellated towers out of a cruel fairytale. That would have been a more appropriate setting for the meeting he was about to have with Sister Gideon's twin.

He walked up the short driveway past the white barriers. A young West Indian with long dreadlocks was shouting to himself outside the entrance, jumping around in his temper. As he got nearer, Father Michael saw that in fact he was conducting a heated conversation with a portable phone. 'I tried,' he was screaming, 'I tried to see 'er, they said, yer name's not on the *list* . . .'

Inside the new harsh red-brick entrance he gave his name to the uniformed receptionist behind her bullet-proof glass. She riffled through the papers on her clipboard to find his appointment, dialled a number and said, 'Father Michael Falcone's here, sir.' She put down the receiver and asked him for some personal identification.

He patted the pockets of his unbelted black gown. 'I don't know that I . . . would a Barclaycard do? Or . . .' He produced from an inner breast pocket the letter he'd received that morning from his Ordinary and pushed it through the aperture in the glass. She glanced at the letterhead, then up to his clerical collar, and handed the letter back.

'Thank you, Father. Will you go into the waiting room, please?' She gestured through the sliding glass doors. He stood with a couple of prison staff waiting for the operator to recognize them and open the door. They held up their bunches of keys on long chains, to show who they were.

There was a lot of spit and polish and shiny bright blue paintwork. A brass plaque on the wall read 'H.M. Prison Holloway WELCOME' and he wondered whether the prisoners polished it to that high state of perfection. A bunch of flowers lay on the low table. During the five minutes he waited, several of the women prison officers glanced hopefully at the card with them. A heavy-set black woman in her late thirties, with slender legs beneath her uniform skirt, grinned at him. 'Who's sent me these, then?'

He finished leafing through *Prison News* and was flipping the lifeboat magazine when a man in white shirt sleeves came down the stairs fast and into the waiting area. Father Michael knew this must be Governor Five, he had the crisp look and manner of a naval officer, his dark beard theatrically streaked with white.

'David Jarrow,' he introduced himself, holding out his hand before he reached the priest. His handshake was brisk and firm and no time wasted. He didn't waste words, either.

'I'm afraid this is something of a pointless journey for you,' he said. 'Kate Downey was released a week ago.'

Father Michael's first reaction was shock – he'd assumed he had found the woman at last. But of course, when he first contacted the Home Office, she had still been a prisoner. Annoyance turned to wry amusement: she'd been inside for fourteen years, and he'd missed her by a week.

'Why didn't someone tell me she was out?'

David Jarrow shrugged. 'Some sort of mix-up between us and the Home Office people – these things go through a lot of hands. I'm really sorry. I think Corinna told you I've been away? Didn't get back till this morning, and by then of course it was too late . . . as I say, I can only apologize.'

The priest said heavily, 'So now, how do I find her?'

David Jarrow beckoned with his head. 'Come on up.' His office was one of a suite on the third floor. He gestured Father Michael to a chair beside a small table. Metal letter trays were neatly aligned, even the papers within them were squared. A single thin foolscap file lay in the centre of the desk.

Beside the desk on a shelf stood a large cage containing a red and blue parrot, hanging upside down from its perch. Father Michael found himself saying, 'There's something ironic in a prison governor keeping a caged bird.'

David Jarrow smiled. 'More irony than you realize, Father. Kate Downey looked after that bird. Now she's out and he's still behind bars.'

'And *he* didn't do anything.'

There was a short pause. An odd expression crossed the governor's face, was gone before the priest could define it. 'You don't know Kate?'

'I know her twin, which may or may not be almost the same thing. But I've simply got to get hold of her, as soon as possible. I suppose she could be anywhere by now.'

David Jarrow shook his head. 'Prisoners don't just wander off into the sunset, and lifers certainly don't. One of the conditions of her release is her place of residence: Kate went to the Bristol area because her father's near there.' The governor got up and went towards the door, talking over his shoulder. 'Come and have a look at the computer. It's just in here.' He tapped in a series of numbers.

'Movement records,' David Jarrow explained. 'Shows at a glance where she's been held.' A file name appeared on the screen and he accessed it.

'Hold on,' Father Michael said. 'Wrong woman.'

'No. Katharine Downey aka Dean. Only senior officials have the password to her real name, though. She's been known as Dean ever since she went into her first secure unit.' He glanced up at the priest. 'You're aware of her crime?'

'Of course, I didn't think – there'd have been reprisals.'

David Jarrow nodded. 'Every so often, something leaks out anyway, however careful we are.' He jerked his head towards the screen. 'That's one of the reasons we move lifers around. And anyone who kills a kid has a particularly rough time, especially the women.'

Peering over the governor's shoulder, Father Michael saw the portion of the screen marked 'Sentence'. In a box were the words: 99 years. He said, 'My God.'

Jarrow said, 'Sure. The sentence means just what it says: life is literally life. If she lives till she's a hundred and four then that'd be the sentence. But when we're programming the computer, it'll only accept ninety-nine.'

'You're saying a lifer is never free? I didn't realize that.'

'No. Neither do the criminals, unfortunately.' He worked on the computer. 'Kate's been released on life licence,' he went on after a moment, 'but any infringement of the law, even being drunk and disorderly, and she could be hauled back to serve a lot more of her sentence.' He pointed to the screen. 'We've got an address for her.' He copied it down on a piece of paper. 'But there's not a telephone number.'

'Damn,' said Father Michael.

'I can do better than that, though. There's a lady called Laura Pegram I think you should talk to.'

She was Head of Psychology, H.M. Prison Holloway. Her office was on the floor below, on a brightly lit corridor behind a door of narrow steel bars. She evidently shared with two other people, by the desks. Waiting, he noticed dark-grey carpet and tall metal filing cabinets. Someone had attempted to soften their effect with a couple of Impressionist prints. A big notice-board was stuck full of bright cards and reminders. Telephones on all three desks rang endlessly but there was no-one to answer.

She arrived two minutes later at what was clearly her customary speed, blond hair standing out round her head wild as a dandelion puff.

'Father Michael? Sorry to keep you waiting,' she said breathlessly. She dumped a capacious shoulder bag on one of the desks. Then she went over to an electric kettle on the window sill. As she passed him, he caught her scent.

'Coffee. I must have coffee. Can I make you a cup?'

'Thank you. No sugar.'

He watched her measure granules into two mugs, charmed by the long faultless legs, the bright colours of her short-skirted suit.

'Now,' she said, perching on one of the desks, 'it's about Kate Dean – Kate Downey – isn't it?'

He went through the story of the twins, their separation, Sister Gideon's illness.

'What I'm after, I suppose, is some idea of what Kate is like now. I'm going straight to Bristol, and I don't quite know what I'm going to face. It's one thing to come here and see her. Here she'd have been . . .'

He searched for the word and she supplied it, 'Contained.'

'Yes. It's something else to start tramping round a city in search of a woman who is . . . who might . . .' He let the sentence slide.

She nodded. 'Who's a convicted murderer on life licence.' She sipped her coffee reflectively. 'I don't suppose . . .' she eyed the black robe and Roman collar he had chosen to wear for the prison, and finished delicately, '. . . you've had much contact with murderers.'

'I've seen killings in my time in Africa. Most of those were tribal feuds. Nothing like this. I'm concerned that I won't know how to deal with her.'

'You'll find Kate Downey isn't at all what you're expecting. She wasn't at all what *I* expected, come to that. The majority of women in here are ordinary criminals – shoplifters, muggers, dealers, credit card fraud, soliciting. We see a good number of arsonists. They all have patterns of crime, their offences are predictable. Often there's a family background of criminal activity, they may well have friends living the same way. They've probably committed petty offences right back from being kids, you know?'

Laura Pegram waited till the ringing telephone beside her had cut out abruptly in mid-ring, then she took the mouthpiece off and laid it on the desk beside her.

'Murderers,' she went on, 'are quite different. They can be of any social group, any age. They're unlikely to have any previous form at all. They do this single, huge act. And afterwards they're lost. They don't know their way around the prison system. And inside it, they often become loners.'

'Did that happen to Kate Downey?'

'Yes. Someone like her has special problems because she's been inside since she was a kid of twelve. There's a lot of what I can only describe as moral contamination in prison. It's bad enough for any lifer. For someone who was brought into the system as a child it is truly terrible. Normally, I'd say they had no chance at all of any kind of meaningful life afterwards. But in an odd way, I believe Kate's character has protected her from much of this. She watches what's going on around her without becoming part of it.'

'I suppose it *is* barbaric to lock up a child for the rest

of her childhood and far beyond. I hadn't considered it before.'

'It's appalling,' she said fiercely, and her hair quivered with indignation. 'If you read the accounts of the trial – and God knows there were enough of them – you'll see what I mean. I was at college when it happened, we discussed the case. It has always seemed extraordinary to me the way British justice works. Or doesn't work,' she added grimly. 'The court was never told anything about Kate's background. So how could her judges have understood what happened? The jury found her guilty without extenuating circumstances. That's what the public demanded.'

He said quietly, 'Perhaps society has the right to exact retribution for the death of a small child.'

She sighed. 'Perhaps. We've learned a lot in the last few years but even so, I bet if Kate were to be tried again tomorrow, the one important question would still not be asked in the courtroom. No-one would ask "Why?". No-one, it seems to me, really took her age into account. No-one searched for whatever her extenuating circumstances might have been. No-one did these things because we were all afraid of the answers, afraid of what they would tell us about ourselves and the way we live and our family lives and our values and our aspirations. So we didn't ask. And we failed Kate.'

'We failed her,' she repeated. She stared out of the window. Father Michael followed her gaze. She had a view of a modern block of prison officers' flats, and beyond, the strangely low, curving perimeter wall of the prison.

'A terrible crime like that is committed because of a personality disorder,' she went on. 'But in Kate there was no discernible physiological abnormality.' She looked back at him. 'There must have been *something*, somewhere in that child's short history, which we should have discovered. Even if it didn't explain what she did, it might have shed fresh light on it.'

'I read the newspaper cuttings last week. You're right, there was almost nothing about her background. Except one article describing the last day of the trial, which said the parents sat just behind her but never touched her, never offered her consolation or comfort. Even when she reached out to them.'

The psychologist nodded. 'Parents like that carry terrible guilt. They can often hardly cope themselves, and they've been unable to teach their own children how to deal with difficult situations. Their grief as they try to make sense of the tragedy is compounded by their own problems, the young age of the victim, the age of their own child.' She paused. 'A guilty verdict is passed on the family as surely as it's passed on the perpetrator. Afterwards, they try to make sense of the tragedy, they go over it and over it. But no-one wants to know – except maybe to daub slogans on their walls, or spit at them in the street. They have to move to a new area, try and start again. I don't suppose many succeed.'

'The Downey family seems to have broken up soon after the trial. And Sister Gideon – Sarah – apparently blocked out the fact that she has a twin. So far as I can ascertain, she's never referred to Kate, not even to the nuns who cared for her when she first got to the convent school, just after the trial.'

'I only once managed to get Kate to acknowledge her sister's existence, and she certainly never used her name. It always worried me. For a twin, that's a denial of self. There are—'

The door opened and a young woman stuck her head

round it, said 'Sorry', and closed it again. Laura Pegram was clearly used to interruptions.

'—some people who can only function with deep grief if they never admit to it. But with Kate, that problem should have been addressed a long time ago. She was self-aware, even at the time of the murder: the papers described her as taking an intelligent interest in what was going on.'

He nodded. 'One of the comments was that she was so self-possessed, it actually estranged people. If she'd shown distress or remorse, she might have evoked a protective reaction from the watching adults. But just the opposite happened, they observed her with a kind of appalled curiosity as if she was in a zoo.'

'Exactly. And she was barely thirteen then. By the time she got to me, it was far too late.'

'Too late?'

'Yes. I never seemed to be able to get any real substance to my reports on her. I thought, I'm not digging in the right places, not asking her the right questions. Then I found, there were no right questions. Kate learned the hard way that in order to get through, she must cover up what happened, hide it away from herself. She learned people will accept answers that cost her nothing to give, that reveal nothing she can't allow to be seen.' Laura Pegram rubbed the top of her left arm with her right hand, an almost consoling movement. 'In the end, she did talk about the killing, about what she believes triggered it. I'm satisfied she understands herself, she's fit to be part of society again.' She slipped off the desk. 'More coffee?' He shook his head, and she made another cup for herself.

'I still don't believe we've really got to the bottom of it, though,' she went on. 'And we won't now, not after fourteen years. If it had been done sooner . . .' She sipped her coffee. 'Too many other things have happened to her, now.'

He was exasperated. 'I don't get this. Kate was in a special unit. Surely she'd have received all the necessary care – that was the point of sending her there.'

Laura Pegram reached back for her handbag and searched through it for a packet of cigarettes. There was one in it. She said, ruefully, 'I'm trying to give them up but . . .' He noticed her lighter was a smooth silver pebble. She exhaled and then said, 'Look, this is just for you, all right? I'm not in the business of changing the system, or even of criticizing it. All I'm saying is, when this killing happened, no-one who had her in their care really knew how to treat her.'

He nodded. 'Go on.'

'The Special Unit that Kate went to is excellent, designed to take about thirty children classed as "asocial". Who've committed serious violent or sexual crimes. When Kate first went there, it was mainly boys. After a couple of years, the number of girls went up to maybe four. Because their offences were less serious, they were only there a year or two. So we know Kate didn't really have a peer group. And I'd argue girls need that maybe even more than boys do, in adolescence.'

'What's the place like?'

'Modern, natural wood, bright colours – bit like a holiday camp with locked doors and panic buttons everywhere. The kids're under constant supervision, day and night.' She saw the look on his face and nodded. 'They're locked in to sleep, and for periods during the day, with observation panels on the bedroom doors. But lessons are fairly normal, they have sitting rooms, a marvellous art room, they're encouraged to read, listen to music, use the gym. The food's fine.'

'So what was wrong?'

'It's the system that's inadequate, not the individual staff. There's a psychiatrist and a psychologist, but they're only consultants, advisers. They don't work as part of the team, and they're certainly not in a position to give direct treatment. So Kate didn't receive any, beyond counselling. It just isn't a medical environment.'

'Well, why wasn't she sent somewhere else for treatment?'

'That would have meant an adult institution. No-one wanted to send her there, and really you can't blame them. There are places around which might have damaged her in different ways. Nowadays there *are* one or two psychiatric treatment units for children. Too late for Kate, of course. So what happened, the authorities worked it backwards. Because they'd nowhere suitable to send her, everyone – and that includes the Home Office – convinced themselves she didn't need such treatment.' She knocked ash from her cigarette with fierce little jabs. 'Which got rid of the problem rather neatly, don't you think?'

'What was the effect on Kate?'

'That's the question, isn't it? Kate puzzles me, and I think she'll puzzle you. You look into her file, and on paper you've got an emotionally deprived girl. You know that her twin – with whom she seems to have been incredibly close until the killing – never once visited her, anywhere. There's no record of any correspondence between them. The mother died not long after the trial. Again, the traumatic effects of this never seem to have been considered. The father's more or less disappeared, the granny came in those days, but in a wheelchair. So Kate relied on the people around her in the Secure Unit.'

Laura Pegram got up and looked out of the window.

Playing with the blind, she went on, 'Some of the people who work in these places are really committed. This might have been a period of much-needed stability.'

'You said the cut-off age was eighteen, though.'

'Yes, on her birthday Kate left the child-care system and went into a young offender's institution. That would have been a hard time for her. The staff obviously have to be tougher. And then at twenty-one she was in the prison system proper.' She brushed a hand over the puff of gold hair. 'Well, anyway, Kate made a couple of friends, some of the staff really liked her. Prison staff have strong views about lifers, you know – they discuss whether she did or didn't do it. In Kate's case, some people would say, I still can't believe she did it, she's so calm, so sensible. And others said, she's intelligent, she watches, she tells you only what she wants you to know, she manipulates you. They see that as proof of guilt.' She was quiet for a minute. 'Maybe they're simply interpreting the same characteristics in different ways, yes?'

He waited a moment, then asked, 'And?'

'Sometimes you just know about guilt or innocence. You look for psychological problems and if you don't find them . . .' She thought for a minute. 'She wasn't too unhappy in prison.'

'I find that hard to believe.'

She said, reprovingly, 'It's all she's known, after all, for fourteen years. She was trusted, a redband, she got on well with the chaplain. There was an incident a year or so ago when she could have attempted to escape, and she actually went back to her cell and closed the door. Very revealing, that. I knew about her panic attacks, when she'd wake with her heart pounding, unable to breathe. I knew about the way she looked after her birds. About the autistic child she taught to swim – did David Jarrow tell you?'

The foot was jiggling again, the glossy shoe sliding at the end of her slim leg. He looked quickly, then forced himself to concentrate on her face.

'OK,' she was saying, 'so is all that evidence of guilt, of the fact that she feels she deserves what she's getting? Or is she a young woman who has come to terms with the hand she's been dealt? I'm damned if I know.'

'So you don't think it was a deliberate killing?'

'All children experiment, test out their power. My own do it, and they're tiny. A cross three-year-old will dig his fingers into your arm and grit his teeth and really *try* to hurt. You give his hand a hard tap and say "No!" and have a cuddle and start another game. But maybe no-one did that with Kate.'

'She wasn't a small child. She was twelve.'

'Scarcely an adult. There was a child not much younger than that, swung another kid over a river and dropped him. Was it a game gone wrong or a pre-planned act?'

The Head of Psychology reached out to the telephone and put the receiver back on its hook. Immediately, it started ringing. She rested a hand on it but didn't lift it.

'You know,' she said, 'if I got emotionally involved in my cases, I'd be no good at my job. Kate's been tried. It's not up to me to judge her again. Whatever I think personally, I've got to be professional. I can't cry over all the awful things I hear and see in here. I'm no use to anyone if I'm down there underneath.'

When he had thanked her and left, Laura Pegram continued to sit at her desk, one hand on the now silent telephone. She was tempted to call Reception and ask Father Michael to wait, go down and say . . . what? She jiggled her high-heeled pump, indecisive. No. After all, it was only a suspicion.

Chapter Twenty-two

''Scuse me, miss!'

Kate turned from the train window with a start – she had been half asleep in the comfortable seat. The man standing over her was big in his dark uniform and peaked cap. She saw his identification badge, heard the familiar clank of his keys on their beltchain as he leant towards her. She pressed herself back against the seat, rigid with terror. The roof of her mouth had dried so she couldn't speak. Outside, rich fields ran yellow and green beside the train. She knew she would never walk through them. They'd come for her. It was all a mistake. They were taking her back.

Kate had heard all about gate arrest. It was one of the prisoner's paranoid fears, bred by confinement. It was also a frequent reality. The law permitted a prisoner to be re-arrested by the police the moment they walked off prison premises and became free women again.

'Don't take no risks, hen,' Joannie had advised her. 'Get a parcel of friends to meet ye. Get a lawyer there, too.' Joannie had been re-arrested three times at the gates. But everyone knew she wanted to stay inside, that was why she refused police interviews during her sentence. She had once confided to Kate that the council had repossessed her flat during her fourth conviction for obtaining credit on false pretences. She couldn't face starting out again to get a home together. 'What's the point of all that sittin' in DSS offices and gettin' grants an' that, when I know I'll only do it again?' She had laughed her wheezy laugh. 'I'm too old, hen, an' that's the truth.'

There had been no-one to meet Kate, though she'd written her father and tried several times to telephone him.

It had taken forty-five minutes to clear the chaos that was Receptions first thing in the morning. At nine-twelve a.m. she walked through the white barrier gates and away. Away from the red-brick buildings and the village green. Away from the cell blocks, and the narrow gaps between, where that morning an enraged inmate had thrown a pink primula, still in its pot, to wilt among the torn magazines and broken plates.

Once through the white exit bars, she had stood with her two suitcases on the pavement of the Parkhurst Road and looked swiftly around.

As David Jarrow had advised, she didn't even glance back at the prison. No-one took the slightest interest in her. A young black woman pushing a pram went past at a run, and an elderly man wearing a black beret and using a white stick tapped nervously round the suitcase. After a moment she tried to hail a taxi to take her to Paddington, as Noonie had instructed her. Her shy waves had no effect on the first two drivers and in the end she had to stand in the road.

Sitting on the edge of the seat, she anxiously counted her money for the thousandth time, stowed her travel warrant carefully in the new wallet, touched the discharge papers folded at the bottom of her shoulder-bag. All the way to the station, she kept looking out of the back window, certain she would see a police car behind them.

But cruel as cats, they had let her run just a little. Just enough. The train swept into a tunnel. There were no lights in the compartment and in the sudden, noisy, rattling darkness, her impulse was to push her way past the officer, escape, leap from the moving train . . . Oh God, she couldn't go back!

Then it was too late. The train burst noisily from the tunnel in an explosion of sound and light and the officer was reaching out for her wrists . . .

'. . . Only want to see your ticket, please,' he was saying.

She stared at him, almost sick with relief. She started fumbling around for her shoulder-bag while he waited with elaborate patience. When he'd clipped the warrant he said, 'Nice nap?' to show he hadn't really minded.

The elderly woman sitting opposite put down her *Daily Telegraph* and fumbled in a carrier bag for a flask of coffee and a KitKat. Kate hadn't thought about eating, it wasn't a long journey. And she'd made herself eat breakfast before she left. Noonie had insisted. 'You know what they say – miss your last breakfast, you'll return to eat it another day!'

It hadn't occurred to her to buy a newspaper. She had been reading *Tess of the d'Urbervilles* from the prison library, and she still hadn't finished it when she returned it. She'd liked the library, with its plants and pictures. They had twelve thousand books, she'd been told by the officer there. It wasn't until later Kate discovered that many of these were picture books, for prisoners who could not read.

She didn't want to read, anyway. She gave herself up to the luxury of thinking about going home. Until now, Kate had not let herself anticipate this meeting. Her father had been asked formally by the probation

221

service if she could stay for two weeks on release, and had agreed.

Dad had not visited her for nearly two years, his sketchy letters had been infrequent. She had told herself he was busy, had hidden even from herself how much she missed seeing him. When she was younger, and in the various secure units in which she'd passed her adolescence, she had looked forward for weeks to his visits, had written down what she wanted to tell him, to ask him.

For a moment, she wasn't on the train at all. She was in the Special Unit sitting room, quite a nice room really, comfy chairs and carpet. Only the windows were reinforced glass, and the doors were opened with security buttons, and she was not even allowed to go to the bathroom on her own.

She saw herself at fifteen, sixteen, hair freshly cut, talking too animatedly, showing her school books, her drawings. And she saw her father sitting opposite, carefully apart from her, hands dangling between his knees, looking at the floor, glancing round, checking his watch, his eyes anywhere but on her, embarrassed and uncomfortable.

Once she'd brought in her guitar to show him. She'd been practising endlessly, to please him: he used to love Julian Bream. She played well, she'd got her first grade. Only after the first piece, although there were still fifteen minutes left, he said he had to start back. She had always wept bitterly after his visits, they had upset her for days.

But the prospect of release had painted everything in rosy colours. She would be welcomed home. Maybe there would be a celebration. Even a bottle of champagne – when Ruth got home, she said, her mum would have one waiting. Kate smiled to herself, hugging the thought. She

222

was longing to see Dad. She would ring him again from the station, maybe he'd come and meet her.

When the trolley came through the carriages, and the uniformed attendant asked if she wanted coffee, Kate had nodded yes, and was shocked to be asked for eighty pence. Almost the cost of getting her hair done in Holloway.

She sipped her coffee and stared out of the smoked glass window, watching an England she had never seen unroll in front of her. Every now and then she leant forward, almost pressing her nose against the glass like a child, craning to catch the last glimpse of some tantalizing sight. Station car parks and garish shopping-centres built from some sort of adult Lego, isolated country houses and industrial estates of windowless warehouses; all received the same absorbed attention.

After a while the elderly woman sitting opposite leant forward, smiling and nodding and speaking very slowly and loudly. 'You must be a visitor to England.'

Kate's eyes opened very wide. 'I . . .' She wasn't sure what to say, the woman so obviously meant well.

'Where are you from?'

If only you knew. She smiled and shook her head, unused to talking to strangers. The woman held out a piece of chocolate, urging her to try it. The sheer silly kindness almost brought tears to Kate's eyes.

She went to the lavatory to escape. The hot little room smelt like the prison loos, of stale pee and people. She couldn't work out how to empty it, till she accidentally stood on the rubber floor knob which worked the flush. She splashed her face with the thin stream of warmish water from the cold tap. There were no paper towels, just a white metal box mounted on the wall. She examined the diagram carefully and dried her hands under a stream of hot air.

Going back to her seat, the door to the compartment – which had been open the first time – was closed. There was no handle. Schooled for so long in obedience, accustomed to waiting for doors to be unlocked for her, she stood patiently in the swaying corridor.

A man inside the compartment kept glancing up at her, with increasing curiosity. After about five minutes he stood up, opened the door and said, 'Don't you want to come in?' He pointed to the large red button beside the door. 'You just have to press this, here.'

Pink with humiliation, certain everyone was laughing at her ignorance, she went back to her seat. She continued looking out of the window, but she saw nothing beyond the glass.

She had spent half her life behind locked doors. All the outside journeys, all the practising in the world, couldn't erase the years of conditioning. She would carry them around on her back for a long time. Kate had brought prison out with her.

Her father was in the yard on his way to feed the dogs when the taxi drew up. She was too excited to take in any details of the house: she saw only his face, pale and stiff. He watched her pay and pick up her bag before he said, 'You made it, then?'

She took a couple of steps towards him. 'Hallo, Dad.'

In the awkward pause, she saw how time had thickened his body and thinned his hair. He had a slight stoop she didn't remember, heavy lines on forehead and under his eyes.

'I've got to feed this lot . . .' he jerked his head towards the kennels, and she became aware of animals barking and whining. 'Jan's out shopping just now with the kids.' He had hardly looked at her. Now he took a couple of steps and leaning forward stiffly kissed the air somewhere in the region of her cheek. She meant to kiss him back, but he moved and the moment was lost.

'You go in and put the kettle on. I'll not be long.'

She stood with her bag in her hand. It was so long since she'd been in a house. Or an ordinary kitchen. Apart from the huge prison kitchens, where even the saucepans were institution sized, she had only seen the toast room on the unit. That was a small room with an elderly electric toaster on a table surrounded by crumbs no-one ever bothered to wipe up. Dozens of packets of sliced white Sunblest were stacked beside the catering-sized jars of marmalade and pickle. Kate used to take hers into the TV room to eat it, with a cup of tea made with water from the hot water boiler in huge teapots.

Although Kate had thought the house looked a bit depressing outside, in here everything was cheerful. The kitchen was painted white, with white cupboards. A kettle and a mixer stood on the long counter underneath, with a bowl of fruit and a mug tree. A bowl held peeled potatoes in water. The fridge had children's paintings stuck on it with magnets. An ironing-board stood with neat piles of ironed clothes. A large plastic box on the floor held toys.

Kate put down her bag and filled the kettle from the tap. She felt a ridiculous sense of disappointment. Everything looked very small to her, and ordinary.

She thought, I don't know about homes. The only houses she had seen since she was a child had been photographs in magazines: of the famous, in *Hello*, and the rich, in *House and Garden*. Or the carefully sanitized interiors of television, a make-believe world.

*   *   *

225

She asked eagerly, anticipating the meeting, 'Will they be back soon?'

'Oh, sure. Soonish. Not sure where they've gone.'

The evasive note alerted her. She wrapped her hands round the mug of tea because she suddenly felt so cold.

'Is Jan expecting me?' She spoke very quietly now.

'She's a bit nervous about having you here. She doesn't understand . . . well.' He lifted his own mug of tea.

'She's not, is she? She doesn't know I'm here. Dad?'

Her father was clearly embarrassed. 'She's a good lass. There'll be no problem.' He got up. 'I'll take your bag upstairs.'

The room was on a half-landing, beside a bathroom, its single window facing over the kennels. Underneath it was a window-seat, piled high with pop magazines. Separated bunk beds stood on either side of it. Both were covered with sweaters and T-shirts, sheets of what looked like essays, and tapes dumped carelessly out of their boxes. More clothes and magazines hid most of the floor, and posters of pop stars were stuck to the pink painted walls with blue-tack.

'That's your bed.' Her father pushed some of the stuff aside and put her bag on top of an obviously used duvet. On the shelf above the bed was a paperback called *Ten Boy Summer* and a bottle of surgical spirit with the lid off and a piece of used cottonwool beside it. Kate picked up a black toy scottie lying on the pillow. It had a tartan ribbon round its neck and a pair of skimpy worn knickers caught on its tail. She put it on the other bed.

'Yes,' she said, forcing the tell-tale quiver out of her voice. 'Thanks.'

'You'll like Denise,' he said. 'When you get to know her. She's a nice kid. Taking her GCSE's this year. She'll be back about four.'

'Good.'

'Anything else you need?' He looked vaguely around, and she didn't answer. 'Right,' he said, 'I've got to get back. We'll have a proper talk later, OK? A good chin-wag. Sort things out . . .' He was already half-way down the stairs.

Kate made no move to open her bag. She was still sitting on the window-seat when she heard the dogs bark and a car pulled up outside. Doors slammed, children shouted.

She looked down. A boy of about five – that must be Tom – ran towards the woven wood gate her father was just locking behind him. Tom jumped up and wrapped his legs round her father's – *his* father's – waist. Roy Downey tugged the peaked cap the child wore until it was back to front, and Kate saw them laughing. Then he carried Tom into the house.

Kate waited fifteen minutes. She was about to go downstairs but the raised voices stopped her. She paused at the closed door, her hand tight round the knob.

Her father was speaking, quick and urgent. The woman answered briefly. Her father, at greater length. The woman's voice, again only for a moment.

Very quietly Kate opened the door, and heard her father say, '. . . through all this, I thought we'd agreed. I've no option. She's my daughter.'

'But not *mine*. I never said yes. It was you talked to that probation woman. You must be out of your mind.' Jan spoke with the soft local accent Kate had noticed people using at the station.

'Jan, for God's sake. Just for a week or two, till I can get something sorted.'

'And how long do you think it takes to . . .' Kate couldn't hear the next bit. But she could guess.

'Don't be ridiculous, love. Nothing like that's going to . . . all behind her now . . .'

Kate could tell from their voices that her father was following Jan from room to room.

'Tell you what . . .' He was cajoling now, 'You take the kids and stay with your ma, just till . . .'

'. . . not be pushed out of my own house, thank you very much.' A door slammed.

Kate shut the bedroom door, found her shoulder-bag and got out her comb. In the pink plastic-framed wall mirror, she was paler than she'd appeared in prison, her eyes shadowed and sad. In this adolescent room, she thought, I look old.

She sat on the window-seat and waited for what she knew would happen. It never occurred to her that she could argue, or demand, or beg her father to let her stay. She didn't belong here.

But even beyond that, she had had half a lifetime of accepting quietly what was meted out to her. Half a lifetime of having no choice. So Kate looked from the window at the caged animals her father kept. Her head throbbed frantically. And methodically, without even knowing she was doing it, she scratched her arms with her fingernails. It was the only visible sign of her distress.

Chapter Twenty-three

'Sing psalms to the Lord, you who love him,' the
  community chanted.
'Give thanks to his holy name . . .'

The light in the chapel was deep blue and turquoise from
the stained-glass windows. In front of her, behind the altar
rail, the candlelit tabernacle housed the hidden Christ.

My body pines for you . . .

Sarah couldn't look at the burdened crucifix above the
altar. His pierced side and bloody forehead, His pinioned
palms and bleeding dusty feet were hard to bear. Her own
hands hurt in sympathy. Instead, she concentrated on the
thick creamy candles: even the flames burned with an
unwavering love of God.

Draw the curtains and light the candles on the birthday
cake she and Kate always shared. Smarties spelling
out their names. White mice and pansies of coloured
sugar.

The child who had been Sarah thought, when Kate
was taken away, that now she would have a cake just
for herself. But by the time her birthday arrived, there
was no-one to make it for her. The house was for
sale and rooms echoed empty. The little family was

lost to each other and the kitten crawled onto the step to die.

Sister Gideon cried in a curious way. The tears – of shame, regret, she scarcely knew, after so long – came without any contortions of her face. Her gold-flecked eyes were wide, the drops welling and falling unheeded down her cheeks.

She cried for the child taken and the child left. For the end of innocence and the lonely dark.

'His anger lasts but a moment; his favour through life . . .'

It had been several days since she was well enough to get dressed and join the others in chapel. It was a joy to be there, part of the community again. They recited as one, knelt and rose as one. When they did so, their habits rustled in unison.

There was someone with whom she was one. Who was not a different person, but another part of her self. The twin, the perfect one, the winner, the centre of the universe.

For years and years, she had shut her twin out. Out of her thoughts, out of her heart. She could not endure the deprivation any longer: a split egg implied a relationship too close ever to break.

But the killing had altered everything, all those cold years ago. It pushed them from each other, turned love away, let in fear and jealousy and suspicion: Was it always like this, and I didn't see?

Now something had changed, the mysterious bond had reasserted itself. She felt Kate's presence all around her, all the time. She could let her mind freewheel and somewhere, somehow, Kate received the message she was sending.

It wasn't a conscious decision. Kate was simply back

in the forefront of her thoughts, as in childhood she had always been, as in her dreams she continued to be. They say the past surfaces in dreams.

'At night there are tears, but joy comes with the dawn.'

They processed from the chapel into the soft April evening. The Infirmarian had suggested she get some fresh air, so she walked down to see the birds in the wire enclosures beyond the kitchen garden. Sister Josse was there already. She had finished milking the goats and was moving them to fresh grass. Sister Gideon passed with a brief wave, leaving her to hammer the metal stakes into the ground and test the chains.

Of all the nuns in this house, she felt closest to Sister Josse, at twenty-five almost a year younger. A Breton like her sainted namesake, she was tiny with sallow skin and eyes shiny black as olives. She was a fierce little thing, all guts and determination. Her faith was rooted deep and unshakeable, nothing ever got her down. Sarah sometimes joked that when it was cold, they could use Sister Josse instead of the boiler to warm the entire house.

The Frenchwoman loved the animals – the goats and the convent's small herd of Beulah speckled-faced sheep, and they were the only ones who ever heard her speaking French. She was talking to them now, calling them 'mes vieux'.

The ducks hurried expectantly towards Sister Gideon, tempted by the conciliatory handful of grain she threw – Sister Josse would be feeding them in five minutes. They waddled round her ankles ungainly as drunken sailors, their voices a watery babble, incessant and soothing. One mother was followed by her brood of five, demure as cartoon creatures, making their comical linear progress on wide yellow feet. Their down had thickened now, they were sturdy and bursting with life.

She knelt and scooped one up. Bright and alert, it peeped from the nest of her laced fingers. Tiny head, eyes glossy as coffee beans, body fluttering warm against her skin.

Mother Emmanuel, crossing the garden with her hoe, saw the crouching figure down among the long grass. She smiled to herself: Sister Gideon and her ducks. Then she frowned at her thoughts. She was more concerned than ever about this young woman, and these brief periods of false recovery were assuming a worrying pattern. Like all the other times, she feared Sister Gideon would be back in the Infirmary within days. So when she glanced up, Mother Emmanuel indicated she should return to the house.

Sarah was making her way back up the garden, she had almost reached the cabbages, when she heard Sister Josse call out. That her cry came in French was a measure of her distress.

'Le pauvre petit! Quel dommage . . . Soeur, Soeur, dépêche-toi!'

She was crouched beside the half-barrel where the brood nested. As Sarah hurried towards her, Sister Josse held out her cupped hands. The duckling she cradled in them was dead, open eyes faintly filmed, tiny beak gaping.

'Oh,' said Sarah, and her eyes filled. 'Little thing.'

Sister Josse said, bewildered, 'There's not a mark on him.' She looked down at the four remaining ducklings pecking round her feet. 'These are all well, non?'

Sarah smoothed the back of a forefinger over the limp body, the speckled fluff already flattening. 'He's still warm. Maybe his mother sat on him by mistake.'

In the distance the campanile bell was chiming Vespers, the office to remind them all of the first gathering in the temple of Jerusalem.

It was still sounding as Sarah gasped out loud. Sister Josse turned to her, black eyes sharp with concern, seeing her press one hand beneath her ribs, and with the other grope helplessly for the air she suddenly could not breathe.

At night there are tears . . .

Chapter Twenty-four

Kate loathed her room in Durrant Street even before she'd seen it, hated it from the moment Miss Duesbury led the way up the steps of the drab house.

The whiff of sardines lingered in the hallway where the notice-board was covered with faded flyers advertising events long gone. She especially hated the little notices posted everywhere. *A gentle reminder: Silence. Make sure you close the front door. Please leave the bathroom as you would wish to find it*. It was like having someone constantly hissing warnings.

Number four was on the fourth floor at the back, and belonged to a distant shabby past. The jumble of furniture must have been collected at small auctions at different times. Some pieces – the wardrobe, the chest of drawers – were older than the others, and the whole room, with the bunches of flowers on the wallpaper, was in faded yellowish colours. The narrow bed had two feather pillows under a brown chenille bedspread with fringes. The central light was a parchment shade exposing the light-bulb, the solitary lamp a cheaply carved wooden candlestick varnished dark brown.

'We've put a couple of people in here before,' said the probation officer, running a finger along the gate-leg table under the window. 'It's very clean, isn't it?' It wasn't a question, and Kate did not answer. Kate liked Fran Duesbury: her clothes were floaty and charming, she wore many bracelets on plump arms, and her hair was caught up on top of her head like a gypsy. She was a wonderful relief from prison officers. On the other hand, Miss Duesbury was looking determinedly on the bright side, just as they all did.

Kate glanced out of the window. The room was set at the back of a narrow oblong formed by the rest of the house stretching out quite a distance on the left, and on the right the high partition wall to next door. So there wasn't a lot of light. She could see dustbins in the yard below, and a tub of geraniums. There was a glimpse of a strip of garden beyond the house, and the trees of adjoining plots.

The landlady had given her the keys downstairs, and said she hoped Kate'd be happy here. Mrs Dennison was like her house, Kate thought. Clean and plain and old and dull. She had explained that Kate was originally going to have a different room, on the floor above, but as she'd wanted to move in earlier than expected . . . Still, she'd added encouragingly, number four was the better room.

'I'll help you unpack,' Miss Duesbury said, 'and then we'll have lunch back at the office. You'll soon brighten this up with your own things.' She looked doubtfully at Kate's single suitcase as she said this.

On her way to her office in the town centre, Fran Duesbury said, 'It's not brilliant, I give you that. Trouble is in Bristol, students snap up anything that's half-way decent. But it's not going to be for long, is it? As soon as we get a job fixed up, you can start planning to move.' She stood hard on her brakes and the Escort rocked to a halt at traffic lights. She went on talking, quite unconcerned.

'It's a pity about that job with the estate agents. They said they just couldn't afford to take you on right now.' She glanced across at Kate. 'I really think you'd have got it, they're a nice firm. But the recession's still affecting people, whatever the blasted government says. They've promised me, if business picks up in a few months, and you're not fixed up, you're at the top of the list.'

While she listened, Kate was watching a girl swinging along the pavement. She looked like a student, with long black legs and unclouded eyes.

'Got your bank account opened?'

Kate replied absently, 'Yes.'

'If you find an unfurnished place, you'll probably get a Community Care Grant for furniture,' Fran Duesbury said.

'I didn't know about that.' Another pretty girl had caught the arm of the first.

'You'll need to register immediately for Income Support,' said Fran Duesbury. The girls kissed each other on both cheeks and started talking and laughing. 'Because you won't get that for two weeks,' the probation officer went on, 'and if you've got a job by then . . .'

The lights changed, she put the car in gear and moved off, but got stuck behind a bus turning right. A young man with long black hair and pale blue jeans who had started to cross the road in front of them shrugged and stepped back.

'You know about the grants and stuff you can get, don't you?'

The young man nearly collided with the pretty girls and one of them dropped the books she was carrying. Kate turned her head to watch them through the back window.

'. . . already got your discharge grant, of course, and there's . . .'

Now they were all talking and smiling at each other, and picking up the books.

'. . . Social Fund only if you're absolutely . . .'

Fran Duesbury stopped talking and glanced at Kate. 'Are you all right?' she asked sharply. 'This stuff's a bit boring, but it's important, OK?'

'Yes,' said Kate contritely. 'Sorry.'

The probation officer added with sudden warmth, 'It's all a bit much, at first. Especially after all that business with your dad. It'll take time to get used to life outside again.' She turned left going much too fast, said 'Oops' and signalled too late. 'Just take it very slow,' she advised Kate, without any apparent awareness of irony. 'It's the only way.'

They spent two hours in Fran Duesbury's office. There were more forms to fill out, telephone calls to try and set up interviews.

'Local paper's OK for jobs, you'll need to get that. I've a couple of people to try for you, so I'll be in touch. And I'll give you a practice interview, if you want,' Fran Duesbury offered.

'Thanks, but I went to the pre-release classes at Holloway. They have a job-club too.'

When Kate left her at three o'clock, she had a list of essentials in her notebook, with amounts pencilled in beside them, which Fran Duesbury had worked out with her. The only thing she had to do today was buy some clothes.

Fran Duesbury had directed her to Broadmead, the busiest area of the town. Kate had to force herself to walk across the roads: the traffic went so fast, her impulse was to dash at top speed.

She wandered around for half an hour simply staring,

intimidated by the apparent efficiency of other shoppers. It took her three hours to buy a pale-grey skirt and long cardigan in Miss Selfridge, a silk shirt in a sale at Pilot. Although she liked colour on other people, she found any but the most neutral made her impossibly self-conscious.

She had a coffee in the restaurant above Next, bought a plant that looked as though it would live even with her, and found her way back to Durrant Street. She'd been feeling almost happy until then, but her room was silent and still.

Kate hung her new clothes in the wardrobe. The hangers were the cheap metal sort from dry cleaners and she covered them fastidiously with clean tissue paper from the clothes. Not for the first time, she wished she'd done as David Jarrow suggested and brought Blue out with her.

When the dinner bell rang, she went nervously downstairs. Walking alone into a room full of strangers was one of the many things she found almost impossibly difficult. It came from all the times she had been moved on, to a different secure unit, another closed prison. There was always the fear that someone would recognize her, know her old name. Then the whispers would start, and the women would stare, and then avoid her.

No matter what crime any inmate had committed, the child-murderer was a lower form of life. It always built up gradually. She would be jostled at rounders or in the gym, at first almost accidentally, later unmercifully, so she was knocked to the ground. When the assaults became life-threatening, she was moved on again.

On the wall in front of her was a handprinted menu: Minestrone soup. Mixed grill. Rice pudding. Cheese.

One of the traditional ways of showing hatred inside was through food. They would tell her they'd spat in hers. And worse. She never ate rice pudding any more.

'Not hungry?' asked a voice behind her. A fattish man of about thirty-five leaned around her to open the door. Kate hesitated for a moment, expecting him to go in first.

Mrs Dennison had evidently made more of an effort with this room: paint instead of the depressing wallpaper, pictures of unlikely lakes and mountains. You helped yourself from a long counter, Mrs Dennison standing over it, presumably making sure no-one took too much. To Kate's mortification, she waved the ladle she was using for mashed potato and announced, 'And this is our new lady, Miss Dean. Say hallo, everybody.'

There was a muttered response. Kate put far too much scrambled egg on her plate. The fattish man said, 'There's a place here,' and she sat down gratefully opposite him at one of the four tables covered in plastic cloths made to look like linen.

By the end of the meal, she had been asked a few questions about where she came from, and what sort of jobs she'd done. Her answers had been vague, but she didn't think anyone had listened anyway. For her part, she'd learned the names of the other seven lodgers, their ages (various), the occupations of those who had them (trainee butcher, assistant in a shoe-shop, building society clerk) and the length of their stay there. There was one very young and dejected pregnant girl, and a man who was going through a bad divorce. It didn't look promising.

For a week, Kate did her best. She got up at seven a.m. each morning, as she always had. She bathed first thing – there wasn't exactly a rush for the bathroom – and washed her hair. She kept her room immaculate and walked everywhere. (She told herself this saved bus fares, but the truth was, she was nervous – would she get the bus going to the right place? Have the right money?) And she spoke to Fran Duesbury most days, though she knew this was not necessary – the regulations stipulated a half-hour meeting with her probation officer every week at first.

When she had imagined – fantasized, really – about how she would use the freedom which was unimaginable inside prison walls, she had never dreamed she would feel lonely outside. Loneliness, for her, came in the middle of crowds of people she didn't like. In all the time she was held, her own company was a pleasure, a relief she desperately needed in all the crush and hassle.

But by the fourth day in Bristol, walking always by herself, knowing no-one, loneliness started to erode her fragile optimism. She'd explored parts of Bristol fairly well by now, she'd been to a cinema, found a reasonably cheap hairdresser. She had acquired a few more clothes, discovered the whereabouts of her local post office, the DSS office and the best local swimming pool.

Even so, loneliness was waiting when she woke. After breakfast she got out her Psychology coursework. There were two essays due this month and she had a lot of work to do. In her cell, she'd had her books neatly arranged, a desk lamp. In this dispirited room it was hard to concentrate. She struggled for an hour with Gross. When she folded her arms on the papers, and rested her head on them, she remembered Miss Dailey saying she couldn't honestly remember the last time they'd had a student from Holloway get her degree. Kate had been determined then that she would manage it. Today, she wasn't so confident.

She had to get out of this room. She felt her identity was somehow slipping away while she was in it. Even in a prison cell, that had never happened. But in here, she had the sensation of being submerged under ancient brown fabrics.

She went to the library and pored through the last three copies of the *Bristol Evening News*. She needed a job, and soon. She'd somehow never totally believed in Fran Duesbury's estate agents, so that particular disappointment had been no surprise. The narrow black columns were discouraging. Bricklayers and hod carriers urgently . . . Nursing auxiliary required . . . Laundry vacancies for two factory cleaners . . . Interior designer seeks upholsterers . . . Office junior for medical centre . . .

She copied out details of that one, though she was probably too old to be a junior. Still, she had a couple of interviews next week, arranged by Fran Duesbury. It was a condition of her life licence that if any prospective employer asked, she had to tell them about her record, or risk being prosecuted for deception. She couldn't imagine who would want her, once they heard. Still, maybe she'd get lucky.

Kate sighed and lifted her eyes from the small print. A pair of pony-tailed librarians were chatting as they sorted books. It reminded her that, apart from Dana at Durrant Street – who was barely eighteen – she knew no-one anywhere near her own age.

Fran Duesbury had given her the phone numbers of a couple of social groups and she must do something about joining some clubs. She looked at the library notice-board: drama societies, mother and toddler clubs, dog training sessions, camera clubs. She didn't think she'd be any good at teaching English to immigrants, but maybe she'd go along to the St John Ambulance Brigade resuscitation course.

You only need a few people, she told herself, you're

being ridiculous. Start. Do something. Make an effort. What are those new clothes for, for heaven's sake?

She got lunch from Boots because she had a voucher allowing 10p off. Standing in the queue to pay for her chicken tikka sandwich, she started thinking that after all, she should have done what everyone had wanted, what everyone else did, and gone to a half-way house, or a hostel, on her release.

She'd wanted so desperately to avoid that. In the end her pleas, combined with recommendations from Laura Pegram, had their effect. In the circumstances, they had said, given her exemplary record . . . So the rules, normally adhered to so strictly, had been put aside. But now she realized she might have been better off there. Sure, she thought grimly, plenty of companionship, anyway. All the ex-cons.

In her room, she unwrapped the sandwich and laid it formally on a plate with a knife beside it. On a second plate, she placed the pot of yogurt and a teaspoon. She ate at the table by the window, looking out at the rain on the dustbins.

She wished – she really wished – she were back in prison.

Stop that. *Stop* it. She washed up at the basin on the back wall. Then there was nothing else to do. She sat in the high-backed chair and rested her arms on its grubby beige rests, but the nubbly fabric was so harsh it hurt her skin. She rubbed the toe of her new black shoe on the dim carpet. It had an Indian pattern, and the bed had been moved to cover the worst threadbare bits; the square marks from its last position were still there.

After a while Kate lay down on the bed. The brown velvet cover caught at her hair. When she rolled over and pressed her face into it, the fabric smelled of closed cupboards. It was sticky under her cheek, and that was when she realized she was crying.

In bed that night, she touched herself secretly. In prison this had brought a measure of solace, some small relief. It confirmed she was human, at least, not just a statistic in their files, a number on the prison computer.

Anyway, it had been all there was, and better than nothing. But in this dim place, hearing sounds from other rooms, alert to other people's lives, it became something shameful. It marked her as another solitary failure.

She was dry and desperate. Maybe the things she wanted so badly were for ever out of reach? It hadn't seemed that way in Holloway. She'd planned and dreamed and schemed, she'd imagined how it would be, how she would act, in the most precise detail. She would meet people, a man, *the* man. He would see her somewhere, she didn't know where. She had conjured up a restaurant she'd seen on television, a box at an opera remembered from a video shown in the gymnasium. She'd even envisaged herself in New York, going into Barnes & Noble for a book, like Meryl Streep.

Lying on the brown bed, she tore her dreams to shreds. It was a vicious emotional self-laceration, as harsh in its way as any Robina Wright had ever inflicted on her flesh. *Life sucks*, Robina's arms had screamed, *Torch me*. It seemed to Kate she must be as easy to read. Idiot, they would see on her, self-deluding fool. Pathetic no-hoper.

There would be no-one for her, after all. The world would always look the other way.

The dark intensified her misery. She had feared it since childhood, back when she'd listened to her parents' bitter fights. Bad things always happened then, especially in prison. It was the time you were off-guard, defenceless. People had to lie down in darkness, and sometimes they died. Mum had died at night.

Other people made love at night, held each other safe while they slept. Their joy increased her loneliness. There was a vast empty space in her life where sex ought to be. Her body was a void she couldn't fill, an ache she couldn't stifle. She put her hand on her breast, over the nightdress with blue and white satiny spots she'd bought yesterday in a Marks and Spencer sale, and felt her heart beat hard and strong. Her hollow heart.

The clamour of her flesh made her whimper and she turned over, pressed her face into the lumpy pillow smelling of someone else. It was so dark. And who could she go to?

Chapter Twenty-five

Culford House sounded imposing. So Father Michael was not prepared for the dispirited smallholding he found outside Bath. The house of greyish stone was built in a dip beside the road. From the pavement he could see into the small windows, the sills crammed with plastic toys. Some of the curtains were still drawn, although it was after eleven a.m.

A high woven wood fence bore a large sign: Culford House Boarding Kennels, J. Burford. Tel: 0225 89762. Beyond the fence, in about twenty large wire compounds, an assortment of dogs barked excitedly.

The man who answered the door was burly at first sight. But it was an impression only, created by his wide work trousers, and sleeveless quilted jacket over a check workshirt.

'Mr Downey?'

'Who wants him?' The tone was both belligerent and nervous.

Father Michael gave his name and added, 'Sorry to walk in like this, but there seems to be something wrong with your phone.' He was pretty sure it had been cut off, the man's lack of surprise – there was no doubt it was Downey – confirmed it. 'It's about Kate,' he went on. 'I believe she's here.'

At this, Downey glanced back uneasily, and said, 'Let's go in the office,' leading the way towards one of two battered caravans on the far side of the driveway. As he went, he spoke in a loud monotone.

'If you're another probation officer, you got it all already . . . no point going on and on asking the same . . . I did my best and it wasn't . . . I'm sorry, all right? I know I promised, I know it was all arranged. But it was different to what we expected.' He went up the step and turned to Father Michael, looking down on him. 'I mean, she's not a kid any more, is she? I thought, it'll just be like having her back, it's just my Kate. But she's not, is she?'

'No,' said Father Michael, 'no, I'm trying to find Kate for a different reason.' He looked around at the chilly little room. It smelled damp. He could see all the fittings were still in place – stove, basin, fridge. There were four large grey metal filing cabinets. The narrow table was covered with what appeared to be mainly bills.

'Who're you, then, the police? That's all I bloody need.' Downey didn't wait for an answer. 'She went off, I couldn't stop her, could I? That social worker woman from Bristol's been on the phone twenty times already, and I said to her, Kate's not a kid any more.' Downey sat down at the table and his shoulders slumped. He was smaller than he first appeared, probably in his mid-fifties. Heavy lines creased his cheeks, his eyebrows grew black and wild. Michael thought, can this man really be Sister Gideon's father?

'I'm not the police. I'm here on behalf of your other daughter. Sister Gideon. Sarah.'

At the sound of her name, Downey's expression changed to one of pure fury. 'Can't you people even leave *her* alone? What harm can she do, stuck away in that place? What in hell's going on? Who *are* you?'

246

Father Michael took a step back. Downey looked ready to lash out. 'No, no, Mother Emmanuel asked me to do this for her. Your daughter's been ill, Mr Downey. Did you not get the convent's letters? They were afraid you'd moved and left no address.'

Downey's anger vanished as swiftly as it had come. Vaguely, he paddled one large hand around among the papers on the table. 'Yes, well, somewhere, I seem to remember . . . things've been a bit difficult lately . . .'

'We've been very concerned.' Father Michael explained again about Sister Gideon's illness. He sat down on the thin mattress of a bunk bed and waited for her father to react.

Downey stared out of the window, the glass streaked with dribbles of old rain. His eyes were the same golden brown as his daughter's, but spoiled by the bloodshot whites.

'Ah,' he said dismissively, 'they've got her now. She belongs with them. I've no doubt they'll look after her better than I ever did.'

The priest began to speak, but Downey was already continuing. 'To be honest, Father, I lost my daughter a long time ago. When April . . . died, I was in a bad way, what with the trial and all.' He patted the papers before him until he found the bulge of a packet of cigarettes, and flipped one out. He lit it with a blue plastic lighter, using his left hand to steady the shaking right. 'Sorry,' he muttered. 'Even talking about it . . .' He inhaled deeply and sat back.

'You've probably gathered, I'm not a Catholic. Not any more. But April . . . anyway, after . . . everything, the Bishop was very good. At least I thought so at the time. Now I'm not so sure. He arranged for the convent school to take Sarah without fees. She was nearly out of her mind, what with losing April and Kate.' He rubbed a hand through thinning hair. 'Sometimes I think, he took her away from me then. Maybe if we'd stayed together . . . who knows? I was in no position to make decisions, that's for sure.'

Father Michael found himself saying, 'She didn't very often spend holidays with you.'

'No. Well. I'd moved in with Jan and her kids were small then. There wasn't really room. Sarah didn't get on with the little ones, there were always ructions. Never her fault,' he added hastily. 'She always was a good girl, I'll give her that. It was Kate had the temper.' He smiled faintly, half-proud. '*My* temper, I'm afraid.

'Anyhow, things just didn't work out. Sarah liked the dogs, all right, but she wouldn't help Jan in the house, wouldn't even tidy her room, left it in a right tip whenever she went back to school. Jan got fed up, I couldn't blame her.' He sat down heavily on the second bunk bed, behind the table.

'Seems like next thing I knew she'd decided to enter the order. I reckoned no harm'd come to her there, and I'm pretty sure that's why she wanted to go in. Know what I mean?' He squinted at the priest through cigarette smoke. 'I've sat in front of that blasted grille of theirs,' he went on bitterly, 'and it could've been anyone on the other side. She's not my girl, not any more.'

'I'm sorry you feel like that. The fact remains, she's in a bad way, and there seems no cause for it. One possibility is that she's enduring the symptoms on Kate's behalf, and Kate is really the twin who's sick. Apparently that's not unknown. That's why I have to get to Kate – she may be at risk.'

'I've no idea where she went. Sorry. Try the social worker in Bristol.'

'I have. Is Kate in touch with you?'

Downey looked at the silent telephone on his desk. 'She hasn't phoned,' he said with sarcasm, 'and I'm not expecting postcards either. We didn't part on the best of terms. So I'm afraid I can't be of much help to you.'

The hell you can't. Michael said, 'You know how the girls reacted to each other as children. Does it sound likely to you, the idea of transmitted symptoms?'

'Christ, I dunno.' He scratched his neck. 'Maybe. I do remember once, Sarah came shrieking down the stairs, we couldn't stop her crying. April ran up to their room and found Kate with a safety pin stuck right into her foot. Just sitting there, she was, real quiet, not making a sound. She didn't seem to mind, even when April pulled it out.' He took the cigarette from his lips and examined the tip. 'Funny kid,' he said at last.

'Can I ask you, Mr Downey – Sister Gideon wouldn't talk about her mother at all. Were they very close? It's possible that has some bearing on her health.'

The other man looked at him. 'Close?' He started to laugh but it turned into a cough. When he could speak again he said bitterly, 'There's no-one gets close to twins, except the other twin. They don't need you to love 'em.'

'I should have thought any child needs loving.'

Downey's face flamed. So he was not so indifferent, Michael noted. 'I didn't say we didn't love 'em, did I? I said, they don't *need* love. They're a unit. A pair. They're complete.' He stared down at his heavy hands, fingers pressed hard into his thighs. He looked up into the priest's face and said wryly, 'You should try having twins, Father. It's an education, believe me. April was overwhelmed by them, she never had a minute to spare for me once they came along. It was put one down, pick up the other. Finish feeding one, start on the other. Change one nappy, straight on to the next one. Never noticed whether I was there or not.'

His voice took on a wistful note, and for the first time Father Michael began to feel for the man. 'The sun shone out of their behinds, far as she was concerned. I could understand, in a way. They were beautiful kids, Sarah and Kate. Wherever she took 'em, people made such a fuss, peering into the pram. April put them in matching clothes. She even dressed in the same colours as the twins sometimes, she was that proud.' He drew on his cigarette. 'I couldn't compete with those two, and after a bit I didn't try. No point, anyway. She'd got what she wanted from me. If I'd been a horse, she'd've put me out to grass.'

Roy Downey stared down at his hands. More expressive than his face or his voice, they were slack now, dejected. 'When they were five or six, April lost interest in 'em. They weren't dolls any more, they were at school. That's when the suicide attempts began. Calling for help, they said. But when *I* tried to help she didn't want to know. Everything I did was wrong. She used to say, the house was never clean when I was in it.' He shook his head, as if he was trying to clear something away. 'And not just me. She'd always favoured Sarah: Sarah was the prettiest, Sarah needed more care when she was tiny. When she got depressed, she took against Kate. Said she was naughty, she was noisy, she made Sarah behave badly. I think she smacked her quite a bit.' He saw the look on the priest's face and added hastily, 'Just smacks, she didn't knock her about that much.' He cradled his left hand with his right in a protective gesture. 'Poor little Kate. I never, like, saw it at the time, did I? Only after it was all over. And I've thought since, maybe that had something to do with it all.'

After a pause Father Michael said, 'I'm sorry. About all of it.'

'What?' Roy Downey was lost in his thoughts. 'Oh. Yes. Thanks.' He drew a deep breath. 'It wasn't a marriage any more. Hadn't been for years. She never . . . she wouldn't even . . .' He glanced across at Father Michael and shrugged. 'Could've been my fault. There were other women, she knew that. But not at the beginning.' There was a kind of desperation in his voice. 'We used to go down the pictures and hold hands even after we married.' The hands moved again, gripped his knees. 'Still, all done with now.' He stood up. 'Well, is that it?'

Father Michael had been listening with growing understanding. He had assumed, like everyone else, that Kate Downey had murdered a child and, in doing so, destroyed her family. But it was becoming increasingly clear that the family had collapsed years before. Maybe Kate's act had been, not the cause of so much unhappiness, but the result of it?

He thought of Sister Gideon, her gold-speckled eyes fixed on him with hungry hope. *Can you help me? Can you?* Pity for both girls swept over him, pity and a kind of love. Pity and anger at the man standing there, already moving dismissively towards the door. He felt the anger grow with something very close to pleasure.

'*Is* that it?' he echoed. 'You have two daughters in as serious trouble as I've seen in a long time. You tell me. Is this the extent of your interest?'

The light in the little caravan was fading. Father Michael was conscious of the smell of the other man: dogs and smoke and work clothes.

'I've done all I can,' Downey said sullenly.

Michael knew he shouldn't interfere: this was none of his business. Then he thought of Laura Pegram telling him in Holloway just how little had been known by the court about Kate's tragic background. He remembered the article in the P.A. Library about Kate's parents sitting far apart behind her during the trial, never touching her.

'I read the reports of the trial,' he said. 'That never came out in court, what you've just told me about your wife's state.'

For a moment Downey was dangerously still. Then he let himself fall back into his chair.

'You could have made sure the court knew about her family life, her mother's suicide attempts,' the priest went on. 'Anyone could see that might have made a difference. The child was living in a nightmare. For God's sake, why did none of you speak?'

There was more hopelessness in Roy Downey's splayed fingers than in his face. He didn't speak for so long, Father Michael thought he hadn't heard.

'We never believed they'd find her guilty.' His voice was strained. 'We just couldn't imagine the law wouldn't be merciful to Kate. She was *twelve*, for Chrissake.'

Father Michael couldn't let it rest. 'The lawyers must have warned you she could be found guilty. You took a terrible risk. And you lost.'

Downey looked up and something burned behind his eyes. 'What do you know about it?' he demanded. 'Someone like you.' He didn't trouble to keep the sneer from his voice. 'I was supposed to stand up, was I, in front of all of them and say, my wife hates my guts, she's been trying and threatening to kill herself for years. She says she doesn't want to spend another day alive with me around. I was supposed to say that, was I? Tell 'em about the slit wrists and the blood and the sleeping pills so they could print it in their poxy newspapers.' There was spittle at the corners of his mouth and his hands were clenched into fists, punching down on his thighs again and again, punctuating the terrible words.

'It was bad enough, for Chrissake, without that. Did I have to tell the whole world, did I have to drag us all down even further? What d'you think it would've meant to the girls, to have everyone know about her and snigger over what life was like for us all? We didn't have much left, by that time. We'd got no privacy any more. No dignity.' He took a deep breath. 'We didn't have any future as a family. I couldn't destroy their past as well.'

Father Michael looked down, unable to meet the other man's eyes. He said softly, 'I didn't realize.'

'Sarah was like . . . like a little sad ghost, without Kate,' her father went on. 'She couldn't speak, some days. So we got her this kitten. He slept on her bed, she said he kept the bad dreams away.' The pain in his voice was tangible.

'The evening the trial ended, and they said Kate was guilty, Sarah found him. Crawling on the step with his guts hanging out.' Roy Downey's hands dropped open in despair. 'I don't know which of us cried more,' he added bleakly. Father Michael thought of Sister Gideon, the way she had asked for his help. Dear God.

'I've asked myself, over and over, how did it all happen to us? What did we do wrong?' Roy Downey seemed almost to be talking to himself. 'Was there something April and me didn't notice, didn't understand about Kate? Something we just – missed.' He shifted on the narrow bench, turning his body sideways to the priest. It was, thought Father Michael, the position of the confessional. 'I never talked much to them separately, see. I never felt they needed me.' He brooded for a minute. 'I didn't really have anything to say to them, not anything that mattered. 'Course, I loved them, I played with them.

But I must of been . . .' again, he struck his thigh with a balled fist '. . . oblivious, not to see what was there inside of them.'

His voice dropped so low, Father Michael could hardly catch what he was saying. 'Maybe it was a gene I passed on to Kate. Maybe it was bred into her, like the dogs. Maybe it's me that's a wrong 'un.' He stared sombrely into space. 'Two boys, I've got now. Christ.'

The dogs brought him back, barking now in earnest. Downey seemed suddenly to hear them and glanced at his watch. 'Bugger. That the time?' He lumbered to his feet. 'I've got to feed the dogs.'

Father Michael got up. As he moved he noticed, half-hidden behind a file-box, a picture of a Welsh sheepdog in a cheap frame.

'Before you go,' he said, 'have you a photo of Kate I could see?'

Her father's face was expressionless. He went back to the table and fumbled around among the papers until he found a battered black wallet. From it he extracted a photograph in a plastic pocket which he handed to the priest.

Father Michael looked at two small girls in a double swing, long hair blowing. Identical check dresses, white shoes and socks. He couldn't make out their faces. And he understood why there would be no pictures of Sarah as an adult, or Kate at any age after she had committed her crime: these were the only daughters Roy Downey wanted.

Even so, following Downey down the steps and across the yard, he persisted, 'But she's just like Sarah, right? They're identical?'

Downey used a key attached to his belt to open the

254

enclosure door, and locked it again behind them. 'Dunno who told you that,' he said.

'I read it, in the papers.'

Downey grunted. 'They're not that simple, those two.' Outside a shed a rusty supermarket trolley contained about twenty orange dog bowls full of meat and broken biscuit. 'They look alike, but not in a spectacular way, more like all sisters.' He opened the first gate, shoving aside the enthusiastic dog which leapt up, its paws against his chest. He slammed down the food bowl, took away the empty one. 'But everything else about them seems to be identical.'

Father Michael followed him.

'So they would have been very close?'

'They were one person, almost.' Downey banged the gate. 'That's it. I can't talk about them any more, OK?' He shoved the bolt home.

'Of course.' They reached the next enclosure. Father Michael added, 'You've quite a business here.'

'Not me. This is Jan's.' Downey unbolted the gate, put another bowl on the ground. 'You honestly think I'd enough nerve left to start on my own after what happened? With everyone knowing who I was?'

At the third kennel, he petted the dog inside for a moment, his thick fingers lost in the collie's curling black and white fur. 'When you've gone bankrupt, it's bloody well impossible. No-one'll touch you. Jan took me on here after her divorce, we run it between us.'

Roy Downey put out more food, filled up a water bowl from an enormous plastic container on the trolley. A child's voice was calling, 'Dad, Daddee,' and a yellow-haired boy, three years old at most, rode a tricycle along the concrete path. It was the first time Father Michael had seen Downey smile. 'This is Sam,' he said, and pride warmed his voice.

'An' Sam's the main reason Kate's not 'ere.' Jan Burford spoke just behind them. It was a country voice, soft drawled vowels, but there was no mistaking the authority in it. Roy Downey looked silently past the priest at the woman, his face now closed and sad.

'One of us 'ad to say it,' she went on. 'An' it was never goin' to be you, was it? All them probation people yatterin' on about rehabilitation and fresh starts.'

She paused. Roy Downey opened his mouth as if to protest, then shut it again. Father Michael caught the look between them and knew this was the ground of old, lost battles.

'Let *them* do it, that's what I say,' the woman went on. Her voice was low, reasonable, almost sweet. 'Let them 'ave a murderer indoors with *their* babbies, see how they feel then.'

Chapter Twenty-six

Mother Emmanuel called a special meeting in the Community Room after Terce.

The prioress was early herself, waiting for her daughters to arrive and seat themselves on the upright chairs. These were always set ready in a large semi-circle for Recreation, when they darned their thick stockings, or embroidered, and talked: they say nobody enjoys a chat so much as a nun in a silent order.

The prioress loved this large room. Wooden shutters were folded back against the floor-length windows, and sunlight warmed the broad polished floorboards and showed up peeling patches on the creamy walls. Beyond the long garden, she could see the dinosaur spine of humped little Welsh mountains rippling to the horizon.

The nuns entered in ones and twos, making the slight obeisance to her which the Rule demanded. When they were all present, she began to speak. She told them that last night, Sister Gideon had collapsed on the stairs, and three people had carried her to the Infirmary. She was once more in great pain, and still there was no apparent cause. Dr Bevan had told her he had never come across anything like it in thirty years of general practice.

Mother Emmanuel paused and looked round at their concerned faces. She told them she had prayed for guidance over this, and then she described how Father Michael had discovered the existence of a twin sister. She waited for the collective intake of breath to run through the group. The sister's whereabouts were unknown, she said, and did not hint at the crime, the trial or the sentence: if Sister Gideon wished to speak of it, that was her affair.

The fact that the sister was a twin was a matter of grave anxiety, she went on, and explained why. They all knew Sister Gideon appeared to alternate bouts of pain with periods of apparently good health. She warned them that in some conditions, decrease of pain did not indicate an easing of the trouble: in the case of a perforated ulcer, or appendicitis, it was in fact a danger signal, and meant partial paralysis.

The prioress confirmed this might happen to one of the twins – or to both. She asked most urgently if anyone could think of anything, *anything*, which might cast a fresh light on Sister Gideon's state?

She waited, but no-one answered. She looked down at the subtle gleam of the amethyst in her ring of office.

'Then we must all pray for Sister Gideon and for Katharine. Only God knows how much time these two young women have left.'

Father Michael Falcone had not been to Bristol for twelve years: nothing had drawn him there since his mother's death. His taxi took him past buildings he remembered and façades he did not: hypermarkets and superstores, hotels and theatres, elegant restaurants and ethnic cafés, The Cello Shop, The Hat Shop, Bristol Blue Glass.

Number twenty-two Durrant Street was a dispirited townhouse with empty flower tubs and dulled paint. Six bells all bore indecipherable names. He rang the bottom one and it was finally answered by a surly shaven-headed girl of maybe eighteen with seven earrings in one ear. For a horrendous moment he wondered – then he took in her T-shirt, which said Dolly Girls Do, and proved it by mounding over a pregnant bulge.

He asked for Kate Dean and was told yes, she did live there and no, no-one knew where she was at the moment, or when she would return. He looked into the dark hallway which smelled of distant dinners, heard a lavatory flush upstairs. Would Kate be back for a meal that night? The girl thought not. Father Michael left a note anyway, and said he would return in a couple of hours. The girl shrugged and closed the door before he had turned away.

Whatever happened, he would need to spend the night here. He found a Bed and Breakfast three streets away and put his overnight bag in a trim bedroom with a pink eiderdown that reminded him of his grandmother's.

He had an appointment with Kate's probation officer in the purpose-built block near the law courts. From the first, they were not impressed with each other. Fran Duesbury shared a bright little office full of plants and case-files. She gave him a polystyrene cup of coffee from the machine and listened with preoccupied politeness. In those professional surroundings, talking to this very practical woman, his tale of pain transference in twins seemed far-fetched even to him.

Then she said, she knew about the twin, it was on Kate's records, but apparently there had been no contact between the two since her sentence began. Kate had never even referred to her sister. It was hard to believe Kate was in serious danger, she seemed very fit. And it all sounded so – she gave him a quick, sideways glance – so over the top, didn't it, honestly?

Fran Duesbury was not expecting to see Kate until her

next appointment the following Tuesday. He must see that it was up to her how she spent her time, she had to take responsibility for herself now. They did not expect to keep track of her every move. He suggested contacting the police and Ms Duesbury dismissed that out of hand: the girl had done nothing wrong, she was fulfilling all the conditions of her life licence. Reluctantly, she wrote a card for him to take round to Durrant Street. She assured him that if Kate called, she would arrange a meeting. She wrote down his telephone number, suggested he check with her tomorrow. She stood up and moved towards the door. Now, if he would excuse her, she had a great deal to do.

Kate, unaware she was the subject of so much activity and anxiety, did not return to her room in Durrant Street at all that day. Its dust-coloured walls seemed to close in on her in a way no cell had ever done. Inside it she was conscious, as she had been more and more lately, of the mysterious vibrations sent out by her twin. She struggled to block them but they were always there beneath normal sounds, of water running into the bath, of music, or voices on a radio programme. Frightening, warning of unimagined danger: 'Screel din. *Screel din.*'

So it was better to stay away. She ate her evening meal in the Thai restaurant she'd discovered on her second day in Bristol, when the proprietor had smiled and bowed as she passed. She had Thai fish cakes with peanut sauce and cucumber, and drank water. Mr Lum could not have been more charming if she had been a party of four eating six courses.

The city made her feel less isolated – and more alone. As it grew darker, she found herself on Black Boy Hill, where narrow streets were lit by the original little lamps.

It never crossed her mind there could be danger for her here. Danger lay within the prisons, where the criminals were. Nor did it occur to her that someone might snatch her bag. So far as she was concerned that, too, was a prison problem: the women stole from the kitchens, or each other.

So naïvety, not courage, let Kate walk without fear late on the streets. And tonight, everyone she saw seemed to be with a lover. She glanced in at an Italian restaurant, Bella Pasta, where in the window a couple were feeding each other eager mouthfuls across the candlelit table.

A little further on, a man and a woman climbed into a taxi and fell into each other's arms even before the door closed: Kate saw the woman's coat dropping from naked shoulders, the man pressing her back against the seat. Awareness of her own unnatural isolation made her so dizzy, she had to stop walking. How would she cope? How would she ever make a life for herself?

She knew nothing about existence beyond the walls and bars of her incarceration. She had been schooled in helplessness, forced into dependency on the massive institution that was the prison system. She saw with awful clarity that she had been buried alive for fourteen years. And the slow passage of those years, the erosion of her self, had turned her into the victim.

Oh, God, if only that part of our lives had never been.

Father Michael returned to Durrant Street at seven o'clock: still no sign of Kate. He asked himself, where would I go if I were her? I haven't much money, so I'll walk. He let the pattern of streets lead him. He passed twenty-four-hour laundrettes and charity shops, galleries selling papier mâché mobiles, undertakers where even the display flowers appeared embalmed.

He peered into vegetarian restaurants, Chinese take-aways, stared in beneath the bulbous fluorescent yellow and orange M of a McDonalds. He walked into a 7–11 store where he noticed a solitary girl buying yogurt and muesli. It wasn't her, and then he remembered the sign in the hall at Durrant Street: NO food in your rooms PLEASE.

He checked the time. At Our Lady of the Snow, the nuns would have finished supper. He found a telephone kiosk, put in his card and dialled Welshpool. When she answered, Mother Emmanuel's voice lifted with relief. He explained he still had not contacted Kate and she sighed. Then she said, 'Sister Gideon's no better, she's in a lot of pain. But she's quieter.'

He heard the subtext. 'Doesn't sound good.'

A long pause. 'No. We're very worried.' The telephone magnified the concern in her voice. 'She's so depressed, she seems to be losing heart in a way I don't like to see.'

'Would it help to tell her I've almost reached her sister?'

'Of course. And we're praying for that.' She added, down-to-earth as ever, 'You sound tired, Father. Have you eaten this evening?'

He couldn't remember the last time he'd done so. He walked down Black Boy Hill in the direction of Whiteladies Road until he found an Italian restaurant. Bella Pasta was packed with people younger and happier than himself, loud with talk and laughter. They found him a table squashed in near a group of students. Even his waitress, he reflected, trying not to eye the tiny black pelmet of a skirt she wore, would have been about eight years old when he was making his vows.

Behind him, a woman was exclaiming in pretended

horror at something her companion was saying. She tossed long scented hair and he felt it flick against the back of his head, his shoulder, in a parody of a caress.

He had chosen to be alone. But everyone needed to love and be loved. The Church itself admitted that the celibate life was against nature. 'A factory for madmen,' a dissenting Jesuit had called it.

He stirred, uncomfortable with his thoughts, and felt the warm body of the woman sitting behind him – and the pleasure it gave him. He pulled his chair away from hers. That was how he lived, he told himself savagely. Caution was his middle name.

There are eunuchs who have made themselves that way for the kingdom of heaven. Let anyone receive it who can.

A eunuch. A castrated man. Christ, was that what he was? He put down his coffee cup and got to his feet. He didn't see the woman rise at the same time, and the two of them collided. She put a narrow hand on his arm to steady herself.

For a single, breathless moment she reminded him of Sister Gideon: something about the way she held herself, the curve of her cheek as she turned towards him, then her stillness when she met his eyes. And in that instant before he realized she was a different woman, he realized something else.

They both laughed and apologized, he paid and left. Out on the street, walking fast in the warm evening, he finally admitted for the first time just why this business with Kate Downey had become so important to him.

He rang the bell at Durrant Street one more time, but no-one answered. He walked the pavement outside the house until just before midnight. Then exhaustion sent him back to the frilly bedroom in Mrs Williams' B and B.

She woke him in the morning, tapping on his bedroom door to summon him to the telephone. Still not awake, he stood in the booth downstairs in his pyjamas. The smell of toast came from the dining room, already overlaid with lemon air freshener.

'. . . spoke to her ten minutes ago,' Fran Duesbury was saying. 'I've arranged to meet her in the square at the centre of Broadmead at eleven. It's easy to find. We'll be sitting on a bench, OK?'

Chapter Twenty-seven

The limited space in the middle of the Broadmead shopping centre was this morning transformed into a miniature market place. Stalls sold candyfloss and vegetable burgers and handmade jewellery. In the centre a small, old-fashioned carousel played timeless fairground music. Painted horses with snorting nostrils and wide black eyes rode up and down their silver barley sugar poles, while children shrieked and clutched the reins. Nearby, sitting alone on a wooden bench, he saw her.

Somehow aware of his gaze, she glanced up from her newspaper and her round gold glasses caught and reflected the sun, so he couldn't see her eyes, or the expression in them. Not that it mattered: he would have known her anywhere. Even without the way she placed herself, as Sarah did, right at one end of the bench with a space unconsciously kept for the invisible other, he would have recognized her. It was Sister Gideon, only wearing something pale and soft. Sister Gideon, but with long hair framing her face. The same face, the same shy and secretive mouth.

And yet even in that split second, he could tell how different she was. She looked older than her twin, there was strain and anxiety in her face. But in the last few days he had thought of her constantly and of course that

265

was to be expected. This young woman may be sister to a nun, but she was one hell of a lot besides. A murderess. A lifer.

He moved nearer. Impatience had brought him here early and there was no sign of Fran Duesbury. He found himself oddly reluctant to approach Kate without her.

He saw now, she wasn't really like her twin. She didn't have the translucent fragility that touched him so. This woman was altogether sturdier, her skin tones warmer. Where Sister Gideon was all cheekbones and jawline emphasized by the stark white band of the habit, here was tousled hair tumbling wildly round her face. Her legs were long and slender and bare, her toe-nails flirtatiously and unexpectedly painted red.

When she took her glasses off, to look up at him, he recognized the intense unfocused gaze, the pale brown eyes with their curious flecks of golden light. They were Sister Gideon's eyes, so like hers he waited for her to greet him.

If the eyes were Sister Gideon's, the look in them was not. Behind this barelegged young woman stretched years of misery and confinement, miles of concrete and iron bars, dim lights in wire cages and keepers with keys on their belts. So he was not surprised to read hostility and apprehension there, to see the tension palpable in the way she held herself. *Emotion shows in all the ways a body moves.*

She slowly put down the big green glass bottle of Perrier water she was holding. Still watching him, she patted her lips with her middle finger, a funny little gesture. She had Sister Gideon's mouth, young and oddly sweet with the slightly dry lips of a child. He was close enough to see the puckered scar on her full lower lip.

He couldn't help noticing there was nothing childish

about her body. She leant forward to put the bottle on the ground and her movement made the wide neckline of her thin cotton jumper fall forward. She wasn't wearing anything underneath.

Standing above her, he saw the faint creamy drop of her breasts, the darker tips. The answering ache in his groin was sweet and sharp. He looked away, shocked and shamed by the rise of desire.

Perhaps it was anger at himself, at his own response, but he directed it at her. The sight of her sitting there was suddenly infuriating: all that worry, all that time, and here she was reading the paper and drinking mineral water in the sun, as if she hadn't a care in the world. It made it worse that she looked healthy, and strong, while back in Welshpool her twin was frail as a shadow.

Just in time, he told himself not to alienate her. He needed her co-operation, he had to make her trust him. And however long it had taken, he'd got her now. He went up to her.

'Kate,' he said. 'Thank God I've found you.'

Because she had her reading glasses on, she couldn't make out his features clearly – just very black, thick hair – but she had noticed him arrive in the square, seen his slight limp.

Fran Duesbury had mentioned that a Father Someone wanted to speak to her, and she had assumed he would be some sort of social worker. But this man didn't look like any social worker she'd ever met, and he wasn't dressed like a priest. She took off her glasses. He had stopped near her, but not close enough to be threatening. He wore denims, a jacket over a white shirt. He had a big, irregular nose and very dark brown eyes under heavy brows: a clever face, a thinking face. The only thing familiar about him was his air of authority – she knew that only too well.

She remembered only that his name was foreign and reminded her of her birds. She expected him to have a foreign accent but he didn't at all. When he finally spoke, he had a beautiful voice, deep and warm.

'Kate. Thank God I've found you.'

And there was something else there, a mixture of anger and relief she couldn't understand. When she didn't answer he went on, 'I'm Father Michael Falcone. Fran Duesbury's told you I've spent a lot of time looking for you?'

She lowered the newspaper and said without any attempt at friendliness, 'Maybe.'

'You've been very elusive.'

She shrugged. 'No. Just had things to do.'

The hostility in her voice annoyed him afresh.

'Look, I must tell you, I've come from the convent. I'm here because of Sarah.'

At the name, the old anger shivered through her, the old resentment. *Oh, God, not again.*

'I don't want to hear about . . . about anyone.'

'Your sister needs your help. Desperately.'

She said acridly, 'I'm sure someone else can help her. She's not exactly alone.'

She seemed calm. He had no way of knowing how she had struggled, over the years, to learn how to handle her anger.

'But it's you she needs. No-one else will do. She's in a most desperate state, they think she could die. That's why I've been looking for you.'

'I know she's ill.' Kate picked up her paper again, a dismissive gesture. 'I've known for a long time.'

He was taken aback.

'How the . . . how? The nuns couldn't find you, we'd no idea where you were. *She* hadn't, either. So how did you find out?'

She spoke without emotion. 'She told me it was coming. She told me months ago.'

'But I thought the two of you didn't . . .'

'Just because we don't meet or write or phone each other doesn't mean we don't communicate. She's been telling me since Christmas, and I've been trying to shut it out.' Kate shook the paper impatiently. 'We haven't seen each other for a long time, and that's how I want it. If she needs something different, tough tittie. If she's ill, I'm sorry. That's all.'

He said, working it out, 'So . . . she's the sender . . . and you're the receiver.'

She shrugged. 'If you say so.'

'But you didn't get all the message. Or you'd know Sarah's not the one who's ill.'

She frowned at him. 'But you just *said* . . .'

'I said she was in a desperate state. Sarah has the symptoms of severe illness. But she doesn't have the illness itself. *You* do.'

She had let the paper fall on her lap, and was scratching her bare arms with her nails, as if she'd been bitten.

'The doctors think the only explanation is that she's suffering your pain,' he went on. 'Enduring it either before you – or on your behalf.' Watching her face, he saw comprehension as clear as if she'd switched on a light-bulb. He waited a moment before adding, 'Your father tells me something very similar used to happen with the two of you, when you were little.'

She drew back her head, her face set. He could tell this made sense to her. But obstinacy wouldn't let her admit it.

'If I get measles,' she said with finality, and he couldn't tell if the indifference was real or assumed, 'I'll send you a postcard. Now please just go away.'

He started to protest. 'Not measles, something much more . . .'

Her words came so hard and vicious, for a moment he was unable to respond. 'Why don't you fuck off.'

She was on her feet, her movements jerky and furious. She flung the paper down on the bench behind her and caught up her shoulder-bag. Then she was running, fast, away from the bright little stalls towards the sound of traffic.

He started in pursuit but she was too quick for him. She ran straight for the turning carousel, slowing a little as it came to the end of a set, the bright organ-grinder music dragging now. She sprang up onto the moving boards as if she'd been doing it all her life and wove her way deftly through the painted horses as they rose and fell, rose and fell on their silver barley sugar poles.

Michael grabbed hold of a pole and started to step up, but a man yelled a warning and he dropped back. He'd never get through those narrow spaces anyway. Instead he ran round the carousel, losing his sense of direction for a moment because of the still turning horses.

By the time he'd reached the place Kate must have been heading for, she had already vanished. There was only one way she could have gone, towards the main part of the town and the busy roads which lay just out of sight.

He ran in that direction, the fairground music still grinding out behind him. Then it was drowned out by the deafening screech of brakes and moments later, the crash of metal on metal.

When that finally stopped, there was utter silence.

270

Even the hurdy-gurdy music from the carousel faded to
nothing. After a measureless time, the hush was broken
by the sound of a horn, the same note wailing on and on
and on.

Chapter Twenty-eight

Dr Bevan laid two careful fingers on Sister Gideon's wrist. Her skin was hot and damp, her pulse tremulous. Above the young woman's head, his eyes met those of the nun who held the office of Infirmarian. He had known her for years and they understood each other very well. The doctor blew out his lips in an expression of unspoken bewilderment.

'Well, Sister Gideon.' His voice was slow and kind. 'I'd expected you should be feeling better by now. But you're not looking as bright as I'd like.'

She opened her eyes and he noted the whites were dull and off-colour. 'I've rested like you said, Dr Bevan. And I'm trying to eat. But it still hurts.' She fumbled in her sleeve for a handkerchief. 'A lot, it still hurts a lot. And nothing helps.'

The tears, once started, were hard to check. He could see her growing visibly weaker. There was less of her in the bed today, after the long weekend.

'Let's have a look,' he said, and pulled back the sheet. Sister Mark helped her open her nightdress, arranging the folds to cover her breasts.

His hands felt very cold against her hot skin. He pressed quite hard beneath her ribs and asked, 'Feel that? That?'

She shook her head no. He pressed again. Sarah lay under the sheet Sister James had pulled up over her and kept her eyes squeezed shut out of embarrassment and shame. Even now, when she should be used to it, the sensation of being touched so intimately, after so many years, was an intrusion to which she couldn't accustom herself. Dr Bevan was middle-aged and kind, but he was still a man.

'Sister, I know this is difficult for you.' He sounded tired. 'Take a couple of deep breaths and relax, let your muscles go. If you're so tense, you see, it's much more difficult . . .'

She licked her dry lips and breathed deeply through her nose.

'That's *much* better,' Dr Bevan said more cheerfully. 'Just another minute and we're done.'

He pulled the sheet back over her and went off to wash his hands at the sink while Sister Mark helped her do up the endless buttons of the convent nightdress. He came back drying his hands on a paper towel.

'It really doesn't look physical to me,' he said to both of them. Then he added, 'Let me have a quiet word just with Sister Gideon, would you?'

The Infirmarian nodded her agreement and he pulled up a chair. 'Look, it's hard to talk when there's always someone listening. Tell me now while it's just the two of us. Are you happy here?'

She just stared at him, without speaking.

'Because', he went on, 'if I thought you weren't settled, contented with your life, then that would be a very reasonable explanation of all this. We could be pretty damn sure it's your mind that's creating the problems. You know about psychosomatic illness, do you?'

'I understand the general idea: it's a physical manifestation of an emotional state.'

He laughed. 'Couldn't have put it better myself. I've been treating you all in this convent for a long time. And I know how many nuns and sisters are leaving their orders these days. I'm sure a lot of them are ill before they admit their difficulties. Could that be what we're seeing with you? I want you to really think, really ask yourself, is your illness a cry for a different life? Better tell me now, then we can sort things out.'

She clasped her hands tightly under the sheet and tried to make her voice strong.

'I love my life,' she said. 'I love it. I'd rather be out on the mission, and Mother's promised I can go back when I'm better. But as long as I'm with my real family, it doesn't honestly matter where I am.'

Her cheeks were pink with the effort of convincing him, and she turned her head on the pillow to see him better.

'This life is all I want. All I ever wanted. I gave everything to God when I entered.' She paused. When Sarah remembered herself in those first years, it was like watching a minuscule figure through the wrong end of a telescope. With almost no emotion she could observe the desperate, lonely, terrified child who in the space of a few short weeks lost everyone and everything she had ever known and loved. 'I've been given such peace and happiness in return,' she went on. 'More than I thought I'd find in my whole life.' Her eyes glowed with feeling, transcending the clichés.

'So it's a yes vote, is it?' Dr Bevan was smiling at her, rather sadly. She thought, it would have been easier for him, if there was an explanation like that.

'Very much so.'

'Well then.' He paused, then said carefully, 'I think we have to talk about someone who used to be very important to you.'

She put out a hand, palm towards him, fingers spread. It was a gesture he had seen her use before, a movement of denial. This time, he disregarded it: she knew what was coming. 'We have to talk about your sister. About Kate.' She looked up at him and those amazing golden eyes – they were actually the colour of good whisky – were full of hurt. But it was all for her own good, sometimes you had to be cruel to be kind, so he pressed on. 'We all think your illness is probably bound up with her, though we've no idea how. We'd like to get the two of you together again, maybe we could try and put things right.' His voice was coaxing. 'Wouldn't you like to see her?'

She swallowed painfully. 'She doesn't want to see *me*.'

'How d'you know that? You haven't even written to each other in years.'

'I just do.' She wasn't being obstinate, he thought. Resigned, that was the word.

'You must have been very close, when you were little.'

She stirred, trying to make herself more comfortable. 'That was then. Now is different.'

He persisted. 'But if we could persuade her, would you talk to her?'

She closed her eyes, seemingly exhausted. 'Yes,' she whispered. 'If you want.'

When Sister Mark came back, Dr Bevan went over to her. 'I'll keep in touch with Mother Emmanuel. Things seem to be coming together one way or another.' He lifted his eyebrows and the Infirmarian gave a faint nod. The physician picked up his bag and walked back to the bed. 'Maybe we can arrange something soon, eh?'

Beneath the narrow ebony crucifix, his patient lay still and quiet. The long cream curtain billowing behind her, and that convent bonnet thing she wore, made her look like the wife of a knight on a marble tomb. He made a quick, exasperated sound. You old fool, he said to himself, she's not dead yet and won't be, if I've anything to do with it.

'Goodnight to you, Sister. Try and sleep. I'll look in tomorrow.'

Her face shone pale under the absurd nightcap. The smile she gave him was all in her eyes. 'Is it night, then?' she asked. 'It feels so early.'

He glanced at his watch. 'Just gone ten o'clock. I was on my way back from a call to one of the farms where there's a new baby. They never arrive during working hours, do they, Sister?' He added this over his shoulder to the Infirmarian.

'I wouldn't know, Doctor,' she said, demurely. It was an old joke between them.

Sister Gideon looked up at him and said seriously, 'Ten's good. Better than I imagined.' Then she added, to herself, 'A new baby.'

He thought it was longing he heard in her voice.

Chapter Twenty-nine

She was back in Holloway. It wasn't a nightmare. It was real. Jesus. She knew because she could hear the familiar sound of an ambulance wailing along Parkhurst Road. She tried to protest, tell them no, make them listen. But the noise got worse, splitting her in two, why did it hurt so much? The ambulance coming nearer every second, blue light flashing frantic behind her eyes . . .

Fingers were holding her head, pulling back her eyelids, *don't*, shining a torch into them, someone wearing a dark uniform cap, who said, 'That's better. Thought we'd lost you for a minute there.'

Faces hanging over her, upside down, peering. What was she doing down here? She struggled wildly to get up but hands pressed her back. Then a voice she knew, deep and reassuring, the priest: 'It's all right, Kate, you're all right. You're safe n . . .'

They spoke in low voices, looking at the green and black X-ray clipped onto the illuminated screen. Even so, some of the words – *acute, perforated, peritonitis* – floated across to Kate where she lay under a blanket on the extremely hard and narrow examination couch.

She kept very still, fearing even to breathe. In just minutes, she had learned that to move was to invite torture, unleash a torrent of raw acid to tear and rip its way through the core of her body.

There had been other words, said as the doctor laid his hands on her abdomen, swollen taut and rigid. Ugly words. *Inflammation* and *haemorrhage*. He had spoken them to try to explain what was happening to her. Only she was beyond listening. She could only hear the furious grating hurt the touch of his hands had brought, the harsh rasp of his cool fingertips on her fiery skin.

'We've caught you just in time,' he had said. 'How long have you been like this? Why didn't you see a doctor?'

She tried to answer, she formed the words. But what came was not her voice. It was not any sound familiar, but as if the scalding, burning pain tearing her apart had burst out from between dry lips.

They asked Father Michael, and he explained. She didn't hear what he said, for she was utterly absorbed by the agony pressing in on her, sucking out her breath, making the blood thud in her ears.

Still, she heard those other words, that other voice, screaming now with fright and fear, warning her, trying to save her.

Screel din!

Sister Mark longed for her bed. It was almost midnight in the Infirmary, and felt much later. She had an extra heater in the room to keep her patient warm, and it was making her sleepy. She yawned and stretched and blinked at the lamp. If Sister Gideon continued to be so restless, she would give her more morphine.

Sister Gideon twists and turns. Drugged against the pain, neither awake nor asleep, she is in a gleaming place she has never seen before. She looks down on a long table draped in green cloths. Someone lies there, gowned in white, hair hidden, face covered. Frightening odours of antiseptic and ether clog the air. On a glowing monitor an irregular blue line blips softly with the rhythm of a hidden heart.

Other figures stand around the table. Gowned and masked, hands of pale rubber, heads bent. They are intent on the supine figure pinned down by the glare of the great operating lamp. Somewhere, music plays. Chopin, a nocturne. The watchers speak quietly to each other.

One of the gowned figures gives an order. The others move. It is a ritual. Then she understands. He is the priest, the figure laid before him is the sacrifice. Body and Blood.

The knife – or is it a scalpel? – lies in its place on a sterile table. It is narrow and sharp and dangerous. Without looking, knowing exactly where it will be, he reaches out and takes it in his gloved hand.

And then the red.

Sister Mark turned her head towards the window. She always left the curtains parted a little, ready for the breathless moment when dawn would streak the sky above the queer little Welsh mountains she loved, and the long night would be over.

Beside her, Sister Gideon gave a great, sobbing gasp. Her body jerked, straightened.

Sister Mark put a hand to her forehead. 'There,' she whispered. 'There.' She felt Sister Gideon relax under her fingers, the tension going out of her as if the pain was dropping away. Quite soon, she was asleep.

The small private room had a glass observation panel in the door. He had glanced through it before he remembered the rooms in which Kate, watched by day and by night, had passed what was left of her childhood.

Now she lay on her side, turned away from him, only the bright tousled hair showing. Under the thick hospital sheet, the cellular blanket, she was curled and quiet.

He saw the curve of her hip, the long sweep of her thigh. In that second, three women blurred and melded in his mind. The saint in stone. The nun given to God. And the child-woman who had murdered another child, and paid for it with the loss of her own youth.

Standing in front of her door, he tried to sort out the emotions Kate aroused in him. Fascination was there. An intense excitement which horrified him even as he acknowledged that it was desire. And pity. A lethal mix. My God, he thought, my God.

If the doctor had not arrived at that moment, recognizing him, wanting to speak to him, opening the door, he would have walked away.

'They won't keep another day,' he protested, trying to amuse her. 'And everyone deserves grapes when they're ill.'

She just looked at him.

He took another grape from the fruit bowl on her bedside cabinet. Her eyes followed his hands, but still she said nothing. She was colourless, mute, a pale reflection of the amber-eyed girl he'd found on the bench by the carousel. He felt guilty, as if his intrusion had brought all this about. Not so, of course: the doctors had told him, she would have been dead in a few hours without medical intervention.

'Don't worry, I'll bring some more in tomorrow.'

She rolled her head on the pillow. 'Don't. I want to get out of here.'

He thought, how she must hate institutions, regulations. Then he hardened his heart. She must be used to them by now.

He said, 'You'll have time to eat them. You won't be going anywhere for at least ten more days. And you really can't go back to Durrant Street, not for a while.' He leaned forward. 'I've talked to Mother Emmanuel. She very much wants you to go to the convent for a month or so. As long as it takes, until you're really well again.'

Fear stiffened her features as suddenly as if he'd slapped her. She stared at him with troubled gold-brown eyes. He hadn't noticed before that her hair was the same colour.

'I'll drive you up,' he offered. 'One weekend. I'd like to see you with your sister.'

She turned her head and stared silently out of the window. He could hardly recognize the fiercely hostile young woman who had leapt on to the carousel. In the oversized white hospital nightdress she was pale, defenceless. And he was aware of the child she had been, the child Roy Downey had described to him in the dingy caravan, failed by the people she loved.

'Let me arrange it,' he urged. 'It'd be good for you and for Sarah. Your father told me how close the two of you were.'

The hospital room was overheated, but Kate gave a quick little shiver. 'Can't you see?' she said, despair flattening her voice. 'Don't you understand *anything*? If you force us together, I don't know what would happen.'

Finally, Fran Duesbury suggested Kate should go to a convalescent home and Father Michael arranged it. Kate did not ask, and he did not volunteer the fact that it was church-owned. He returned to London, and twice a week spoke to the social worker, who told him Kate's

281

companions were mainly elderly ladies, and that she spent much of her time sleeping.

He sent her postcards, once he had flowers delivered. But mostly he stayed in the attic flat, trying to work. The weather was growing warmer, and the plants on the roof terrace needed watering in the evenings. He would lean his elbows on the stone parapet while the city below him flashed its lights, beckoned and invited him. He found it increasingly difficult to keep his mind on his book and his pilgrims, trekking their way hopefully across Europe. Then, after almost three weeks, Kate telephoned him herself.

'I'm going mad here,' she said. 'I've got to leave. I'm going back to Durrant Street.' Father Michael picked up the postcard he'd received from Zoe Schon.

'Don't go back there yet,' he said. 'I've been invited to spend the Bank holiday in the country with some friends. Will you come with me?'

He hired a car, drove to Bristol to collect Kate, and took her on to Suffolk. He remembered May days like it from childhood, stretching warm and endlessly promising. Winding roads edged with white cow parsley divided flat fields the colour of brilliant mustard. Through the village of colour-washed cottages, past the Post Office Restaurant with the Michelin badge, and there were the gateposts of the Old Rectory.

Daze of summer in a quiet garden: sunlight and open windows and tubs of orange and yellow nasturtiums. A black and white sheepdog panting in the shade barked without much conviction at their approach and the figure in a frayed cricketing pullover and baggy cream chinos waved.

Father Michael had forgotten the cordial warmth of

Victor Schon's welcome, the broad smile as he took Kate's hand between his own and said, 'We're so glad you're here.' He left them on the terrace under a sun-umbrella and disappeared into the shuttered house.

Kate, white and strained from the heat and her first excursion since leaving hospital, seated herself quietly on a long swingchair, looking across the garden to where a sandpit was littered with buckets and spades. Beside it bright blue water glittered in a plastic paddling pool shaped like a giant turtle.

She turned her head and lifted her chin to the sun in what Michael now recognized as a characteristic gesture, closing her eyes in pleasure as it warmed her skin. He thought she was like a cat, sensual and quiet.

The professor returned with a bottle in a bucket of ice. 'Zoe discovered a couple of elder trees and found an ancient recipe and now we're addicted to the stuff: nectar of the gods.' He finished pouring and handed a glass to Kate. Handing another to Father Michael, he exchanged a glance with him, eyebrows raised: she was curled up in the right-hand corner of the six-foot-long seat.

The two men chatted for ten minutes, they all drank some more cordial. Kate, who'd scarcely spoken, got up and wandered down the daisied lawn. She walked slowly, on bare feet, seemingly not conscious of their gaze. The late afternoon sun was behind her. It turned the soft fabric of her dress into a misty blur, showed the shape of her body, the high breasts and narrow waist.

Victor Schon did not miss the way Michael's eyes followed her. He smiled to himself. 'Hard to imagine her in Holloway,' he said.

She was asleep on the grass in the shade when the family came home an hour later. A yellow Renault with a large cartoon duck on the bonnet came down the drive and stopped in a spray of gravel. The sheepdog, suddenly full of energy, rushed round it in protective circles. Zoe, heavily pregnant now in a flowing smock, unlocked the doors and undid seat-belts. The children tumbled out and raced across the grass to hurl themselves on their father. He disappeared beneath the bundle of bodies with ferocious growls which they greeted with shrieks.

Father Michael got to his feet and went towards Zoe. She took his outstretched hand and kissed his cheek warmly. Because of her condition, because she was surrounded by another man's children, she posed no threat of any kind: that must be why he could enjoy the small encounter, kiss her back and tell her, 'You look wonderful.'

She beamed at him, glossy with health. 'Nothing to do with me,' she said. 'It's all those blasted hormones. Everything shines. It's nature's way of getting you ready for the ghastly twelve months to come.' Still talking, she picked the youngest child out of its padded seat. 'Exhaustion,' she said to him, with mock annoyance, 'getting up five times a night. Never having time to eat a decent meal all in one go.' She kissed him soundly. 'Much you care.'

Visited by a new anxiety Michael said quietly, 'Zoe. One thing. It honestly never occurred to me till now. You know what Kate did? Why she was in prison?' Zoe nodded. 'Well, I hadn't thought, but all these children – should I have brought her here?'

Zoe, Hugh in her arms, said, 'Of course. She'd not be released if they weren't certain of her, of her self-control.' She set Hugh down on the grass and the small boy staggered a few feet and sat down suddenly, chubby legs buckling beneath his own weight. He was dressed in denim dungarees sewn all over with flowered patches. A white sunhat protected his head and he'd pulled it at a rakish sideways angle. He was laughing and his cheeks were round and golden. His eyes were triangular and the same deep blue as his T-shirt.

Michael smiled at him. Hugh must be what – eighteen months. Two on his next birthday. Just as he thought that Kate, woken by the noise, sat up. She was only yards away, near enough for him to see the look on her face. He knew she'd noticed Hugh – the rigidity of her pose as she supported her weight on her flexed arms told him so. Her expression was absolutely blank, her eyes wide and wild.

Then she was on her feet and hurrying away, down the garden. He thought, she'd have been running if she had been capable of it. Even so, she moved with astonishing speed towards the gate at the bottom of the garden, the dense tangle of trees and bushes.

Kate woke, as she had so many times, on a flood of old fear. Just like before, just the same. She was being dragged back, dragged down, and nothing had changed, after all.

She recognized the nightmare by the children's voices, just as she always did, when the little boy's family chased after them through the garden and there was no way out. And then the voices were all round her, insistent and shrill, and it was real, all these children. All these people. She struggled, fighting up through the fog of despair, to get away from them all, to be alone again. She tried to run, somewhere, anywhere.

After the blinding sunshine it was mysterious in here, damp and cool. Long shafts of light broke through in places, clouds of transparent insects wheeling within

285

them. Kate followed the almost invisible path between the trees, not caring that the bushes caught and snagged her thin dress, wanting only to be away from them all.

Then the ground sloped steeply. Below her lay a hidden pond, so deeply green it gleamed black. Trees crowded round, leaves trailing low. It could have been a painting, the water so still and glassy in the heat, it was impossible to tell which were the reflections.

Just looking at it soothed her, quieted the shrill jangle in her head. She went to the water's edge, crouched down and cupped her hands. It smelled fresh. She held them to her face, her throat, the back of her neck. Gradually, her breathing slowed.

She could hear only bird calls until, high overhead, a light aeroplane buzzed silver across the pale sky before it was hidden by the leaves. A huge dragonfly, iridescent turquoise, hovered on helicopter wings beside her. Something small scurried about its business in the bushes, oblivious of her presence.

With delicate fingers, she unbuttoned the front of her dress of Indian cotton, and probed the scar that ran thin and long and livid still, across her abdomen. It was sore when she pressed there, so she knew it, at least, had been real.

It was all over then, all done with. The warning had been sent, and she had received it. The danger was past. Only if it was over, she didn't understand why the trees seemed to be closing in on her, why the surface of the pond was feathered by a furtive wind.

No more. She couldn't endure any more. But even as she rebuttoned her dress with trembling fingers, and stood up, realization gathered. How could she have been such a fool, not to see? It wasn't over. The threat had never gone away. It had changed its nature, that was all, it was different – and this time it terrified her more than any illness. This time, the danger was of discovery.

And then she did, she did understand: the warning was about the priest. Already Father Michael had uncovered so much that had been hidden. He could learn everything. If he did, the secret she and Sarah had mutely kept for half a lifetime would be exposed. And what would happen then?

Oh God, if only that part of our lives had never been.

She couldn't obliterate the memories. They were worse now she was back in the world, they darkened even this green and quiet place. She clapped her hands over her ears and squeezed closed her eyes and screamed aloud in a vain effort to shut out the images she never, ever wanted to see in her life again.

As he pushed open the gate, Father Michael thought he heard the screech of some large bird. He made his way cautiously over exposed roots and clumps of nettles. It was chilly and damp here after the sunbaked garden, and he was worried.

He began to hurry, following a path he could scarcely make out, heavy undergrowth scratching his arms. Perhaps it hadn't been a bird, after all, perhaps Kate had fallen. He called her name, but there was no reply. It was two minutes more before he reached the green glade and the hidden pond, and his heart lurched.

She stood far out in the dark water. For a terrible moment he assumed she was bent on self-destruction, like her mother before her. She was wading in to drown herself. Her back was towards him and her neck, under the bundled-up hair, was slender and vulnerable. She must have heard him, because she turned then, moving carefully, as if the pond bed was slippery.

His first emotion was relief, for she held her skirt in both hands, bunched up in front to keep it dry. She was in way beyond her knees, her thighs were white and wavery beneath the bottle-glass-green of the water. He couldn't help himself, his eyes went down to the exposed V of pale underwear at her crotch, as erotic to him just then as if she had been naked: his genitals stirred at the sight, he felt himself grow and stiffen, and the breath caught ragged in his throat.

There are decent parts of a woman's body, less decent, and indecent.

He should feel shame. He did not. His gaze travelled to her face and she met it steadily. She was not provocative, or teasing. She appeared neither shy nor angry – she showed none of the emotions he would have expected. She was unsmiling, solemn, as if he'd disturbed her deep in thought.

He was puzzled at first. And then he was able to interpret her look. She did not mind, because she saw only the priest watching her. She did not see the man.

A single bird called, piercing and sweet, and again. The third cry came from somewhere else as it fluttered above them. It was almost a shock, after the sun-baked silence of the garden where – until the children arrived – the loudest noise had been the strumming of bees at work.

She raised her head to follow the sound. When she looked back, her eyes were glistening with tears. 'God,' she said softly, and her voice trembled. 'I'm such a bloody fool. I thought about it all for so long. When you're inside, everything out here becomes a fantasy. I imagined I could do anything, I had such plans. I was going to get out and achieve all the things I haven't been able to do, I was going to make it all happen straight away and it was going to be so wonderful.' In a childish gesture, she lifted one shoulder,

288

wiped her cheek on the sleeve of her dress. 'But it's not. I don't even know where to start. I just brought the fantasy world out with me, didn't I? And now it's all falling to pieces. I just can't handle it.'

He knew what she meant. Freedom, the thing you never noticed until you lost it. He wanted to say, don't be silly. It'll be all right. But this woman needed more than platitudes.

He took the few steps to the edge of the pond. She cried in a curious way, the tears forming and falling without any contraction of her face. He saw the lights and movement of reflected water in her golden eyes, the gleam of her lashes. He saw, God help him, the sweet shadowing at the top of her thighs.

She was too complex for him to understand. She had endured experiences he could not even imagine. Words, always his tools, his weapons and his defence, deserted him. And what was there, for him, but words?

'Come on,' he said, and it was all he could think of to offer. 'Get out. You'll catch a terrible cold.'

Chapter Thirty

Sister Mark had already opened the curtains on the far side of the room. The creamy cotton billowed and twisted either side of the opened window and the sky she glimpsed between was dazzling and pure. It was the colour of the old-fashioned blue bags the nuns used to whiten the sheets. It was the colour of heaven.

It was Tuesday, she remembered now. Washing day. 'I'm feeling much better,' she told Sister Mark. She said it before she was certain, but it seemed to be true.

'Would you like a bath, then?'

The bathroom wasn't warm, it was too high, and the floor was linoleum, cracked by so much washing, so much water. She took down the cardboard box in the cupboard where they kept the long slabs of harsh green soap. She hacked off a piece with the knife kept for the purpose. Standing on the square of matting, she unbuttoned the front of her thick nightdress and pulled it off, dropping it over the old-fashioned wooden clothes horse. She was accustomed to cold water in an enamel bowl in her cell, and a hot bath should have been a pleasure. But she had filled it only a third of the way up, and even climbing into that made her hold her breath with anxiety: ever since she could remember, she'd been terrified of water. Ridiculous, but just one of those things.

When she was little, so many things had frightened her, no-one had bothered much about one more. And as long as she hadn't been alone, she could face her fears. She thought of two little girls sharing their bath, sitting back to back on the same chair afterwards to read to each other . . . No. No more.

She slid her hands down her thighs and felt her bones sharp just beneath the skin. Even for her, she was far too thin. She made herself slip lower in the water to keep warm.

The bath in here was old-fashioned enamel, wide and deep with splayed claw legs. The house possessed two spartan bathrooms for everyone except Reverend Mother to use: she had her own, one of the privileges of her rank. The rest of them took turns once a week according to the list pinned to the board outside. Those baths both had old wooden lids, with a hole cut for the head, which you pulled down once you were in the water, so you couldn't see your own body. They were ridiculous but no-one seemed to mind, or even to notice. Only the novices were horrified at first. One girl, who had left before her postulancy ended, declared they were the most absurd anachronism she had ever come across in religious life. But the lids had been in place eighty years and more, ever since the order came to this house, and this gave them a virtue beyond their function.

Sister Gideon started to wash her cropped hair with the harsh soap, and as always it didn't lather properly. It would leave her hair feeling dry and coarse and, if she could have seen it, it probably looked awful. She didn't know, for there were no mirrors in the convent. And of course, it didn't matter what her hair looked like, it would be covered anyway.

It was hard, though, not to care at all how you looked.

291

Most of the nuns kept the lid of a vaseline tin, which they polished until they could use it as a mirror, to check they were tidy. But it only showed a tiny portion of your face: it hardly counted as vanity.

Before she went out to Guatemala, she had often helped make the convent's special soaps with oils from garden flowers. These were carefully wrapped by hand in waxed paper and tied in ribbon. They sold well to Clover Connection in Welshpool, along with the knitting wools the convent produced. They supplemented the convent's meagre income, and the nuns never used these for themselves: it would have been uneconomic. Besides, bathing was not a luxury but a necessity. On this blue and billowy day, the soap was not even a tiny penance.

She rubbed her hair thoughtfully, then lay back in the water to rinse it clear. Washing day.

She got dressed slowly. Fresh vest that reached well down, pants that went almost to her knees. A long, heavy petticoat cut without fastenings in the medieval way. Thick tweed underskirt with its five-inch hem and capacious pocket. Her robe and then the sleeveless scapular, slipping over her head, reaching the ground back and front. She put on the serre tete, the white linen cap, pulled tightly round her head with a drawstring at the back, secured under her chin. A fresh white linen band low over her forehead. She picked up her veil. To hold this on, the nuns kept berries from the garden in tins until they hardened, then strung them on to cords. Fastening these, Sister Gideon reflected that they were the medieval equivalent to safety pins.

By the time she had finished, and wiped down the bath, Sister Rosalie brought up her breakfast on a tray: a white napkin, a single marigold in a tiny bottle, a covered bowl

292

of cornflakes, a piece of homemade wholemeal bread, honey, a mug of sweetened tea.

It was the first meal she had eaten with appetite for days. She sat opposite the open window, watching Sister Dominic raking the gravel and carefully pulling up dandelions. Sister Dominic abhorred waste, and tonight the washed leaves would be served in a salad with chopped spring onions. If she could even think about food, she must be getting better.

She sat in the window for a while, with a book on her knee. C.S. Lewis, *The Screwtape Letters*, from the convent library. But she was too restless to concentrate.

She waited until ten o'clock, when Sister Mark came back from chapel and her reading. Sister Gideon said, 'I'd like to go down to the laundry, just for half an hour.'

Sister Mark's eyebrows went up questioningly and she held up one finger. Sister Gideon nodded. Yes, she would be all right on her own. Sister Mark signed yes, tapped her watch to signify, no longer. If you were a patient, you could speak, but the rules of silence must not be broken unnecessarily, even in the Infirmary.

Silence of the lips. And of the heart. The daily search for God.

The nuns used the laundry which had always been part of the old house. It stood away from the main buildings, near the stables where the horses and carriages were once housed, beside the old dairy which was now the guest room. Normally, they used the twin-tub washing machine which had been gifted to them many years before. It was a cumbersome contraption; dripping clothes had to be lifted by hand from one tub and placed in the other to spin. Some months ago it had shuddered to a stop and all the efforts of Sister Peter had been in vain. As a last resort, Mother Emmanuel had telephoned the local electrical shop.

'I'm afraid we charge forty-five pounds for a call-out fee,' Mr Sutton had said. And added, hearing Mother Emmanuel's stunned silence, 'And to be honest with you, Mother Emmanuel, a twenty-five-year-old washing machine isn't even worth a prayer.'

Now the convent was saving hard for a new machine. They had held a special meeting to discuss the problem, for every spare penny was already spoken for. The previous year they had started giving up milk on Fridays, and sending the money they saved to a children's charity. However, the money that came from the sale of their eggs (constantly checked for salmonella and what a performance *that* was) had already been donated to the washing fund. Several of the oldest nuns were busy making and painting polystyrene models of cells which they put in the outer hall for visitors, hopefully, to buy.

In the meantime, they were using the old equipment which had been in the house when they arrived. They were doing, as old Sister Godric would have said, exactly what the Little Flower of the Carmelites, the little Thérèse, had done all her short life.

As Sister Gideon walked along the covered way that ran round the courtyard, she could see the steam already rising from the low stone outhouse. The door was open to let in the air. Inside, there were four deep pottery troughs, each with a ridged scrubbing board in the middle. Here, the heavy convent sheets and pillowcases, the white veils and the thick underpetticoats, the drawers and shifts and vests, were all soaked overnight. First thing that morning, even before prime at six a.m., the old-fashioned copper had been lit by Sister Rosalie. By eight a.m. the water would have been hot enough for work to begin. It would take much of the day.

Sister Gideon stopped in the doorway. On the other side of the broad stone sill, the flagged floor was already awash with soapy water. Amongst the steam and the clothes, the nuns moved in high wooden clogs to keep them out of the water, skirt hems caught up in their broad leather belts.

Enveloped in enormous plastic aprons, the women were working four to a trough, slapping clothes and sheets against the scrubbing boards, the water opaque with green Fairy soap. When she saw Sister Gideon looking in, Sister Rosalie waved the wooden paddle she was using to stir the sheets. Young Sister David looked up and beamed and nodded through the steam.

Sister Gideon stood watching for a moment. She was worried about the water, she never remembered it being so deep. She checked quickly in case it had risen to the height of the grating through which the steam escaped.

Beside the centre one, there was a loose brick. She'd found it one day soon after her arrival here in January. Over maybe two months, whenever she'd been well enough, whenever she could slip away, she'd hollowed out a space behind it, just big enough to take the one thing that had to be kept secret. Silly of her: no-one ever entered another's cell. But she had to be sure.

She perched on the low stone wall. The courtyard was sheltered from the wind blowing over the wild little Welsh mountains. She relaxed in the sun and held her pale face up to its warmth. She turned her head and lifted her chin. It was a characteristic movement, unself-conscious and sensual.

She could feel her skin warming up, her muscles relaxing. Sitting out here, watching her sisters work, she felt enclosed by their presence, their affection, their concern for her. This was her family. This was where she belonged.

Sister Antonia was putting the clothes through the mangle near the door, holding the wet mass of material, feeding it into the voracious rollers. Sister John was working the green-painted metal handle. The clothes went through puffy and full of air, emerging the other side of the two great rollers stretched flat for Sister Antonia to catch them again. Sister John's round face was ruddy, her hands red and wrinkled from the water. Her glasses kept steaming up and in the end she had to take them off and drop them in the pocket beneath her scapular.

A handbell sounded. Sister Peter, who was in charge, moved beside one of the troughs. Eleven a.m., time for the midday prayer. Yet the work had to be completed, so they would not leave the laundry.

Everyone stopped what they were doing, let the clothes drop back in the water. They stood absolutely still, very simply. Their eyes were closed, their soapy hands hung empty at their sides.

'Lord we offer our work this morning in union with your divine intent . . .'

'. . . For your glory and the sorrows of the world,' finished the nuns.

Beside her wall, Sister Gideon prayed with them. Everything they did here was used for the world. Work was an expiation of sin and this included every act, every deed, every task. Even the washing. Especially the washing.

When work began again, after a moment's silent prayer, Sister Antonia started bringing out the huge sheets to pin up on the clothes line. She had on the apron sewn like a deep pocket and filled with the wooden clothes pegs they bought from the gypsies twice a year.

Sister Gideon lowered the wooden pole that held the line high and helped fling the heavy sheets over the line. Buoyant as sails in the wind, white as the clouds, they had a life of their own. One wrapped itself around her and, caught up in its warm damp folds, smelling the fresh soap, she almost laughed aloud.

Sister Antonia, eerily tall on her high wooden clogs, tapped her on the shoulder and frowned, and shook her head: that's enough, you mustn't do too much. Obediently – she was feeling tired now, after all – Sister Gideon went back to sit on her wall in the sun.

Inside the laundry, they were washing the underwear now. Fresh water from the copper was poured into the troughs. The clothes were rubbed and pounded up and down the scrubbing boards in the steaming water.

As she watched, bubbles of Fairy soap, lifted on clouds of steam, floated out of the door of the laundry and drifted towards her. Round and perfect in the sun, quivering rainbow colours. Against the clean washed blue of the sky they rose, shimmering like souls.

Chapter Thirty-one

'Kate – champagne?'

Victor Schon held the bottle wrapped in a tea-towel, a shallow glass in the other hand. Kate took it obediently.

'What are we celebrating?' Father Michael asked.

'There's a choice. First we'll drink to Kate's recovery . . .'

'And then . . .' Zoe went on for him, 'we'll toast my new job. I've just heard I've got an enormous research grant . . .'

'Not enormous,' Victor interrupted. 'Comfortable.'

'. . . and,' she continued, ignoring him, 'next year, when the baby'll be a respectable size, I'm taking everyone to Vancouver for a year. Victor's doing some lectures, but the rest of the time he'll go around showing off the children to numerous relatives while I work.'

'So I'll be mother.' Standing behind his wife, holding the champagne bottle, Victor made as if to pour it over her. 'Marriage,' he said in sing-song sanctimonious tones, as if he were reciting a prayer, 'has many pains.'

'But celibacy,' Father Michael finished for him, 'has no pleasures.' Both men roared with laughter. Zoe rolled her eyes at Kate and held up her glass.

'To Kate – and her future!'

She did not tell them she'd never tasted it before. She

298

drank and smiled and thanked them all, and raised her glass. She felt the lift of true happiness – until she sipped. Three weeks before, she had anticipated Dad opening a bottle of champagne to welcome her home. The sweet dry foaming wine was suddenly tart on her tongue, bitter as the recollection.

It was dark before they sat down to dinner at the long pine table. The jumble of geraniums, newspapers and children's tea-sets was swept to the far end. Candles burned in elegant, tarnished silver holders, and Zoe served a fragrant casserole from a curved yellow marmite pot.

'Delicious,' said Michael. 'Did you make it, or did Victor?'

Zoe giggled. 'Me. I told you, Victor just does the showy stuff. Not your actual *meals*.'

'Certainly I do,' said Schon, passing the long stick of bread over to Kate. 'If you want crêpes suzette, bananas flambé, I'm your man.' He looked at her appreciatively: old enough to be avuncular, attracted enough to flirt a little.

Kate gave him a warm smile, but didn't answer. After Michael walked her back from the pond, Zoe had taken her up to her room. She had drawn the curtains and fallen like a child into sleep. Now she accepted another glass of wine – the glasses, she noticed, were beautiful, obviously old, but none of them matched – and let herself float on the talk and laughter.

No-one seemed to notice her surreptitious glances to see which knife to use next. No-one could tell this was the first time she had ever attended a dinner party, and listened to Haydn ('No, Scarlatti,' Michael whispered when she asked), with people who made jokes about politicians and argued easily, without acrimony or anger. And didn't,

299

she added to herself, wait for you afterwards outside the bathrooms to tear out a handful of hair if they disliked your attitude or the way you talked.

'So what *does* Kate think?' Victor Schon was watching her with amusement.

'Sorry, I was miles away.'

'We were talking about Vancouver and saying individuals do assume different roles, within a partnership.' Victor spoke more as if he was musing aloud than holding a conversation. 'Maybe not so overtly as our Vancouver year. A wife may seem to be totally involved with domestic things, but really she's exerting an awful lot of pressure on the husband.'

Kate found she was drawn in despite herself. 'You're talking about power?'

'And how it operates in a partnership.' He poured more wine into her glass, though she noticed he refilled his own with mineral water.

'I don't know anything about marriage,' she said stiffly.

'But you do know about twins.' His voice was very quiet. 'And that's the most fascinating partnership of them all. Isn't that so?'

When she remained obstinately mute, he added, 'Has Michael told you about my work? That I'm particularly interested in twins?' She gave a brief nod, shifting her weight very slightly in her chair, away from him. He noted her reaction, and went on, 'There can be a sort of pseudo marriage, you know, between them. A kind of exclusivity. It can make forming other relationships very difficult, later on.'

She rubbed her fingers along the stem of her wineglass. Behind her, she could actually feel Father Michael's silence. It was a long time before she answered.

'Not exclusivity,' she said reluctantly, 'more like a conspiracy.'

'Your relationship felt like that?'

'Always.' She hesitated again and admitted, reluctantly, 'Mum and Dad fought. Maybe not all the time, but it seemed like it. And if they weren't fighting, they weren't speaking. So . . .' she almost spoke the name and broke off. 'So we were always whispering and hiding and keeping quiet and looking after each other. Trying to be good, to do what we thought they wanted. Trying not to be noticed.'

Zoe returned to the table with a large cut-glass bowl topped with chocolate and cherries. 'What we were saying about swopping roles.' She picked up a serving spoon. 'Twins often copy each other's behaviour in all sorts of ways – they make themselves even more alike than they already are. Some pairs do it deliberately, but with others it seems to be quite unconscious. Did that happen with you two?'

'I don't know. I can't remember how it was.' Her voice very low.

'I think you do,' Father Michael interjected. She shook her head, but he pursued it. 'It's possible to lie by omission, you know.'

She sparked back. 'I said I didn't remember if we swopped roles.' The glance she gave him was evasive, graphic as a shrug. 'If it's possible to lie by omission, then lies can sometimes tell the truth.'

Michael opened his mouth to protest, but Victor Schon put a restraining hand on his shoulder as he placed Kate's dessert before her.

'Probably one of you was more noisy, more of an extrovert than the other one?' Victor suggested. Kate dipped a finger in the chocolate and licked it. She wiped her mouth with her napkin, patted her lips with her middle finger.

'Me,' she said. 'I was the one who rushed around and talked to people, I was more social. Mum said I was the naughty one. The aggressive one.' Her voice dropped. 'That's what everyone said.'

'It's almost,' said Victor softly, 'as if you were programmed by your family to do what you did.'

Kate went very still. When she raised her head and looked across at Father Michael, the haunting pain in her face drove everything else out of his mind: he just wanted to put his arms around her.

Zoe was watching her, too. 'Often the dominant person isn't the one you *think* it is,' she observed, and her voice was quiet. 'Not the obvious one. That's something you can't see on the surface, it occurs between themselves. But you know all about that, don't you, Kate? Did Sarah make the rules for the two of you?'

For a minute, Kate held her breath. Somewhere in the back of her mind, a child couldn't breathe for the weight of emotion building inside her. She gave a curt nod and dug her spoon into the rich ice-cream with all the fierce concentration of a child. Without looking up, she said with finality, 'I'm not going to talk about her any more.'

Victor and Zoe exchanged a look, and included Michael. 'I'll get the cheese,' Zoe said. 'Michael, could you bring the tray?'

They were discussing where Michael should drive Kate the following day when Zoe stopped suddenly, as if she'd heard a noise.

'What?' Victor Schon glanced towards the door. 'Is someone . . . ?'

'There's someone,' Zoe said, 'but using a different door.' She let herself down into her chair again, put a hand to her waist and rubbed gently.

'Whoops,' said Schon softly. He and Zoe shared a long, loving smile. Kate and Michael, aware of the strong current suddenly present in the room, glanced from one to the other.

'Yes?' asked Schon.

'Definitely,' Zoe replied.

'Ambulance? Or suitcase and car?'

Zoe gave her irrepressible giggle. 'Ooh, Professor, you've done this before, I can tell.'

'Yeah, but you're the boss, Boss. You say which we need.'

'Um. Well.' Zoe relaxed, her shoulders went down. 'I'm sure I've time for a cup of coffee.'

Victor Schon pushed his chair back. 'No way. I remember what happened with Hugh because you were so laid back.' He glanced at the others. 'Just one baby born in a Volvo at seventy miles an hour is quite enough for a lifetime, thank you very much. So I don't know about you, but I'm driving to the hospital *now*.'

'Oh, all right.' Zoe pulled a face. 'I do love masterful . . .' The sentence finished in a gasp and Schon said, all business now, 'Michael, get the car round, would you?' He threw the keys across the table. 'I'll get your jacket, darling. Bag in the usual place?'

'Under the stairs. But I have to pee first. And kiss the kids goodbye.'

'Better not, you might wake them.' He kissed the top of her head. 'You'll be back here in forty-eight hours. Don't go all maternal on me.'

Zoe kept moving, but slowly. 'Bit late for that particular warning, but I'm sure it was kindly meant.'

303

She paused to get her breath. 'Couldn't make it up the stairs anyhow.'

Kate said, 'What can I do, please?'

'Stay near her,' suggested Schon, 'just in case. I'll only be a minute.'

Michael nodded. 'Fine. Um – one thing, Victor, we've been drinking and . . .'

Schon waved a hand. 'No sweat. I had one glass and about seventeen of fizzy water.'

Five minutes later, Victor Schon drove towards the gate, while Michael and Kate watched from the step. Suddenly the car reversed smartly, back into the circle of light cast on the gravel by the open hall door. It stopped beside them. Schon stuck his head out of the window.

'We seem to be leaving you with all the kids. Sorry. Is that . . . ?'

Michael looked across at Kate and they said, together, 'Of course . . .' 'Get to the hospital for God's sake!'

'The only one who might wake you is Hugh.' Schon turned on the windscreen wipers, although it wasn't raining. 'Just get Louise to deal with him, she won't mind. She's only ten but she handles him better than anyone.'

'My Ma'll come over if there's a problem,' Zoe told Kate, leaning out of the passenger window. 'Janet. Number's programmed into the phone. 06.'

Victor let out the clutch. 'You might give her a buzz for us,' he added, over the engine noise, 'tell her what's happening. And the hospital number's on there too. I'll call you in the morning, if I'm not back.'

The car rolled down the drive. Kate waved and called, 'Good luck, Zoe, good luck!'

Victor Schon stuck a thumb out of the window and shouted, 'We're in control!'

Michael started running down the drive after them. 'Lights!' he yelled. 'Switch on your headlights!'

Chapter Thirty-two

Rain fell light as mist and the night garden trembled as it revived. They walked without speaking, savouring it. Kate bent and rubbed her hands over the soaked grass, put her wet palms to her face, inhaling the smell. Then she slipped off her shoes and pressed bare feet into the grass, the little spikes coming up between her toes. He remembered Holloway: the smell of disinfectant, cheap talcum powder. Harsh walkways of grey cement. In a moment of intuition he understood all she had lost, in those incarcerated years. For different reasons, they were both of them quite alone.

Behind them the house waited lit and quiet, the children asleep, the cats fed, the dog lying as he always did in the porch. Out of his thoughts, Michael said, 'I wonder sometimes, how it'd be to have your own house, a family.' He glanced back at the Old Rectory. 'It feels pretty good from here.' He had hoped she would follow his lead, say something personal, something revealing. He had reckoned without Kate's hard-earned expertise. He didn't recognize the armour she had grown against years of professional questioning.

'Most married people don't have houses like this, though, do they?' she asked. He thought for a second it was sarcasm. When he realized she genuinely did not

306

know – how could she? – he said, 'Very few, I'm afraid,' but already she was pursuing his statement.

'That's not the sort of thing you expect a priest to say,' she told him. 'Surely you decided you didn't want those things.'

He had his habitual little black cigar between his lips. 'My grandfather was the only person who opposed me, when I decided to have a go at being a priest. He'd known too many broken men, he said, surviving on alcohol and kidding themselves they were doing God's will. He said I'd end up lonely and bitter.'

'And are you?' But when it came to asking questions, her directness continually discomfited him. She never dressed them up with polite frills. Protected by darkness, he was able to tell her the truth.

'Getting to be, I'm afraid. I envy Zoe and Victor what they're experiencing tonight. A birth, a new life, a *confirmation* of love. It makes what I call love appear a very dried up emotion.' They reached the low wall and the gate leading to the small wood, the hidden pond. 'Much of the time I feel I'm doing work that matters. It's a privilege and an honour and an inspiration. I stand before the altar and maybe God speaks through me.' He paused and added heavily, 'But sometimes He doesn't. God's silences can last a long time. And if you've given up everything for Him, they can be very hard.'

After a while Kate said, 'I wonder what it's like, living like that.'

Curious, the way she seemed sometimes to be continuing a previous conversation. It must be a habit of twinhood. Out of that thought, he knew at once what she meant.

'Sarah? She seems contented. Of course we've only talked under difficult conditions, when she was weak from her illness. Or rather, yours.' He waited, but she didn't ask, so he added anyway, 'She's recovered at about the same rate you have. She's much better now.'

Kate said, almost sulkily, 'I didn't ask her to make herself ill. It was nothing to do with me. I don't *want* that kind of involvement with her.'

'I don't believe she had any choice.'

She picked a long grass stem and put it in her mouth. 'I never used to think about being a twin, it was just a fact of life, there was no other way to be.' She tried the gate, but it was jammed.

Michael said, 'Victor and Zoe keep it locked, they're afraid the smaller children might get in there when they're alone.'

'It's just like the Secret Garden,' she said. 'D'you remember, in the book? Hidden away and overgrown and beautiful. A private world.'

'How extraordinary you should say that. While I was looking for you, I did some reading about twins. Does the name Professor Zazzo mean anything to you?'

She shook her head. 'Who is he?'

'A French psychologist. He described the bond between twins as their Secret Garden, the place only the two of them could enter.'

Kate absorbed this. 'Like the book – the only ones who could find their way in.' She thought for a minute. 'I sort of imagined it was just us. A special place only we had.'

'But this doesn't make it less special. Your garden was yours. Another twins' garden would be quite different.'

She turned her face towards him, but he couldn't make out her expression. 'You need to feel special,' she said quietly, 'when everything you have is shared with someone else.'

Talking to this girl was like treading on shells: everything so fragile. He tried again. 'Professor Zazzo also describes the ways twins develop a private language. Called an ideoglossia, apparently, a sort of shorthand only the twin understands. He says in all the cases he came across, they used a free word order, with the important word coming first.'

Kate laughed delightedly. 'Lin odo beer,' she said.

'Good God,' he said comically, 'how extraordinary. What are you saying?'

'It means, *Kate goes to school*.'

'So you really do have a private language.'

'It wasn't ever meant to be private,' she explained. 'They were sort of baby words. I don't know where they came from. I don't even remember them all now. Yab was bird, I think. And kak was something we wore, perhaps it meant socks. It was fun to speak it, a game, because no-one else understood. But the teachers hated it, as we got older. They said it disadvantaged us.'

On the ease of her laughter, he asked casually, 'What does *screel din* mean?'

Beside him, she seemed to shrink into herself.

'You must remember that,' he said. He had to move closer to hear the words.

'Watch out, something terrible is coming.' She turned away as she spoke them, as if she couldn't really admit to them, and grasped the wooden struts of the gate with both hands. In the half dark, in her pale dress, hair curling wildly round her head, she looked like an angel locked out of Paradise.

'When I was eleven,' she said finally, 'I won the year essay prize, I had to go up on Speech Day, all that. I wrote that being a twin was a miracle. Waking up each day knowing – even if you're not in the same room – there's another part of you waking too.'

Eventually he prompted her. 'And now?'

'I feel it's a curse. A curse on both of us. It might have been a Secret Garden when we were little. But now it's turned into a trap, another sort of prison. And all I want is to get out.' He couldn't tell whether anger or grief put the quiver into her voice. 'Shall I tell you the worst thing? I'm afraid in case we even share the same soul. It's always frightened me.' Her eyes gleamed in the darkness as she waited for his reply.

'Every individual is unique,' he said. 'Of course your soul is your own.'

She turned her face away, as if in rejection.

'That's no answer for me. Maybe you don't realize it, because we don't look exactly alike, we're not mirror images. But we shared almost everything. Eyes, skin. Our hair was almost the same then. We were always the same height and weight, but maybe that's changed now. We've both got a bent little toe on one foot.' She lifted her bare, narrow left foot. He peered at it, pale in the darkness, and laughed, despite her seriousness.

'I'll take your word for it. But you say you're not identicals.'

'No. They think we're probably a third sort of twin where the mother's egg splits before it's fertilized, instead of afterwards. So almost identical but not entirely.' He saw her fingers rake down the fine skin of her arm. 'We owe our similarities to Mum and our differences to Dad. Only, as we got older, we realized that in fact we even thought the same way. Our parents told us we'd come into a room separately and ask about someone we hadn't seen for eighteen months.'

'You were the same age, you'd had the same experiences. Perhaps that's not so strange.'

Kate sighed and said, 'She broke her leg once.' Again that reluctance to speak the name. 'At least . . .' Doubt darkened her eyes. '. . . I *think* it was her. They let me stay in hospital too. When we got home it became a game: I was the patient and she was the ambulance man. Next time we did it the other way round. So later on, we could never remember who really had the broken leg.' Her voice dropped. 'Even our memories don't belong to us separately.'

He asked carefully, 'If it *was* Sarah, did you feel the hurt of her broken leg? Did you experience sympathetic pain?'

She frowned in concentration. 'It's too long ago, I can't be sure. But usually, it was her feeling for both of us.'

'I wish you'd said so sooner.' He tried not to sound accusatory but she reacted at once.

'I couldn't believe she was still doing it! All these years later, for God's sake. I thought it was all over.' She tried to shake the gate, to release her feelings. 'I'll never get away from her! Never! Never!' Fury flushed her cheeks, her voice was harsh with it. 'Damn her to hell!'

He understood suddenly. 'It's still happening. She's still trying to reach you.'

She let out a long, whistling breath. 'How'd you know?'

'I've been listening to you,' he said drily. 'Tell me.'

She shrugged. 'The same. I hear her calling to me. Only now it's when I'm awake, too.'

'And the message?'

'Just like before. *Screel din*. Something dreadful coming.' She shook her head in protest. 'But it's

311

happened, it's done with. She warned me and she was right. What *else*, for God's sake?'

'Perhaps she couldn't help it,' he suggested. 'You say how much you shared. Perhaps it's out of her control.'

'You're right.' She took a deep breath, consciously calming herself. 'It is, it's out of control.' Her face screwed up like a desperate child as she remembered something else. 'But that's why I'm so frightened of it, don't you see? If we share all that, why not a soul too?'

She sounded almost frantic. He understood finally, how deeply this worry must have been gnawing at her for years.

'Because ensoulment is the moment true human life begins. So even the most identical of twins must have separate souls.'

'Are you *sure*? Twins aren't ordinary babies, are they? And no-one really knows about our sort of twin anyway.'

How could any man be sure of such a thing? He wasn't even aware if any theological debate had ever covered the question. But she needed to be reassured, she didn't need doubts. He could hear in Kate's voice the fear that her twin might also be tainted by what she had done.

'I am sure,' he said, and saying it, knew it must be so. 'You and Sarah are not one body divided by two. You are two bodies. Two separate people. And believe me, two souls.'

He was aware of the tension going out of her. She let go the bars at last.

'Thank God,' she said.

Victor phoned at eleven o'clock: Zoe was fine but still had a way to go. 'Don't wait up,' he said. 'This one's going to be a dawn baby.'

Long after midnight they finally went upstairs. Kate was in the room he'd occupied on his first visit, up a winding staircase on the attic floor. He was below her, the children's rooms further along the corridor.

In bed, he tried to read, but his thoughts obscured the words. He kept seeing Kate's face, blank and stiff as Zoe picked little Hugh from the car.

And he saw her standing up to her thighs in the dark green pond, her back turned to him, her neck bent beneath the piled-up hair. Longing opened up in him, a huge ache. For a moment, he didn't understand – and then he did, it all flooded in on him. Another woman, her back turned, her hair caught up because of the heat . . .

He had gone one night to visit Francesca Gardelli. They had met three times, in public places. It was almost impossibly difficult to get away alone from the seminary, especially in the evening, but he planned carefully, invented an imaginary relative.

He had leaned in the doorway of her kitchen with a glass of wine, talking to her as she cooked. She had on a top and skirt of soft grey knitted silk and he thought he could see the points of her nipples. His hands tightened on the glass as he imagined himself reaching out to touch them.

They listened to music while the city darkened around them. Sitting across the room from her he had asked hesitantly and almost inaudibly, 'Would you – Francesca – would you . . . will you undress for me? I only want to look at you. Nothing more. Only to look.'

She considered him without speaking. Then she put down her coffee cup and got up to close the balcony windows. Still with her back turned, with a single movement which seemed to him utterly feminine, she pulled the loose top over her head. Her back was bare, the knobs of the spine delicately outlined in the smooth flesh. Her neck curved like a stem beneath the weight of her hair. She reached back a hand to the fastening of her skirt. He heard, almost with terror, the sound of the zip opening.

She asked him, finally, 'You don't want me, Michael?'

She had put on some sort of filmy garment, loose. He wanted to say, if you would just, if you would only, lift your slip a little, so I could see . . . then he would have been lost, there would have been no argument left to him. But instead he found himself uttering pompous, incredible words.

'It's very nice of you, but I think I'd better say no.' He thanked her politely for dinner – and went back to the seminary.

For two weeks, he drove himself mad. What was he thinking of? What about his vows? How could he have behaved like that? He must have hurt her feelings, she would have seen only rejection.

And mixed up with all of it was the terrible fear that he wasn't a man any longer. Maybe all the years of denial, of suppressed sexuality, meant he could no longer respond to a woman as a normal man. Maybe something had been killed in him.

Lying in the Schons' guest room, Michael found the recollection as agonizing as the events had been. In the end, after the heart-searching and the appraisals and the wrestling with himself, he had gone to her. She had understood, and it had been all right. It had been wonderful. And then it had been over.

He had not experienced these emotions in ten years and more. And now he was in their grip again, as shaken and confounded as if it were the first time.

314

It had started months ago, though he hadn't allowed himself to acknowledge it then, sparked by the sight of Sister Gideon lying lovely as a saint in stone, her head averted, her long hands still. Whatever he might have felt for her he'd stifled, disallowed. It was unimaginable. Forbidden.

Then, Kate. In more ways than one, he had moved closer to her with every step of his long search. He had found the same woman – and not the same at all. The same hands, only not white and fine, but strong and capable. The same remarkable eyes like clear amber. But a different expression. The same voice, speaking of other things. *Do we share a soul?*

He started to sweat. My God. My *God*. Bad enough that he wanted her, that he was lying here seeing her thighs white in the water beneath the bunch of her skirt . . . But to desire a woman who had killed a baby, a murderess, an ex-convict? How could he feel as he did for Kate, who was all these? What had she done to him, how had she got to him?

Michael sat up, unable to lie still any longer. She had done nothing, nothing. This was all on his side, and his alone. There were no excuses for him. But perhaps there were, for her. Many years ago, a child had committed a crime and paid for it in full. He would maybe never understand the stresses that had pushed her to that act, though in Roy Downey's dingy caravan he had glimpsed the half-destroyed world of the young twins.

There is no evil. The Jesuit precept. *Only an absence of good.*

The thought calmed him and he lay down again. He must get to sleep, there'd be a lot to do tomorrow. Five minutes went by, ten – then something jerked him back from the very edge of sleep. Drowsily he wondered if a telephone had rung. Nothing more disturbed the darkness and he drifted off.

When it came again he sat up and switched on the light. Still silence, only this time he knew he'd heard a sound. He got out of bed without turning on the light and pulled open his door. The hall was lit, as he had left it for the children.

He tried to shout, heard the croak in his throat as he started forward. Kate was going stealthily into Hugh's room.

Chapter Thirty-three

Compline is the last, the most intimate, office of the day.

Protective of her left hand in its sling, Sister Gideon put on the choir cloak of unbleached cream wool. It had belonged to three nuns before her, and each of them had worn it throughout her religious lifetime. The number embroidered inside was 158. The number, too, had belonged to others before her. God knew how many. It had been allotted on the day she entered, written into the order's Book of Names. The Novice Mistress had explained then that if she were to leave, it would be passed to the next postulant who entered. But she knew now, that would not happen. She would be 158, God willing, until she died.

The day of her death was the day – she prayed for this – when she would enter heaven. What remained would lie uncoffined in the bare earth, as all their order did, their names known only unto God.

Here, if it is hard to live, it is most sweet to die.

Some orders celebrate a death, for the soul longs to see God. Theirs did not: the body may suffer. The nuns were buried at the end of the garden, beyond the orchard and the raspberry canes, for even in death they kept their enclosure.

Later, the number 158 would be written beside her name in the Ledger of the Dead, in some quiet office of the Curia, within the Vatican.

Sister Gideon pulled the heavy cloak round her shoulders. She did up the clasp at her throat, the long pin through the square buckle. It was a medieval design. Two hundred years ago, three, five, nuns had fastened their choir cloaks exactly as she was doing now.

In all those years, nothing here had changed. The tide that was the affairs of the world rose and fell far from the rock on which the Priory of Our Lady of the Snow was built. There had been world wars and the collapse of nations and the death of kings. There had been famine and atomic bombs, natural disasters and medical wonders. Through all these things, the nuns had moved serene and untouched, because they were there *Dieu seul*. For God alone.

Sarah thought of Saint Theresa, telling her Carmelites to keep their eyes and hearts upon the mountain, ignoring the news of the plain. Or the author of *The Cloud of Unknowing*, advising that their response be prayer, for: A naked intent directed upon God, without any other cause than Himself, sufficeth wholly.

It sufficeth wholly, Sister Gideon told herself, as she lit one of their thick beeswax candles, hand rolled in the Candle Office. She stuck it firmly in the stubby holder of black iron.

All along the corridor, nuns were opening the doors of their cells and joining the long procession. She stepped out and took her place beside Sister Rosalie.

'Save us Lord while we are awake . . .'

The candles were creamy white. The colour of love, she thought. Everything and nothing at all. The smoke, caught by the wind of their passing cloaks and drifting

318

up into the old stone arches, scented the air very faintly with musk.

'Protect us while we are asleep . . .'

In the nuns' choir, she knelt. She heard the familiar soft susurration of fabric as all the nuns simultaneously crossed themselves. All around her, women were lost completely in their prayer.

The golden vials full of odours, which are the prayers of saints.

Some knelt, others half-leant, half-lay against the dark wood choir-stalls. Here in the chapel, these women made formal and measured prayer. But there was nothing stilted or self-conscious about their relationship with God: this was where they were most at home.

After a while, Sister Gideon rested her head on her arms.

> *That we may keep watch with Christ*
> *And rest with Him in peace.*

She opened her eyes. In their soft poses, their long robes, the nuns resembled an old, dark Spanish painting: grey and cream and black against the muted reds and deep blues of the chapel.

High and clear then came the antiphon: 'Guard us, Lord, as the apple of your eye.'

In unison, they made the response: 'Hide us in the shadow of your wings.'

The words comforted and sustained her, as they were meant to do. As they always would.

An hour before, Mother Emmanuel had told her she would soon be sent back to the mission. And in five years, or ten, she would return to this house. She belonged to the order. These women were her family. This was where she was meant to be.

At the end of the service, Sister Gideon moved with her sisters out of chapel. By candlelight, walking two and two, the nuns passed through the courtyard, where the air was heavy with the perfume of tobacco plants and night-scented stock. As Mother Emmanuel reached the old house, the chimes of the campanile bell rolled rounded and perfect through the darkness.

The Great Silence had fallen now. It would last until Nocturnes at four-forty-five a.m. next morning.

Guard us, Lord, as the apple of your eye.
Hide us in the shadow of your wings.

Chapter Thirty-four

Kate turned in the doorway of Hugh's room and saw the horror imprinted on Michael's face.

Then the child's grumbles escalated into a long, wailing cry.

'Duce! Duce *now*!'

'He won't stop,' Louise said despairingly from her post beside his cot. 'I'll have to get Mum.'

'Mum's not here.' Kate looked back at the child, absorbed again by the immediate problem, uncertain how much Hugh would understand. 'There's a special package on the way,' she said, meaningfully. 'The little one you've been waiting for. Mum's gone with Dad to arrange . . . things.'

Louise's bewilderment immediately gave way to comprehension. She went scarlet with excitement and gave a loud gasp. 'When? When will it be here?'

'Sssh,' Kate warned her, keeping her voice to a whisper. 'We'll talk about it in a minute, when Hugh's settled. Tell me what he wants.'

Louise nodded, her eyes huge. 'He means juice – can you get his drink? It's in the fridge in a jar thingy.' She held out a plastic beaker with a spout. 'It has to be in here and you add a teeny bit of boiling water first.' She turned back to the cot and started lifting the child out. 'I'll put him on the potty.'

'Let me,' Michael said, reaching past Kate for the beaker. He stumbled down to the kitchen.

After a few minutes, Kate followed him. He was waiting for the kettle to boil. Without turning, he said, 'Kate, I'm so sorry. I thought . . .'

She interrupted. 'I could see what you thought. You didn't exactly hide it.' She spoke defensively, 'I heard Hugh crying and crying, I couldn't just leave him. I didn't know Louise was in with him.' Her voice went flat, suddenly bleak. 'I don't blame you.'

He kept his eyes on the kettle. 'It was unforgivable of me.'

She reminded him, 'Those children are in your care.'

'Yes.'

'Only I couldn't possibly have hurt him. I love Hugh, I really do.' She gave a wobbly laugh. 'Duce,' she said, mimicking him. 'Duce *now*!'

He turned to look at her.

'I was going in to look after him, for God's sake.' There was a break in her voice, but she seemed calm. She was holding herself in, making a tremendous effort to tell him this. 'Something . . . something terrible happened all those years ago. A baby died for no reason. A *baby* . . . And it was all my fault. My fault,' she repeated, bleakly. 'I deserved what was done to me.' In the silence, there was the sound of the kettle heating, the old Aga creaking to itself. In one corner of the room, a hamster ran frantically on its wheel.

'I didn't understand what was happening,' she went on, finally. 'I didn't know how to cope. But because of it, no-one has loved me in all this time.' She wrapped herself in her own arms. 'It's left me . . .' she struggled for the word, '. . . empty. A void. I feel as if I've been poured out.' She desperately wanted him to understand. 'I must

322

have something for myself, or I won't exist any more. I've thought and thought, and it's not a job I want, or a house, or a holiday . . .' She almost laughed at herself. '. . . it's love, I just want love. I don't mean sex . . .' she dismissed it with a gesture, as unimportant, '. . . I mean, proper love. Holding and caring and looking after and being taken care of.' There were tears in her eyes. 'Not great passion. I don't imagine I'll ever have that, not now. I'm not expecting it. I just want . . . ordinary love.'

Michael was suddenly out of his depth. He was used to confessions, he was trained for this, not to be judgmental but to absorb. Only there was a quality here that almost scared him, a depth of feeling that embarrassed, demanded a response he didn't know how to make.

He struggled to see past this moment to all the meetings, the therapy sessions, the questionings, to which she had been subject for half her life. She had faced herself in a way few people ever did. He felt she was trying to show him her soul.

He said, finally, loathing himself for his caution, but not wanting her to be hurt any more, 'I don't believe there's such a thing as ordinary love. It's all extraordinary.' This woman was like an uncertain adolescent, he felt she'd run to anyone who showed an interest. He said, putting it as delicately as he could, 'For a bit, you might have to make do with less. But there's a joy in the wanting and not quite having of love.'

Her disappointment was tangible, he could have touched it: he'd failed her. When she spoke, her voice was tart. 'I'm sure I've read that somewhere. I didn't believe it then, either.'

Not such an adolescent after all. He spread his hands

323

in a rueful gesture. 'It's late and you're right and you don't need me to preach to you.'

Kate pushed her hair back from her face. She was exhausted and cross. She'd felt so well these last few days, she'd forgotten they had warned her, it took many weeks to really recover from surgery. And Father Michael was trying to help her, he hadn't deserved her scorn.

She thought of what he'd just said, about the joy in the not quite having of love. He was either an emotional stoic – or a desperately lonely man. And perhaps the truth was neither of these. Perhaps, like her, he had been damaged in some way beyond his control.

He gave a weary smile. 'God. What a night.' Under the heavy brows, his eyes were warm and dark and tired.

They made her, suddenly, very aware of the skimpy soft orange T-shirt she'd hurriedly pulled on. Instinctively she tugged at the hem, and his eyes followed her movement down, lingered. Until this moment, she hadn't noticed he wore only blue pyjama bottoms. She saw the muscles of his neck and shoulders, the dark fuzz of curly hair across his chest. She could smell him, those little cigars he smoked, the coffee he'd made for the two of them after dinner. And that indefinable male smell that made her want to breathe differently, that came to her all the stronger for its unfamiliarity.

Formal in the black soutane and white collar, he had been a priest, invested with the authority of his office. In his jacket and shirt he had just been a man, older than herself, with a clever, thinking face, still hedged about by his title, his role. Like this, he was younger than she had thought, more masculine.

Almost against her will, she was conscious of him now. Dramatized by the black robes, he always held himself straight and tall. But she recognized the characteristic way he stood, with folded arms: she'd learned enough of body language in prison to see it was defensive. She heard the intimidating assurance in his voice – and saw the hesitation in the slight flicker, the nervous tension, of his eyelids. He was struggling too, just like her. He was uncertain, as she was.

It hit her like a hammer blow. She was accustomed to the rough and ready relationships of prison, the formalized behaviour of senior officials. Her only friends were from her prison past, and she was fearful of any intimacy with people ignorant of it.

Father Michael knew, and she had never read censure in his face. He knew about her and her twin, and did not compare them. She had thought she was responding to his interest in her, his desire to help, his kindness, the sensitivity with which he treated her. What a fool she was.

Kate grabbed the beaker of juice from his hand and hurried back up to the children.

She waited in the hall while Louise gave Hugh his drink. When he was settled, Kate brought the doll she found on the carpet, and tucked it in beside Louise. The girl turned it upside down, showing the two faces: the rosy smiling one under yellow wool curls, the sad-mouthed face under straight black hair, with painted teardrops on white cheeks.

'She's nice,' said Kate, only because that was what Louise wanted her to say. It was hateful, deceitful. Double. The child heard the strain in her voice and asked, 'Can I have a kiss?'

Surprised, Kate asked, 'Really?'

Louise put up her arms. Kate leant to kiss her cheek. 'You were so good with your brother,' she said. 'Maybe you'll have another by the morning.' Louise squeezed her neck excitedly. She smelled of toothpaste and clean hair. Something hard in Kate softened, finally, and slid away. How long since she had kissed someone goodnight, who smelled like that, and curled close?

Later, Kate stood in front of her door, not looking at Michael.

'Lock me in.'

'I can't.'

'Do it. I told you, you're responsible for these children. If anything happened it would be . . . I *want* you to.'

He said reluctantly, 'Christ, Kate, I hate to do this.'

She tested the key in the lock. 'It works fine.' She opened the door again, stepped through. As she pulled it close she repeated, determinedly, 'Go on, lock it.' But when she heard a key turn once more behind her, she started to shake.

Chapter Thirty-five

'Zoe's done it again!' Victor Schon was jubilant. 'Another boy . . . looks like me, for a change . . . she was wonderful, just . . . yes, yes, I will, I'll tell her, she's right here . . . can't tear myself away for a bit, I'll be home after breakfast, OK?'

When Michael put down the phone and looked at the clock, it was almost four. He went up to his room and pulled back the curtain. The edges of the sky were already lightening to pale green. Deep bars of mist banded the fields, trees floated on it and horses slumbered, invisible from the hocks down, in a milky sea. Someone on a speeding bicycle – an early milkman on his way to work? – whistled down the high-edged lane behind the house.

There was a sound from above, a movement. He must tell Kate. He went quietly up the attic stairs, and knocked. He called her name, but no answer. Nor the second time. Then he heard the sharp splintering of glass. He told himself something might be wrong, though in truth he was looking for a reason, any reason, to go in. He turned the key and opened the door.

The room was in darkness but a light was on in the tiny blue-tiled bathroom. Kate was in there, holding a broken glass. She had just showered, and she was still naked.

He felt like a voyeur, standing in the shadows peering

at a woman in a lighted room, and just for those brief seconds he knew the voyeur's secret sensations.

Her hair was pinned close to her head so she looked almost like a beautiful boy. But there was nothing boyish about her body, her creamy limbs. Above the sway of her hips, the sleek waist, her breasts were pointed, brown-tipped, tender. Below the faint ripple of her ribs was the thin dangerous line where they had cut into her flesh, the uncovered scar almost healed. For some reason he couldn't define, that seemed to him unbearably erotic – it made her vulnerable, it made her real. The blemish brought her within his reach. When she went down on one knee to pick up the rest of the glass, his eyes followed the tensed curve of her round thigh, the chestnut spring of pubic hair.

He didn't stir. He could not. If his life had depended on it, he could not have turned from this room, this woman, the sight of her. He wanted only to watch, to experience her quiet movements. *Emotion shows in all the ways a body moves.*

And at the same time, there were a whole lot of other, different emotions. Deep dislike of the way he always behaved. Again, he was on the sidelines, observing other people, never involved. All his life, it seemed, he had been taught that love could be expressed through words alone. And the words at his command, God knows, were beautiful.

But with this woman, he wanted more than words. He wanted to reach out and touch her. And if he did so, was he more terrified of her response – or of his own? He said, quietly, 'Kate?'

Shocked, she dropped the glass she held and her hands went to her face. She brought her elbows together to hide her breasts. He realized she couldn't see him clearly –

328

she was in brightness, he in shadow – and he added, 'It's me.'

With her relief, anger flared. 'What the *hell*!' Furious, she spun round, snatched at a towel.

He put his hand over his eyes, a little boy's gesture. 'Jesus, Kate, I didn't mean . . . I came to tell you about the baby.'

She said nothing for a minute, then her voice lifted, lightened, 'The *baby*? Just a minute.'

He heard movements.

'All right. I'm decent. Tell me.'

There are decent parts of a woman's body, less decent, and indecent.

She had wrapped herself in the white bath towel, tucked a tight roll round the top of her breasts. With it, she had put on another, glowing face.

He told her about Victor's call. She asked excitedly, 'What does he weigh?'

'Weigh?' He was perplexed. 'I've not the slightest idea. Victor'll be home in . . .' he glanced at his watch 'about five hours. He'll probably know.'

Her hair was still dripping from her shower. Two or three drops rolled down the side of her neck into the soft dip of her collarbone. The moisture sparkled against matt skin. She saw him looking and said in a small voice, 'Don't.' Tissue in hand she knelt, as if eager to get away from him, and started collecting the bits of broken glass. Under his gaze she was self-conscious, jittery. She gave a sudden gasp and drew back sharply.

He dropped on one knee beside her and caught hold of her reluctant hand. It was the first time he had touched her, and he felt her astonishment leap and tremble. Then she steadied herself. A sliver of glass was embedded in the fleshy part of her first finger. He prised it from her

329

skin, squeezed till he was sure it was clear, till he saw a drop of blood.

'I'll have to wash it,' she said. For answer, he lifted her finger to his lips, and sucked away the blood. All the time he watched her face, her reaction, and she refused to meet his eyes.

It was the single most intimate thing anyone had ever done for her. She shivered.

'Are you cold?' he asked.

She shook her head.

He examined her finger. 'Do you want a plaster?'

'God.' Despite herself, she started to laugh. 'You Jesuits ask a hell of a lot of questions.'

'Do we?' He meant to smile at the joke but he couldn't. He was so close, the drips from her hair were making dark splotches on the knees of his pyjamas. He put both hands on her upper arms. Her skin was incredible, soft and smooth and cool as cream.

He moved slowly, expecting a rebuff even now, unable to believe she was not about to push him away, fight him off. But these things did not happen. In her golden eyes he could see himself, a tiny figure reflected in the glossy iris. As if she had absorbed him already.

What he felt for this woman was a sin in the eyes of the Church. Something a priest must crush and subdue in himself. Subdue and overcome. But he could not do it. He did not wish to. What was happening had the inevitability of a piece of music, building note on note.

They were both of them alone. There were no partners, no children, no lovers, no linked lives to be touched on, or destroyed. He opened her left hand, took the tissue with its fragments of broken glass, and put it on the edge of the bath. He would not hurt her in any way, he wanted her to be enriched. If anyone must suffer from this, then let it be him.

They were still kneeling, facing each other. When he lifted his hands, and took her face between them, she could feel his palms quiver. And she understood what he could not say.

He didn't even try to kiss her. There was an intensity in him, in the way he studied her skin, the curve of her eyebrow, the line of her jaw, her eye. He was treasuring her, she realized, storing up her image against his future loneliness.

He took his hands from her face. Water was still dripping from her hair onto her shoulders and he tracked a drop with a finger, down the curve of her cheek, the side of her neck. Down the slope of her shoulder, onto the pale swell of her breast.

She held her breath, willing him, don't stop. In the hush, a bird in the ivy outside the window stirred, fluted for a moment, fell silent.

Michael leant forward, put his forehead against her collarbone, his hair thick and black and warm against her skin. He said, 'Kate.' She heard desire and despair. She remembered who and what he was.

With a little groan of impatience, she dragged at the end of the big towel, where she'd pushed it between her breasts, pulled it loose from the tight fold. The fleecy material fell away, settled round her hips as she knelt on the blue tiles.

At her movement he sat back on his heels, arms slack at his sides. He was hungry for her, and frightened. This time, there'd be no turning back. No second chance. This time, the waters would close over his head.

She said, questioning, 'Michael?'

(A gentle, Venetian voice. *You don't want me, Michael?*)

331

'Christ,' he said quietly, not as an oath. He did not stir.

She put her hands beneath her breasts, pushed the soft flesh towards him, in a gesture at once provocative and disturbing, innocent and erotic. She must have seen it somewhere, God knew where, this lewd enticement. It filled him with pity, that she was reducing herself to this. And shame, because she was doing it for him.

She offered herself with awkward allure. But her amber eyes were clear and trusting as a child's. She stared at him, the gold darkening as the pupils grew huge, deep pools opening up for him. 'Michael,' she said again, desperate with wanting. He had never heard his name spoken in just that way before. His mind – his clever, trained, analytical, considering mind – shut down. It wasn't pity for Kate he felt now, only his own overwhelming physical need.

He reached out to her pale brown nipple. Under his palm it stiffened, puckered. His hand smoothed over the swell of her breast and Kate made a little sound of assent deep in her throat, and her thighs parted slightly. That galvanized him. He caught her roughly to him, pushed her back onto the thick towel, on the tiles. He heard her sharp indrawn breath – he must be careful of the scar – and then he couldn't think at all. Her arms were round him, her body tense and yielding all at once. He found the other nipple with his lips, and began to drown.

He didn't know anything. He wanted – he'd never wanted anything so much – to know what would make her happy. What would make her love him. Which movements, which caresses, would bring her delight?

He rubbed the secret skin between her legs, and she whispered, 'I'm all wet, you don't mind?'

A little later, limbs wound round him, she stiffened and clung as if she would forge their two bodies into one. Her short nails raked down his back as she bucked against him and sobbed aloud. 'Oh, God, lovely, lovely, lovely . . .'

And when he could go on no longer, when her hidden muscles tightened their tender, merciless grip, when he felt himself coming in her, he heard almost with surprise the sound of his own ecstatic release: a single, harsh cry, raw with feeling.

He didn't think he had slept, but when she stirred, flexed a cramped leg, he woke.

Sunlight was streaming into the tiny bathroom, falling full on the back of his head, and her face. It was so strong, it killed the bright neon strip over the basin. Her eyes were full of light, full of love, her skin shiny now from sweat, not the shower, she gleamed beneath him.

She touched his face with the tips of her fingers. 'And I thought,' she murmured, 'people only did it in the dark.'

Chapter Thirty-six

Dr Bevan drummed his fingers on his desk and pushed out his lower lip in thought. When his eyes met Sister Mark's, he stopped.

Sarah was considering her own left hand. The fingers were curled and rigid, ugly as a claw. 'I can hardly use it at all, some days. I haven't been able to straighten my fingers for two weeks.' Her eyes were anxious. 'And now my whole arm's hurting as well.' She ran her right hand up the limb to the shoulder, which she pressed. 'It's a burning feeling, it throbs all the time.'

'No swelling at all though,' Sister Mark interjected. 'Nothing glandular, I think.'

'We'll do a blood test, then, just to eliminate rheumatoid arthritis and one or two other nasties,' Dr Bevan said. He sounded more cheerful than he looked. 'But I don't believe we'll find anything.'

'What can it be?' Sarah asked. 'I was getting so much better and now . . . it will improve, won't it?'

'A trick of the mind,' he said, answering a different question. 'That's my reading of it. Another manifestation of your emotional links to your sister.'

Her body tensed in denial, her shoulders went up. Sister Mark said hastily, 'We hear Kate's very well, considering she had her operation just over two months ago. Certainly there's nothing to tie in with the hand.'

The doctor looked at the two women over the top of his glasses. 'We'll wait for the test results. If they're negative, then I think we have to look deeper for the cause this time. Psychoanalysis, y'know? This can't go on, can it?'

Sister Mark observed the younger woman's apprehension, saw the already pale skin blanch. She was vulnerable, exposed, she seemed to lack the self-protective layers most people develop over the years. And she aroused all the Infirmarian's maternal instincts.

Sister Mark leant forward.

'Don't worry about all that now,' she said firmly, and was rewarded by Sister Gideon turning to her with transparent relief. 'We'll think of something.'

Mother Emmanuel telephoned as Father Michael was finishing breakfast. 'Hope I'm not too early, Father Michael.'

He caught the suspicion of superiority in her voice: like all members of the Priory of Our Lady of the Snow, she rose before five every day of her life. He swallowed his last piece of toast. 'Indeed not, Mother. I'm not long back from mass.'

There was a lot of crackling and he realized she was in the garden, calling on her mobile phone. She said without preamble, 'We're desperately worried about Sister Gideon. It's all flared up again.' She made a sound of anxiety and exasperation. 'We'd thought that wretched twin business was all over, but apparently not. Sister Gideon's unable to use her left hand, or arm, and it's getting worse each day. The Infirmarian and Dr Bevan can't find any physical cause this time, either. They're both convinced this is all in her mind, too.'

'I read an article recently about a study on separated twins. It seems that if one dies even at birth, the other can continue to mourn well into middle-age.'

'Well, Sister Gideon's obviously doing it – or something very like it. So strange.'

'Among older twins,' he added, 'the surviving twin often adopts some of the characteristics of the lost one.'

'A dreadful thing,' she said, after a moment, 'to have separated those girls.'

'Alternatively,' he said drily, 'a pity they weren't encouraged to be individuals a bit sooner. That might have prevented a tragedy.'

'As it is, we've still got our original problem with Sister Gideon. She's virtually lost the use of her hand. We're at our wits' end here. The Infirmarian did have an idea, though. Tell me what you think.'

It had been planned months ago that three members of the Priory of Our Lady of the Snow should travel to Lourdes in mid-August. Now, Sister Gideon was allocated one of the places. And Mrs Glyn of Welshpool once more footed the bill.

This elderly lady used to make retreats with the nuns. Believing her to be a poor woman, knowing she had no family to help support her, they never accepted any more from her than homemade jam. On one visit she suffered a heart attack and the sisters nursed her for a month as she stayed in their guest house.

After her death some years later, the nuns were astonished to receive a formal letter from her executors: whenever members of the order wished or needed to make pilgrimage to Lourdes, the money would be sent to them. In the seven years since then, fifteen nuns had been to the

French town, and Mrs Glyn of Welshpool was warmly remembered in their prayers.

This year, the weather had broken early and morning fog greeted the nuns at Dover. They had journeyed from Wales the previous day and spent the night at the house of another order. Tired though they were, they had found it hard to sleep in unfamiliar beds: Mother Antrobus had not been away from Welshpool in forty-five years.

The ferry terminal was jammed, and beyond the concrete quays Sarah caught a glimpse of surly grey-brown water. A surprising number of people were wearing the blue and white Catholic Association badges declaring they were pilgrims. An elegant black woman and her sister carried a small baby each, their pushchairs strung about with bags of plastic nappies. There were several older children and a number of wheelchairs including that of Mother Antrobus.

A woman with cropped white hair was telling Mother Antrobus about somebody's brother who had been losing his sight until . . . Mother Antrobus, too deaf to make out the words, smiled politely. But Sarah saw she had been distracted by the wheelchair beside hers in which a young boy of about twelve was held upright by a contraption of straps and braces. A soft leather band around his forehead pressed him back against the padded chair. His hands were long and limp. The woman with him, obviously his mother, smoothed back his fine blond hair. Poor child, Sarah thought, I hope Lourdes helps him. But he was surely an incurable. What kind of miracle would that have to be?

She saw him again in the first lounge, parked in his wheelchair beside his mother's seat. She was chatting to him, looking round and describing what was going on.

Aware of her glance, the woman caught her eye and

smiled. Then she said something to the boy, rose, pressing his shoulder as she did so, and came over to the nuns.

'I don't want to bother you,' she said, 'but I need to use the ladies and I don't like to leave Ross alone for long among so many people.'

Sarah got up immediately. 'Of course.'

She sat beside the boy. His head, in its leather harness, was turned slightly away from her, and when she said, 'Hallo, Ross,' there was no response. She chided herself, she must not expect any from him.

He was getting restless, his body quivering with involuntary little spasms behind the cage of straps and buckles. Sarah glanced round. The lounge was packed, there was probably a long queue for the ladies. More to reassure herself than him, Sarah said, 'She'll be back soon, I expect.'

The slight body continued to flicker its signals of distress, and she knew that, like Mother Antrobus, he had not heard. She leant forward.

'Ross?' she said more clearly. On an impulse, forgetting the habit of so many years ('Touch no-one,' said the Rule, 'even in play'), she covered the boy's boneless hand with her own. It felt surprisingly warm and soft. Unused. She looked into his face to see if he reacted.

Communication and warmth sparked in the boy's eyes, more eloquent than words. She saw where he was looking and touched her white headband.

'I have to wear one, as well!' she said.

Ross's face worked, and this time she knew he was trying to laugh: intelligence and interest and fun shone out of those speaking eyes like a beacon.

She talked about their trip from Wales. She was willing him to hear her, though she saw now it scarcely mattered whether he did so. The important thing was the attempt, and his realization that someone very much wanted to speak to him.

All around them, people were talking, ordering drinks, eating sandwiches and crisps, exclaiming over their Duty Free purchases. Like them, the nuns were travelling to Lourdes in total faith. They were not hoping blindly for a miracle. They craved the hope the place would give them, the inspiration to get through whatever their future held. Still, they were human enough to secretly imagine that maybe, possibly . . . Many people declared how much better they felt, told how the miraculous waters really did heal and inspire.

Perhaps for them, too, this would be the case. Perhaps, after all, their act of faith would receive a gift? Perhaps Mother Antrobus's stiff knees would unlock and her bad hip ease. Perhaps Sister Andrew's flaking skin would be controlled. Maybe she would get back the use of her hand.

But it seemed to her now that the look in the eyes of a twelve-year-old boy was a greater miracle than any she would see in the Pyrenees.

'Is he all right?' Sister Andrew's earnest face was peering at Ross. Sarah's attention had drifted for a moment. The boy was now having difficulty breathing. He was gasping, mouth open with the effort, his body twitching frantically.

'Did his mum tell you what to do?'

'No.' Sarah touched the boy's hand again, leant towards him. 'Ross, have you got something you should take? A pill?'

'Looks like asthma,' Sister Andrew volunteered. At that moment, the mother reappeared.

'Sorry I was so long,' she said breathlessly. 'The queues were just . . . Ross, you need your inhaler!' She turned to

Sarah. 'Didn't he have it on his tray? I was sure I'd left it in case . . .' She opened the bag slung on the handles of his wheelchair. 'I always have spares, thank God.' She pulled out the cylindrical maroon inhaler, held it to Ross's lips. 'There, darling, easy does it.' As he breathed in the fine spray she explained, 'He must've got anxious about where I was, that could trigger it. He'll be fine now.' She saw the worry on the nuns' faces. 'Don't worry,' she added. 'He must have dropped the other one somewhere.'

Rouen. They spent two days and a night on the French train. *Tours*. None of the nuns needed the specially adapted ambulance cars for the sick pilgrims, but shared the couchettes. *Poitiers*. At regular intervals, the whole train echoed to the broadcast prayers, a decade of the Rosary. *Bordeaux*. On the afternoon of the second day they reached the High Pyrenees.

When they were within sight of Lourdes, everyone who could walk left their seats and crowded to the windows to see the Gave du Pau, the river which flowed through the Grotto, and here ran beside the train. A stooped Welshman who claimed he had taken the waters fifteen times was telling everyone who would listen that there were the baths, see? Sarah watched a yellow glow from the candles of the pilgrims, and beneath the looming bulk of a steep cliff face ('there's Massabielle, see?') the Grotto itself.

Inside the train, over the excited voices, the loud-speakers had started to play again. Men's voices singing a tune which was already familiar, trite and sentimental, and yet immensely moving.

Immaculate Mary, sang a dozen male voices, *our hearts are on fire . . .*

'Sing that every night in the torchlight procession, they

do,' the Welshman shouted to be heard. 'Sixty verses,' he added proudly at the top of his voice, 'an' I know every one of 'em.'

Sarah and Sister Andrew exchanged glances. The Welshman had already told them he was staying at their hotel.

'I bet,' muttered Sister Andrew, 'we hear every one of them before tomorrow morning.'

Chapter Thirty-seven

Their hotel was called Mon Refuge. It boasted a pink-washed exterior protected from the street behind ornate iron railings and two palm trees in pots. The red-carpeted front hall was decorated with pink-tinted glass lit with pink fluorescent striplighting. Madame, bulky in her good black, behind a high mahogany desk, sized them up with a practised eye as they approached.

Michael was certain it was only then she allotted the rooms. He signed after Kate, without using any title. Walking upstairs behind her he said quietly, 'I have the distinct impression she knows there's a Roman collar in my luggage.'

'She probably sees an unearthly aura round your suitcase, like a halo.' It astonished her that she was able to tease him. It astonished her even more to discover he liked being teased.

He answered wryly, 'It'll have to do for both of us.'

Neither of them had spoken of their lovemaking. It was there between them, an accomplishment, but they hadn't the vocabulary to discuss it and they feared to lose it. They moved around each other tentatively, learning each other's likes and dislikes – jogging in the early morning, thick-cut marmalade, Monty Python,

HP sauce – without admitting why it mattered they should know.

Because it had been unpremeditated, each separately believed it wouldn't happen again. They were uncertain of themselves, burdened with so many problems of their own. They were not people capable of casual intercourse. Kate had imagined, back in prison, that all she needed was a man's body. She'd discovered a lot about herself, in the weeks of release. When she told Michael she wanted ordinary love, she was already acknowledging that for her, it was the relationship which underpinned the sex, not the other way around. If Michael was not free to love her, she would have to find someone else.

She understood she had been an occasion of sin for Michael. On the day of their encounter (she didn't know what else to call it) he had driven miles to find a Catholic church where he could confess himself. She did not know what had happened in the confessional when he heard the question: do you have any sins of the body to confess?

Many years ago, his spiritual director at the Greg had advised him: 'Penance is a wonderful sacrament. You should use it to ensure you can return to a state of grace.'

He had thought of Kate's face, as she looked afterwards, smoothed and calm and warm. How much he had wanted her, what delight she had brought him. He had not responded to the confessor's question. He was not prepared to bring what had taken place between them down to the level of a 'genital act'. He would have to face God for his disobedience – but he would do so alone.

They had adjoining rooms in a dark, narrow corridor, the heat of which made him decide to check the fire escape. Kate opened her door first.

343

'Crikey,' she said, and started to laugh. Although not large, it contained a double bed, two single ones and a variety of chairs. A curtained recess held a collection of hangers on a rudimentary rail. The only bit of wallspace not occupied by a bed had a tiny cubicle with sides and floor of plastic, housing a shower and a small basin.

Michael tried his room, and came back. 'Mine's just a cupboard.' He grimaced. 'I was told they crammed visitors in at Lourdes, but this is ridiculous. We could try somewhere else.'

Kate stared round at the rough-plastered walls full of foot-high niches. They were shrines, each containing a tinselled statuette – the Virgin, St Joseph, St Bernadette – and beside each was a handwritten prayer in a little gold frame. The shower had its own prayer, she noticed, also in a gold frame. On inspection, this proved to be a warning about the exceptional heat of the water. Even here, it seemed, she couldn't escape notices. 'I rather like it,' she said.

They walked that evening through the streets of the high town. There were hundreds of hotels here, squashed as close together as ingenuity would allow, all named after saints or holy places. ('Golgotha?' Kate repeated to Michael, stunned. 'Calvary?')

Even at this hour the neon-lit souvenir shops were open and busy, their goods piled on tables on the pavements, packed into great baskets beside the doors: votive candles in the Marian colours and all possible sizes, plastic grottos encased in snow storms, devotional pictures with pious mottoes in a dozen languages, including Flemish, crucifixes, television sets which, wound, produced pictures of the Apparitions.

There were medals and flags and more rosaries. But

most of all, there were Virgins. These were carved in wood, cast in plastic, set on plinths. Some were in modern dress, some crowned in what appeared to be tinsel. Kate even found Lourdes pastilles, with the outline of the Virgin imprinted in the sugar and a guarantee they contained the miraculous water.

'Pilgrims dine early,' Michael observed, as they searched in vain for a restaurant prepared to serve them. They finally settled on one where the tables outside, beneath a low striped awning, were still occupied.

Kate picked up a local Bigourdan newspaper on its long wooden roller, and studied it while they waited for their order to arrive. The headline read 'Assassin Sadique' below the photograph of a lumpen-faced man. She asked, not really caring, 'What does it say?'

He craned to see, as the waiter set down their plates. 'It's a bit different in English. The literal translation is, cold-blooded killer.'

Her tone was light, conversational, disconcertingly at odds with her words. 'That's what they called me.'

His breast of duck ceased to look inviting. He put down his fork. 'Kate, I shouldn't have . . .' He could literally see those headlines again. He attempted to repair the damage. 'But they didn't know you.'

'They knew *about* me. They called me a monster with a pretty face. I never thought I was.'

He said, hating to hear her, 'You're no monster.'

Her smile was a mixture of pain and sadness. 'I meant, I never thought I was pretty.'

'Ah, Kate.' He reached across the little round table and stroked her hair back from her face. 'It doesn't matter what they said about you. None of that matters any more.'

345

She said, painfully, 'They wrote I was an evil freak of human nature.'

'You were a little girl. It was a terrible thing to say.'

'Not so little. Twelve isn't little.'

'You were only just twelve. It happened soon after your birthday, didn't it?'

'The week after. Mrs Keller said, eleven's too young to babysit. Wait for your birthday, she said, then we'll see. Mum didn't want us to, anyway, she didn't like us going anywhere.'

Michael had spent two hours going through the trial reports in the PA library. He said, working it out, 'But she drove you to the Kellers' house. That's the way it was reported. Why do that, if she didn't want you to go?'

Kate tasted her lamb before she said, as if talking about something that had happened yesterday, 'Sarah made her, because it was such a cold night. Mum always did anything Sarah asked. Anything.' She kept her eyes on her plate. 'She loved her best.'

'Ah, Kate,' he said again. She was heartbreaking, the more so because she said these forlorn things in a matter-of-fact tone, as if it did not cost her to utter them. 'This business with you and Sarah, it can't be allowed to continue.' She made a movement of rebuttal. 'No,' he said, 'this is important. You said yourself, you're trapped by your joint history.'

'In our Secret Garden.'

'It must always have been exclusive, it must have seemed wonderful. But it's become a dangerous place.' Her anxious expression made him want to reach out to her. Not only the public gaze but the habit of so many years prevented him. 'And because of circumstances, the key was taken away. But until you find it, and unlock yourselves, I don't see how either one can hope to have a real life.'

'How do we do it?' She sounded as if she had no hope.

'Meet, face up to each other – how else? Communicate properly, not in this weird extra-sensory way you're doing it now. Tell each other the things I believe you both need to hear. That you love each other, that you've missed each other.' His voice dropped. 'That you're sorry.'

Her laughter was harsh, a brittle sound he hadn't heard from her before. 'I'm damned if I'm going to play psychological games with you. I've had enough of them.'

He spread his hands in appeasement. 'You've had enough time behind real bars. You can't afford to spend any more trapped by emotional ones.' He stopped, in sudden comprehension. 'I think that's what you want, though, Kate. It makes you feel safe, it's more of the same.'

'No,' she said. 'No!'

'Then do something about it,' he said. 'If you'll just talk to her, about whatever you like – but *talk*.'

She gave a weary smile. It had been a long day, a hot evening. 'All right, perhaps I will. When we get home.'

He said, briskly, 'No time like the present. What's wrong with tomorrow? Sarah's here, I can arrange it.'

Her head went up sharply, suddenly alert. 'I don't believe it.'

He nodded.

'She's in Lourdes – and you knew!' She was on her feet, her chair scraping on the pavement, falling behind her. 'You brought me here for a holiday, you said . . .' Her voice rising, fury growing, she was incandescent with rage. It was the first real intimation he'd had of how that

347

terrible event could have happened, all those years ago. '. . . for the experience, you *said*, because you wanted to do some research here. And . . .'

He had never seen such anger, he marvelled that her slight body could contain it. He attempted to deal with it as he would have controlled a furious child in his classroom.

'That's enough!' he said sharply.

She went on as if she hadn't heard, '. . . all the time it was just a bloody *plot*!'

He did what would have been impossible for him a few weeks before: he reached out and grabbed her wrist. He tried to pull her into the chair beside him, but she resisted. He kept his voice deliberately low. 'I should have told you before, and I'm sorry.' She was breathing fast, her face flushed. 'I do understand,' he went on, trying to be conciliatory. 'You've had years of being pushed around. It was too much to get the same treatment from me. I don't blame you for being so upset.'

Kate leant forward so her face was inches from his. She hissed the words viciously, wanting to wound him.

'Are you looking for excuses for me? Another chance to patronize me? You did this without any warning, and then you have the nerve to tell me it's only my unfortunate past that "upsets" me.' She invested the word with massive scorn. 'Your own lousy behaviour has nothing to do with it, of course. I'm to blame – as usual.' She paused, and went on in a whisper, 'You've got problems too. You're the priest. Screwing a woman must be bad enough. Screwing one who's committed a mortal sin must be much worse.'

He released her wrist without a word, too stunned by her attack to answer it. His was the response of the child who had learnt too soon to be fearful of investing in emotion, in case the person you loved left you. There was no answering rage, only a kind of resignation: he had been at fault himself, that was why it had turned out this way.

And Kate left. She grabbed her shoulder-bag and strode away from the table, her last sentence scarcely addressed to him. 'You manipulative *bastard*!'

He'd never dreamed anyone could make such a scene in public. Her behaviour was beyond his comprehension. His meticulous, controlled personality would never have permitted such excesses, he was acutely embarrassed for her and by her. He lifted his glass of wine to his lips, and found his hand was actually shaking.

He became aware of silence around him: the other diners had clearly been listening keenly. He kept his eyes on his plate, on his now congealed duck.

No-one, ever, had aroused so much feeling in him. No-one had come so close. Gradually, as he sat there beneath the awning and watched the comings and goings on the street, he grew calmer. And he forced himself to try to comprehend her open display of emotion. He thought, she has lived all her life in public, she has never known privacy.

The waiter came, removed Kate's plate without being asked and poured him another glass of wine. He finished his meal alone. But he was used to that.

She returned as he was drinking coffee, cool again, in charge of herself. 'May I join you?' She asked it like a friendly acquaintance. Equally formal, he rose and pulled out a chair, nodded at the waiter, who brought a second coffee.

'Where did you go?'

'I walked by the river. I looked at the weir.'

He asked, quizzically, 'Did you come back because you'd forgiven me? Or because you didn't want to get wet?' He gestured with his head. Behind them, beyond the deep striped awning, it was starting to rain, hard and fast.

'I thought about what you'd said.' She spooned some of the froth off the top of her cup.

He'd told himself he would play it differently this time, keep his distance from this too volatile woman. He leant back in his chair, saying nothing, smoking one of his little black cigars.

'You're right,' she went on, 'and I will see her. I have to. It's as if we were locked in handcuffs. We can run and run, but we'll always end up side by side.' She looked him straight in the eye. 'So I'll meet her. But I won't apologize, not to her. And not to you.'

'You don't owe me an apology, you don't owe me anything. I don't know what you have to say to Sarah. But I just don't want you to think I'm patronizing you.' He found he couldn't keep his distance, after all. He reached across the table and put his hand on hers, as it rested beside her coffee cup. His voice deepened with feeling, but he kept it very low. 'And be clear about one thing. It wasn't screwing.'

She was stiff as a board, he could feel it in her hand. And then she did something so unexpected, he couldn't react for surprise.

She turned her hand over, caught hold of his, and lifted it to her cheek. She held his palm cupped there for a moment, her eyes closed. He could feel the delicate warmth of her cheekbone, the little flutter of her lashes. Then, still holding his hand between both her own, she pressed her lips against his knuckles.

He drew a sharp breath. It was a gesture both of penance and of passion.

A waiter, conscious of the hour, had already started towards them to ask if he could get them anything else. He stopped short, arrested by the intimacy of the couple, the look of trust on the woman's face, the way the man bent so tenderly over her bright tousled head. Then he shrugged and went back to polishing glasses.

That was how they were sitting, aware only of each other, when the three nuns – one of them in a wheelchair – from the Priory of Our Lady of the Snow hurried beneath the awning. They were making their way back from the torchlit procession round the Domain to their boarding house, and Sister Andrew had led them in here to shelter briefly from the rain.

It was she who – curious as ever – happened to glance behind her at the tables. She recognized Father Michael immediately, but seeing him with a woman – and my goodness, what was going on – she discreetly turned away, saying nothing to her companions.

Only Sarah, standing beside her, watching the water stream down the gutters of the narrow street, noticed her quick movement of surprise and followed her look. And so Sister Gideon saw her twin again, for the first time in fourteen years.

Chapter Thirty-eight

The little note stuck to the painted pastel blue robe said simply: 'Please heal Susie.'

The Virgin was sweet-faced, sentimental, her white and blue grimed by smoke from so many supplicant candles. Sarah, passing through the Grotto on her way to the baths, had waited half an hour just to reach it, moving slowly through the crowds gazing at it, praying before it, or simply sitting on the rows of benches before the Grotto.

The Grotto of the Apparitions reminded Sarah of a school visit she had made once to an aquarium: the cave had the same watery atmosphere. Only here it was the child Bernadette's spring and the green plants around it which were exhibited behind brightly lit glass. The stone walls shone, polished by pilgrims. They smoothed it with their bare hands, rubbed it with their rosaries.

Sarah leant her forehead against the dark stone, seeking consolation. This was the place to empty her mind and her heart, to rid herself of the bitterness that rose in her throat until she thought she would throw up.

So many prayers had risen through this recessed Grotto, full of hope and longing. But she could not ask for what she wanted in a prayer.

She wanted her twin punished. Kate – sociable,

difficult, angry Kate, the one she needed in order to dominate, the one who made her complete – was stealing Father Michael from the priesthood and from God. Sarah had seen it with her own eyes in the café in the high town, had read their faces, the way their bodies leant towards each other like plants to the light.

Sarah, trained to introspection, to question her every thought and action, failed to do so this time. She could not acknowledge a heart flooded with jealousy, that unacceptable emotion: she did not see what she could not bear to look at.

Sarah was no longer needed, when they took Kate away from her. She lost her role as the strong twin. In private, between the two of them, Sarah – the last-born by minutes – had always been the one who laid down the rules for both of them.

So she chose to mirror Kate's existence, as nearly as she could, in order to undergo similar experiences, to keep the psychological thread taut between them. In the convent she too was solitary, hidden from the world, essentially alone. She had never asked when or whether Kate would be released. When it happened – if it happened – they would be re-united. For more than a year, she had been communicating with her, tugging the thread. But now she was conscious only of a sort of humming inner silence.

A life without Kate was beyond imagining: she was the perfect one, the focus, the loving conspirator. Yet suddenly, last night, she found out Kate was moving towards a new existence without her, not needing her. And she, Sarah, would be left alone.

She had watched her twin and the priest, oblivious to everything. Oblivious to her. And something in Sarah finally snapped.

The press of people behind forced her, finally, to

move on through the Grotto with them, obedient to the 'Silence' placards. Reverently they touched the Virgin's robe, kissed it, and produced their pieces of paper. There were literally hundreds of others, in every language: Sarah even saw one in Japanese. But the plea for Susie was the one she remembered. She stuck her own note beside it.

The Miraculous Baths were low stone buildings further along the Domain, containing thirteen tubs for the ritual of bathing. The nuns waited again outside one of the entrances to the women's baths, the long queue of morning pilgrims patient and cheerful, joining in the prayers booming out over the relay system.

'Salve regina . . .'

Together with five other women, Sarah was shown into the entrance hall. She went into the changing cubicle behind the blue and white curtain and undressed. The tiled floor was wet and water stood in the little channels. On a hook was a blue cloak for her to wrap herself in.

Still in silence, she and another woman were beckoned forward through into another room, to the piscine, a huge rectangular trough like a Roman bath filled with water. One of the two or three *piscinières*, a stout middle-aged woman with burly forearms, held another cape round her, already wet from the many women it had covered that morning, unpleasant against her skin, but it didn't matter: this was a spiritual exercise, a penance. The woman took the dry cape on her arm, gestured Sarah to go down the steps.

At the far end, on a ledge, was a little statue of the Virgin and before it, prayer cards, some in Braille, some in languages she did not recognize. Sarah murmured her prayer, leant back and let the *plongeures* lower her, take

354

her swiftly right down, plunge her in the water up to the neck.

For Sarah, terrified from childhood of water, unable to swim, it was a dreadful, drawn out torture. Eyes and mouth and nostrils clenched against it, fifteen seconds going on for ever, weightless, endless, only her own body sounds in her ears.

She had expected it to be cold but it was blood heat. It must be freezing only first thing in the morning, when it was clean, and again when they changed the water at midday. The rest of the time, it was gradually changed by hundreds of immersed bodies to the colour and texture of soup.

Her rational mind knew the waters were just those of an underground mountain spring, no different from a thousand others. It was not magical, even the town guide wrote that it did not even contain many minerals. Only she so desperately wanted to believe.

This was the place for healing; bathing was in itself an act of faith. This was the point and crux of this busy, packed, overwhelming little town. Many cures were documented, the nuns knew of them. People saw again, walked again, recovered from incurable diseases. They regained the power of withered limbs, of speech, of hearing.

So Sarah held her breath. If a feeling of great warmth rushed through her body, it might be a cure, a miracle, the end to these months and months of pains not her own.

But there was only the lukewarm water streaming from her body as the women lifted her upright again. She climbed out of the other end of the bath, and the whole thing had taken little more than a minute.

The wet cloak was taken from her, the dry blue one given back and she returned to her cubicle. No towels were provided, it was said that Lourdes water had this magical property also, there was no need to dry oneself. Her skin tingling, she dressed as fast as she could, the habit always took ages to put on – the long drawers, the vest, the underskirts, robe and scapular, the business of the head-dress: serre tete and drawstrings and veil.

Sarah waited for Sister Andrew and together they walked back through the Domain of Our Lady, across the Boulevard de la Grotte over the torrent of the Gave du Pau.

She was reborn. Cleansed and empty of sin. *I am poured out like water.*

Chapter Thirty-nine

At nine-fifteen the next evening, Kate looked up from the table where she was writing and listened. Somewhere, voices were singing the Ave Maria. The long windows were wide to the warm air, the shutters pushed back. It was almost dark, bats reeled soft under the streetlights.

'. . . Maria, Ave, Ave . . .' the sound swelled and then faded, but she still couldn't see them.

'What's that? Is it the loudspeakers again?' At the window, she peered down into the narrow grey street. She could see only a man pushing someone muffled up in a wheelchair, the wheels scraping as he negotiated the pavement.

Michael muttered into the pile of papers he was working through. He and Kate had spent two hours photostatting them that afternoon: they were a small selection from the Lourdes Medical Bureau's records of Proclaimed Miracles. Then he looked up and checked his watch.

'The Torchlight procession must've started, it's nine o'clock every night. We must go and see, it's amazing. Thousands and thousands of pilgrims, all carrying candles under special hoods, walking round the Domain.'

'Can we go?'

Michael smiled at her, indulgent of the incredible

enthusiasm she brought to everything, a child discovering limitless possibilities.

'Not tonight, because of Sarah. But we can take part tomorrow, if you want.' He turned a page, then added, 'If you stand outside, you might see them.'

She considered the wrought iron balcony, with its waist-high sides. Even the floor was curlicues of iron, but it was strong enough to carry a chair and a tub of geraniums.

'I hate heights,' she explained, 'always have.' She went back to her writing. In the silence, a radio played the sort of music no-one danced to any more, and occasionally the wind blew a faint 'Ave' to them from the invisible procession.

Kate lifted her head eventually. 'D'you still think she'll come?'

As if it had been a cue, there was a knock. Kate looked at the door but made no move to open it. She got up and went over to the window – the furthest point in the room – and stood there watchful as a cat. He said quietly, 'Shall I leave you two together?'

'No! No, stay.'

Even before she came in, he could sense that Sister Gideon – Sarah – was more tense than he had ever seen her. The decisive features were sharply drawn under the broad white headband, the body taut as wire beneath the folds of the floor-length black and grey habit. One hand was in a small sling, the other folded decorously in her sleeve. But Michael knew Kate now, and he was beginning to understand how closely these women were linked. So if he could see Sarah's hands, they would be clenched – as Kate's were – with the force of emotion.

'Sister Gideon,' he said courteously. 'Please . . .' he held the door wider. He was surprised and a little perturbed that her brief nod of thanks held no warmth, no acknowledgement of him. As if he were a complete stranger she took four steps beyond him, into the room.

Nothing had prepared him for the shock of seeing both women together. Even as he realized they were not identical, he sensed they were two shoots from a single stem. There was something extraordinary here, something mysterious and inexplicable. For the first time, he understood why twins were the source for ancient legends of pagan powers and dark fears. And because of his involvement – no, he forced himself to admit it – because of his love for Kate, he found it an extraordinary moment, brimming with feelings he couldn't quite bring himself to acknowledge.

Both of them were entirely unconscious of him. They had eyes only for each other. Their faces were still and calm, almost without emotion. As if, he thought with sudden insight, they were examining their own features in a mirror, not responding to someone else. Then Kate said, on a gasp, 'You never used to wear glasses.'

'Nor did you.' Slowly, without taking her gaze from her sister, Sarah slipped her right hand from her sleeve, took off her glasses. She carefully rubbed the bridge of her nose for a moment, as if they had been uncomfortable. The tiny metal frames quivered in her hand. Then she dropped them into the big pocket beneath her scapular.

A moment later, Kate did the same. Her movements were the most precise repetition of her twin's, except that her glasses went into the pocket of her skirt.

He must have made some sound of surprise, because both women turned simultaneously to look at him. Two pairs of amber brown eyes flecked with specks of gold regarded him. One set were cool, detached, the other warmer, softer. That was the only discernible difference.

The shape, long and full, the spray of lashes, the pale curve of the lid, were the same.

Now they were together, so he could compare them, he noted Kate's face was fuller, rounder, her mouth more curved, more voluptuous. Sarah's features were finer-drawn, her narrow nose more aquiline. But essentially the same. He couldn't help it, he said, 'I thought you said you weren't identical, but you are incredibly alike.'

'Apparently we were almost identical babies,' Kate answered. 'As we got older, people said, when you're apart, we think you're alike, then . . .'

'. . . when the other turns up, we realize you're not,' Sarah finished. Her voice sounded like Kate's, but quieter, less inflected. He looked from one to the other, like a spectator at a tennis match.

'They say,' Kate went on, 'twins actually become more alike if they're separated. We're supposed to follow our immediate inclinations and talents . . .'

'. . . rather than responding to the other twin's needs. That must be what's happened to us,' Sarah finished. The two women waited gravely for him to answer.

Not tennis, he thought, an end-of-the-pier double-act. Though he had no desire to laugh.

'Look,' he offered, 'I think I ought to leave you two alone. You've a lot to talk about.'

'Yes, thank you,' said Sarah. And Kate said, 'No, please.' She gave him her most beseeching look.

He smiled at her. There was something intimate in it, something sexual, and Kate responded. Sarah caught, not the look itself, but the subtle current flowing strong between them. She felt it in the air, and without really comprehending the emotion, the depth of it, she understood completely what it meant for her. It meant that these two were moving together, and away from her.

Nothing of this showed on her face as she waited. Michael said, 'I'll just be next door, if you need me. Perhaps in half an hour we might all go and have a coffee?' He opened the door. The twins watched him. But even before he closed it behind him, he saw they had already turned to each other at the same moment, and he was forgotten.

They looked at each other as if they could never look enough. Each saw a face she had recognized before she recognized her own reflection, a person she knew better than she knew herself, a twin she loved more than anyone in the world.

In the end, it was Sarah who held out her good arm. Kate hesitated. Reluctantly, moving slow as a sleepwalker, she submitted to the embrace. For the space of a long breath she held herself stiffly, as if it was all against her will. Then Sarah murmured something, so soft only she could hear, words just for her, and she let her head drop on her sister's shoulder, with the tired sigh of a child lost and then unexpectedly and thankfully found. She slid both hands round the broad leather belt clasping Sarah's narrow waist, reunited at last with the person who once had provided all her emotional caring.

'Baby,' Sarah said, and her eyes were closed. 'My little love.'

Through the open window, the singing voices soared, sentimental, rapturous:

'. . . ia, Ave, Ave, Ave Mariiiaaa . . .'

'Listen,' Sarah said. 'They must have gone all round the Domain. You should have a wonderful view from here.'

'I couldn't see anything before.' Kate released her sister. Sarah went to the open window and peered out.

'Yes,' she exclaimed. 'Look, over the roofs, there's the basilica all lit up, and oh!' Her voice, normally so soft, rose enthusiastically, 'Even from here, you can see all the candles, rivers of candlelight, Kate!'

Kate moved reluctantly to the window. She had lost interest in the procession for the moment. She had given herself over to this meeting, she wanted to settle it all, whatever it was, and start her real life. She didn't want to be distracted.

The Sarah she remembered wouldn't have been particularly interested, anyway. But that didn't surprise her, she accepted it easily. It had always been like this: they had borrowed each other's behaviour as casually as they swapped toys.

Kate did her best. 'I can see the glow in the sky,' she said.

Sarah took her hand. Then she stepped onto the balcony, tugging the hesitant Kate after her. 'Come on, look, through that gap, between the houses, see? Millions of candles!' Still Kate would not step over the sill. Sarah grasped her arm, urging her forward. 'Come on, don't be silly, they're fantastic, Kate. All bright and golden.' She was up on tiptoe, craning to see. She turned to her twin, her face alight with excitement. 'Just like fireworks!'

The word was enough. Instinctively Kate drew back. But Sarah's grip on her was so strong, so determined, she couldn't free herself.

'Let go,' she said sharply but Sarah wouldn't. Her fingers dug deep into Kate's arm, really painful now as Kate struggled and wriggled. And it was like being little again, all the years between vanished. She was four or five, or six, and it was just like always. Sarah – the other Sarah, not the one who loved her so – was bullying, hurting, forcing her to do something naughty so she'd be blamed. Then Mum would belt her till she cried. And then Sarah could cuddle her.

Kate had looked back on all that, after the trial, and understood how she had been dominated, how Sarah had operated her unspoken power, made herself needed. Only now it was happening again and it seemed not to matter that she was grownup, because all the old grief was welling up inside, reducing her again to helplessness.

'No! Let me go!' Kate sobbed her protest. 'You know I can't bear heights, don't . . .'

But Sarah wouldn't release her. The merciless grip tightened on her flesh, she was being dragged over the sill, onto the terrifying balcony. Kate couldn't keep her eyes off the way the streetlights shone up through the open pattern in the wrought iron floor.

For a moment nothing happened, the two of them held steady by their combined weight.

Kate lifted her head and met her twin's beautiful, golden gaze. And what she read there made her scream her sister's name aloud.

Sarah was mad. Something had broken in her, some desperate dreadful misery had snapped a deep spring that would never be mended. The open agony she saw in her sister's eyes dragged Kate back to a fathomless place where she had only ever dared look once before. It had been dark then, too, and a little boy had died, and Sarah had held her bloodied hands . . .

Kate screamed again. Michael, already out of his room in answer to her first cry, raced the short stretch of corridor and tore at the handle of her door. He was just in time to see the two women locked together in the travesty of an embrace as Sarah tried to haul the protesting Kate onto the balcony.

'What in God's name . . .'

Kate heard his yell of protest and gave a last desperate wrench. She freed herself from Sarah's clawing fingers and half fell back over the sill. She crouched there, white and panting from exertion, and then she felt Michael behind her.

Alone on the narrow balcony, Sarah staggered heavily as she tried to regain her own balance. Michael saw her face, the crazed eyes, and he caught Kate to him, protective.

Sarah was staring at them both, facing into the room, so she didn't notice the low tub of flowering geraniums before she stumbled against it. Trying to right herself, she trod hard on the edge of her long habit. The fabric made her foot skid on the slippery iron floor and she fell hard against the delicate wrought iron side.

It was freshly painted, but very old. Rusted through, the police pointed out later, though who could have known? The whole balcony side simply gave way beneath the sudden impact. There was nothing to save her. Kate cried out and reached for her, but there was no time, no time for Michael, lunging forward over the sill, to catch hold of her.

Sarah grabbed desperately at the geraniums as she fell past them, tearing the flowers root and earth from the tub as she tumbled.

She fell without a sound into darkness, her eyes wide and blank with shock, her mouth open as she stared up at Kate. Then the dreadful heavy muffled thud as she landed on her back, impaled on the wrought iron railings two floors below.

The coroner said death would have been instantaneous: her eyes were still wide when they reached her, as if full of wonder. She lay across the bars, a great black and grey bird caught on a spike.

A single black iron fleur-de-lys, one of twenty forming the top of the railing, penetrated her back. It missed the spine by half an inch and exited just below the base of her throat. A second went straight through the palm of her left hand, free of its sling and flung out as if to save herself.

Her skin was as white as her coif. Only the blood blossoming from her mouth was scarlet, and the geranium still clutched in her right hand.

Chapter Forty

The pool was empty, lit from beneath impossibly blue water. She was a strong, not a spectacular swimmer. Michael dived in and churned powerfully up and down the roped off lane for fast swimmers.

Kate did one length, then two more. She switched from breaststroke to overarm, relishing the weight of water against her body, face and hair streaming. She thought of nothing but the sensation of the moment, the pleasure of it.

She was near the middle of the pool when it happened. One minute she was travelling smoothly towards the deep end, the next she had lost momentum. It was as if she didn't know any more what to do, how to move her limbs. And the water itself became an alien element, dark and deceptive suddenly, very cold.

It must be a sort of cramp, she thought, although she felt nothing. She tried to call out but Michael, moving in the opposite direction with his back to her, was oblivious and there was no-one else.

She was in panic now, flailing around wildly, her head going under, water filling her eyes and ears and nostrils. She swallowed a great mouthful and spluttered, retching and coughing, blinded and afraid.

She felt herself going down and opened her eyes

underwater. It was blue again now, the colour of forget-me-nots. Forget-me-not.

It went through her fierce as an electric current. Christ, no, she hadn't forgotten. She made a huge effort and burst up to the surface. She hadn't forgotten how terrified Sarah had always been of water.

The fear Kate felt was not her own, and never had been: it was Sarah's. Something was happening to her, something over which she had no control. She couldn't tell if it came from her own subconscious mind or from outside, but it made no difference. She realized only that she must summon all her will if she was to save herself. Don't go under. Don't drown. Not now.

She forced herself to put her hands together, to push her arms forward, kick her legs. It took forever, there was no strength in her any more, she never knew how she got to the side. Gasping, she clung to the curve of tile, rested her head against the hard, reassuring surface.

When she looked, Michael was just reaching out a hand to turn at the far end of the pool.

'You've been in such a rush lately, I'm sure that's the reason it happened.' He put his arm round her. 'It's only four months since you were in hospital, don't forget.' In the short pause, she heard his thought as clearly as if he had uttered it. *And Sarah died just eleven weeks ago.* 'You must slow down a bit,' he finished.

She shivered and nodded and drank her tea. There was plenty of time to tell him she would never swim again.

'Tell you what.' His arm tightened and he murmured into her neck. 'You may not be the world's greatest swimmer, but you can save my life any time.'

It had begun as a joke between them, that very first morning in the Schons' blue-tiled bathroom. Kate had started to get up, and Michael found he couldn't bear to let her go, to move away from him, in case this was the only time he would have her, in case it never happened again. He had sung her the refrain from the Dory Previn song, '. . . stay awhile and save my life.'

She had said, suddenly serious, 'It was you. You saved *my* life.' She fitted herself against him, pressed her mouth on his until her ardour left them both gasping.

'Kate,' he had pleaded with her, half-laughing, entirely smitten, and she had stared into his eyes, absolutely still, glittering with excitement and anticipation and love, until neither of them could wait another moment.

He was discovering with her – through her – that he was, after all, both priest and man. His vocation was a gift from God. But so was his sexuality.

In the past, he'd repeated blandly that marriage was a sacrament. It had never even occurred to him until now that lovemaking was sacred too, that there was mystical beauty in the union of lovers' bodies. The sensual and erotic pleasures he experienced with her turned him into a different person.

It was not the priest but the man who exulted in the way Kate responded to him, in the damp unfolding of desire, the sounds she made deep in her throat that excited him to the point of frenzy. It was not the priest but the man who lay with his face between her thighs, inhaling the rich warm smell their bodies made together. He accepted at last that men and women were beautifully made by God. Their bodies were good, their sexual needs were good, they brought joy.

And having experienced it, he was forced to acknowledge that the absence of a loving relationship with a woman was a loneliness which no religious belief, however strong, could overcome for him.

Celibacy, he reminded himself, had never been part of the early Church but an afterthought, grafted on by old men who no longer even remembered the body's urges or the cravings of the heart. He had prayed about it, written endless letters, spoken at length to his superiors. Finally, he had decided to request dispensation from Holy Orders. He was suspended from all priestly functions. He could not say mass or hear confession or recite the psalms in public. He could not receive the holy Eucharist, marry the living nor bury the dead. Still, in the eyes of the Church, he would remain a priest until the end of his life.

He said now, 'Kate, won't you save my life?' and buried his face in her hair. To utter the words, hum the melody, was shorthand between them for 'I want you'.

At first, it had provided an easy way to say what both of them found so hard. Michael's only romance had been the brief affair with Francesca ten years before. He had to learn how to sustain a relationship, continue a loving dialogue over days and weeks. He was a bachelor by habit now as much as circumstance: meticulous, set in his ways. It was difficult for him to tolerate any other person around him all the time. Even Kate.

Prison had taught her how to be alone and calm in the midst of chaos. She could shut her mind to the radio, to people talking across her, and carry on with whatever she was doing. She never noticed untidiness, her own or anyone else's. She tried hard when she was with him, knowing how he disliked it. But free at last of all constraints and rules, she never closed doors or screwed tops back on bottles.

The reason was clear enough: fourteen lost years gave an urgency to everything she did now. It all had to be crammed in, savoured immediately. She was always in a rush, eager to move on to the next thing.

He realized how far he'd come with her one morning, when he found she'd brought their combined washing back from the laundrette and dumped it in his tiny, immaculate kitchen. He picked a pair of lacy knickers out of the bread basket and felt nothing but amused affection.

Kate had no template for loving a man at all, but it was easier for her. Despite everything that had happened, everything that had been done, she came sooner than Michael to the expressions of love. Somewhere she still had deep, stifled memories of closeness, total harmony, sharing. These things were instinctive, and somehow, Michael tapped them.

She existed on a plane of emotional and physical joy she had never dreamed possible. She wanted Michael with a breathless longing that was never satisfied, no matter how often they made love. Just the sight of him opened up a hungry ache. Only his body covering hers, the feel of him inside her, his taste, his touch, his smell, cancelled it out.

But only briefly, for a few hours, perhaps a day, until the physical sensations of their last lovemaking began to fade. While her thigh muscles still quivered from encircling his back, and her nipples were sore from his sucking, and her cunt still ached from his thrusts, she was sated, content.

Then the yearning would begin again, the longing to telephone, hear his voice, arrange a meeting, see him walking towards her. She didn't even want to live with him. Through a friend, a former priest now working for the BBC, Michael helped her find work as a part-time researcher. Then they arranged her move to London, a room near his flat. That was as much as she would do for the moment, fearing that together always, they would lose the wild core of their lust.

They would lie for hours looking at each other, tracing the curve of an eyebrow, the line of a shoulder. Fused at groin and breast and mouth, legs wound together, arms entwined, fastened perfect, they stopped time.

Even her dreams were physically explicit. She would be somewhere so humid she felt sweat trickle between her breasts, run down her forehead into her eyes. There were birds everywhere, flights of them, brilliant green under a harsh metallic sky. The leaves of huge plants were the same vivid colour, moist and cool between her fingers.

She dreamed the moon. Its round golden face glowed cold, an implacable goddess waiting for Kate to remember her old name, from forgotten time. She understood then that these were not her dreams. She was looking out of someone else's eyes. Sarah's eyes. And because now she was also Sarah, she almost had the name, it was in her mouth, she could taste it . . .

The phone rang and rang. Michael answered, his voice blurred with sleep. And then he got out of bed, and stood there talking. She lay and thought how she loved him naked. Leaning over, she ran a finger down his back, down to the cleft of his buttocks, fondling him. But he reached back and grabbed her hand, and held it so she knew he was being serious, and she heard him say, 'All right, Mother. Yes, yes.' He listened. 'I'll catch the first train in the morning. And I'll bring Kate with me.'

Mother Emmanuel took both Kate's hands in hers and examined her face closely. Michael wondered what she would see there, this unworldly but experienced woman, who knew so much about the sisters in her care, and had lived in silent enclosure for more than forty years.

'I feel I know you, Kate. An illusion, of course. Although . . .' she shook her head. 'I don't know.

Your eyes . . . a different expression in them, though. A different soul looking out.' She released her with a sigh. 'We miss your sister very much. This house is not the same, without her. We are a small family, and close.'

Mother Emmanuel turned to Michael and gave him a searching look. One of the first letters he wrote when he decided to leave the priesthood had been to her. Her reply had been sympathetic, though she had not hidden her sorrow. She understood his reasons, but still it was a defection, and she had not expected it of him. *All of us will lose*, she had told him, *and we won't be able to replace you*. Now she gestured towards the chairs and seated herself behind her desk.

'This is really why I asked you here,' she went on, 'though I hope I haven't wasted your time.' She touched the small brown paper parcel on her blotter. 'We found this diary in the washhouse. We never would have, only Sister Peter had her arthritis again and couldn't manage alone, so we got a workman in just for the wall. He insisted on doing the whole thing properly, you know how they are, and did the part we hadn't even touched. The diary was behind a loose brick.'

She unwrapped a small book. It was less than four inches by seven, and folded in a plastic bag. 'There is no name. No names appear in it either, so far as I can tell. I'm assured by the community, it belongs to none of them. And it can't have been there too long. It's in such good condition, you see, and the laundry gets so steamy.'

She looked at Kate. 'We thought it could only belong to your sister. Do you recognize it?'

Kate shook her head without speaking.

'What's that on it?' Michael leant forward and took the diary from the plastic bag. The leather was dark blue, stamped all over with small gold fleurs-de-lys. It would have been a pretty thing, but for the words gouged black all over the front cover. He turned it in his hands. 'Looks as if these letters have been burned in somehow.'

'That's what we should do with it,' Mother Emmanuel exclaimed. 'Burn it. I'm sure it belonged to Sister Gideon, and we none of us want to pry. Unless . . .' she turned politely to Kate '. . . you would like it, my dear?'

This time, Kate shook her head violently.

'There are one or two other things belonging to your sister,' Mother Emmanuel added, opening a large shoe box. 'Clothes and so on belong to the order, her ring and crucifix. But there are a couple of photographs you might like?' She picked out a small wooden frame and held it towards Kate. 'This one is of you.'

Kate gripped the arms of her chair. 'No, please. Burn everything.' She turned impulsively to Michael. 'Would you do it?' As if she couldn't trust anyone else to see this thing through.

'Excellent idea.' Mother Emmanuel looked relieved. 'When you're ready to go, there's a gate into the garden from the drive. I'll have it unlocked for you. There's a shed near the kitchen garden, we've all sorts of things in there. White spirit and so on.'

The prioress started to put the lid on the box when she stopped. She reached in again for a small maroon cylinder. 'Sister Andrew found this in Sister Gideon's pocket after her . . .' a delicate pause '. . . after her fall. It's a Ventolin inhaler – you know, the sort asthmatics use, only we've no record of her ever needing one, and Dr Bevan never gave her a prescription. We thought it might belong to you?'

Kate said, 'Not me.'

'Oh, well.' Mother Emmanuel smiled sadly. 'It doesn't matter now.'

Chapter Forty-one

The light was starting to fade as they went through the unlocked gate opening from the drive into the long garden. Once out of sight of the house, Kate tucked her hand into Michael's.

They walked down past the flowerbeds, empty now of everything but the last shrivelled chrysanthemums, tall spikes of Michaelmas daisies, past the rose garden and the espaliered fruit trees, until they reached a part of the garden where the ground fell away to the plain below.

They could just make out the outlines of the humped Welsh mountains, comical as pantomime giants, running to the horizon. In the valley, three linked rivers were made of dimpled pewter, reflecting the heavy September sky. Scattered house lights showed on the hillsides from farms and isolated cottages. As they looked, there was a distant whine and an arc of coloured balls – red, green, gold – burst overhead in a frenzy of stars.

Kate gasped. It was only some kid anticipating Bonfire Night, letting off a solitary rocket. But it brought back the nightmare of almost a year ago, the smoked-out cell at New Hall, her burned skin and singed hair. She had never told Michael any of it, she just grasped his hand tighter, for reassurance.

But Michael took the moment as another reminder of

what had been lost to her. Over the last two months, as they spent more and more time together, he kept coming across these unexpected gaps. It had been oddly difficult to grasp that a woman could reach the age of twenty-six without ever having a date, or spending a day at the seaside. She'd never walked on a beach, eaten candyfloss, lost money in arcade games. She'd only ever been to a disco in a prison gym, and rock concerts were for other people. She had never seen a play in a theatre, or heard an orchestra play.

Almost despite himself, Michael was enchanted by her appetite for experience: it delighted him to be able to open so many doors for her. Taking her to a restaurant, to the Tate, the South Bank, more than doubled his own pleasure. He even took her to a couple of gigs in Hammersmith, though the names of the groups meant nothing to him and the music meant less. She watched his face and laughed at him, and said afterwards, she'd manage on her own next time.

When they reached the kitchen garden, behind its high old brick wall, they found the logs Mr Dunbabbin chopped for the Aga and picked out small pieces for a fire. They balled up his old copy of the *Daily Sport* and Michael found the white spirit stored in the shed and set the paper alight.

While they waited for the wood to catch, Kate sat on a long garden seat, arms wrapped round denimed knees, the collar of her bulky cream sweater turned up round her face for warmth. Michael emptied the shoe box. He held out the handful of photographs – he recognized Roy Downey, this must be April, there were several of Kate – for confirmation, and she waved them away without looking.

He dropped them on the little fire and opened the diary,

flipped through the pages. Several times he stopped to study one. They were covered in writing so small, so intense, it was almost impossible to make out. He could read just enough to see that it was oddly written, without much punctuation, but with a certain rhythm almost like poetry. Some of the sentences were childish – *Mum loved me the best. She was always the naughty one* – and he assumed it must have been started when Sarah was very young. Odd phrases were curiously perceptive. *I learned to read first so she didn't need to. When she saw I had mud on my shoes she took hers off.* And, *One of us nearly died when we were born, it should have been me.* Some of the observations were adult, demonstrating real under-standing: *Impenetrable closeness, primitive and powerful. Genetic burden.* And, *Nature's own genetic experiments.* A few could have been copied from medical books: *EEG's and brainwave patterns in twins are often so alike they could be superimposed one on the other* . . . One of these he found particularly chilling: *Genetic control extends through life, to age at death. And cause of death.*

And then, in the last few pages, something strange, a recurring phrase, bothered him. Obviously important, it was written with capital letters, but apparently mean-ingless. He flipped back through the pages, but couldn't find it anywhere else. He found the part he wanted and handed the diary, open, to Kate. 'Could you read this?'

She took it so reluctantly he said, impatiently, 'It won't bite.' She flinched visibly and he almost told her, don't, it doesn't matter. But then she started to read it aloud, deciphering the difficult script in the darkening garden as easily as if she knew it by heart.

'Now is the time and the place for the telling. I must confront the Never Said.' Her voice was low, she read without emphasis, giving each word the same weight, as if that would make them less dreadful. 'To write will make it real, give it breath. All these years I've squeezed it down under a lid. But I've felt the hurt tight in my throat. I needed to speak of it, I whispered it to myself at night, but that didn't help. If I could tell all the true things about me no-one knows, it would stop the pain.

'They said it had no logic, none of it made sense. They churned up my mind. They told me a story and said, this is a true story. But it was another lie. Then years went by and gradually it did become the true story.

'It became the only story I could tell.

'When the Never Said happened, I didn't know what was real and what was made up. They told me afterwards my sister had done it, my twin. But how could I be sure? They said the other stories were true. But they never were.

'He cried and cried. That was true. When I touched him, tried to soothe him, he only cried harder. He pushed away my hands, he turned his face from me. He wouldn't look at me. I put all his toys in a row at the end of his cot but he scrambled out of his covers and threw them all away. His screams hurt my head, on and on. When I picked him up he kicked his legs and wriggled out of my arms, struggling to get away from me. I loved him so much and he hated me.

'He cried so hard he was nearly breathless. It made my teeth hurt and then I was sick. I fell down and he was still in my arms and I went over on top of him. Then something in his leg was sharp and he screamed worse than ever.

'I put my hands over my ears to shut out the crying. Then I couldn't, I couldn't see, but I heard the gurgling scream of someone waking in a nightmare, a kind of bubbling shout.

'I dreamed vampire dreams. I was the swooping shape in darkness, seeking something I had never had. Vampire hand becomes a knife, gleaming and cold. Stroke across the silk of skin with a touch smooth as love.

'I pushed the knife in hard. But when I pulled it out, the holes in his skin were so small, much smaller than the blade.

'He didn't bleed at first, then it started to spread. Over his bright pyjamas and the little grey elephants. They skipped in blood, rode their bicycles over blood. They were all spoiled and I cried. But he wouldn't even look.

'Blood red. I looked it up afterwards, and the words in the thesaurus were so beautiful. Cardinal, claret, crimson, carmine. Venetian, rosaniline, wine-dark, Tyrian. And other words. Incarnadine. Liquescent.

'Words are supposed to tell what things are like, but those words don't. It's not beautiful, it's hot. On television, or films, they just use ketchup or something. Nobody can know what it's really like, to have your hands covered in somebody's hot blood.

'It has a dark smell, an animal smell, it makes the little hairs stand up on your arms. It gums the insides of your fingers together as it dries, like another skin.

'He bled scarlet sequins. I heard them explode as they hit the floor. He went quiet and sweet then. He let me touch his cheek and it was cool. So I held him close and warmed him against me. His heart was beating like my heart. Then it stuttered, stammered.

'I carried him round his room, cuddling him. When I looked down, there were pretty red exclamation marks all over the floor. After a while they dried brown and crusty. Then I saw what they were.

'I kissed his dear little head. His face squeezed tight as a bud, hair duckling yellow. I would not wake him. He lived while he slept. To awaken would be to die.

'He bled a lot. I thought of all the people who have died. I was bleeding too, woman's blood. All the people still to be born.

'His blood tasted salty. Mine tasted like tin. Warriors used to drink it. If you die from lack of blood, then to drink it must mean you will live for ever. Just like in church. Body and Blood.

'Tidy up. Wash his face, his tiny hands. Wipe away the blood from his body. It was just oozing out now, little dots pinging on the floor. Grownups have eight pints. I expect babies must have nearly that much.

'I changed his clothes, put him in nice clean pyjamas. I brushed his hair and the brush tinkled. It played Baa Baa Black Sheep and I sang it to him.

'It had gone very quiet, the silence was thick and misty. I stroked his back softly, smoothing out the transparent bubbles of his life.

'I laid him gently in his cot and made his hands go neatly together, so his mum and dad would be pleased.

'Then she came back. My sister, my twin, the person most like me in all the world. She had a big bottle of Pepsi and a plastic carrier bag, I could smell the vinegar. She was laughing. "You'll be sorry you didn't go for the chips," she said. "Guess who was in . . ."

'When she saw us, her mouth went a different shape. A screaming shape. It had no sound, but still it was louder than the ringing at the edges of my mind. It went on and on in my head. I heard it for years.

'She went very still and watched us. In just those few minutes I saw her face change. She looked like Mum, all lines turning down, her mouth so sad. All of a sudden she was old.

'When she spoke her voice was soft and white. "Let him sleep. Poor little boy." Her face all wet, but there was no rain. "Dear little boy, he'll sleep now. He'll be quiet now."

'She washed my hands, very carefully, and my face. The blood went brown on the tissues, and made swirly lines in the warm water. She said What will Mum say? but to herself so I didn't answer. Her hands started shaking then.

'She washed round my mouth and kissed me on my lips. My sister, my dear. And then she helped me take off my jumper and my denims. Knickers too, she said, and bra, in case there's anything on them. We changed clothes. We shared them anyway, dressed out of the same drawers, the same wardrobe, everything was ours.

'She told me what she would say, and what I must say. She said it and said it over and over. She said, I don't think they'll let us be together any more. Don't forget what I told you. She put her arms round me. I didn't want to hug her then because she had blood all over her clothes. So she kissed me. Then she went to the telephone.'

Kate's voice faded to a whisper and the book drooped in her hands. She brushed her forearm across her face, wiping away the tears, and then her voice was stronger.

'I am healed now. It was so long ago. I am sane and whole these days. I am even happy, much of the time. I live in God. I am a different being.

'But so are you. My sister, my twin, the person most like me in all the world. You gave me the time for this to happen. You gave me back my life. You gave me a future at the expense of your own. I see now the price you paid, and it was too great. It was a gift I should not have taken. Forgive me.

'I love you more than I can say. I will never forget what you have done.

'I will never forget what I did. If I could only burn it from my brain with their fine electric current, cauterize memory. I would welcome that.'

Kate's voice shook and she let the diary drop to the ground. 'I have faced it now, the Never Said,' she finished. 'This was the time and the place for the telling.'

Her tears were falling onto the tissue thin sheets, blotching the ink, making the writing finally indecipherable.

Unable to speak, Michael reached out blindly for her. They sat side by side on the garden bench, while night closed in around them.

He understood, at last, why he had never been able to reconcile the way she was, the way she looked, with the huge, brutal fact of what she had done.

He understood what it meant, to be twinborn. In the substitution of one child for the other, when they were twelve years old, in Kate's acceptance of her sister's guilt, lay the true meaning: one heart in two bodies.

When he could trust himself to speak he started to say, 'We must show this to . . .' but she moved very close so he could feel her warmth against him in the cold evening air, pressed urgent fingers over his mouth to dam the words.

'No,' she said quietly. 'If you do, it'll all have been for nothing.'

'Kate . . .' he protested, '. . . for the sake of your family, then. Your mother would have wanted people to hear the truth.'

Her eyes flickered, amber, ambiguous, and she glanced away from him, looked down. Telling him, the mother had known it, had encouraged the substitution, either deliberately or by simply never denying the lie.

He realized, it was he who wanted a pardon, public exoneration. Kate had always been innocent, as she was determined the world should believe Sarah had been.

'As long as you know,' Kate said.

Michael tore the pages from the diary and dropped them onto the voracious little flames. The first pages crumpled and darkened before they burned. As the fire flared stronger, they caught immediately, the thin paper disintegrating, curling to nothing and finally blowing away. When the last one had gone, he held out the cover. With a shudder, she gestured that he should do it.

It took several minutes for the flames to sear the leather, scorching the golden fleurs-de-lys. It seemed a long time before it was finally consumed, before the words vanished. The words the child had scored into the blue and the gold all those years ago. So much hurt and guilt and horror. Nothing was left now but smoke.

DON'T LOOK

DON'T READ

TURN AWAY

Chapter Forty-two

Michael Falcone watched his sleeping wife. She lay on top of the covers, too hot now towards the end of her pregnancy. As always, her right hand was beneath her cheek, the left tucked neatly under her pillow, in the way he found so childish and endearing.

He pulled the curtain a little, to shield her from the afternoon sun. Beside the bed he paused. He put a hand on the swell of her belly, feeling it tight and hard and full beneath the flowered smock. Full of life. He'd never known what it meant until now.

He bent, not to kiss but to inhale the scent of her, milky and innocent, at the base of her throat. A pregnant smell, unlike any other, of warm young things growing. It made him incredibly happy, rich beyond belief. *His* wife. *His* child.

He was in that stage of love where her sexual power was enhanced by familiarity, by the undreamt of, incredible ordinariness of married life. Of waking up together, eating breakfast, talking about plants for their bit of garden, a film they wanted to see. She had yearned for ordinary love and she'd been right. He couldn't take his eyes off her. She had only to make a gesture, pick up a plate, to fill him with longing. *Emotion shows in all the ways a body moves.*

She stirred and murmured, as if aware of his presence. Her smock pulled back and he noticed she had been lying on top of the diary she'd bought only the other day. She planned to record everything about the birth and the baby's first year.

He could never rationalize, afterwards, just why those particular words came into his mind at that moment, when they never had before. The words from that other diary.

What was extraordinary was the clarity with which he could recall them, though he'd only flipped through the pages, that horrible November night. But he could see them in his mind's eye, in that odd, cramped writing, without space or indentation on the thin paper, so different to his wife's huge, flowing, generous script.

Both of us recall childhood incidents. But who did they happen to? We experienced everything together. Now we cannot tell apart our memories.

Michael Falcone sat down on the edge of the bed where Kate still slept on, her gentle breathing the only sound in the quiet room.

He could not think, he could not breathe.

Sometimes, she had told him once, lies can tell the truth.

THE END